MW01633258

Titles by Todd Borg

A DARK ROAD SUSPENSE SERIES:

WILDERNESS VACATION
WILDERNESS JUSTICE
WILDERNESS PUNISHMENT
WILDERNESS THREAT

THE TAHOE MYSTERY SERIES:

TAHOE DEATHFALL
TAHOE BLOWUP
TAHOE ICE GRAVE
TAHOE KILLSHOT
TAHOE SILENCE
TAHOE AVALANCHE
TAHOE NIGHT
TAHOE HEAT
TAHOE HIJACK
TAHOE TRAP
TAHOE CHASE
TAHOE GHOST BOAT
TAHOE BLUE FIRE
TAHOE DARK
TAHOE PAYBACK
TAHOE SKYDROP
TAHOE DEEP
TAHOE HIT
TAHOE JADE
TAHOE MOON
TAHOE FLIGHT
TAHOE RESCUE

WILDERNESS PUNISHMENT

Josie Strong
A Dark Road Suspense
Book 3

by

TODD BORG

THRILLER PRESS

Thriller Press First Edition, September 2024

WILDERNESS PUNISHMENT

ISBN: 978-1-931296-77-9

Manufactured in the United States of America

For Kit

ACKNOWLEDGMENTS

I owe a great deal to my editors, Liz Johnston, Eric Berglund, Christel Hall, and my wife Kit. They find and fix countless mistakes. They make much-needed suggestions for improvements. If my book reads well, they get the credit.

Graphic maestro Keith Carlson produced a spectacular new look for this new series. So beautiful I want to keep staring at them. I can't thank him enough.

Kit also serves as initial reader, story coach, last reader. She has an unerring ability to find and take out my misjudgments. I can't thank her enough.

ONE

"Here's something to know about death in medieval wars," Professor Josie Strong said to her lecture class. "When medieval warriors went into a major battle, many of them—maybe even most of them—expected to die."

There were microphone stands in the middle of each aisle of the UCLA lecture hall. A student stood up from an aisle seat. He walked to the nearest mic.

"Yes?" Josie gestured at him.

"How could a general get any respect from the troops if the troops thought they were marching to their deaths?" the student asked.

"Boys were raised with the knowledge that when they became a warrior, going to war meant that they would fight to their death. Many of them even relished it as the goal of a warrior. Because death was assumed, warriors were much more effective. They didn't shirk from battle because of fear. The captains and commanders, which is what generals were called back then, benefited hugely from that perspective."

A student in one of the front rows called out from his seat. "How could so many die when they had such crappy weapons? A typical soldier today has an M-Four carbine, a grenade launcher, a pistol, a knife, and he can still put his thumb in another jarhead's eye. But all the Romans had were swords. Woo hoo!"

There were multiple chuckles throughout the hall.

Josie said, "While medieval weapons didn't have the advantages of modern weapons, it was the warrior's commitment to their battles that produced a catastrophic casualty rate. In a fight to the death, that is exactly what happens. There is an enormous amount of death. And to your mention of swords, I should add that in medieval times, warriors had many other weapons in addition to swords. They had other stabbing weapons such as daggers and pikes. They had swinging weapons in the form of axes and spiked balls on chains and war hammers. They also had throwing weapons like javelins and spears, launching weapons such as catapults and sieges, boobytraps like caltrops, punji sticks, snares, shooting weapons such as longbows and crossbows, and various ways to burn you with chemicals such as quick lime and Greek fire. And in addition to those weapons, they had effective armor. So think twice before you carry your M-Four into battle against a medieval warrior who expects to die fighting you."

One guy in back shouted down toward the student who'd said woo hoo. "Yo, Leatherneck, if your carbine gonna take down a charging knight on horseback, his comrade on the horse behind gonna stomp you into the ground."

There were laughs and jeers from the crowd.

"Okay, students, point made." Josie turned around and spoke to her aide, who sat at a computer. "You can start the slides."

While Josie waited for the photos to come up on the two screens above her on the left and right, she put both hands on her podium and leaned forward to see her audience better. The UCLA lecture hall was large enough to hold 800 students. There were only scattered empty seats, confirmation that her class was the most popular in the history department. Josie knew it wasn't her charisma or her speaking style that drew her students. It was her discussion of medieval weapons that motivated the curiosity. And in the last year, a popular fantasy author, whose violent books were set in the fifth century after the fall of the Roman Empire, had put multiple mentions of Josie's class on her social media pages. She claimed Josie's class as the inspiration for her series. Josie knew that a portion of the crowd sitting in front of her had read those addictive books.

Josie noticed someone who stood out from the crowd, someone sitting in the aisle seat on the left side of the front row.

He was in his thirties, substantially older than most of her students. He wore a black suit jacket over a white shirt. Although his collar was open, his dress was nothing like one would expect at an undergraduate history class. It looked like he was part of a wedding party. Or, Josie thought as she remembered a scene recently on the national news, he would fit right in with the Secret Service. He had brown hair, parted on the right and combed to the left. He sat very straight. And he looked excessively serious. Too serious. He made Josie uncomfortable.

The first picture came up on the screens.

Josie looked back down at her notes and resumed her talk.

Through periodic glances, Josie could see that the man in the nice clothes watched her with a kind of intensity that few students had. And unlike most of the students, he wasn't doing the constant thumb dance on a phone or gazing off into space.

Josie finished her lecture, and the projection screens went dark. "Any more questions?"

A woman in camouflage Army clothes, her sleeveless shirt exposing muscular, tattooed arms, walked over to one of the mic stands. Her pants were tucked into the tops of heavy black boots that thumped as she walked. Like the well-dressed man, she looked to be substantially older than most of the students, maybe in her late thirties.

Josie gestured and nodded toward her. "Yes?"

The woman hesitated, telegraphing nervousness. "Thank you for taking my question, Professor. You talk about when warriors expect to die and how that can give them advantages on the field of battle." The woman paused.

Josie nodded at her. The woman's polite demeanor was not what Josie expected after seeing her military clothes and tattooed arms.

The woman continued, "It sounds like what you're really saying is that the commitment of medieval warriors was their ultimate advantage. That in any battle, it's not the soldier with the best weapons but the soldier with the greatest commitment who's likely to be victorious."

"That's exactly right," Josie said. "You've all heard a version of the phrase about perseverance and commitment being more powerful than genius. It applies not just to wartime battle but to all of life's struggles. Another word I like for it is grit. The person with grit usually succeeds, where someone who is only armed with intelligence and talent fails."

There were a few more chuckles from the students.

"We can all learn from medieval warriors," Josie said. "Slouches and slackers need not apply. Commitment and focus rule."

Josie glanced at the clock. "Before I close, I want to remind you all that while I seem to speak casually about weaponry and the deaths of warriors, we should never forget the significance of each life lost. To that end, I'd like to read part of a poem written by a Canadian physician named John McCrae during the First World War.

"It's called 'In Flanders Fields,' a reference to the Flanders region of Belgium where the Germans launched one of the first poison gas attacks. The poem takes the structure of a rondeau, a common poem form in medieval France in the thirteenth and fourteenth centuries."

Josie put on her glasses and leaned in close to see her notes.

"I'll read the second stanza.

'We are the dead. Short days ago
We lived, felt dawn, saw sunset glow,
Loved and were loved, and now we lie,
In Flanders Fields.'"

Josie closed her notebook. "As we learn about medieval weapons, let us never forget and, especially, never laugh about the lives lost in human warfare."

She flipped a switch on a panel near her lectern, and the lecture hall lights got brighter.

"The next lecture is tomorrow, nine a.m. I'll be bringing an example of a deadly medieval weapon. Read chapters twenty-four through twenty-six. Thank you for coming and thanks for your interest." She turned off the mic, put her notes back into her briefcase, and turned to go.

The man in the black suit was now standing off to the side, looking at her. Josie felt uncomfortable, wondering if he wanted to talk to her, hoping he didn't. Despite it still being morning, it already felt like a long day. She had no more classes for the day, and she wanted to go home.

Not far from the man was the polite woman in the black boots and camo clothes. The two of them seemed to be the only people in the lecture hall who weren't immediately leaving. The woman wasn't looking at Josie but was instead watching the man in the black suit.

Josie didn't know what to make of it.

Josie walked out the side door. The man in the nice clothes appeared next to her in the hallway. His shoes were polished black. The bulk of the students went straight to the front of the building. Josie turned left down a short passage to one of the building's side doors. She began to open the door when the man quickly grabbed it and held it open for her.

"Thank you," Josie said as she walked through.

"Professor Strong, I have a message for you," he said.

She slowed but kept walking. She didn't answer, knowing that he would continue to speak. They were on a sidewalk that led to a street that was off limits to all vehicles other than service trucks and campus police.

"I work for the governor," he said.

Again Josie didn't respond. She'd heard all the recent talk about state budget cuts and how the governor was lobbying university faculty to get behind his proposals.

Josie was in a hurry. From the service street, she could access a diagonal sidewalk that cut across campus toward her bus stop.

"The governor would like to speak to you," the man said.

Josie tried not to scoff. It reminded her of those come-ons in the mail or email. 'Please join the governor's task force on education. Your voice is so important to our cause.'

Josie glanced at the man. She saw for the first time that he wore one of those little ear pieces with the curved microphone wire that reached halfway to his mouth. Like the Secret Service. She felt a jolt of fear.

She kept walking. Except there was a vehicle in her way. She turned to make a small detour. Josie realized the vehicle blocking her way was a black limo, the tall SUV style. A heavily tinted passenger window rolled down.

"Professor Strong?" A man's voice. Vaguely familiar.

Josie turned toward the voice in the limo. A man was visible in the open window.

It was the governor of California.

She stopped walking.

"May I speak to you, Professor Strong? Please?" he added.

The center door on the limo swung open. The inside of the limo was bigger than the breakfast nook in Josie's Santa Monica condo.

Josie's impulse was to ignore him and hurry away. The man with the earpiece seemed to crowd her. She had the sudden thought that if she tried to leave, he might stop her. She felt her heart speed up. These kinds of surprises were not good for her blood pressure. Josie stopped, took a deep breath, and held it as she had learned in meditation class. What to do?

The governor sat at the rear of the limo, facing forward. He was in shadow, hard to see. Facing him, lit by the sun coming through the tinted windows, was a woman. Like the man who'd approached Josie, the woman in the limo was also wearing a suit, dark gray over a white shirt. Her shoes were low black pumps polished to a high sheen. She had short hair, no apparent makeup, and she radiated efficiency and competence. Unlike Josie, she had no excess. She wasn't very thin, but she was trim and looked muscular. She was about Josie's age, older than the earpiece man by ten years and younger than the governor by ten years. She sat opposite the governor.

Josie breathed out. She leaned forward so she could see the governor through the open door. "What can I help you with?"

"We have a situation I'd like to talk to you about. Would you please join us in here?"

Josie's instincts told her no. Her instincts told her to ignore the governor. She'd recently been involved with several state law enforcement organizations, and the experiences had mostly been disastrous.

"There is no trouble," the governor said, obviously perceptive about the impact his sudden appearance could have on a private citizen's life. "This visit is official business. A request for your service to the state of California. If you decline to speak to us, we'll be unlikely to find another person with your knowledge and skills."

"How long will this take? I have a bus to catch. I can't miss it because I have to meet my daughter." It wasn't exactly true.

"We'll drive you to your daughter. We can talk while we drive."

Josie looked left and right as if checking for trouble. There were no police, no other governmental vehicles. Josie looked again at the woman. Josie had always been a good judge of character. Maybe if she heard the woman's voice...

"You work for the governor?" Josie asked the woman.

"Yes. I'm Sonja Gonsalves. I'm the outreach liaison in the governor's office. I can answer any questions you have."

Josie didn't reply for several long seconds. "Can we make this fast?"

"Yes," the governor said.

Josie got in and sat in the forward portion of the compartment, next to Sonja Gonsalves and diagonally opposite the governor. Josie faced toward the rear. She held her briefcase on her lap.

The man with the earpiece shut Josie's door, opened the rear door, and got in next to the governor, directly across from Josie. Just before the man shut the rear door, Josie saw the student with the tatted arms, camo clothes, and black boots over by a tree. She was standing straight and square with her weight on both feet as if at attention, and she was watching Josie. She held a phone near her waist and seemed to be angling it as if to take pictures without carefully aiming it.

The young man shut the rear door, and the limo pulled away.

TWO

"Thank you for speaking with me," the governor said. "Now you've met Sonja, my outreach liaison. You should also meet Taylor Cooke, my valet. His name is spelled with an E, not that it matters to you."

Josie made a little nod toward the young man with the earpiece, and he nodded back.

"Sonja takes care of the big stuff in the governor's office, and Taylor takes care of the details. Without them, I'd be shipwrecked, marooned on a distant shore."

Again, Josie had to force herself not to scoff. It was just like the governor to speak in such a grand, over-the-top manner.

"Can your driver hear me?" Josie said. "I'll give him my home address. I'd like to go there."

"No, she can't hear you," the governor said. "But I believe she has the address. Is that correct, Sonja?"

As the woman responded, a distant truck horn sounded, drowning out her words.

"I didn't hear that," the governor said.

The woman spoke again, taking care to enunciate. "Affirmative. The driver has Professor Strong's address. We plan for all eventualities."

The governor pressed a button. "We're dropping our passenger at her home." He let go of the button.

"You looked up my private information," Josie said. She tried not to sound too judgmental, but it bothered her that they hadn't asked her for permission.

"Sorry if that seems intrusive," the governor said. "I don't know where you live, for what that's worth. But it's part of my staff's safety protocol. The governor's aides always make a point of knowing the basics about people who our office deals with."

Josie didn't reply. It sounded like invasion of privacy wrapped in the supposed cloak of government security.

The limo started up gently. The vehicle had some kind of special sound proofing. Josie could barely hear anything from outside the vehicle.

"So why are you contacting me? I'm a medieval history professor."

"You've recently done a great service for the state, catching a cop killer and others. You've become legendary in certain circles. People are talking about you."

Josie knew he was referring to murderers she was able to catch, partly by using her knowledge of medieval weapons and strategy, but mostly by using common sense and being persistent.

"We have a crime situation near Lake Tahoe that has baffled local law enforcement," the governor said. "They haven't been able to solve it. Your name was mentioned. Once we looked into you, it seemed clear you would see this crime in a way that law enforcement does not. Will you please consider helping us? You could apply your special analysis. I have no doubt that you can discern possibilities that have eluded traditional law enforcement."

Was the governor pleading with her? Or was he schmoozing her?

Josie kept her voice low. No doubt her skepticism was obvious. "I'm sorry. My schedule is overflowing. You'll have to get someone else."

"Please?" the governor said. "Could you just consider our situation? California depends on its most educated, skillful, and concerned citizens to help solve its intractable problems."

Josie made a deep sigh. She turned and looked out through the tinted windows. The mountains behind UCLA looked lush from inside the limo.

She inhaled and let the air out slowly. "What is this situation?"

The governor looked at Sonja. "Ms. Gonsalves? You are versed in the details. Could you please explain the situation to the professor?"

Sonja shifted slightly in her seat so that she faced Josie at a three-quarter view. The woman wore some kind of scent that smelled of sea salt and sandy beach, and it wafted toward Josie. The motion of the limo also made the woman's necklace move and catch the light. It was a beautiful stone of variegated blue, hanging from a thin gold chain, a feminine touch on a woman who didn't telegraph much femininity. Josie was so distressed and distracted by the sudden disruption in her day that she tried to do a meditation focus like she had learned in a seminar that UCLA provided for overworked professors.

She took more breaths as she stared at the stone on the woman's necklace. It was an irregular shape an inch or more long and the width of a wooden pencil. One end was quite pointed like a pencil that had been broken at an angle. Although the stone was polished smooth, it wasn't rounded. It seemed more like a shard of rock than a gemstone for a necklace.

Sonja had some sheets of paper on her lap. She lifted them up and read from the top sheet. "Three days ago, on December thirteenth, a Forest Service ranger was killed near Lake Tahoe." The woman scanned her notes. "It happened near the west side of the lake. Are you familiar with that area?"

"I was at Lake Tahoe only once, and it was years ago," Josie said. "I'm not familiar with the area."

Gonsalves nodded. "I'm not familiar with Tahoe, either." She looked again at her notes and continued reading. "The ranger lives part time in a cabin above Emerald Bay. Lived. He was found shot to death in the snow on the mountain which rises behind his cabin."

Despite Josie's attempt to stay calm, she flinched at the words. She'd recently been around too much death. It was not possible to think about it and remain calm.

Sonja Gonsalves continued. "The victim was on a path that led up to high mountains, a wilderness area called Desolation Wilderness. The closest road to Emerald Bay is Highway Eighty-nine.

"Based on tracks in the snow, the killer parked near a side

road that leads to several summer cabins. In the winter, the side road is not plowed. The cabins can only be accessed by snowshoeing or skiing in from the main road. Which means the cabins are largely vacant from November until April or May, when the snow melts. The suspect parked next to a snowbank on the main road. He broke into one of the cabins, took clothing and camping gear and ski gear. After his theft, he apparently left by skiing up into the forest, away from where he'd parked his car. It appears the ranger, who often stays in his cabin even in the winter, saw the burglar leaving the burglarized cabin with the stolen goods. The ranger put on his snowshoes and followed the burglar. The ranger caught up to the man and apparently accosted him. Unfortunately, the burglar shot the ranger, one shot to the heart and one to the head. The ranger died. And…" Sonja paused as if not wanting to read the next words. "This report says the head shot was execution style. A single bullet to the back of the head."

Again, Josie winced.

Sonja glanced up at the governor.

The governor didn't say anything.

"Do you have an idea of why the ranger was shot?" Josie asked.

Sonja Gonsalves shook her head. "No." The motion made her necklace shimmer. Gonsalves looked down at the papers on her lap and ran the tip of her finger over the printing. "The report speculates that the ranger probably tried to arrest the burglar, and the man resisted."

Josie asked, "Do rangers phone their arrest intentions into headquarters?"

The woman scanned the sheet of paper. "There was no call that we know of. If the ranger had only been asking casual questions, there wouldn't have been cause for the burglar to have a violent reaction, don't you think?" Sonja Gonsalves suddenly looked embarrassed. "I'm sorry, I shouldn't be making assumptions." She glanced at the governor. "The governor is asking for your help, not my help."

Josie made a slight nod. "You said the burglar was skiing

up the trail. How do you ski up? Skis are for going downhill, right?"

Sonja frowned. "That's a good question. I don't know the answer."

"This is something I know about," the governor said. "I have a friend who served in the Tenth Mountain Division of the Army and was deployed in the Zagros Mountains in Iraq. He's been a backcountry enthusiast ever since, and he took me out once. It turns out that backcountry skiers ski uphill by putting skins on their skis. Or else they use skis with a grip-type pattern on the ski base."

"I've never heard of the Zagros Mountains," Josie said, aware that the statement was immaterial even as she said it.

The governor looked out the window as if thinking about a fond memory. "My friend likes to say that the Zagros range is twice the size of the Sierra Nevada and almost as tall."

"What are skins?" Josie asked, back on subject.

"In the old days, they were made from animal skin. If the fur is short and stiff, and if you tie a strip of the fur onto the base of your skis, it allows the skis to go forward with the grain of the fur. But the skis won't slip backward because the fur grabs at the snow. Modern skins are synthetic. But the principle still applies."

Josie thought about it. "Despite your glowing opinion of my investigative abilities, I don't know anything about law enforcement, so forgive my naive questions. What is the difference between a ranger and a police officer?"

Sonja Gonsalves gave the governor a questioning look.

The governor said, "I actually don't know much about the distinction. I think of rangers as a certain type of police. It's my understanding that the U.S. Forest Service hires their own rangers to patrol national forests. I think rangers have similar peace officer powers as most cops. They carry guns like cops. They can detain and question and arrest suspects. But instead of a jurisdiction that might be a town or a county or the state highway system, the ranger's jurisdiction is the national forest."

Josie said, "Lake Tahoe is in a national forest?"

"I believe that much of Tahoe is in the Tahoe National Forest. But maybe not all of it."

"So rangers aren't able to patrol the entire lake?"

The governor shrugged his shoulders. "Maybe not. In addition to forest service rangers, Tahoe has sheriff's offices in the five different counties that make up the Tahoe area. The city of South Lake Tahoe has its own police force. Also, the FBI has an office in Tahoe. And the Coast Guard has jurisdiction over the lake itself."

Josie paused. "You're saying there are lots of different law enforcement agencies, and this man who was murdered was just one type."

"Right. Tahoe law enforcement is complicated." The governor turned toward Sonja. "Did I explain all that okay, Sonja?"

Sonja made a weak smile. "Based on what I've read, yes. But I don't really know."

Josie said, "You said the killer parked his car on the highway. Did they learn anything from that?"

Sonja shook her head. "It turned out it was stolen from a gas station in Reno. A woman left her car running when she went inside to pay for gas. When she came back out, the car was gone." Sonja Gonsalves took a drink from a shiny metal canteen that was similar to the one Josie's daughter Samantha used. It made Josie like the governor's liaison. Like Josie's daughter Samantha, the woman cared enough about the environment to avoid using plastic bottles.

"Do they know where the killer went?"

Sonja shook her head. "Only that he drove the car from Reno to Lake Tahoe. It snowed two feet that night. They were able to get a vague sense of where the killer's ski tracks went through the trees near the cabin. Apparently, the trees provided enough wind protection that the snow showed a dip of sorts where the killer had skied and left a trail of compressed snow. But once the man moved out into the open, the wind erased all traces of his movement."

"Where do they think the killer went on his skis?"

"The mountains to the west of Emerald Bay go up to a wilderness area called Desolation Wilderness," Sonja said. "I read about it on Wikipedia. So I'm now an armchair expert, right?" She made another shy smile, and then glanced at the governor as if worried what he might think. She looked down at her notes. "Desolation Wilderness is sixty thousand acres of high country, mostly exposed granite, from seventy-five hundred feet to ten thousand feet. Because of the elevation, it's pretty much buried in snow for much of the year."

"Why would someone go there in winter?"

Sonja shrugged. "Good question. I suppose it would be a good place to hide because there's no one there. Or maybe it would just be a good escape route. From what I saw online, once the killer got up to the top edge of what they call the Sierra Crest, he could have skied downhill to practically any point on the western slope of the Sierra. I looked on the map. The western slope goes gently downhill for forty miles. Of course, when he got to the warmer temperature of a lower elevation, he'd end up skiing out of the snow. But then he could hike anywhere. There are very few roads to speak of. It's mostly wilderness until you're almost to the Sacramento suburbs."

Josie rubbed her forehead with her fingertips. She suddenly felt very fatigued. "I still don't see why you'd contact me over all the other possible choices," Josie asked. "If your goal is to find someone who isn't biased by law enforcement perspective, you could find dozens of wilderness experts and backcountry ski experts." Josie looked at the governor, then at Sonja. "I don't know how often police officer murders are solved. But I bet they're rarely solved by a history professor."

"Until you came along," the governor said. "Yes, officers die in the line of duty. It's always a tragedy. But this was particularly brutal. Whenever we have a cop killer, we consider it a top priority. Often, federal agencies like the FBI get involved. State agencies get involved."

"Like California's Bureau of Investigation…" Josie felt stomach acid burning her esophagus as she said it. They had caused her so much misery...

"I know that must be a painful subject for you after what you recently went through," the governor said. "But yes, our state bureau gets involved. Local law enforcement agencies try to coordinate their response. Everyone worries about another killing. So we go to extraordinary lengths. Including calling on other experts such as yourself."

"I understand that it is particularly upsetting when someone kills a cop. And I don't mean to sound insensitive. But police officers get killed quite often, right? So why is this particular killing so significant that the governor of California is calling on a history professor for help?"

The governor took a deep breath. Josie thought it seemed like he was trying to decide whether to give a cursory explanation or something more thorough.

"Last year, a man named Don Lassey died. Don was not just my campaign manager but my longest friend. When he was on his deathbed with lung cancer, he asked me to look after his daughter Mary Jo."

Josie thought the governor seemed more melodramatic than sincere. "I don't mean to seem dense, but who is Mary Jo?"

"Mary Jo Telman. The widow of Ranger Francis Telman, the ranger who was shot."

"What made Mary Jo the focus of her dying father's concern?"

"Nothing in particular. She was just… special."

"Special like an only child?"

"I suppose one could say that. I think Don actually had a couple of other kids. I never met them. They scattered a long time ago. Don stayed very close to Mary Jo. Before Don died, I told him I would do my best to look after her. Don was hoping to make it until Mary Jo's and Francis Telman's wedding. But he died two days before they got married. I ended up being the one who walked Mary Jo down the aisle. It was three months ago but seems like only yesterday." The governor turned and looked out the limo window. In the distance was a narrow view of the Pacific. "Now that Mary Jo's husband has been killed, I want to do whatever I can to help. But the main motivation for calling you was that Mary Jo asked me to contact you."

Josie restated it. "The widow wants me to help find her husband's killer."

The governor nodded. The governor glanced at the woman next to Josie. "Then my aide said that she had heard you are tenacious and creative, and she said she could coordinate your involvement if I wanted."

The governor stretched his neck left and right as if he were under lots of stress. He reached his hand up and rubbed the back of his neck. "So I'm putting Sonja in charge of this." He gave the woman a long look. "Sonja, you should probably take it from here, don't you think?"

Josie felt awkward. She was being called in to help someone who got the kind of devotion that few daughters ever got. As Sonja Gonsalves looked down at her lap, Josie had the sense that the governor's aide felt the same way. She might have been an appreciated employee, but she would never receive such attention from the governor. Probably never got it from her father, either. Or maybe, like Josie's daughter Samantha, she didn't have a father to speak of.

Josie found herself staring alternately at Gonsalves and then at the governor. She glanced at the governor's valet, Taylor Cooke, who hadn't moved.

Sonja was shifting papers and hadn't said anything else.

Josie felt the awkwardness. In the momentary silence, Josie again thought how much she didn't want this sudden job. "I appreciate your concern and desire to help Mary Jo. But you can't possibly think I can be of use in finding this man. I know nothing of snow. I've never been to this Desolation place. I wouldn't have a clue about the mountains in winter."

The governor spoke up. "From a report I read, it was your very inexperience that motivated you to come up with innovative ways to find a suspect who was on the run in Yosemite Park. I believe the report said you did some kind of data analysis from satellite images?"

Josie knew that what the governor was referring to was, in fact, analysis that her former tech-savvy student Cumberland

Durand had done at her request.

"That technique was useful in the confines of Yosemite where the mountains are like walls," Josie said. "There are only a couple of roads in and out of the park. But the mountains near Lake Tahoe aren't closed in like that, are they? A person knowledgeable about the territory and skillful on backcountry skis could go anywhere. Or am I wrong about that?"

The governor shrugged. "You may well be right. Which is why we think you are the person for this job. You would approach this in ways that might never occur to traditional law enforcement. In return, the state would provide a substantial reward for your efforts, whether successful or not."

"I'm sorry," Josie said. "I'm a history professor. The idea of tromping around in the snowy mountains is so far beyond my experience, I can't even imagine it. You'll have to find someone else."

The governor's face seemed to harden. "Frankly, I'm surprised at your reaction. I don't know if you've ever met Royal Stanters, one of UCLA's board members? He knows of you, and he told me he was certain you'd be eager to help. His fellow board member Bertrand Marmosa agreed." The governor gave Josie a warm smile.

Josie suddenly realized she was being squeezed. Both Stanters and Marmosa had been part of a faculty fight over a faculty restructuring controversy. The press had depicted Josie as Stanters' and Marmosa's opponent. There'd been talk that the board of directors was split, and several faculty members told Josie she should back away from her position. The two men also served on the tenure committee. If they didn't support her, she might find her tenure track in jeopardy.

Josie took a deep breath. She was determined not to be blackmailed into some backcountry search for a killer. It was an outrageous pressure tactic on the part of the governor. She loved her job at UCLA, and she would do most anything to maintain her tenure track. It was very upsetting to have the governor pull such a tactic.

"I simply can't," Josie said. "I don't have the appropriate

skills, and my schedule is out of control, partly because I'm trying to make up for the impact of the Yosemite situation. It nearly destroyed my career. Again, I'm sorry."

"We can help with your career," the governor said. "I'm certain that Stanters and Marmosa would speak to your dean and anyone else appropriate. My office has the ability to intervene in many matters."

The governor gave Josie a cold stare. She understood that he was trying to wear her down. But she didn't understand why he cared so much. She held his eyes without flinching.

"We especially take law enforcement matters seriously," he said. "For example, the resolution of incarceration cases like that of Jabari Moreau often depend on the governor's office."

Josie gasped. How could he bring up the case of Samantha's father?! He was a terrible man that Samantha didn't even know about! It was an obvious travesty for the governor to use that man's name in relation to a request for Josie's help. There was no connection between Jabari and Josie's current life. To mention him was a grotesque effort to make Josie think that the governor would stir up a nest of trouble if she didn't agree with his demands. Josie had devoted her life to making Samantha's childhood happy and secure. That meant keeping her from having contact with a man who couldn't care less about her, other than to brag to his prison mates that he had a daughter who was a volleyball athlete. If the governor were to pass on Samantha's cell number or email address to Jabari… The very idea was disgraceful!

"I can't believe you would mention that man. He has nothing to do with my life or my daughter's life. He's been absent in every way for over a dozen years!"

"Easy, Professor Strong. I meant no harm. I only mean to point out that we try hard to do what's right for society. Our number one job is to ensure the safety of Californians. When prisoner parole hearings approach, the parole board often looks to the governor's office for guidance. In the case of Jabari Moreau, he is up for parole in a few years. We would want to make a thoughtful and considered recommendation for how the parole board should proceed."

"The only thoughtful recommendation would be to keep that man locked up for his entire sentence!" Josie realized she was shouting. But such an outburst was to be expected when a mother is backed into a corner. Josie thought that not only should Samantha's father remain locked up, but that Samantha was still too young to even know of his existence.

She took another deep breath. "I'm sorry. I didn't mean to shout."

"No problem," the governor said in a voice that was sweet to the point of sickening. "You are only looking after the well-being of your daughter. A mama bear protects her cub, even from the cub's father. So you protect Samantha."

Again, Josie nearly gasped. They knew her daughter's name! Did they know everything about Josie's life? Did they know the details of what Jabari did? Did they know that right before he went to prison, he basically sold Samantha to Josie for a very high price?

Josie looked from the governor to the young man next to him. Both had hardened looks on their faces. She glanced at Sonja. At least, her face showed kindness and understanding.

Josie shut her eyes and tried to find some small hint of tranquility. But it was impossible. Although the governor's words were calm, his blackmail was obvious and, to Josie's point of view, unforgivable.

But between the threat to her tenure track and the threat to reveal to Samantha details of her father, Josie felt trapped. She bowed her head and took many long, deep breaths.

She opened her eyes and gave the governor a hard look. "Okay, what else should I know about the case?"

THREE

The governor looked at his aide. "Sonja, you prepared an information file to give to Professor Strong. But is there any other information that you should explain while she is here?"

Sonja Gonsalves opened the folder on her lap and moved some pages. She scanned the sheets of paper. "The address of Francis Telman's cabin is here. We've included a key to his cabin. I'm not sure the details of his death are helpful, but the autopsy on Francis Telman says he was killed with a nine millimeter round. I don't know exactly what the number means, but when I talked to the pathologist, he said it's a common type of ammunition."

"Nine millimeter is the size of the bullet," the governor said. "And yes, it's very common." He looked from Sonja to Josie and back. "You've probably also heard numbers such as thirty-eight and forty-five and three-fifty-seven in connection to bullets. The numbers aren't standardized and don't make much sense. They've evolved over the decades as new types of ammo have been developed."

Sonja continued, "Forensics could not establish anything about the gun that fired the shot. Apparently, it's a gun that's not in the database. The Reno gas station where the Camry was stolen did not have functioning security cameras."

"So you know nothing about the suspect," Josie said.

"Correct."

Josie glanced at the sheets on Sonja's lap. "Where is Mary Jo's and Francis's home?"

Sonja looked at the governor.

He said, "I'm embarrassed to say that I haven't kept current on their situation. After Mary Jo's father's death and her marriage to Francis, she and Francis moved into her father's house in the Sierra foothills. But when Mary Jo called me to ask about getting you to look into Francis's murder, she said she was staying at a house belonging to some friends. I suppose she felt too uncomfortable to stay in the father's house. Perhaps staying at the house of her friends had fewer painful memories."

"She's at the friend's house now?"

"I think so." The governor looked at Sonja.

Josie pointed at the folder and papers in Sonja Gonsalves' lap. "Is the address of the friend's house in there?"

Sonja scanned the papers. "Yes. It's a house in the Sierra foothills, near the town of Placerville."

"You said that Francis Telman often stayed at the cabin in Tahoe?" Josie said.

"Right. But he actually reported to work at the Forest Service office in Foresthill, which is in the foothills north of Placerville. Apparently, Francis was based both in the foothills and in Tahoe. Foresthill is where Mary Jo's father lived. So after Mary Jo's father died and the house became hers, it made good sense for the two of them to move into the father's house. I understand it was a nicer place than the apartment where Mary Jo lived."

"Do you have contact info for Mary Jo Telman? Email and such?"

Sonja ran her fingertip down the papers on her lap. She looked on another sheet. "Here is her phone. Let me write it on this first page." She wrote with careful precision, perfectly formed letters. Josie was immediately aware of the contrast between the woman's perfect penmanship and her own sloppy scrawl.

Sonja looked again at the papers. "We don't seem to have an address for the friend's house where she is staying. We only have directions. I'll write them down, as well."

The governor said, "You want to talk to Mary Jo Telman? Do you really think that's necessary?"

"It seems prudent," Josie said, trying not to sound like his question was ridiculous.

"I suppose it is. But I just want to leave the poor woman alone. Do you think the death of her husband at Lake Tahoe could have something to do with Mary Jo, even though she was down in the foothills at the time?"

"I doubt it. But it makes sense to consider all possibilities."

The governor seemed conflicted. He frowned. "The thing is, Mary Jo is very shy, very reticent. And I understand that she's skittish since her husband's murder. Which is probably why she's staying with friends. If you contacted her, she might well disappear before you showed up."

"Do you think I should just show up at the house unannounced?"

"That would probably be best." He hesitated. "What, if I may ask, would you hope to learn talking to her?"

Josie thought his question was dense. "I have no idea," she said. "Maybe her husband's murderer wasn't just a criminal resisting arrest. Maybe Francis Telman was targeted. Enticed into coming out in a winter storm."

The governor looked shocked. "I can't imagine that scenario."

"You contacted me because you thought I'd think in ways that typical law enforcement doesn't." It was a snarky comment, but Josie was very frustrated. The governor was acting dumb. She said, "It appears that the man was killed because he was a Forest Service Ranger and he was doing his ranger job. But things are often not what they appear to be, right? So it makes sense to consider all other information."

"Yes. You're right. That's probably why Mary Jo wanted me to ask you. She'd heard about the other cases you worked on. She thought you'd be the perfect person to look into her husband's murder."

Josie thought about it. The idea that the widow requested her help softened her resistance. Josie looked out the window of the limo. The Santa Monica Mountains northwest of Beverly Hills made a crisp green line against the blue sky.

"I'll have to talk to the dean and the administration to see when I can get away," Josie said.

The governor spoke. "We've already made arrangements, correct, Sonja?"

"Yes," she said. "We've been in contact with the UCLA history department. Your class will be canceled after your next lecture. You can explain to your students that you've been called away on emergency business for the state."

Josie was shocked. "You can't intervene in my life without my permission! And I can't just leave suddenly like that. My daughter has her school as well."

Sonja made a slight nod, as if being polite.

The governor said, "We've also been in contact with the headmaster at your daughter's school."

"You spoke to my daughter's school before you even asked me?! I'm appalled!"

"Sorry," the governor said. "Official business of the state requires advanced planning. My office felt we had no choice. Many times we have to move forward on multiple fronts at once. If we waited for approval from UCLA before we got approval from your daughter's school, the process would take too long. The suspect would have that much more time to disappear."

"So now the headmaster of my girl's school knows everything about us and what we're doing and what we did before!"

"We were very careful," he said. "We explained that you would be helping us on a project of great discretion. The headmaster was very understanding. And, in any event, you only have a couple of days left before the university goes on the holiday break. Same for your daughter's school."

Josie was aghast at the loss of privacy.

The governor looked out the window at the forested slope below the Getty Museum. "If you'd like, we can swing by the school and pick up your daughter now."

"No. Absolutely not. I can't imagine what all the kids would tell their parents if they saw Samantha get into this huge limousine."

The governor made a single nod. "As you wish."

A few minutes later, the limo came to a stop outside of Josie's condo building.

"I can't think straight," Josie said. She was being pressured—menaced—by an implied threat against her job future, her tenure track, and the possibility that they might tell Samantha about her father. There was no opportunity for discussion about whether Josie would be a willing participant or not. It was as if the governor's personal whims were forcing Josie to do something she wasn't prepared for, something she had no training for.

Josie wanted to appeal to Sonja for help, but she knew the woman's job was to help the governor in any manner he wanted.

"I have no idea of what I need to know or what I need to ask," Josie said. "How can I even begin to find someone whose name you don't know, a person that no witness has ever seen up close. You don't know anything about his history, and he apparently vanished into the wilderness."

"It's a real puzzle," the governor said. "But as we just discussed, we believe you will be able to figure out what law enforcement hasn't."

Sonja handed Josie a card. "These are direct numbers to my office and my cell. Below that is my personal email address. We don't want you to feel hemmed in by any schedule, but we'd appreciate a periodic update on your progress. Every day or two, if possible. If we don't hear from you, we'll stress."

Josie was speechless. The governor's impertinence, and thus Sonja's in acting as his agent/employee, was shocking to Josie.

Josie took Sonja's business card. She looked at the governor, then realized there was no way she'd be given his number. They knew all about her. She knew nothing about him other than he was an overambitious politician.

Josie looked at the card. The phone numbers had prefixes that were common to the Los Angeles area.

"I thought the governor's office was up in Sacramento," Josie said.

"Yes, my official office is not far from the capital building," the governor answered. "But most of the state's population is down here. So we operate out of the L.A. office much of the time."

Josie reached for the door handle, gripped it, but didn't immediately open it. She felt more like she was being sentenced for a crime than being recruited for her skills. She had so many thoughts on her mind, but she couldn't form them into words. She eventually stammered, "I've learned that cell service is spotty in the Sierra." It was a lame statement.

Sonja Gonsalves said, "If you text or email and hit send, I think most phones will keep trying to send the message until you get into an area with coverage."

Sonja neatened the papers, put them in a folder, and slipped the folder into a large manila envelope. "We expect that you will have substantial expenses. In the folder is a Visa debit card. The debit account has forty thousand in it. There is a Post-it note with the debit card password. It would be best if you memorized the password and tore up the Post-it. You can use the card to get cash, pay for lodging or car rental, and pay for whatever supplies you need. After you're successful in this mission, we'll bring the debit card balance back up to forty thousand. That will be your fee for up to a month's worth of work. If this project runs longer than that, the governor's office will consider a larger fee."

"What do you want me to do if I succeed in learning who this killer is and where he is?"

The governor answered. "Contact us with his location, and we'll send a team to arrest him."

"I'll think this through."

Sonja nodded. "Any questions you have, any support you need, any information you'd like, just let me know."

"I don't know what I'll need. But I'm guessing I'll need to talk to law enforcement agencies. They might not be very eager to help me."

"That won't be a problem," the governor said.

"Then what I'd like," Josie said, speaking more toward Sonja Gonsalves than toward the governor, for whom she'd already developed a strong dislike, "is for you to call the local law enforcement agencies and clear the way for me so I don't have to struggle to get information. The Forest Service. The sheriff's office or whoever provides law enforcement for the area in Lake

Tahoe where Francis Telman was killed. I'd like the appropriate contact numbers and a letter of introduction that I can show to anyone I talk to about this case."

The governor answered. "We'll tell them that they should be forthcoming with any information you want. You are acting on our behalf, so responding to you means they are simply complying with a request from the governor's office." He turned to his aide. "Sonja, can you prepare a list and email it to Professor Strong?"

"Yes, of course. In the folder, there is already an authorization on the governor's stationery. It explains that you are working with this office. That should provide some access and credibility, should you need it."

The governor looked at Josie. "I hope you will work on this right away and develop a plan for how to proceed, a plan you can put into motion twenty-four hours from now."

Sonja handed the manila envelope to Josie. Josie put it into her briefcase.

The well-dressed, young man who hadn't said a word jumped out of the back door and opened the center door.

Josie got out. Before the door shut behind her, she looked at Sonja Gonsalves. Because Sonja was going to be her main contact, Josie felt she should have a bit more personal connection to the governor's aide. But she didn't know what to say. Finally, she once again looked at the woman's jewelry.

"Your necklace is quite beautiful," Josie said. "May I ask what kind of stone that is?" Josie sensed the governor rolling his eyes as if he thought women focusing on something as prosaic as jewelry was evidence of weak minds and a preoccupation with silliness.

Sonja Gonsalves gave Josie a bright smile. "It's called Tanzanite. From the country of Tanzania."

"In Africa," Josie said. "Very nice." Josie nodded, gave her a genuine smile, and turned away, pleased that she'd made some kind of personal connection to the one person in the limo who didn't act like a slick politician or a politician's bodyguard. Josie walked toward her condo building without looking back.

FOUR

Josie slowly walked up the flights of stairs to the third floor. She unlocked the door and went inside. Her small dog, Unknown, was at the door, sniffing Josie, no doubt noticing the myriad scents associated with the governor's limousine. Unknown still didn't wag except in the most unusual circumstances. And she didn't bark, qualities that Josie and Samantha ascribed to the trauma from the murder of her former owner. But Unknown showed her pleasure at Josie's homecoming by turning a circle, swiping her paw at Josie's pant leg, sitting next to Josie, and leaning against her leg.

Josie set down her briefcase and bent down to pet Unknown.

When Josie straightened up, she felt strangely awkward. The intrusion into her world by the governor and his demands was very unsettling. All Josie wanted was a calm, normal life. Beach walks with her daughter and Unknown, quiet evenings at home with homemade dinner or Chinese takeout, and maybe watching a movie in their living room with the partial view of the Pacific Ocean and the Santa Monica Pier out the window. She loved exploring with Samantha, taking in the occasional concert at Disney Hall, visiting the Getty or the L.A. County Museum of Art. Josie liked the routine of teaching, the simple pleasures of a brown bag lunch in UCLA's sculpture garden. She even enjoyed her open office hours when students could stop by to ask questions and review assignments.

But now to be, once again, thrust into the dark and twisted world of crime was very stressful. It all started because she and her daughter had been targeted by a killer, and Josie, and Samantha too, had demonstrated a creative aptitude for finding and taking down the monster.

It was too much. It was too painful. No matter how valuable some officials considered their crime-fighting contributions to be, Josie didn't want any part of it.

Yet once again, she was put into a no-win situation against her will. And having the governor threaten to tell Samantha about her incarcerated father and interfere with the UCLA board members who could possibly disrupt her tenure track was too much!

Josie wanted out. She put water on to boil for tea and pulled a legal pad off her desk. When the tea was ready, she sat down at the dining table and began making some notes.

Ten minutes later, Samantha came home from school. Unknown trotted to the door before the lock turned. Samantha came in, hugged Josie, and bent down to pet Unknown.

"Oh, Sam, I can't tell you how glad I am to see you," Josie said. She stood up and hugged Samantha. Samantha's head towered over her mother.

"Mama, what's wrong?"

"I had a visit from the governor today."

"Do you mean the governor as in the state of California?"

"Yes. He wants us to do another project for law enforcement."

"What?! No, Mama! This must be why the headmaster spoke to me when I left school."

"What did he say?"

"He did that thing where you say something unclear. What's that called? Enig-something."

"He was being enigmatic," Josie said.

"Right. I was leaving and he said goodbye and that he'd see me again eventually. I knew it meant something bad!"

"I'm so sorry," Josie said.

"Mama, I don't want to do another project. I just want to go to school and play volleyball. I just want to be a normal kid!" Samantha suddenly looked horrified. "Is this because of my smuggling screw-up?"

"No, Sam, this has nothing to do with that, other than the authorities were impressed with how we found the bad guys, and they want us to do it again. Let's take Unknown for her walk and I'll tell you all about it."

Josie picked up a pen and wrote on the pad. 'We're back to our lives being split between public and private.' She turned the pad toward Samantha.

Josie knew that Samantha would remember the routine. When they wanted to put on a facade for anyone who might be monitoring, they would bring phones but not talk about anything private. When they wanted to be certain no one could monitor them, they would leave their phones behind. The governor wasn't a crook like the last guy who hacked Samantha's phone. But there was no way to know what the governor might do in pursuit of his own selfish interests.

It was clear that Samantha understood. She nodded, took out her phone and put it on the table. Josie did the same, grateful that she had eventually gotten her phone, and her car, back from the Mariposa Sheriff's Office after they'd been taken during the Yosemite debacle.

With no electronics, they left the condo, took Unknown to the beach, and walked the trail where dogs were allowed on leash. Apparently, there were no major storms out in the Pacific, for the rolling breakers were relatively small. The sound of surf was mild, and it was easy to talk.

Josie explained about what had happened, but left out the governor's mention of Jabari Moreau, Samantha's father.

"So they're blackmailing us into looking for another cop murderer," Samantha said. "You have to do this or they'll talk to those school board member guys and they could mess with your future tenure."

"Yes. It's a really cheap shot to get us to do their bidding."

"But this sounds impossible, Mama," Samantha said. "With the Yosemite killer, we at least knew roughly where he was hiding. We had some information about him. You're saying we know nothing about this killer? We don't even know where he might be?"

"Right."

Samantha spoke slowly. "Cumberland used his computer

skills to hack into satellite images and find the guy hiding in Yosemite. Could he even do that with this guy?"

Josie shook her head. "No. There's nothing to go on. The guy could be in Tahoe. But he could also be in Reno or the Bay Area or New York for all we know."

"Then how could we possibly find him?"

"I don't know, Sam. I have no idea."

"When do they want us to look for this guy?"

"Immediately. They contacted my department and got the dean to cancel my medieval history class without telling me in advance. I go in tomorrow and tell my students it's over. I'm so angry about it. But I don't have a choice."

They walked in silence. Unknown meandered, pulling lightly—politely—at the leash, sniffing out beach detritus, never going fast. Josie watched her, wondering once again what kind of trauma had taken away the characteristics that nearly all dogs had. Unknown didn't bark, didn't wag, didn't run. And yet she seemed content, if not happy. Maybe there was a lesson there about adapting to trauma. Finding some kind of contentment even when circumstances have stripped the excitement of life away.

"We're going back into the dark forest, aren't we?" Samantha said, her voice heavy and depressed. "It's just like you used to say about children's fairy tales. We're never going to get our life back. And it's all because of me. My presence. My mistake." Samantha sounded like she was about to cry.

"No, Sam, no." Josie put her arm around Samantha's waist as they walked. "That's not true. We all have both dark experiences and cheerful experiences. If you're going to think about any possible negative results from your actions, then you have to also acknowledge any possible positive results from the things you do. I could do a never-ending talk about the upside you bring to most everything you touch."

Samantha squeezed Josie's arm against her side.

Josie said, "I'm sorry, Sam, I forgot to ask. How was your day?"

Samantha made a small grin. "Today was a volleyball day.

We had two practice games. I did my first successful pancake!"

"What's a pancake?"

"A pancake is when the ball gets past you and is about to hit the ground. So you dive to the ground like a belly flop in the sand, and you reach your hand out where the ball is about to hit the sand. Before the ball can hit, you slap up with the back side of your hand and blast the ball into the air. It's very hard to succeed at it. But I did it!"

"That's great, Sam. You don't just love to eat pancakes, you perform them, too!"

"But spiking is still my best move. After the game, the coach said I was the best spiker she'd ever coached. Of course, she's only coached kids."

"Sam! Stop that. She said you're the best. She didn't say, 'for a kid.'"

"Right, Mama."

"Anyway, wow, that's great! You got the chops, girl. I'm so sorry that this new project means you'll be pulled away from school and volleyball. So sorry." Josie felt like crying. "At least, we're coming up to the Christmas/New Years break, so you'll only miss a few days of school."

After a minute of silence, Samantha seemed to shake herself out of her funk.

"Okay, Mama, let's do that priority thing you talk about when we confront a dark forest. Even when you don't know how to navigate the forest, you can usually figure out your first step into the woods. What's it gonna be?"

"I go back to school tomorrow and tell my class it's canceled. Then I'll figure out the next move."

"Do you have an idea what it is?"

"No. What about your next move?"

Samantha walked in silence, staring down at the sand. "I guess I do the same thing. I'll tell my teachers I have to go away. What's that called?"

"A leave of absence?" Josie said.

"Right. And from what the headmaster said, they'll already know it by tomorrow morning. But it'll be hard to tell my coach.

She's counting on me. And she's not part of the headmaster's inner circle. So she probably won't get the word about my absence until I tell her."

Josie reached down and pet Unknown as they walked. "She's still going to want your skills. Everyone counts on the best spiker, right, Unknown?" Josie stopped, faced Samantha, took Samantha's hands in hers, and said, "Seems to me like a captain with spike and pancake skills can conquer the world."

"Aye, Matey," Samantha said.

FIVE

When they got home, Josie's phone rang. She picked it up from the kitchen table. The readout said it was Amelia Gomez, the ambitious girl from Peru who wanted to start a coffee roasting company.

"Hi, Amelia," Josie said.

"Hello, Professor Strong. Is this an okay time to call?"

"Yes, and remember, please call me Josie."

"Okay." Amelia hesitated. "Josie. It takes me time to change because my parents are so insistent on using Mr., Mrs., and Ma'am. They say you have to be extra formal and polite if you want to find a way in a new country."

"I understand. What can I help you with?"

"Remember when I told you and Samantha that our landlord was making us leave?"

"Yes, of course. We said that if it took you awhile to find a place, you could stay with us."

"Yes. That was so kind. And I never thought I'd have trouble. But there is an issue with my status. The government is going back on some of their promises to Dreamer kids."

"Children who were brought to America when they were very young and, hence, mostly only speak English yet don't have citizenship," Josie said.

"Yes. They keep telling me it will only be another month. How many times have I heard that..."

"You are still welcome to stay with us," Josie said. "You can sleep in Samantha's room."

"Oh, profess... Josie. Thank you so much! I am so grateful!"

"You're welcome. However, I should tell you that Samantha and I have to leave in a day or two to work on a project for the governor. So it would be best if you come and get settled in very soon. We can show you what is involved."

"Yes, thank you. Very much. When would be good?"

"Today or tonight."

"Oh, perfect. I'm on the day shift at the coffee shop. So I can come after work. Would that be okay?"

"Sounds good," Josie said. "See you then." Josie clicked off.

"Amelia's finally moving in?" Samantha said.

"Yes. Does that still seem okay to you?"

"Yeah, totally."

"Do you think it's okay to give her a key and let her stay here when we're gone?"

"Absolutely. Amelia is, like, the most reliable person I know."

Josie nodded agreement. She also thought that Amelia was a good role model for Samantha. At 19 years of age, Amelia was five years older and very ambitious. Being an immigrant from a poor family, that ambition was very good for children of privilege, like Samantha, to witness.

That evening, Amelia showed up bringing coffee shop bakery treats, which, Josie was glad to see, were in a coffee shop bag along with the receipt. Josie never doubted that Amelia was an honest employee, but the receipt was nevertheless reassuring.

Samantha went out with Amelia and Unknown to get Chinese takeout, which they ate at the kitchen table. Later, decaf coffee and pastries for dessert finished off a nice evening.

Samantha had previously made up her room with a makeshift bed that used a sleeping bag pad along one wall.

That evening, Josie, Samantha, and Amelia went over every detail that Amelia might want to know about living with Josie and Samantha.

"I am so happy you are doing this for me," Amelia said before going to bed. "I can't thank you both enough."

"We're happy to have you," Josie said as Samantha nodded.

The next morning, Amelia left for her job. After Josie and Samantha walked Unknown, they left the dog in their condo then got on the public bus that went near Samantha's school. When Samantha stood up to get off, Josie gave her a hug and kissed her. "We'll get past this, Sam," Josie said.

"Sure, Mama. Sure." Samantha hopped down the bus steps.

Josie could tell Samantha was just saying it and didn't believe it. Josie's heart broke a little bit.

Josie transferred buses at another stop, then rode to UCLA and walked to her office.

An hour later, Josie had spoken to the dean and two of her colleagues about her problem. The dean said he'd already been contacted by the governor's office, and the dean professed his desire to find a good solution that wouldn't leave Josie's students without an option. Like Josie, the dean didn't have a clear plan, but he thought it might be possible to manage without a substitute teacher. There was only one lecture left before the holiday break. And they had two weeks to come up with a plan for winter classes, should Josie's assignment last that long.

While the dean was agreeable about it, Josie sensed his frustration at having the program disrupted. Maybe the governor had given him a veiled threat as well. It still bothered Josie greatly that the governor had intervened with her dean before she'd had a chance to tell him. It seemed patronizing on the part of the governor's office, a clear violation of basic decency for him to create a problem for Josie and then attempt to insert himself in the issue without consulting her first.

Josie walked across campus to the lecture hall.

At the start time for her class, she stepped up to the podium, and looked out at several hundred students. She swallowed, forcing back the emotion of the moment.

"Good morning. I had hoped to continue where we left off yesterday. Unfortunately, life intervenes in ways we don't expect. After class yesterday, I was approached by the governor of California. They have a crisis and the governor has asked me to provide assistance. The final classes are canceled, and I won't return until after the holiday break. You will be given full credit for your attendance and your classwork. For those of you who are scheduled to start the next class after the holiday break, I'm hopeful that I will be available to teach it. If not, we hope to find a replacement. Thank you very much for your understanding. If you have any questions, I'm happy to answer as best I can."

There was a strong hum of disappointment in the audience.

Two students made their way to the microphones in the aisles and asked questions about class credits. Josie gave her best answers, which were a variation on 'I don't know.'

A student shouted from the back of the hall. "Hey, Prof, does this mean the governor wants you to teach him how to use medieval weapons against his opponents?"

Laughter rippled through the hall.

"That would be effective, no doubt," Josie said. "But it looks like he's in need of medieval strategy more than weapons, which, of course, would be a huge step up in sophistication from current politics."

More laughter.

Josie apologized again and turned off her microphone.

When Josie was outside, walking toward Bunche Hall where the history department offices were located, a woman fell in next to her. Josie turned to see that it was the student she'd seen the previous day. The woman was wearing a different sleeveless shirt but still wore camo pants and the big black Army boots. Her tattooed arms were once again bare. The woman was twenty years older than most of Josie's students, but was younger than Josie by several years. She had dark brown hair in a short buzz cut. She was substantially taller than Josie and had more muscles than most men.

"Hello," Josie said without breaking stride. "I remember you. Yesterday you stepped up to the microphone and commented about commitment as an advantage in battle."

"Good memory," the woman said. "I'm real sorry your class is canceled."

"Thanks. I am, too. I also remember seeing you when I got into the governor's limousine."

Josie sensed the woman nod as she walked alongside. The woman didn't respond.

"Did you have another question?" Josie asked.

"Not really. I just wanted to be sure you're okay."

"That's kind of you. Yes, I'm okay. A little frazzled. But okay. Why do you wonder?"

"I'm not sure how to say it. Since I got out of the military, I've taught self defense to women. One of the things we always stress is for women to learn to recognize certain thresholds that are danger zones. Women almost universally aren't good at seeing them. They always try too hard to do what people want, especially when men want them to do something or go somewhere that isn't smart."

"Like getting into a strange vehicle," Josie said.

"Yeah. Sorry if that sounds—you know—in your face."

"Not at all."

The woman said, "When I saw them urging you into the limo, my warning lights lit up. I sensed they wanted something from you that was dangerous. At the minimum, I thought it wouldn't be in your best interest."

"You were right on both accounts," Josie said.

"But you're okay," the woman said.

"That remains to be seen. Can I ask your name?"

"Cor. Cor Kontos."

"Cor," Josie repeated. "I remember seeing your name on the roster."

"It's short for Corinthia."

"Isn't that a Greek city?"

"You know your geography," the woman said. "Yes, a city at the entrance to the Peloponnese. I was there once when I was fourteen years old. My dad wanted me to see my heritage. It was amazing."

"I remember learning about Greek column designs," Josie said. "Doric, Ionic, and Corinthian. Same Corinthia?"

"Yeah. History and architecture. I guess it makes sense you'd know that, what with the whole medieval thing."

"Kontos is obviously Greek as well."

"My dad was originally from Athens, but spent a lot of time in Corinthia. Mom is from San Juan, Puerto Rico. I'm the resulting mix. Stocky, muscular. Brown skin. And a Greek chip on my shoulder."

"You wouldn't be considered very brown in much of my world," Josie said.

The woman made a brief glance at Josie. "I suppose not."

They walked in silence for a few moments.

"Teaching self defense to women is admirable," Josie said.

"Thanks."

"You were in the Army?"

"Yeah." Cor laughed. "How did you guess, ha, ha. I always wanted to be an Army Ranger. But they didn't let me into that program. Now a bunch of women have graduated from Ranger school. That's the ultimate cool."

"Why didn't they let you in? You look fit enough."

"I was, but twenty years ago was several lifetimes when it comes to opportunities for women. However, the bigger problem was that I was convicted of second degree burglary when I was seventeen."

"I'm sorry to hear that. That put the Army Rangers out of reach?"

"Yeah. The general Army gave me a waiver because of the circumstances and allowed me to enlist, but the Rangers wouldn't touch me. The Rangers are a small specialty branch of the Army. Very exclusive."

"We all make mistakes as kids," Josie said.

"Mine was a big one. I accompanied a boy on a store burglary. He told me his dad owned the store, which wasn't true. Second degree burglary is what they call a wobbler crime. They can charge it as a felony or a misdemeanor depending on how the DA feels. So I went up as an adult, but for a misdemeanor. I was convicted, sentenced to a year in county jail and a thousand dollar fine. When I got out, I went into the Army thinking it would get my head straight. Not sure that worked. But I tried. Anyway, if you need help with anything, I'm volunteering. You're kind of a role model for me, teaching at UCLA. Not like I could ever be a professor. I can barely get up the courage to speak in front of people. Asking that question in the lecture hall yesterday was way out there on the bravery scale. But your world requires the whole public speaking thing."

"Do you live around here?" Josie asked.

"I'm over in Hollywood. Not the nicest neighborhood. But I can pretty much hold my own."

Josie couldn't imagine anyone who could hold their own better. The woman radiated toughness and was polite besides. Josie's instincts told her she could trust Cor Kontos.

"Do you go to UCLA full time?" Josie asked.

Kontos shook her head. "No. I take extension classes. Maybe I can change up my game in the future and get into a degree program. They say extension credits transfer. But it's tough to get accepted into this school as a regular student."

"Now your job is teaching self defense?"

"Yeah. I put in my twenty years in the Army, got my pension, and decided I should better myself in other ways. So I go to school in my spare time."

Josie was interested. She wanted to keep the woman talking. "What did you do in the Army?"

"It's more like, what didn't I do. My last six years were in Afghanistan. They had me working on logistics and supply chain issues. Then they shifted me to help in teaching heavy weapons and artillery to new recruits in the Afghan army. Near the end of my gig, I was providing security for visiting military advisors. But through it all, they had me studying reconnaissance, threat assessment, and a bunch of other skills."

"Military skills are a long way from the experience of most people."

Cor Kontos turned and looked at her as they walked. "Maybe if more people studied those history books, we wouldn't have so many wars, and we wouldn't need to put so much focus on the military."

As Josie got close to Bunche Hall, she decided that she would go a step further than was normally comfortable for her. "This thing the governor wants me to do..." Josie said. "I'm not sure what it entails, but I might need some help. You said you would volunteer to help. Would that be about self defense?"

"It could be. Mostly, I'm kind of looking to expand my

world. You are somebody, and you're going places. If being useful to you meant I could come along for part of the ride… I'd definitely help in any way I can."

Josie thought about it. "Okay. But this is definitely not going the kind of places I want to go. I want to teach medieval history. I don't know that there'd be anything in it for you. It looks like they're going to give me an expense account, so I might be in a position to pay you a fee."

"Put it this way," Cor Kontos said. "The governor is requesting your services. For a Joe, that's way up the ladder of going places."

"What does that mean, 'for a Joe?'"

"A Joe is just another word for a soldier. Especially a new recruit."

"Like GI Joe?"

Cor nodded. "Yeah. I was told that soldiers in World War Two started calling themselves GIs because it stood for Government Issue. And there was a comic strip called GI Joe. Then the whole Government Issue thing faded away. A guy I knew who went to Vietnam said the soldiers there were called Grunts. In my part of Afghanistan, soldiers were just Joes. Some places, it's considered a slam to call someone a Joe. But the guys I was around? A Joe was just a name badge for someone who was part of our brotherhood. Same for the Army women." Cor slowed her pace a bit, looked behind them for a moment as if checking something, then turned back and resumed walking.

"Anyway, I'm willing to help," Cor said. "And I don't care about money. My pension is almost nineteen hundred a month, so I'm set."

It took a moment for Josie to comprehend. Nineteen hundred a month would barely pay for Samantha's charter school tuition. It wouldn't touch rent for most L.A. apartments. Even in Hollywood. Maybe the woman had roommates.

Cor Kontos pulled a very thick wallet out of her rear pocket. It was stuffed with cards and photos and folded pieces of paper and receipts and other bits and scraps of things that Josie couldn't identify. The woman removed a business card. "Here's my number. Just call or text or whatever."

Josie took the card. It was printed with the name Cor Kontos, a phone, and an email.

"Thank you. It was a pleasure to meet you, Cor." Josie held out her hand, and they shook. It felt like Cor was trying to be delicate, but, nevertheless, was about to break Josie's hand bones.

"I may be in touch," Josie said.

"Remember," Cor said. "Always mind your danger hunch. It's never wrong."

"Do you often get danger hunches?"

"All the time," Cor said. "That's why I wanted to see if you were okay."

"Because of me getting into the limousine yesterday."

"Yeah. You maybe weren't as aware as I think you should be. But I was."

Josie stopped walking, turned toward Cor, faced her and looked up at her. "And your warning lights lit up because I wasn't very aware of the pitfalls of getting into the limo."

"Well, yeah, but I was also thinking about the guy who was watching you."

"What guy?" Josie asked. "The governor's guy in the black suit, who ushered me toward the limo?"

"No. The other guy in blue jeans and black leather jacket."

"I didn't see that guy. Where was he?" Josie felt a little sick.

"He was on the sidewalk some distance behind the limo. He followed you when you walked out of class, watching both you and the governor's man."

"What was he doing?"

Cor paused a moment before answering. "Watching, judging, taking photos of you and the governor's limo with his phone. He had his phone down low, doing the cowboy quick-shot aim."

"Why would he take photos of me?"

"Because, for some reason, you're his mark, his target."

"You kind of scare me when you say that," Josie said.

"He kind of scared me," Cor said.

SIX

Josie frowned as she looked up at the Army woman's face. She took her time as if trying to see into the woman's mind.

"Tell me about this man who was watching me." Josie said to Cor Kontos.

"Caucasian male, five-ten, thirty-eight or forty, about one seventy-five, brown over brown, self-cut hair buzzed at the half-inch setting, three-day beard, worn blue jeans with a tear in the left knee, white T-shirt, Dodgers baseball cap, black Oakley sunglasses, dirty Nike Air Trainers, cheap black plastic watch on his left wrist worn with the face to the inside, black Samsung Galaxy phone. He's never been in the military. He's paunchy, soft, and probably doesn't do anything more physical with his hands than type or take phone photos. And he's left handed."

Cor again glanced behind them.

"His attention was split between watching you and watching the governor's limo. I couldn't tell if his focus on you was about who you are, maybe because you're a UCLA professor," she said, "or if his focus was on you being a person the governor was contacting. It could be he was just observing everyone who came near the governor."

"How do you know his eye color with him wearing sunglasses?"

"He took them off to rub his left eye."

"What makes you think he's never been in the military?"

"Sloppy posture. Of course, that can be feigned."

"I wonder if it could be someone I know. Someone from the university."

"That's easy. Take a look." Cor pulled out her phone.

"You took a photo of him? I'm… I don't know. Surprised,

I guess." Josie remembered how quick Samantha was to take photos. Josie never thought about it.

"I learned surveillance in the Army. We were trained to notice anyone who stood out from the crowd. Especially if they were trying to blend into the crowd. That's why I noticed him. He was trying too hard to be incognito. So I held my phone at my waist and took my own cowboy quick-shot pics." She handed her phone to Josie. "There's four or five pics you can swipe through."

Josie scanned through the photos. As Cor had said, the man held his phone at belt level. He seemed to grip it with tension. Like it was dangerous. Like it was a gun.

Josie handed Cor's phone back.

"Ever seen him before?" Cor asked.

"Not to my knowledge. How is it that you noticed things that aren't even in the photos? Like his shoes."

"Army trains us to do that." Cor paused. "What do we do next?" she asked. She sounded like a diligent soldier asking advice of her Commanding Officer.

"I need to think about it," Josie said. "I'll consider what's happened and what you've said. When I get home, I'll see if I can come up with a tentative plan."

"A plan," Cor said slowly, "about whatever it is that the governor wants?"

"Yes. Depending on what happens, I may call you some day. But I don't want you to expect or anticipate any contact from me. It could be that I have an epiphany that would help me reject the governor's request. Or maybe I will realize that I have to do this alone."

Cor nodded, her face very serious. "Okay. No expectations. If you do call and get my voicemail, it'll be because I'm teaching the ladies."

"I'm curious," Josie said. "Is teaching self defense about showing them how to use mace or a taser? Things like that?"

"We have three levels. The first is about learning to yell. A large proportion of women are incapable of vocalizing when they're in trouble."

"So they practice yelling?"

"Right. 'Stop right there! Don't come any closer! I'm armed and I'll kill you!'"

"That sounds… Very commanding."

"It is, and that's the point. The second level of class is basic physical defense. How to immediately run, and if that doesn't work, where to kick, where to claw, how to use your thumb to take out their eye, how to break a hold."

"You said there's a third level."

"Yes, if women are really committed. That group is usually women who've been assaulted. Some of them are radicalized by the assault. They want to make sure that if it ever happens again, they can subdue their attacker. We teach them what weapons to carry, how to use them, how to disarm and then disable an attacker, and, if necessary, how to kill him."

Josie watched Cor as she said it. She sounded so matter-of-fact.

"I assume you know how to do all those things. Even kill."

Cor reached up to the left side of her sleeveless shirt and touched a medal that was pinned there. "They awarded me the Combat Action Badge for performance under hostile fire. There were four of us. We had to use all of our skills."

Cor's words made Josie tense.

"Where do you give your self-defense classes?"

"We teach at a community center in Hollywood. It's in an old school building. The center offers a range of classes. They call it A-to-Z school. From Art to Zen Buddhism."

Her statement made Josie think of the former Green Beret blacksmith Ralph Ellison, whose warehouse artist loft had a sign that said, 'From Artemesia to Zorn,' which were famous artists.

"You refer to 'we' with regard to teaching self-defense. You're not the only teacher?"

"I started by myself. There was so much interest that I asked another Joe to help me. Diane Day. She was my battle buddy for several years in Afghanistan but she was assaulted by a fellow soldier. It was so traumatic for her that she quit the Army, came home to L.A. and pretty much went into hiding. Eventually, she decided to take charge of her life and become powerful enough that not even a male soldier could take her down unless he surprises her with a gun and is willing to use it. So she became a firearms instructor and got into martial arts. Diane is a little flower. Small and blonde and pretty, but lethal if she wants to be."

Josie pointed to an embroidered patch that was sewn on Cor's shirt just above the Combat Action Badge. It showed a human stick figure standing on one leg, leaning back with the other leg thrust up, higher than the figure's head.

"What does this mean?"

"That's a Pencak Silat symbol." She pronounced it 'Penchak.' Cor continued, "It's a type of Indonesian martial art. Diane got me into it. Kind of like karate. In the military, we studied hand-to-hand combat, which often involves weapons. But Pencak Silat is more of an art form. Pencak fighters can use weapons, but it's mostly an open-hand fighting approach, which allows the fighter to block blows but also slap and grab."

Something about the name sounded familiar to Josie. "Is that the one with the matriarchal origin story? From the fourteenth century, I think?"

"Yes! That's so cool you know that! The legend is about a woman named Rama Sukana who had been assaulted. So she got interested in how tigers and eagles fight and then developed fighting techniques with similar characteristics. One day, a group of drunken men attacked her, and Sukana was able to fend them off. After that, her skills began to be widely taught. I was drawn to it because it had female roots." She paused and then exclaimed. "But I never thought about the fourteenth century aspect. That makes it a medieval art, doesn't it? That's so cool!"

Josie noticed that cool was one of Cor's most useful words.

"Yes, it is cool," Josie said. "I suppose I should point out that we mostly use the term medieval history just to describe what went on in Europe. In many ways, cultures in the far east were much more developed than cultures in Europe, especially before the fifteenth century and the Renaissance. But it's still interesting to note similar time frames."

"You know so much stuff," Cor said.

"Until this moment, I never knew about Combat Action Badges and Pencak Silat fighting and observers who stand out because of how hard they try to blend in."

Cor grinned. "And you know about how to make someone else feel worthwhile." She reached out and gently touched Josie on her forearm. "Thank you for that."

Josie wanted to ask about the woman's arm tattoos. The largest one showed a rifle, a helmet, a flower, and the words 'Maria. Gone but not forgotten.' But Josie realized it might be too personal. Maybe some other time.

Josie nodded and held up her hand in a little wave.

SEVEN

When Josie got home, she greeted Unknown, made some tea, then sat and pondered what the Army woman had said.

Unknown sat at Josie's feet and swiped her paw down Josie's leg. Josie knew she was eager for a walk, but Josie waited, knowing that Samantha would be home in minutes.

Before Josie finished her tea, Samantha arrived, swept Unknown up in an embrace, and then gave Josie a kiss.

"You okay, Mama? You look stressed."

"The governor's demands have me upset, but I'm okay. My main concern is your school. When it comes time to travel to Tahoe or wherever, maybe you could stay with your friend Christy so you don't have to leave school. Or you could stay home with Amelia. Having her here makes me feel you would be safe."

"No, Mama. I'd rather run into the fire with you than hang out someplace easy. And anyway, Amelia Gomez sent me a text."

"I'm curious," Josie said. "She didn't text me. I wonder why?"

"She said she's worried that her presence will make me unhappy, especially considering she's staying in my room. So I wrote her back that I like having her with us. Plus, I can probably learn stuff from her because she's very focused on developing her business plan for her coffee shop and roasting company. Anyway, when I go with you, that will make her feel less like she's disrupting our world and more like she's watching our condo for us. Watering the plants and all."

"You sound so grown up." Josie felt her eyes sting with tears of pride. "How'd I get a kid like you?" Her thoughts went to the sordid past with Samantha's father Jabari Moreau and secrets Josie had never told Samantha.

"Just lucky, I guess." Sam reached her arms around Josie and pulled her close.

Josie got out her phone, silently gestured with it, then put it on the kitchen counter. Samantha made a knowing nod and set her phone nearby. Josie pulled open a drawer, reached in and pulled out the burner phone they'd used a few weeks before. Samantha raised her eyebrows.

They took Unknown out on the beach walk as they had the day before.

"Do you think the governor has hacked our phones and is listening to us?" Samantha asked.

"Probably not. I'm not sure I trust him. But no way could he be as bad as the previous evil we dealt with. Maybe that is me being blindly optimistic. Nevertheless, I feel like we can't go wrong if we occasionally try to be more private than normal, regardless of who we're concerned about. Cumberland Durand taught us that tech-savvy people can monitor people's phones. And anyone with authority could connect to tech people."

Unknown stopped to sniff what looked like a dead crab.

Josie said, "I think the governor's desire is merely about getting the results he wants. He wants me to catch the ranger killer, which will make him look good. His hold on me is the veiled threat about my tenure track." As Josie said it, she knew the governor's implied threat about revealing information about Jabari Moreau was a stronger motivator. But she wasn't ready to tell Samantha about him. Not yet, anyway. "Even so," Josie said, "I'm pretty sure the debit card they gave me will trigger a computer alert of some kind the moment I use it."

"You can take cash from the debit card account while you're here in Santa Monica and then use that if we travel. Especially," Samantha added, "if they're doing the double-cross, secret-agent thing."

"Like in the movies, Cap'n," Josie said, smiling and bumping her elbow on Samantha's hip.

"Basic life info from the movies, Matey," Samantha said

with a straight face.

Josie said, "I think using cash is a good approach to prevent them from knowing every move we make. However, when we need to go somewhere, we should probably book a room with their card so they don't get alarmed about us. We want them to think we're doing exactly what they want, even if our inquiries take us in directions they might not want us to go."

"What kind of directions do you imagine that will be?" Samantha asked.

Josie forced a grin. "Secret-agent directions."

"I brought my dog pack," Samantha said. "Wanna go down on the sand?"

"Yes."

Samantha unfolded her dog backpack, picked up Unknown, and tucked the dog into the backpack. When she was done, Josie helped her get the pack up on her back. But Samantha was strong, so a 20-some-pound dog wasn't that difficult.

Samantha shifted and made a couple of bounces to get the pack and dog into position. "Can she see okay? Does she look comfortable?"

"I think so," Josie said. "Her head is out. She's already staring at the birds near the surf."

Samantha nodded, turned, and headed down the beach.

The law didn't allow dogs on the beach sand, leashed or not. But Josie and Samantha had found no specific wording that forbade dogs from riding in a backpack. And the many times they'd walked with Unknown in the pack on Samantha's back, no one, cop or citizen, had complained.

From the first time Samantha put Unknown in the pack, Josie had noticed that Unknown was compliant, seemed happy, and made no sound or fuss when riding on Samantha's back. It was as if Unknown understood the trade off. If she wanted to be near the surf, she had to ride, not walk.

They walked on the firm water-soaked sand, just up from the sea foam line.

"I'm glad you don't think the governor and his cronies will be spying on us." Samantha said.

"Cronies?"

Samantha grinned. "I learned that word at school. Cool, huh?"

"Cool, indeed." Josie remembered that the Army student Cor used the word cool.

Samantha said, "If we rent a car, they could track the car."

"True. Remember what Cumberland said, that our old Prius is a dumb car that doesn't phone home. So unless someone puts a tracker on it when we're not looking, then we could drive it without broadcasting our location."

Samantha spoke slowly. "If the credit card tells them what hotel we're staying at, they could come there in the middle of the night and put a tracker on our Prius."

"We'll have to find a hotel with a shopping center nearby, and we can park there."

"Secret agent-style," Samantha said. "It sounds like you assume we'll be traveling."

"It's very likely, yes."

"Do you know where?"

"Not yet where or when. All we know is what they told me about the ranger who was killed. We'll have to look up that ranger and see what we can learn about him."

"Wait," Samantha suddenly said. "What if the killer had some previous connection to the cop! Before he killed him."

"It's probably a long shot, but we should consider it."

"In that case…" Samantha was staring down at the sand as she walked. "In that case, we should try to figure out why the governor is focusing on this."

"He said the ranger's widow is the daughter of his friend who recently died."

"So there's a connection between the governor and the cop."

"That's good, Sam."

Sam started doing a kind of slow-motion hopscotch step in the sand. She took care to avoid bouncing so that Unknown didn't get jostled. "Like, what if the cop had some kind of dirt on the governor, and the killer got that info from the cop before he killed him! The governor could be trying to orchestrate a cover-up!"

"I love it." Josie was nodding. "Orchestrating a cover-up would be another one of those lessons you talk about."

"Basic life info."

"But I've noticed that you sometimes watch horror movies. How can you get life info from those?"

"Every kind of movie is instructive, Mama. Horror movies teach you to stay away from vampires with fangs who bite your neck and suck your blood."

Josie nodded. "Definitely a good lesson for me. I have trouble avoiding vampires."

"We should call Cumberland to help us," Samantha said. Her voice was so dry that it was as if Josie's comment about vampires was not remarkable at all. "You brought the burner phone. It could be like Yosemite, where Cumberland does his magic from here while you and I head out into space and look for alien life forms."

"Or vampires." Josie pulled out her burner phone and dialed new friend Ralph Ellison's home number at the warehouse loft where Josie's former student Cumberland Durand had moved with his young siblings when they and their mother lost their Beverly Hills house.

"Hello?" came the soft, warm, baritone voice.

"Hi Ellison, it's Josie," she said.

"Thought so. No caller ID either means a robo-call or you on your burner. Am I right?"

"You certainly are."

"I'm thinking the burner's not a good sign." Ralph Ellison's voice sounded so reassuring, it helped Josie. The world was a better place when he was near, in person or on the phone.

"Things aren't great," she said. "But first, how's your head doing?" Josie had remained worried ever since the psychopath had clobbered Ellison with a log up in the San Bernardino Mountains.

"I'm still alive," Ellison said. "Which is always a good indicator of brain status. Brain and heart are funny that way. Of all the organs, they're unique in that, if they stop functioning, most everything else stops pretty quick. Back to the burner phone. How come?"

Josie told him about the events of the last two days.

"I'm so sorry. I imagine you're not eager to get back to—what would you call it—field work."

"Correct."

"And this time it's the governor calling," Ellison said. "I guess that's a big deal by definition. How can I help?" he asked. "Remember, even though I'm the clichéd, dreaded black man that society reviles, I'm old. So people look past me. I'm the perfect invisible man."

"It's so nice of you to offer your help. Especially after what happened last month."

"Old guys look for purpose same as young guys. Helping a prof who's hot in her field is good purpose." After a slight pause, he added, "Maybe hot was the wrong word choice. I just meant, you know, having a big-time career."

"You don't need to worry, Ellison. I'm a short, chunky woman who only gets hot in the summer when the air conditioning isn't turned on."

"That's not the way I think of you. Or wait. Sorry. More bad phrasing."

"It's okay," Josie said in a breezy, dismissive manner as if a prelude to changing the subject. "Anyway, having purpose should at least be safe. Purpose shouldn't get you hit over the head. And I don't know the shape of this new job, yet."

"Cumberland is good for determining shape, right?"

"How is he?" Josie asked.

"The same. Never met such a strange, shut-in guy. Super smart, though. He kind of lives inside his head. He seems to have a direct connection from his head into the world of computers. He doesn't even notice anything outside of that world. Sometimes, he comes down the loft stairs to the kitchen area wearing a shirt and sweatshirt and looking like a regular guy from the waist up. But from the waist down, he's wearing boxer shorts and slippers with no socks. He can barely focus on mundane stuff like putting on pants or eating."

"I'm guessing he's not there now, considering what you're saying."

"He walked down to the corner market. Probably to get more Saltine crackers and Diet Coke."

"What about Aiden and Cara?"

"His siblings are normal kids, that is if you can be real smart and still be normal. Shy as can be. But they are functional. They get fully dressed. They eat actual meals instead of just nibbling on crackers continuously all day. They seem to have adapted to the local school. Sometimes Cumberland walks with them to school. But sometimes that seems beyond him. If so, I walk them."

"Any word from their mother?"

"She talks to the kids a bit. She's still staying with her friend in Little Armenia, west of downtown. I heard the Beverly Hills house was sold by the bad guys who were involved with the criminal dad who caused all the trouble."

"I hope Cumberland is still able to do his work."

"Yeah, best as I can tell," Ellison said. "I was gathering up a bunch of loose papers he'd left on the rolling counter in my kitchen. I wasn't prying, but I noticed a sheet that listed what seems like strange computer stuff from the last month. There were several lines of description with dollar figures to the right. The total was ninety-three thousand dollars. It was dated a few days ago. I realized it was a payment report. It had Google printed on it. I don't know if they're the company that paid him or if they're just some other kind of reference. I never made half that much money in any year of my life. This kid gets paid that for three week's work."

"That's out there in my world too," Josie said. "UCLA professors get paid quite well. But not like that. I suppose those are payments for finding security flaws in software?"

"I guess so. I didn't ask him about it. Whatever he does with hacking, he obviously does it well."

As Josie talked on the phone, she and Samantha walked closer to the water line where the sand was firmer. Unknown seemed to scan the beach as they walked, craning her head out of the pack. Samantha veered toward the water when the foamy edge ran out, then turned back when the water surged back up the sand.

Josie explained the basics of her situation to Ellison.

"So this gig the governor wants you to do," Ellison said in Josie's ear. "You got a plan?"

"No. I haven't any ideas at all."

"When you get an idea, let me know."

"You're too kind," Josie said.

"Naw. But exciting as pounding molten iron is, your world brings new surprises. I'd like to be part of it. Oh, here comes Cumberland now. You want to talk to him?"

"Yes, please. Thanks, Ellison."

"Welcome."

Josie heard Ellison calling Cumberland's name. She visualized Cumberland coming through the huge, rolling door into Ellison's cavernous top-floor warehouse loft.

After a moment, Cumberland came on the line. "Hello?"

"Hi Cumberland. It's Josie Strong."

"Oh. Professor."

The standard dry response for Cumberland, Josie thought. Not especially brusque, but always socially maladroit. With Cumberland, there was no decorum, no salutation, no pleasantries. But he was earnest and sincere and endlessly helpful.

"I'd like to come visit and ask you about a problem I have."

"You want to come to Mr. Ellison's loft?"

"Yes, please. If you'd rather meet someplace else, that's fine."

"Let me ask him."

Josie heard voices in the background.

In a moment, Cumberland said, "He says come any time."

"Great. Tomorrow morning at about nine would work well for me."

"Okay. Bye." There was a click on the line.

Samantha gave Josie a questioning look. "It sounds like he

hung up on you again," Samantha said, a bit of amazement in her voice. "Did he really do that?"

"Yes, he did. He's not intending to be rude. It's just his style. I believe it's kind of an autism spectrum characteristic. It's happened quite often, so I'm getting used to it."

Samantha said, "He's a genius with tech stuff, but a total deficient otherwise."

"What is a total deficient?"

"You know. Human emotion stuff. He can't do emotions."

"That's not derogatory?"

"Not at all. Well, maybe a little. And he's gorgeous. Not that it has anything to do with being a deficient."

"He does look like a model, that's true. Is that what the other kids call it? Total deficients?"

"Yeah. We've got a few of them at our school."

"Are you giving Cumberland a pass for being good looking?"

"No way. Okay, sort of. I'm just saying a person can have flavors. Some good, some not." Samantha had walked toward the waves, and one came rushing up the sand. Samantha took running steps to stay dry. The water receded, and the foam made a slight hissing sound as the water disappeared into the sand.

"I bet Ellison wants to help," Samantha said.

Josie noticed in past months that Samantha had always called him Mr. Ellison, even after he'd requested that she drop the mister salutation. Like Cumberland, Samantha had a hard time losing the more formal approach. But now it seemed she'd gotten comfortable with just using his last name, which is what he preferred, even over his first name.

"Yes, he does. But after getting clobbered on the head up by Big Bear Lake, he might have lost some enthusiasm. Another possibility for help is a woman I met today at UCLA. She was in my class that was canceled. Her name is Cor Kontos. She saw me when the governor visited. She said her warning lights lit up, as if the whole situation was dangerous. She could tell I was stressed and said she'd be happy to help if I needed anything."

"Her name sounds cool," Samantha said.

"It's Greek. She seems pretty cool, too. In fact, that's kind of her word. Everything good is cool. She's retired from the Army. Late thirties. If she's half as tough as she looks, she could help us in any physical situation. The main thing is that she saw me getting into the governor's limousine yesterday, and she picked up on the stress of the situation. This morning, she approached me and basically said that she could tell I was in a tough spot. It's as if she read my body language."

"Watching you get into the limo."

"Right."

"How could she help?" Samantha asked.

"I'm not sure. She teaches self defense to women, she learned lots of skills in the Army, and she radiates competence. So there are many things she could do."

"Being retired maybe lets her be flexible and she could come with us out of town."

"Maybe. I imagine her flexibility depends on her self-defense teaching schedule. It's like Ellison. His flexibility is subject to his metal fabrication orders."

Unknown was looking down out of the backpack at a strange gelatinous mass that had washed up on the beach. A large jellyfish, maybe. Unknown's nostrils were flexing as if smelling the jellyfish. All Josie could smell was the salty sea and sand. It reminded her of the perfume the governor's aide was wearing. It took Josie a moment to recall the name. Sonja Gonsalves.

Samantha said, "Even though both Ellison and Cor Kontos are retired, they still have expenses, right?"

"I assume so. If they helped, I could pay their expenses with the governor's debit card. Although Ellison probably wouldn't let me."

"Yeah, he's kind of old-fashioned," Samantha said. "I don't think he'd take money. What's our next move?"

"I will go to Ellison's warehouse tomorrow morning and talk to Cumberland to get ideas on how to proceed."

EIGHT

The next morning, Josie had planned to drop Samantha at school before she headed across town to Ralph Ellison's warehouse loft in Montebello.

"I want to come with you to Ellison's," Samantha said.

Josie looked at her without immediately responding.

Samantha said, "The headmaster has officially relieved me of school duties for whenever you have to leave town to find the ranger killer. Leaving now to go to Mr. Ellison's loft is part of your official governor duty, so I think that qualifies."

"Aiden and Cara will be in school, so you won't be able to see them."

"True. But I also like Cumberland and Ellison. It's good for someone like me to not spend all my time with kids. Talking to adults develops important social skills." Samantha gave Josie a winning grin.

"Where do you come up with this stuff?" Josie said, then, "Wait, no need to answer that. Basic life info from the movies."

The winning grin expanded.

"Okay," Josie finally said.

"Oh, goodie," Samantha said.

They packed a bag lunch, took Unknown, and left in the Prius.

The day was the kind that made visitors from the rest of the country decide to move to Southern California. Although it was close to Christmas, the SoCal sky was impossibly blue, the sun was hot, the temperature in the shade was in the low 70s, and the breeze was just enough to rustle the fronds of palm trees and waft the enticing scents of never-ending flowers into the air.

Josie was surprised at how well the traffic was flowing on

the 10. Normally, she felt boxed in on all sides. Today, she left a good space between her and the truck in front of her, yet no one cut in to fill the gap, as was the norm. And to the rear, there were no tailgaters pressuring her. There was just a black pickup hanging back many yards, being polite, Josie thought, which was an unusual experience on L.A. freeways.

They crossed from Santa Monica through L.A. and found the path through the spaghetti tangle onto East 60 toward Montebello in less than 40 minutes. The black pickup was still behind her, keeping a safe distance, oddly reassuring in its presence.

Josie found her exit and worked her way over toward Ralph Ellison's warehouse loft. Another glance in the rearview mirror showed the pickup had taken the same exit. Josie was pleased. And then concerned. Was it possible…?

Josie made the turn onto the side street that led toward Ellison's building, then looked again in the mirror. The pickup was gone. She moved her head to shift her view and looked out the side mirrors. No pickup. That was good. Or was it?

Josie saw Ellison's warehouse building up ahead. She pulled into the lot and parked.

"C'mon, Unknown," Samantha said as they got out of the car and headed toward the big ramp that led into Ellison's building. Unknown trotted.

Josie watched with delight as Samantha skipped. But the delight was fleeting as Josie realized that such joys of childhood were nearly over for her daughter. Josie herself hadn't skipped in decades except perhaps to show Samantha how to do it when Samantha was very young.

Josie took her time. She knew there were four flights of stairs to climb. And unlike the stairs at her condo, these flights were very long. No need to get prematurely winded.

Josie took the steps at a steady—if slow—pace. Were it not for the daily exercise of climbing the short stairs to their own condo, this much longer climb would have really taxed her. No wonder Ellison was in such great shape. From far above, Josie heard Samantha running up the stairs and then knocking and calling out. "It's Mama and me, Ellison." Her words echoed through the stairwell. The next sound was the deep bass rumble of the rolling door.

The truck-sized door was to the side as Josie came up the last flight. She made a little courtesy knock on the side of the open door as she walked through and into the huge atrium with the glazed roof. Josie stopped in front of the 8-foot sculpture of Athena—goddess of wisdom—that Ellison had sculpted in his metal fabrication shop. It was as dramatic as she remembered.

"Good to see you, professor."

Josie turned as Ellison walked up to her. The tall, thick man was a commanding presence. Although in the three weeks since he'd helped fight the evil men in the San Bernardino Mountains, his tight helmet of curly hair looked a little whiter, a striking contrast to his walnut skin.

"Good to see you, too," Josie said. She reached out both her hands to shake his, then abandoned her motion and stepped forward to hug him. He bent down and wrapped his arms around her.

"You look strong and confident as always," she said.

"And you are like Thena, here. Wise enough that even the governor wants your help."

They made some small talk as Samantha and Unknown explored. Soon, Cumberland ambled down the stairs from the upper loft. Unknown saw him and watched, but didn't attempt to meet him because the metal-grate steps were not comfortable for dog paws. Unknown made a slow wag as Cumberland got close.

"Look, Mama!" Samantha said. "Unknown is wagging again! She only wags for men. I wonder why."

"Me too."

Cumberland bent over and carefully touched the top of Unknown's head. "Hi dog," he said. Then he straightened, walked to Ellison's refrigerator, and pulled out a Diet Coke.

Ellison offered tea, and both Josie and Samantha accepted. Ellison took Samantha over to two big chairs that were upholstered in forest-green leather. They faced two windows and looked out toward the distant skyline of downtown Los Angeles. Ellison spoke to Samantha in low tones. Josie thought it was great for Samantha to get to know a man who was so thoroughly outside of her world of school and volleyball, a man who almost never used a cell phone.

Josie sat down at the big rolling table, alone with Cumberland. She told him about her situation. Cumberland didn't even grunt acknowledgment. But she kept talking as if he were paying attention. She gave him the circumstances of the ranger killing and explained that she had no other information about his death or the killer.

She said, "I'm thinking that because the killer vanished and we have no information about him, maybe there is something about the ranger that I can track down that would reveal lines of inquiry to pursue."

"You mean, maybe he wasn't killed just because he was a cop," Cumberland said. "Maybe there is something specific to this particular cop."

"Right." Josie sipped tea, making a conscious effort to not say too much. Best to give Cumberland the basics and then let him think.

He said, "And whatever is specific to the murdered cop might give you a hint about the identity of the killer."

"That's a good summation."

"You have his name." It was a statement, not a question.

Josie said, "A Forest Service ranger named Francis Telman. He lived in Tahoe near where he was killed."

Cumberland reached over to a laptop computer that was near the corner of the table. He tapped some keys and moved his fingertip on the trackpad.

"What does a ranger do?" he asked.

Josie noticed that it was the same question she'd asked the governor and his aide. "Apparently, a ranger is a type of law enforcement officer who works for the Forest Service and patrols Forest Service land as opposed to a city or a county."

Cumberland made a single nod. "Do you have some time? I could look up some stuff."

"Yes, please."

Cumberland didn't appear to notice that she'd answered. He remained bent over his computer, typing, tapping on the trackpad, moving his fingers.

Josie didn't know if she should stay at the table or leave and let him work alone.

Cumberland interrupted her thoughts.

"This forest ranger was married," he said.

"Yes. Just a few months ago."

"Was his wife Mary Jo Tclman?"

"Yes."

Cumberland continued to focus on his computer.

Josie waited.

"Was she Mary Jo Lassey before she was married?"

"I believe so. The governor said her father Don Lassey died just before her wedding."

Cumberland was again silent.

Josie leaned sideways to glimpse his computer screen. It showed an unusual configuration of information, dense columns of words. No header. Nothing at all like any website she'd every seen.

"Some points of interest," Cumberland said.

Josie waited.

"Francis Telman was kind of an ordinary guy. No social media pages. Like a lot of guys who aren't real young, he didn't use it. But the traditional databases have the normal stuff about him. Date of birth, Social Security number, credit history, driver's license number, employment history, property he owns. Stuff like that. But here's something weird. Mary Jo Telman, or Mary Jo Lassey, if we search on her maiden name, pretty much doesn't exist."

"You mean, no social security, no DMV information or anything like that?"

Cumberland nodded. "Yeah."

Josie frowned. "I think the governor has known her since she was a child."

"I don't mean she doesn't physically exist. I just mean, she mostly doesn't exist online. She's not in the databases. I can't find the normal stuff about her."

"Why do you think that is?" Josie asked.

"Either somebody has put a lot of effort into scrubbing her data, or else she exists under a different name."

"I don't get it," Josie said.

Cumberland looked puzzled. "Maybe she's in the witness protection program? No, they would create a fictional background for her. Or maybe she's always operated under two names. Mary Jo Lassey/Telman could be a fictional name she uses for some things. Her real name that attaches to her data is likely something different."

"How would I figure that out?"

"I don't know. I only know about computers and databases. Maybe if you can learn about real estate she owns or something else where the records are in the public domain... Then I could look it up. Of course, if she's very industrious, she might try to own property under an alias."

Josie recalled that the governor's aide, Sonja, didn't have an address for the house where Mary Jo was staying. She had written down directions for how to get there.

"If I meet her, I can ask," Josie said.

"Sure. Then I can look her up."

Cumberland's laptop started beeping. Cumberland clicked on something and the beeping quit. "Time for me to pick up Aiden and Cara at the school. It seems like a safe neighborhood for them to walk to school by themselves. But Mr. Ellison says no way. It must be that something happened." Cumberland walked to the big door, which was still standing open.

"Wait, Cumberland," Josie said, wanting to stop him from heading down the stairs. She walked over to the door.

He stood there waiting.

"I just want to thank you," Josie said. "You've helped me a great deal in the past. Of course you know that. But now you're offering to help me again. It's really appreciated."

"Sure. You helped me, too. It was kind of scary, mom and us losing our house to those loan sharks that dad scammed.

You made it so Mr. Ellison took us in. I'm pretty sure he wasn't looking for kids to live with him."

Josie noticed that Cumberland said it with a straight face and no sarcasm.

"Yes, that's probably true. But he likes you guys."

Cumberland nodded, very earnest. "I should tell you that Aiden and Cara think their new school is pretty neat. Aiden says it's more real than Beverly Hills."

"Really? What makes it more real?"

"I don't know. Aiden said he met a poor kid, and the kid was nice and offered to let Aiden ride his skateboard. So maybe that's it."

"I'm very glad."

"We'll be poor, too, if they stop paying hackers to find back doors."

"I don't know what that means," Josie said.

"Back doors are just the software flaws that allow hackers to sneak into a system."

"I remember now. You called it penetration testing. Companies want to see if you can penetrate their computer defenses. And if you can, they pay you to see how you did it."

"Right."

Josie nodded and smiled.

"Okay, bye." Cumberland said again, then turned and walked out the door and headed down the four flights of stairs.

NINE

That evening, while Amelia was still at work, Josie and Samantha headed out for their beach walk.

Josie had been wondering if she should be in her Private World or Public World mode. After their previous case with the Bureau of Investigation, when some bad men had installed malicious software in Josie and Samantha's cell phones and monitored their conversations and movements, Josie was hyper sensitive to the possibility it could happen again.

She had wanted to be done with those concerns about which phones to bring and which to leave behind. But the governor's request for help brought it all back. Sometimes it seemed like too much to figure out.

She decided to play it safe. They left their regular phones in the condo but took her burner phone.

They stayed off the sand so Unknown could walk on the leash and not have to ride in Samantha's backpack.

The burner rang as they walked.

"Hi Cumberland," she answered.

"I found out some more stuff about the ranger," Cumberland said.

"Great."

"Francis Telman was forty-four years old. He grew up in Sacramento. He worked as a ranger for eighteen years. He was married to Mary Jo for a couple of months before he was killed. He'd never been married before. I don't know if his wife Mary Jo had been married. I'd have to know her real name. No kids, obviously. Oh, I guess that's not obvious." Cumberland paused. "I've got some work I have to finish for Apple. After that, I have some other ideas I can look up. Will you be, um, waiting?"

Josie realized that Cumberland was feeling pressure. "No,

I've got plenty to do. You take your time. Call me when you have something?"

"Okay. Bye." Cumberland hung up.

Samantha turned her head and stared at Josie. "Did he hang up on you again?"

"Not really. He said 'bye' just before he disconnected. I'm getting a little more used to it."

"It's jarring, Mama. Admit it. Just because he's a genius doesn't excuse being rude."

"Maybe. But I need to remember that he's been such a huge help to us. And now he's helping us again. And I don't think he's being rude in his mind. He's just being efficient. To him, little verbal niceties are a waste of time."

"But they're not to people like us," Samantha said. "I've watched you. You use emotional stuff to figure out—you know—other stuff. Cumberland couldn't begin to do that."

"No, he probably couldn't. He's not wired that way."

"Like I said, a total deficient. A beautiful total deficient." She grinned.

Josie stopped walking, turned, and gave Samantha a disapproving stare. "He's just different. He could view us as deficient for all the things we don't know."

Samantha thought for a moment and said, "You're right."

Josie said, "Let's find a place to sit and plan our next move."

There were no unoccupied benches. They found a pair of palm trees at the edge of the walk. There was a small patch of sparse grass against their trunks. They were about to sit, when Samantha said, "Stop, Mama. Look at Unknown. She's sniffing the palm trunks."

"Oh. We know what that means. Lets put Unknown in your dog pack and go over to the high-tide sand crest. Not too much crapola there. That sand was washed at the last high tide."

"Crapola, Mama? Professor speak is changing, huh?"

"Old professors can learn new tricks."

"You're not old."

Samantha got Unknown into the pack, hoisted it up onto

her back, then walked over and sat on the tide crest. She settled down into the sand enough that the pack and Unknown's weight were supported by the sand, not Samantha's shoulders. Josie joined her. Unknown's head extended out of the pack, and she stretched out her nose to give Josie a sniff.

Josie delicately rubbed the very top of Unknown's head.

Josie had brought the envelope that the governor's aide, Sonja Gonsalves, gave her. She flexed the envelope to peer in at the pages and flipped through until she found the sheet on which Sonja had written with her precise handwriting. She pulled it out, handed it to Samantha, and pointed at the directions to the house where the widow was staying.

"We need to talk to this woman, Mary Jo Telman," Josie said. "In person, if at all possible."

"Because in person you can read her emotions," Samantha said.

Josie continued, "The woman knows the governor and asked him to contact us to help find her husband's killer."

"Not us," Samantha said. "You."

Josie said, "I think the governor referred to us. We're a team. Our success in this crime-fighting business belongs to both of us. Anyway, the governor doesn't think we should call her because she's skittish. He thinks she might decide to go into hiding."

"Even though she supposedly asked for us."

"Right."

"So we should just show up at her door?"

"I think so, yes."

Samantha was looking down at the sheet Sonja had given Josie. She said, "The lady's spread appears to be in the middle of nowhere."

"A house is a spread?" Josie said.

"In the movies, yeah." She looked down at the paper. "And this one's near a river with a funny name." She spoke slowly, sounding out the syllables. "The Co-sum-nes River." Samantha shook her head. "Never heard of that river. Watch, Mama, there won't be any cell coverage at all. We're gonna be cut off like we're back in the Quetico Wilderness in Canada."

"We'll find out."

A large wave crashed on the sand, and foam raced up the slope. Samantha jumped to her feet as if the backpack with Unknown in it weighed nothing. "C'mon, Mama, hurry!" She helped pull Josie to her feet, and they ran back from the sand crest just as the wave flowed over it and spread foam down the back side.

"Whoa, that was close. You can move pretty fast, Mama, if you have to."

Josie nodded. "Perhaps. But now my knees hurt."

They resumed walking down the beach.

"Mama, you only brought your burner phone because you wanted to keep things private. What would be an example of things you'd want to keep private from the governor?" Samantha asked.

"Let's imagine that we learned something that suggested where the killer was hiding," Josie said, "but we still didn't know who he was or what he looked like. We might want to sneak into the area and take a closer look. But if the governor's office knew our intentions, they might tip off the cops, who might want to rush in."

"Spoiling any chance for subtle investigation," Samantha said.

"Yes, exactly."

As the wave foam disappeared into the sand, they once again angled down closer to the water.

"When do we set sail?" Samantha said.

"Would tomorrow work for you, Cap'n?" Josie asked.

"Aye, Matey."

TEN

That evening, when Amelia came home from work, they double-checked their routine with her, made sure she knew how to find the hidden key, and was comfortable being left alone.

"If I have a question or even just get lonely, I'll call," she said.

Josie had a strong sense that Amelia was competent in all ways.

Because it was December, and they were heading toward the northern Sierra, they packed clothes for cold weather. And because winter days were short and they didn't want to drive in the dark, they got up early and left at 6 a.m.

Their bags filled the rear hatch of the Prius, leaving the back seat for Unknown.

The air in Santa Monica was hazy with Pacific moisture. As the 405 climbed up past the Getty Museum toward the San Fernando Valley, the air became clear. They crossed the valley, crested the mountains to the north, and dropped into the south end of the giant Central Valley of California. The sun turned bright and hot, and its light seemed to scour the landscape. The Central Valley was hemmed in by coastal mountains on the west and the Sierra Nevada on the east. There was no more ocean haze in the sky.

Two hours later, they were following the two concrete canals that carried water from the Northern California rivers to the swimming pools and golf courses of the much drier Southern California. They cruised past the endless orchards that supplied the country with almonds and pistachios and walnuts, along with every kind of fruit, from oranges and lemons to nectarines. Farther north were endless vineyards.

The Central Valley is 50 miles wide, making the mountain ridges on both sides visible. Although the winter storms hadn't yet hammered the southern portion of the state, the Sierra mountains to the east were white with snow.

"Sam, it's like you're attached to your phone," Josie said as she glanced over at Samantha, who was slouched down in the passenger seat.

"At least I have a cell signal," Samantha said, not looking up from her phone. "Unlike when you dragged us to the Canadian Wilderness in the fall."

"That was a valuable mother-daughter bonding exercise. Not having phones was part of the experience," Josie said.

"Right," Samantha said, her words sarcastic. "We were both almost murdered. That would have been a major bond." Samantha's words were harsh, but she spoke them with a matter-of-fact tone.

Nevertheless, Josie felt stung. But she had learned that Samantha was rarely sarcastic unless she'd been provoked. Still, Josie needed to be a mother now and then. Right or wrong, an attentive mother went out of her way to shape her daughter in the way she thought best.

"Despite the glory of cell phone reception, you might want to look outside the car window now and then. Check out those mountains to the east. The Southern Sierra Nevada mountains are the highest in the United States outside of Alaska, higher even than the Rocky Mountains."

Samantha glanced out the window. "Pretty snow. But they're really far away. The San Gabriel Mountains in L.A. are lots closer." She looked back down at her phone.

"Are you learning anything on your phone?" Even though Josie tried to say it with an uplift to her voice, she realized the question would just push Samantha away.

"No, Mama. I'm just reading gossip, writing gossip, and watching gossip videos. And, yes, I know the gossip world won't help me get into college. But it helps me understand how people think."

"Mindless thinking?" Josie immediately regretted saying it.

"Yeah, Mama. Totally mindless."

Josie felt shut out. It was her fault for not understanding how young people connected to each other.

"Sorry, I didn't mean to pry."

"I know that," Samantha said, never looking up, doing the thumb dance even as she talked.

Two hours later, there was a sign that announced the road that cut across the valley toward Merced. "Here's the turnoff to Merced. If you look at those mountains to the east, that's where we were in Yosemite a few weeks ago," Josie said.

"Another pretty place that I may never go back to again," Samantha said.

"That's a harsh judgment of a place as beautiful as Yosemite."

"What happened there was harsh enough to keep me away forever."

"Bad things happen everywhere."

"Not like that," Samantha said, still looking down at her phone. "Not in Santa Monica." She paused. "Well not usually, anyway."

"Same for Yosemite," Josie said. She had the impulse to explain how negative experiences can create an inaccurate picture of a place. But she realized that Samantha would think she was using what Samantha called professor speak. Josie decided it was best to drop the subject.

Except for a stop at a rest area to walk Unknown, they were mostly silent for the next hour.

"We're coming to the Mother Lode," Josie said. She pointed out across the foothills to the east.

"What's that?" Samantha asked.

"You know about the Gold Rush, right?" Josie quickly worried that Samantha's answer would be 'no.' So she continued, "In eighteen forty-eight, gold was discovered in the foothills just north of here. When the word got out, hundreds of thousands of people came to California from all over the world. By the very next year, in eighteen forty-nine, the Gold Rush was huge. Over the next several years, the population of California exploded."

Josie paused, hoping to get a sense that Samantha was interested. It didn't seem so.

"Anyway," Josie said. "The biggest gold-producing areas were in the Sierra foothills just north and south of what is now Sacramento. So those areas are referred to as the Mother Lode."

"Oh," Samantha said and looked back at her phone.

Josie felt wounded. But she'd long been aware of the challenges of raising a teenager.

When they got to Sacramento, Josie turned east on Highway 50, a ten-lane freeway. Almost as busy as L.A. freeways.

"Look," Josie said after they'd gone about 20 miles. "Normally, roads gradually wind up into the foothills and then the mountains. But we're on the flat here, and up ahead is a huge, dramatic slope where the highway angles up the hill. It's like someone drew a line. Central Valley ends here. Foothills begin."

"Yeah," Samantha said in a bored voice. She looked up and stared vacantly out the window.

Josie felt that her efforts were worse than ineffective. Instead of enticing Samantha to care about geography or history, she seemed to be having the opposite effect, reinforcing Samantha's view that anything of interest in life came through her phone, not through hands-on experience.

They pitched up the giant hill and began climbing. Josie floored their Prius to try to stay with the traffic flow.

"Mama," Samantha said, "do you have a plan for talking to this lady? Because she seems kind of weird. First, she asks the governor to get your help. Then she hides out so that you can't even call her without worrying that she'll disappear."

"I don't want to judge. The poor woman just lost her husband to murder. That would drive almost anyone into hiding. Especially when the killer hasn't been caught."

Samantha said, "I wonder how she got your name?"

Josie shrugged. "You know our Yosemite case was extensively written up in the media. That Merced TV station did a story on it. I assume she saw one of those articles. And no, in answer to your question, I don't have a specific plan. I just want us to talk to her. See what she thinks. It's only been a few days since her husband's murder. I'm hoping she'll remember something useful. Maybe you will pick up on something useful even if I don't."

"Like what?"

"I have no idea. Maybe the woman got a call from her ranger husband before he found the suspect and was killed. If it was one of those short, reassuring I-love-you calls, maybe she didn't think to tell the authorities about it."

Samantha nodded. Then she spoke with excitement. "Or maybe the husband told her something that the cops would think was innocent but was really code speak! A secret message!"

Josie smiled. "You are imaginative."

"Like, maybe the killer had him at gunpoint, and he forced the ranger to say something about where he was going, and the ranger said something the opposite of the real direction!"

Josie kept smiling.

"It happens all the time, Mama!"

"In the movies, no doubt."

"Movies are simply mirrors of real life. Magnifying mirrors."

Josie nodded, still grinning. Her daughter was growing up very quickly. She routinely made statements that surprised Josie with their high degree of perception. Perhaps Samantha had heard the line somewhere. But to remember it and use it like she just did showed how engaged she was, regardless of her focus on her phone and what she called the gossip world.

After they'd driven up a couple of thousand feet in elevation, Josie found their turnoff in a town called Placerville. The road was a two-lane road with the number 49. On the map it was called the Gold Country Highway.

The road went south and crawled up and down through the foothills without an obvious direction. Josie thought it was probably built on an old gold mining road. Or a stagecoach route. After ten minutes of following the directions provided by Sonja, they found their turnoff. They ended up on a gravel road that wound past vineyards that stretched over steep slopes.

Although the heavy traffic from the freeway was gone, there were numerous vehicles including a dark one with yellow running lights that seemed to follow them a good distance back. When they went around a tight curve, it disappeared. When they came out on a straight section, it reappeared in the rear view mirror, always back a good distance, unlike most vehicles. Because the sunlight was getting low, she couldn't see what kind of vehicle it was, only that it had yellow lights. But as she went around a curve, she got a glimpse in the rear view mirror of the vehicle. It was a pickup. Maybe black. Something about it seemed familiar. She tried to remember. Then it came to her.

When they drove to Ellison's warehouse loft a couple of days before, there was a black pickup that followed them. It always stayed a good distance back.

Josie decided not to say anything. It was no doubt a coincidence. And even if there was a remote chance it wasn't a coincidence, there was no point in alarming Samantha.

"Help me remember this route," Josie said. "We'll be coming back this way after dark."

"Uh huh," Samantha said, staring at her phone. "I've got it on my GPS. I can backtrack us using the app. Unless of course I lose cell coverage. But now that I think of it, GPS services only require a view of the sky, not a cell tower. But I think my app needs a cell tower."

Josie was always amazed at what Samantha knew.

The last turn was onto a one-lane gravel road that was substantial for a driveway. The drive had hair-pin turns and steep grades both up and down. It eventually crawled out on a ridge top and ended at a blacktop parking area and a modern house that perched on a point of the ridge. There were steep drop offs on three sides.

The sun was nearly set and shined a golden glow on the forest and reflected off the house's windows, which were so large they were like transparent walls. As Josie came to a stop in the drive, the rays from the setting sun glinted off a twisty river at the bottom of a canyon that must have been a thousand feet below.

Josie parked, and they got out.

Samantha looked down into the river canyon. "Wow, Mama, you can't see any other houses."

"Yes, it's very secluded."

"And sure enough, there's no cell signal. It reminds me of our camping trip in the Quetico wilderness. Totally remote. The forest is creepy."

"Instead of creepy, maybe we should think of a remote forest as a welcoming refuge for wildlife."

"You mean bears and mountain lions? That's even creepier."

"From what I've read, bear will come near people, as they occasionally do in Yosemite. But they don't bother you. However, mountain lions prefer to stay hidden. Unless you bicycle or run by quickly like their prey. It's probably good that Unknown doesn't run."

"You're making it worse, Mama."

"Oh. Sorry."

The house was a modern assemblage of box shapes, made with walls of contrasting materials. One type of section was made of vertical boards that looked like maple. The boards were about 3 inches wide, and they were separated from each other by a dark, half-inch space as if the maple boards had been attached to a black panel. The dark recessed stripes looked very dramatic and, to Josie, like ideal sheltering places for bugs and other small critters. Josie had often noticed designs like that, where the architecture was so focused on a certain look that it ignored practicality. To keep the boards looking nice, one would have to regularly clean the recessed stripes with a broom or a leaf blower.

The wooden wall sections alternated with large panels of weathered, corrugated steel, the corrugations of which ran horizontally as if to heighten the contrast with the vertical boards of the wooden walls. The corrugated metal had substantial rust and other corrosion. Part of the look.

The third type of wall was glass, huge windows set in polished steel frames similar to those on a city skyscraper. Behind the windows were cream-colored blinds made of vertical slats. The flat roof was comprised of multiple planes that projected six feet or more out over the walls. The only interruption to the roof line was a satellite dish.

There was a large maple garage door, wide enough for two cars and more. A flagstone walkway led to the front door of the house.

Samantha kept Unknown on the leash as they walked to the door, which was a wide, smooth slab of maple under a broad horizontal overhang. The entry area was dark under the overhang. To one side above the door was a small camera that wouldn't be noticeable except for a tiny red light. Samantha pressed a lit doorbell button. A distant chime sounded.

A minute later, the wall sconces to the sides of the door turned on, and the door opened.

ELEVEN

The person in the doorway was an attractive woman about Josie's age wearing soft blue dress slacks, soft blue leather shoes, and a thin sweater in a lighter sky blue color. She was not tall like Samantha and nowhere near as thin. But she was tallish and thinnish. The woman's skin was pale with a thousand freckles, and she had short, curly red hair that had been parted in the middle, with the curls pressed flat to either side. The look made Josie think of pictures of 1920's flappers. Her eyes were a soft blue that seemed reinforced by the blue clothes.

"Hello," Josie said. "My name is Josie Strong, and this is my daughter Samantha. Are you Mary Jo Telman?"

The woman made a tiny nod. Josie thought the woman seemed as if she were in a fog. Slow to process. Slow to react. Like what one might expect if someone had taken a sedative. Or suffered the shock of their spouse being murdered.

"The governor asked me to stop by and see if I can be of assistance in finding the person who took your husband's life. Apparently, you requested my help?"

It was a moment before the woman reacted. She frowned. "I don't want my husband's death to be sensationalized. I don't want the press. And I don't want the governor involving himself in my life. It was a mistake to ask for his help. Your help. I just want to be left alone."

Josie said, "I have nothing to do with the press. I'm a history professor at UCLA. The governor told me he was very close to your father and that your father was close to you."

The woman narrowed her eyes and looked off at the forest with a withering scowl. "Right. My father, King Lear. A messed-up man who was fixated on what would happen to his meager estate when he died. A pathetic man who continuously wanted me to profess my love for him. He kept saying how excited he was to walk me down the aisle. And then he wanted to back out because he didn't like my colors."

Josie was puzzled. "You mean the colors you chose for your wedding?"

"Yes. I was doing a blue ensemble, and he hated blue. Of course, when your father is a tyrant, you automatically like anything he hates. I think he willed himself to death before my wedding just so his absence could once again make him the center of attention."

It was, Josie thought, a brutal assessment, but one which may well be true. Even Samantha, normally unflappable, widened her eyes in surprise.

Josie said, "Regardless of your issues with your father, the governor obviously cares deeply about you. I think he's worried about…" Josie stopped.

"About my mental health? He should be if he's going to interrupt my solitude. He should have known that my request was desperate flailing. He shouldn't have automatically tried to get you involved just because I asked. Where is his internal editor? Where is his sense of restraint? When someone says, 'I'm so upset, I want Wonder Woman to rush in and solve all my problems,' you don't blindly call in the fantasy troops. You're supposed to hit the pause button."

"I'm not Wonder Woman."

"I can see that. Anyway, I'm trying to cope with my husband's death. I'm also trying to cope with a distressing range of issues in my life. I appreciate your effort. But your sudden presence is very disruptive."

"I'm sorry. But what else could I do? You asked the governor to get me involved."

"I did. And I'm sorry about that. I now realize that nothing will change. Nothing will bring my husband back. Even if you found the killer… Hell, even if you killed the killer, like I read you did a few weeks ago in the San Bernardino Mountains, I still wouldn't be made whole. I'll never come full circle. My life is shattered into pieces, and no miracle could ever put me back together again."

Josie nodded. "I understand." But as she said it, she realized that the governor would say the opposite. He would point out that Mary Jo was under enormous emotional stress and that Josie should see through that and persist in helping. Only by catching the killer would Mary Jo really start to heal.

"As long as we're here, may I please talk to you? These kinds of tragedies can never be softened or ameliorated. But if we can possibly find your husband's killer, there would be a chance at justice. A killer shouldn't be allowed to just vanish. A killer should be locked away forever so that no one else has to experience what you're going through."

The woman took a deep breath and let it out in a big sigh. She pushed the door open farther. She leaned out for a moment and glanced at the forest behind Josie and Samantha. Her face showed weariness and worry as if her husband's murder had created pervasive fear. "Come in. Maybe we can make this fast." She stepped to one side.

Samantha looked down at Unknown as if not knowing what to do. People always commented about Unknown's presence and possible entry into their house, whether pro or con. But not Mary Jo Telman.

Josie looked at Samantha, raised her eyebrows, and then tipped her head toward the house's interior as if to say, 'let's give it a try.'

Josie and Samantha and Unknown walked past Mary Jo into a wide, spare entry with a slate floor. To one side was a large contemporary sideboard made of maple. In the middle of the entry was a pedestal and a shallow, water-filled stone bowl that was shaped like a bird bath. In the center of the bowl rose a stone chalice decorated with intricate filigree in endless repeating patterns. Josie remembered patterns like that in medieval Moorish design. From the chalice came the gentle burble of water flowing down into the larger bowl. It reminded Josie of a small fountain at Alhambra in Spain, a place she'd visited back during graduate school. It was a dramatic contrast to the modern house, and yet the spare geometric designs seemed at once to be both traditional and oddly modern as they had been for 2000 years. Above the chalice and flowing water was a hanging basket with a long cascade of ferns, and above it a skylight that would make a wonderful illumination during the day.

"We can talk in the living room," Mary Jo Telman said. She walked down a long, open space with an off-white marble floor that was elegant with its dramatic gray veining. The floor angled from the entry past the kitchen. It was as if the big box shapes that made up the house had been joined to the others at 30-degree angles, which added to the modern feel.

The inside of the house had tall walls, some covered with vertical maple boards with black spaces between them, echoing the maple walls outside. Other wall sections were covered with heavily textured plaster in swirling patterns and painted yellow like daffodils. On the walls hung large abstract paintings with intense contrasting colors.

Mary Jo glanced toward a grouping of furniture in a large living room with floor-to-ceiling windows along two sides At the far side of the room was a modern fireplace with a hearth and mantle made of slabs of polished black granite.

There was something in the woman's glance, Josie thought. A furtive look. Tense. At first, Josie thought the look revealed something about the woman's past experiences in the room. Then Josie realized the glance was directed out the windows. As if the woman wondered about someone looking in.

Although it would be dark in minutes, the blinds were open. But the ground outside the house dropped steeply away. No one could easily see in without clinging like a climber to the house's outer wall, which would make them obvious from the inside. Josie walked forward and looked out the windows. Beneath them was the dark canyon with the glinting river far below. In the distance to the west stretched the Central Valley. Many miles away, silhouetted by the setting sun, were low mountains, what Josie thought were the coastal ranges near the Bay Area. Josie saw no people, no houses, and no vehicle headlights, near or far. They could have been in a wilderness.

"Quite the beautiful view," Josie said.

"Yes. My friends use this as their vacation home. They want to move from the Bay Area and live here full time, but work prevents that for the next several years at least. After my husband's death, I needed a change of scene. So they offered to let me stay here."

The woman pointed to several leather chairs and a couch. "Have a seat." She didn't even glance at Unknown, so it seemed that she had no concerns about a dog in the house.

Josie took a chair. Samantha sat on the couch and had Unknown sit on the floor next to her.

Mary Jo held out her hands in an awkward way. "I could probably find you something to drink." Her voice was a depressed monotone.

Josie saw Samantha glance at her. "No thanks," Josie said. "We're fine."

The woman sat across from Josie. Her posture was prim, back straight, ankles crossed. The glow from the sunset hit her face and showed the contrast of her red, swollen eyelids around the blue irises. The woman had obviously been through enormous grief. After a long silence, she spoke.

"Despite my discomfort, I'll probably come to appreciate you coming here to try to help me," the woman said. "Although I didn't realize they would send you to this house where I'm staying. In fact, I didn't think they knew I was here. I must have told them. But I would have thought they'd call and tell me you were coming. Although there's no cell reception here. And I suppose they don't know the number for this house's landline."

Josie didn't want to say that the governor's office thought that Mary Jo might get cold feet and flee if they called first. Josie nodded and said, "The governor suggested I just show up and knock. I'm sorry for that intrusion."

The woman nodded. "When my husband was killed, I was so distraught I couldn't function. The governor called to express his sympathy. He asked if there was anything he could do to help. I'd been interviewed by multiple police officers. None of them seemed to have a plan how to proceed. There were no clues about who had killed Francis. Although I'm not informed about crime investigation, I could sense that they'd already decided that finding Francis's killer was a lost cause. It was as if they thought the killer was a mountain man who might be hiding in the wilderness and not be found for years, if ever. Then I remembered an article I'd read about you two." The woman glanced at Samantha. "The article said that the two of you had solved two murder cases even though you have no criminal investigation background." The woman looked from Josie to Samantha and back. "Am I right about that? You've never been in law enforcement?"

"That's correct," Josie said. "I'm a history professor at UCLA. Sam is a middle-school student in Santa Monica. When we were confronted with those cases you read about, we only did what seemed logical. On the first case, a killer came after us. We had no idea why. We fought for our survival. We did some things right and some wrong. In the end, we caught the man. On the second case, we got pulled into an elaborate fraud. We did some research, asked questions. Eventually, the things we learned led us in the right direction. We were lucky that we met some people who helped us. I don't think either of us felt like we were doing anything extraordinary. And, to be fair to you, I don't believe we have any kind of special skill in this regard." Josie didn't want to add that she feared for her tenure track if the governor's friends on the UCLA Board of Directors didn't like her response to the governor's request.

"However," Josie added, "the governor thinks we might have a different perspective than the police regarding how to find your husband's killer."

"So you don't have a plan of how to proceed with my husband's case?" The woman's voice seemed imbued with a great sadness and despair.

"Not specifically, no," Josie said. "But we can do what we did before. Start by asking questions."

Mary Jo Telman seemed relieved. "How can I direct you? Do you want the names of Francis's work colleagues so you can question them?"

"Eventually, sure. But first, I'd like to talk to you."

"You have questions for me?" Telman's voice went up in pitch as if she were surprised. "But I don't know anything about what happened."

"I understand. But you can help us get to know your world."

"Fine. But that's not going to help you find my husband's killer." Mary Jo Telman's words had a biting edge to them. "His killer was some kind of a madman cop killer. It was pure randomness that had my husband chasing him instead of another ranger or cop. When the killer realized my husband was after him, the man shot and killed him."

"You really think it was random?"

The woman made a jerk of surprise. "Of course."

"What if your husband knew the killer?"

"But he didn't! The idea is ridiculous."

"Is it? Did your husband tell you about every single person he met during his work?"

"No, of course not. I asked him not to talk about every detail of his encounters with bad people because it could be depress…" Telman stopped as if catching herself being too informative. "Depressing," she finally said, finishing the word. "Anyway, how could he know this guy? Francis just saw someone burglarizing a neighbor cabin. Then the man put on skis and began heading up a snow-covered slope toward the Desolation Wilderness."

"How do you know this? Did your husband call and tell you?"

"No. He would have, I'm sure, if he had a spare moment. I know what happened because the police on the scene made notes about the tracks in the snow. They could tell what had happened. The burglar pulled off the highway at Emerald Bay up at Lake Tahoe. He parked where there is a forest service road that isn't plowed during the winter. Francis must have watched out his cabin window as the man left the neighbor's cabin and skied past on stolen skis. He must have gotten curious about why someone was out there at night, curious enough to put on his own snowshoes and follow him."

"And you know this from what the police deduced from the

tracks."

"Right. The tracks led up a long, open slope, then entered the forest. They told me the ski tracks periodically traversed left and then right, zigzagging up the slope. Whereas the snowshoe tracks Francis made went straight up the slope. He was like that. Always into fitness. Snowshoes made it so he could catch the burglar."

"Snowshoes are faster than skis?" Josie didn't understand.

"Faster when you go straight up a steep slope. Skis, of course, are faster when you come down."

Josie made a single nod. "What can you tell me about Francis's job?" Josie asked.

Mary Jo Telman shrugged. "He worked as a ranger for the Forest Service for two decades. Before that he spent a year as a cop in Salt Lake City. When the Forest Service hired him and said he'd be working out of the Foresthill office and spending significant time in the Tahoe Basin, he was ecstatic. He called it his Tahoe beat. After three years, he was able to buy a small, one-bedroom cabin on the West Shore above Emerald Bay. At the time I met him, he'd been on the Tahoe beat for many years, and he still thought it was a dream come true."

"You said his work base was in Foresthill?"

"Yes. It's a little foothill community north of here. Not far from Interstate Eighty."

"What did Francis like about being a ranger?"

"He often said it was more like being a camp counselor than a cop. Sure, he carried a gun, and he had to enforce the law. But he thought that patrolling campgrounds and making periodic forays into the beautiful high country was more play than work. When he first became a cop in Salt Lake City, he went to school at night and finished his degree in Environmental Science. When he was hired by the Forest Service, he was so pleased to work in the forest world he loved."

"Does a ranger have much contact with criminals?"

"Not the way typical cops do. His worst encounters were with drunk campers."

"Did he get along with his colleagues?" Josie asked.

"Yes. It was a good crew, the Forest Service guys. He said the bureaucrats, site managers, firefighters, and volunteers were all mostly focused on managing the forest for the public good. Nothing at all like being a big city cop."

"Did he have disagreements with any colleagues?"

"Not that I ever knew about."

"What did he do in his spare time?" Josie asked.

"He went hiking and camping and fishing. He climbed all of Tahoe's major peaks. He hiked the TRT. In the summer, he kayaked, and in the winter, he skied."

"What does that mean, the TRT?"

"The Tahoe Rim Trail. It's a route that follows the highest mountains around the edge of the Tahoe Basin. Almost two hundred miles of high country."

"Did he ever mention any difficulties? Or things he struggled with? Either with work or not?"

"I don't understand. He was in perfect health, if that's what you're wondering about."

"I'm thinking more about career or ongoing life frustrations. Hopes and dreams that were thwarted for whatever reason."

"No. Nothing. He had his act together, if you want to call it that. I can't think of anything that would give someone motive to kill him."

Josie was thinking the same thing, but she was glad that Mary Jo was the one who put it into words.

"It's clear to me that his killing was a random act of violence," Mary Jo said. "When murderous psychos get chased by cops, they kill them. It happens all the time."

Josie knew Mary Jo was right. But it didn't give her anything to go on.

"May I look at his cell phone?"

"Sure. The police just returned it. They wanted to catalog his call history. But apparently they didn't find anything useful." Telman stood up and walked over to a small desk area in the kitchen. The desk was a spare, modern maple writing surface with no drawers or organizer bins. The backdrop of the desk was like the maple walls, vertical boards spaced with half-inch intervals. The recessed spaces were black. Mary Jo reached under the desk, feeling with her fingers, and moved something. A portion of the maple-board backdrop swung open, apparently hinged in one of the black recesses. The open door revealed a hidden cupboard with three shelves.

Josie heard Samantha make a stifled gasp. She turned to see Samantha staring at the secret cupboard, amazement and delight in her eyes.

On the shelves were paper pads, an appointment calendar, some pens and pencils. Mary Jo reached in and picked up a phone, then swung the cupboard door shut. It clicked into place and once again became invisible.

She brought the phone over and handed it to Josie.

"Does it need a passcode?"

"No. Francis hated having to have passwords and codes for everything. So he didn't use one on his phone."

"Would you mind if I wrote down the phone numbers that he called and that called him?"

"No."

Samantha spoke. "I could just email them to you, Mama."

Josie looked at Mary Jo Telman. "Is that okay?"

"Sure. Whatever you want."

Josie handed the phone to Samantha and turned back to Telman. "When we first came, we couldn't get a cell signal," Josie said.

"Mama, it's connecting through wifi."

"Oh." Josie felt she'd never understand how it all worked. "What about email? Did Francis have an email account?"

"Just his work email. But he rarely used it. If he wanted to communicate, he called someone. But feel free to look at his email. His phone has one of those email buttons. The police said I shouldn't use the account or delete anything in it. But it's okay to open incoming emails. He has the setup where his email always shows on his phone."

Josie looked at Samantha. "Sam, is that also something you could email me?"

"Sure." She looked at Mary Jo.

"You have my permission to do that as well."

Josie nodded. "Was Francis in good shape financially?"

Mary Jo frowned as if she didn't like the question. "Yes. A Forest Service ranger doesn't make much money. But it pays the bills, and the job comes with benefits like health insurance."

"Did Francis have any major debts?"

"No. He didn't believe in debt. He was very frugal. If he needed to replace his old car, he would save up and buy another used car, just not so old."

"Did Francis ever associate with people who were in trouble financially or with the law?"

"No. His few friends were other rangers. He mostly kept to himself."

"Did Francis gamble?"

Mary Jo seemed to recoil. "You are asking questions that suggest Francis was of questionable character." Her voice got louder as she spoke. "I can tell you that Francis was a good man, stable with his finances, his friendships, his career. With me. He didn't gamble. There is nothing that you can find that could somehow be twisted around into explaining why some murderous psycho would kill him."

"I'm sorry," Josie said. "I meant no offense. I'm only trying to be thorough in pursuing your desire, which is to find out who killed him."

Mary Jo Telman stood up. "My desire is justice. If you're going to try and disparage my husband's character, then I will find someone else to track down this killer." Telman took a step toward the door.

Josie realized she'd used up the woman's tolerance for questions. She stood. "Again, I'm sorry. I wasn't trying to make you uncomfortable. I was just trying to learn anything that might help me find the killer."

Samantha handed Mary Jo Telman her husband's phone.

Telman was talking loudly. "You're looking for a murderer. Why would you try to slam the character of my husband?"

"I didn't mean it like that. We'll leave and give you some peace."

TWELVE

Josie moved toward the entry and the front door. Mary Jo Telman walked ahead. She opened the door and walked out onto the parking area, heading toward Josie and Samantha's Prius as if trying to hurry them into leaving.

Although it was now dark, the parking area was lit by yellow lights on low posts. The lights shined down at the ground and cast a yellow glow that mimicked the earlier glow from the setting sun. The dramatic lighting made the Prius look like an advertisement next to the short stone wall, with the dark canyon and distant mountains behind.

Josie and Samantha and Unknown stepped out of the house and took several steps toward their car. Samantha unhooked the leash, and Unknown walked slowly out onto the parking area. She lifted her head as if to better sniff the air. Josie turned and faced the woman.

"Thank you, Mary Jo. I appreciate you taking the time to answer questions. I hope I am able to be of use to you and the governor."

Mary Jo Telman spoke in a loud voice. "I never should have called the governor. Nothing will come of it. The killer won't be found. And you're already making negative suggestions about my husband's character." She was now shouting. "I won't have any closure." Her voice caught in her throat as she shouted, "Drop the case. Just go away!"

"I'm sorry, Mary Jo," Josie said. "We'll leave."

"I'm sorry, too," Samantha said. Samantha was holding her phone in front of her as if it were a mini shield.

Unknown seemed to react as well. She turned her head as if listening to the dark forest and did her version of a growl, no rattle in her throat, just a smooth low-pitched whine.

Josie reached into her purse and pulled out her car key. Her lipstick accidentally came out and fell to the drive. It rolled away. Josie took several fast steps and bent down to grab it. In her peripheral vision she sensed Mary Jo Telman lunging toward Samantha as she made a hard, coughing grunt of effort. As Josie straightened up and turned, she saw Telman strike Samantha. Samantha made a sudden cry as she was knocked backward.

Samantha, and then Mary Jo, hit the short wall with their feet and legs. As they tripped, their momentum flipped them over the wall, heads down. The women bounced and slid down the steep embankment.

Josie ran to the wall and looked down into the darkness.

"Sam? Sam! Are you okay?" Josie called out louder. "I can't see you in the dark. Say something, Sam!"

"I'm okay, Mama," came a soft, traumatized voice.

"Thank God."

Josie could tell that something was wrong with Samantha. She sounded wounded.

"Mary Jo," Josie called out. "Where are you?! How could you do that! We could have all been severely hurt. Where are you? Speak up!"

Samantha called out, "What happened, Mama?"

"Mary Jo pushed you over the wall and down the slope!" Josie raised her voice. "Mary Jo, get a flashlight, and come help us right now!"

"Mama, I'm stuck! My arm really hurts. Come and help me."

"I'm coming." Josie lifted her leg, got her knee on the stone wall, got her other knee up, and began lowering one foot down into the dark on the other side.

There was a whimpering sound. Josie realized it was Unknown.

"Come here, Unknown," Josie said. When both of her feet were on the ground, Josie bent over the wall and picked Unknown up off the driveway. She lifted the dog over the wall and set her down on the steep slope on the other side.

"That's good. I'm going to unhook your leash so you don't get tangled." Josie raised her voice. "I'm coming, Sam. Unknown's with me. Call her, and she'll find you in the dark."

Samantha's voice was weak. Almost feeble. "C'mere, Unknown. I'm down here in the dark. C'mon, girl."

"Keep talking, Sam. I'll come to your voice." Then much louder, "Mary Jo, where are you?! Come help us." Josie went down the slope. It was as steep as a staircase.

"I'm over here, Mama."

"Oh, I'm going the wrong way." Josie turned to crawl across a rocky slope that was so steep she worried she might slide off into the canyon below.

Josie said, "Can you turn on your phone so I can see the light?"

"I don't have my phone. I must have dropped it when Mary Jo hit me. I can't feel it anywhere. And my left arm is numb, except my shoulder hurts worse than I can say."

"I'll be there in a minute. Keep talking. I'm crawling toward you. The slope is steep, so I'm going slow."

"Okay, Mama. Keep coming."

Josie rolled onto her hands and knees. It felt like the sharp rocks were tearing into her skin. Her purse was still slung around her shoulder. It dangled beneath her neck, swinging as she crawled. She got one of her arms through the strap so that most of the slack was taken up.

"This is scary," Samantha said, "being down this hill in the dark."

"I'm very close," Josie said. "Don't let me startle you. I'm reaching toward you, but it's cave black."

Her fingertips brushed fabric. "Oh, Sam, I found you." She started to bend down in the dark to hug Samantha.

"Ouch. Careful, that hurts."

"I'm sorry," Josie said. "I can't see a thing."

"Do you have your phone?"

"Yes. It's in my pocket."

"It has a flashlight."

"I don't know how to use it."

"Here, I'll show you. I'm reaching up with my hand."

Josie waved her arm. They touched hands. Samantha got hold of Josie's phone.

Samantha talked as she worked Josie's phone with one hand.

Josie was glad for Samantha to have a distraction from her pain.

"You swipe up from the bottom," Samantha said. "There's a flashlight symbol. Just tap it. Look away so it doesn't blind you. I'm turning it on."

A brilliant white-blue light came on. It was facing away from Josie, off to Samantha's side. There was just enough light spilling beyond the main beam to throw light on Samantha. The girl lay sideways across the slope. Unknown was lying next to her.

Josie was so glad to see that her daughter was in one piece.

But then she saw blood.

Josie tried to muffle her gasp.

Samantha was covered with blood. It was all over the front of her shirt. It was splashed across her neck and all over her face.

THIRTEEN

Josie struggled to stay calm. She couldn't seem to breathe. "Samantha, where's your pain?"

"Just my arm. My left shoulder. It hurts so bad. And I can't move the arm at all."

"Is it numb?"

"The lower part is. The shoulder has a deep, throbbing pain. I can barely stand it."

"I'm going to take the phone out of your hand so I can use the light."

Josie took the phone from Samantha and shined its bright light on Samantha's shoulder, taking care not to shine the light in Samantha's eyes. There was no blood on the shoulder. The injury must be internal. Samantha probably hit a rock when she fell. Then Josie noticed that the shape of the girl's shoulder was not normal. The outer curve was all wrong. Josie knew nothing about medicine, but it looked to her like Samantha had dislocated her shoulder. Josie had heard it was one of the most painful injuries.

"Your shoulder isn't bleeding," Josie said. "So that's good." Although as Josie said it, she realized that Samantha could be bleeding internally.

"Does anything else hurt?" Josie asked.

"Just the front of my chest. On the right. Up high. Under the collar bone."

"I'm going to look at it with the light, but I worry I'll shine it in your eyes, so you better close them tight."

"Okay, Mama. My eyes are shut."

Josie shined the light on Samantha, just under her collar bone. Her shirt was soaked with blood. There were soft bits of material like minced flesh. Josie's heart thumped. She couldn't imagine what kinds of injuries Samantha had.

"I'm lifting up the neck line of your shirt to see if I can tell what hurts." Josie said. There was a thick, dark bruise, a dull purple black that stood out from Samantha's rich teak skin. There didn't seem to be any break in the skin.

"You have a nasty bruise. But I don't see any place where you're bleeding."

Samantha lifted her right hand to her chest and pressed with her fingertips here and there, palpating her chest to gauge the injury.

"I don't understand. My shirt is all wet. Sticky wet. Did I roll through water or something? I have no memory of what happened."

"You have some blood on you." Josie didn't want to add that there was other material as well.

"What?!"

"Don't worry. It's probably just one of those skin wounds that bleed a lot. But we obviously need to get you to the car and take you to a doctor." It took all of Josie's concentration to maintain control. Only the knowledge that Samantha's life was at stake helped to keep Josie's focus.

"Can you lie still a minute while I take this light and look around?"

"With this shoulder pain, I don't think I can do anything but lie still until the pain goes away."

"Okay. I'm going to stand up and get a sense of this slope we're on. You hold Unknown with your good hand. She'll keep you calm."

"I'll try, Mama. Hurry. My shoulder really throbs."

Josie shined the light away from Samantha's eyes and slowly stood up. She took care to make sure she had good footing so she didn't trip and tumble down the mountainside. She had worn nice leather shoes to the meeting with Mary Jo Telman. Which meant they provided very little support.

Josie turned the light to the left and the right, scanning in the dark. Even though the light was very bright, it was hard to tell what she was looking at. There was a big rock to one side.

Josie realized it was partially blocking a shape that didn't look like rock or wood. Josie walked that way, shining the light down at the ground, being careful with her foot placement.

When she got near the boulder, she was able to illuminate the rock.

On the far side was Mary Jo Telman. She was lying on her back, head down the slope. Her eyes were easy to see in the bright light. They were open as if in shock at what happened. They were dull and non-reflective. The front of Mary Jo's blue sweater was dark with blood that looked shiny black in the phone light. Even though the sweater fabric did a good job of covering the skin beneath it, Josie could tell that the woman had been shot. There were many bits of tissue protruding from a dark spot in the center of her chest. Tissue like what Josie had seen on Samantha's shirt. At least that helped Josie worry a tiny bit less about Samantha. But the knowledge made her feel panicky and light-headed. She could barely breathe. Her heart thumped faster.

Josie stood in the dark, trying to force herself to focus and figure out what happened.

Mary Jo had been facing Samantha when she lunged at her. The sudden movement must have occurred when she was shot. Because she was facing them, the shot must have come from behind her. Up the slope behind the house, probably. Judging by the messy wound on the front of Mary Jo's chest, the bullet must have gone all the way through, splattering Samantha in the process, maybe even hitting Samantha someplace that Josie hadn't seen.

Josie didn't know about guns, but from what Ellison had told her in Yosemite, a major bullet wound without a very loud gunshot noise, meant the shooter was a long distance away and using a powerful rifle. That might indicate that the shooter wanted to keep his distance, which might be a good thing. However, it might also indicate that the shooter could stay where he was and wait for Josie and Samantha to reappear so he could shoot at them also.

Josie turned and made her way back toward Samantha.

She turned off the phone light, then bent down and touched Samantha's cheek.

Josie whispered. "We need to talk quietly. Mary Jo is dead, hon," Josie said. "She was shot. The bullet is what pushed her into you."

"Somebody was waiting to murder her?" Samantha's voice was a whispered wail. "But they couldn't have known that Mary Jo would come out of the house. Meaning, they were probably trying to kill us! I can't believe this is happening again!"

FOURTEEN

"I'm so sorry, sweetheart," Josie said. She didn't want to worry Samantha any more than necessary. But when someone starts shooting at you in the dark, you can't exactly minimize it. "Our first priority is to get the police. Then we have to get you to a doctor."

"But I can't move! And if you move, the shooter will see you and shoot again! This time he might hit you!"

"I'll be very careful."

"Can you look at your phone again?" Samantha asked. "Maybe there's cell reception down on this slope?"

Josie looked at the screen. It said, 'searching' in the upper corner.

"Nothing," Josie said.

"What do we do?" Samantha's anguish was intense.

"We don't have much choice. We could hide down here in the dark and wait until dawn and then try to escape. But that much time will make your shoulder worse, not better." Josie didn't want to say what she was thinking, which was that if Samantha was bleeding internally, she might not last until dawn. "And I worry that the shooter might find us down here anyway. It's critical to get you medical care as soon as possible."

"But you have no cell reception." Samantha's voice had risen in volume.

"Shhh," Josie said. "There is a landline in the house. After Mary Jo opened the door, and we went out, she didn't lock it again. I can get up this slope to the parking area, run into the front door, and lock it behind me. Then I can call for help on the landline."

"How long will it take?"

"I don't know, sweetheart. But I'll go as fast as I can. Once the nine-one-one call goes through, it will no doubt be awhile."

"What should I do?"

"The critical thing is to stay silent. No matter what happens, you can't call out because that would let the killer know where you are. I'll try to get to the landline and call nine-one-one. It took us quite a long time to drive here, so the police and ambulance won't be showing up anytime soon. After I make the call, I can sneak back down this slope to you."

"Mama, that sounds like forever!"

"Right. So let's both of us remember that trick we learned for passing the time."

"About the Grimm's fairy tales?"

"Right. When you were very young, I would read you four of them at night. That was usually fifteen pages. Usually you were asleep by the end."

"And it usually took an hour," Samantha said.

"Right. So I want you to imagine that I'm reading the fairy tales. Think of your favorite ones. Imagine four of them and then imagine them twice. That's two hours."

"I can do that. But what if the killer shoots at you?"

"He's probably long gone. Either way, he won't know when to expect me. Or, even if I'll show up at all. And he'll be surprised by how fast I move. So, if you hear gunshots, just visualize him missing me. If the landline doesn't work, maybe I'll jump in the car and drive to a place with cell reception. He won't know what to expect."

"Mama! You can't drive away and leave me alone on this mountainside in the dark! I would die of fright!"

"Shhh. I would only do that if I couldn't get through on the landline." Josie leaned in close so her lips were near Samantha's ear. She whispered, "You are the most important thing in the world to me. I will be here for you always. No matter what happens, the way you can protect us both is to not react. Stay completely silent. If you do that, he may even think you slid off the mountain. You'll be safest that way."

Josie took her purse off her neck and shoulder, lifted Samantha's head a few inches off the rock, and slid the purse underneath for slight cushion. Then she pulled off her ¾ sleeve suit jacket and draped it over Samantha's body.

"This will help keep you warm. And keep Unknown next to you. I'll clip her leash back on. She'll help you stay warm. Remember the fairy tales. Four stories, twice. I'll be back by then. I love you. I'll love you forever."

Josie could hear Samantha crying, in pain, afraid, and lonely.

Josie gave Samantha a long hug, being careful not to touch her injured shoulder. She kissed Samantha twice, stood up to leave, and began hiking up the slope in the dark, trying not to let Samantha hear her sobs of despair.

FIFTEEN

Josie stayed bent, her hands on the ground in front of her. Because of the steepness of the slope, she used her feet, not her knees, to crawl up the mountain. She hit numerous obstacles. Boulders. Trees. Bushes that seemed impenetrable. But she dared not take her phone from her pocket and use its light. Even if she'd had light, she'd probably be unable to see anything, so thick were her tears.

The sounds of night permeated her distress. An owl hooted. A distant coyote made a shrill yipping cry. Scurrying sounds seemed to emanate up from the dirt. The night world was alive, and Josie's city perspective made her think every sound was threatening. She remembered the night earlier in the fall, hiking through the Santa Monica mountains, trying to save Samantha from the first killer. Now she was doing something similar. The emotional angst threatened to crush her spirit.

But she had to forge ahead. She had to save Samantha.

In a minute, Josie got close to the short wall that separated the parking area from the mountainside that dropped down below it and the house. The glow of the short, yellow lights became more obvious. Josie slowed to a stop as she reached the wall and put her hands on the stones.

She stopped moving and stayed below the wall while she listened for any sound that wasn't from non-human wildlife.

No sound came to her. But she knew that meant nothing. A killer had hidden somewhere over on the forested slope above, waiting for a long time. Patiently waiting for Josie and Samantha to come out of the house. And when they did, he killed Mary Jo Telman. Did he want to kill Samantha and Josie as well?

Josie slowly rose up and peeked over the short wall. Nothing had changed. Just as she thought, the front door of the house stood open, light spilling out to the sidewalk entryway. Moths fluttered near the doorway.

As Josie visualized a killer in the forest, able to easily scan all of the area, the front door seemed a very long distance away. Much farther than she'd remembered. If Josie climbed over the wall and ran for the door, how long would it take? How hard would it be for the shooter to pick her off? Josie didn't think it would be difficult at all. In fact, from the moment she hitched a knee up on the wall to climb over, she would be fully illuminated by the parking area lights. The shooter couldn't possibly miss her.

Josie's impulse was to run for the door, anyway. But she thought of Samantha lying down the mountainside in the dark, with multiple serious injuries, covered in blood. Anything Josie did was going to be very risky. She accepted that. But there was no justification for taking additional risks. The door was too far away to risk sprinting toward it. It would be better to get in her car and drive it close to the front door.

Josie thought about where Mary Jo had been standing when she was shot. Josie imagined how the bullet had hit Mary Jo and propelled her into Samantha and Josie. As Josie remembered their positions, it gave her a very rough idea of where the shooter had been. Maybe he was still there.

Josie looked at the forest. She thought about a point that would fit the source of the trajectory of the bullet. But there was nothing to be gained from the idea because the forest was black-dark with only the faintest light from stars above. Josie could see nothing. She estimated that it had been ten or fifteen minutes since the rifle shot. It was possible the shooter was now a long distance away. Maybe he'd even driven away. But if he had immediately started hiking down toward the house, he could easily be near the house and parking area. In fact, he could be inside the house. Josie still didn't think it safe to step out into view and run across the open parking area.

Josie looked at where she'd parked the Prius. If she moved farther along the outside of the stone wall, she could possibly crawl over the wall in a place where the Prius would block the shooter's view of her.

Josie stayed crouched behind the wall as she moved that way. When she got near the Prius, she peeked out again. She realized she could still be seen from most places.

Unless she went over the wall near the rear of the Prius. In that case, the car would give her some coverage.

Then what would she do? Had she locked the car? The key was in her purse! She felt the pocket where she often put the key. She could feel the outline of the key fob. She must have put it in the pocket when she picked up her lipstick.

If she unlocked the car with the key fob and ran around to get in the driver's door, she'd probably be in full view of the shooter. Unlocking the car would flash the car's lights, making her presence obvious to the shooter. Even if she ran fast, he'd have some time to fire a shot at her.

However, if she unlocked the car and opened the hatchback, she might stay blocked from the shooter's view by the car. The car's flashing lights would alert him that someone was getting in the car. If she opened the hatch with the key, that would keep the exterior lights from flashing. But opening the hatch would turn on the light inside the hatchback. It would still be harder for him to see her crawling in through the back than it would be to see her running around to the driver's door. Once she got the hatch raised, she could hit the switch next to the light and turn it off.

It was a stressful decision, but it seemed the hatch was the best way into the car.

Josie chose the place on the wall that had the most cover from the slope above. She stayed low, and moved as quietly as possible. She stayed bent as she lifted her knee up and put it on the top of the wall. Then she made a sideways sliding motion, trying to slither her body over the wall. Her clothes caught on the rough rock of the wall. She heard ripping as she lowered herself to the ground. When she was down on the blacktop, she crawled across the asphalt to the rear of the Prius, pulled the key fob out, and pressed the unlock button. She'd forgotten to use the key!

The car lights flashed so bright she was confident the entire nearby foothills were illuminated.

The click of the doors unlocking was loud enough that anyone would have heard it.

Josie quickly rose up just enough to open the hatch. She still believed it would be harder for the shooter to hit her crawling through the car than entering through the driver's door.

As the lid rose up, she crawled inside the back of the car and got the hatchback light turned off. She left the hatch open and tried to scramble over the seats to the front. But what would have been fast and easy for Samantha was difficult at best for Josie. She wasn't thin enough to snake her way into the driver's seat. She settled for doing a kind of head dive into the front passenger seat and then tried to get turned around and into the driver's seat. She was just getting into position when the windshield exploded.

SIXTEEN

Josie gasped. The windshield glass didn't completely collapse, but a large hole appeared and pieces of shattered glass fell onto her lap.

She started hyperventilating. She focused on Samantha to avoid losing control. Her daughter needed to be rescued.

Josie got the car started, shifted into reverse, and backed up. She aimed for the front door of the house. Another shot blew through the windshield, making a huge star in the glass. The Prius bumped up from the asphalt to the stones of the entryway. Josie drove backward up to the front door. She slowed and stopped a few inches from the door.

Josie set the brake, turned off the car, and slithered back over the seats as fast as humanly possible.

She crawled out the hatchback, shut it, hit the key fob to lock the car, then ran inside and shut the front door. She turned the deadbolt, then dropped down and crawled on hands and knees to the living room, then to the kitchen.

The house lights were still on from their earlier meeting with Mary Jo.

Josie remembered seeing the landline phone on the counter. While still kneeling to present as small a target through the windows as possible, she reached up and slid her hand along the counter top. There was no phone. And the house had so many windows that it was probably easy for the shooter to see her crawling around looking for the phone.

She stood up to see better.

There it was. A portable standing upright in a holder on the little kitchen desk. Josie grabbed it, then looked for light switches. She found the kitchen light switch and turned it off. Still holding the portable, she practically ran on sore hands and knees through the living room, looking for another switch. There. By the entrance to a hallway. She reached up, hit the rocker switch, and the living room lights went off. There was still light. Two lamps in the living room. Josie scrambled over to them. Found the switches and turned them off.

Yet more light spilled from the kitchen. Four lights under the cabinets. They must be on a switch.

Josie ignored the pain in her knees as she pounded across the marble floor. She found three switches up by a counter. She pressed the first one. Ceiling lights came on, bright as stage lights. She flipped it off. She hit the next switch. The under-cabinet lights went off. She was now in relative darkness.

She sat on the floor with her back against what she thought was an inner wall and dialed 911.

"State your name, address, and emergency."

"I'm Josie Strong from Los Angeles. I don't remember the address. I'm in an unfamiliar house. This is a landline phone. There must be an address connected to it. The house belongs to friends of Mary Jo Telman, whose ranger husband Francis Telman was murdered a few days ago. I'm in the foothills near Placerville. Just off the Gold Country highway. It's a modern house on a ridge top."

"What is your emergency?"

"There is a shooter outside. He shot Mary Jo Telman. She's dead. He also shot at me and my daughter. I think the shooter is the person who killed Francis Telman. Please hurry. He shot at me in my car, which I've backed up against the front door as a barricade. My daughter is seriously injured. She's outside, hiding in the dark. I'm hiding in the house. The shooter is obviously serious about trying to kill us. Please hurry!"

"Stay on the line. I have the police en route to the address connected to this phone line."

"My daughter needs an ambulance. She has a broken shoulder among other injuries."

Josie was hyperventilating again. She couldn't get enough air. The stress seemed too much to take. All she could think about was Samantha, down the slope, injured, probably freezing.

There was no way she could be reciting fairy tales to herself now that there'd been more gunfire. She'd be shivering and shaking with terror.

"Please be patient," the voice said in Josie's ear. "The police will be there soon. I have paramedics on the way as well."

Josie tried to focus, tried to stay strong. But she started crying for Samantha. That poor girl was in such pain, and she was lying in the dark, hearing gunshots. She must have been terrified beyond belief.

Josie sat in the dark. The time seemed to stretch out forever. Ten or twenty minutes. Maybe more. She didn't want to look at her phone to see the time because the light would impair her night vision. It felt like it had been an hour when she heard sirens. She crawled toward the sound, found a window with blinds. She pulled them aside and looked out. Two cars with flashing blue and red lights came up the drive and into the parking area.

Josie hurried through the dark house to the front door. She unlocked it and pulled it open just enough to look out. It took some time for her to convince herself that the officers were real and not bad guys impersonating officers.

Doors opened on the cop cars. Deputies got out of each of them. Three total. The cops and the forest beyond were illuminated by the pulsing red and blue lights.

Josie called out as two deputies trotted up to the Prius, which was still blocking the front door.

"I'm Josie Strong." She was speaking through the narrow crack where the door was ajar. "The shooter was somewhere over toward that area of dark forest. We were standing near that low stone wall when Mary Jo was hit. She fell toward my daughter Samantha and the two of them went over the wall and down the slope below. Samantha is down there with our dog. Please help her! Mary Jo's body is down there, too."

The officers ducked down behind the Prius and looked across at the forested slope. They shined flashlights up toward the forest. There was nothing to see but trees and brush. One cop turned his flashlight on the windshield of the Prius.

"Toss me your car key, and I'll move this car away from the door."

Josie threw the key. The man got in the Prius and drove away from the door.

Josie stayed beneath the front door overhang where she thought she was out of sight. "I have to get down to my daughter!"

"We'll come with you."

One cop stayed in the drive and two cops stayed on either side of Josie as she crawled over the wall. They shined their flashlights, and Josie used her cell phone light as she scrambled down to Samantha, who hadn't moved.

"Sam, Sam, are you okay? Are you freezing? The police are here. You're going to be safe!"

"I'm okay." Samantha sounded very weak, very scared.

Josie got to Samantha, bent down, and caressed Samantha's face.

Josie leaned close to Samantha. "The paramedics are coming to help you."

One officer kneeled next to Samantha. The other said, "Where's the shooting victim?"

Josie pointed toward the darkness where Mary Jo's body lay. "She is over there."

The cop got on his radio as he hiked across the slope toward the body.

Josie couldn't hear all of what he said, but it sounded like he was calling in reinforcements.

There was another siren, distant but growing in volume. An ambulance arrived a minute later, as evidenced by a new set of lights flashing red across the dark forest. Two paramedics came down the slope. They both had lights attached to forehead straps. The beams bounced as they came through the brush.

"Over here," Josie called.

The paramedics took a quick look at Samantha. One asked her some questions and shined a small light in Samantha's eyes, which Josie knew was a way to check for certain kinds of brain injury. Then he shined his light on her shoulder, and touched it very gently, feeling the shape of her injury.

One man ran back up the slope. A minute later he came back with a stretcher.

They strapped Samantha to the stretcher while Josie held her good hand. They used a brace to immobilize her damaged arm. Samantha was shaky, but she seemed to Josie to be very strong considering what they'd been through. Josie could tell that the slightest movement made Samantha's arm hurt. But the girl was a stoic. Josie let go of Samantha's hand while the men carried her on the stretcher, up the slope and over the stone wall. Josie followed with Unknown.

Samantha was shaking violently. Josie thought it was a combination of pain and shivering from cold.

One of the cops came up the slope as the paramedics loaded Samantha into the ambulance. A paramedic pulled up Samantha's sleeve, swabbed the back of Samantha's right hand and started an IV.

He said, "This has a mild pain reliever. It will dampen the pain and help you relax."

Josie pushed next to Samantha on the other side.

"I'm scared, Mama," Samantha said in a tiny voice, filled with pain and terror and vulnerability.

"Just another minute, hon. You're going to be okay."

One of the paramedics reached to shut the rear doors of the ambulance. "I need to ride with her," Josie said. "I have to be next to my daughter."

The paramedic looked at the cop. His manner suggested that they weren't supposed to take anyone except the injured patient. "We have a policy…"

"My car is shot up," Josie interrupted. "I obviously can't drive it. I'm serious, I'm riding with my daughter. My name's Josie Strong. I'm a UCLA professor on an assignment from the governor. Call his office. Ask for his aide, Sonja Gonsalves. I'm sure they'll explain to your boss if necessary. I have the number right here in my…" Josie looked around. Where was her purse? "Oh, God, I put my purse under my daughter's head when she was lying on the rocks."

"This purse?" the cop said.

"Yes. Thank you." Josie took it, pulled out the governor's card and authorization letter, and handed both to the officer.

The cop looked at it. He looked at the paramedic and shrugged. "You guys should probably let her ride in the rescue rig. They'll be stuck at the hospital. We've got another rig coming to collect the body. One of our units will be stopping by later to get their statements."

The cop turned to Josie. "Where do you want your car towed?"

"I have no idea. I'm from L.A. There must be someplace that can make the appropriate repairs. The car was shot at least twice, maybe more."

"I'll see what we can do." He still had the key Josie had given him. He held it up.

Josie thanked him.

The paramedic was waiting.

Josie had dropped Unknown's leash. She looked around in the dark. "Unknown? Where are you?"

Unknown appeared next to Josie.

"Now you want to bring a dog?" The paramedic sounded put out.

"A member of the family," Josie said. "A service dog for my daughter. The governor would insist. We don't want him making irritated phone calls to your boss."

The driver looked at her, his face passive.

Josie coaxed Unknown up into the ambulance. "Unknown is right here, Sam. Right next to you." Josie got in and held Samantha's good hand as they drove away.

Josie leaned over toward Samantha and nestled her face at Samantha's neck. She could hear her daughter struggling to breathe slow and deep like they'd practiced for falling asleep during Samantha's childhood. Josie synchronized her own breathing with Samantha's. Josie tried to push away her thoughts of the shooter who'd caused all this misery.

But she couldn't stop thinking that when the shooter was aiming at the three women, it was possible he couldn't distinguish between Josie and Samantha and Mary Jo. So the shooter just fired, trying to kill whomever he hit, trying to create the maximum terror. Maybe his plan had been to kill all three of them, and he didn't expect that hitting one would knock one of the others over the wall and out of his sight. But he waited until one reappeared, climbing back over the wall, and he began firing again.

When Josie considered that the killer might have only been targeting Mary Jo, or even herself, she could keep a certain emotional distance. But to think that the killer might have wanted to kill Samantha as well created a constriction in Josie's throat and in her heart. The pain and terror made her rigid as she thought of what might have happened. Was this like the first killer they caught? Someone who thought that Samantha had witnessed something that made her death necessary?

Sitting on a little fold-out seat in the back of the ambulance, Josie felt a rage grow. It was the rage of a mother who wants to protect a child, the rage of a lonely frightened person fighting for the one person in the world who means more than everything else combined. The anger swelled until it choked Josie's own breathing. It squeezed her soul until her perception was reduced to a single, focused thought, a knowledge that Josie would do whatever it took to find the person who shot at them.

Josie resolved that she would find him and kill him.

SEVENTEEN

They brought Samantha to the Emergency Room of a local hospital. Samantha's stretcher was a kind of convertible gurney. They pulled it out of the ambulance, pulled a lever, and the wheels dropped down. They wheeled her in through a door that was wide enough to drive through. Josie carried Unknown.

The woman at the admitting counter looked at Unknown and said, "Do you have a service dog certificate?"

"No. But..." Josie couldn't brazenly lie. "Our car was hauled away. We live in Los Angeles, and I have nowhere to leave my dog. I'll hold her. I won't even set her down."

The woman frowned for several seconds.

"Okay. You hold her. In your lap. You don't let go."

"No, I won't let go."

Josie carried Unknown as they took Samantha to an examination room.

Josie tried to resist her impulse to make comments about every little thing. It was hard to watch as they treated Samantha like an ordinary patient and not the world's most treasured child.

A female doctor attended to her. She was a pudgy, red-faced woman in her thirties. She acted uncomfortable but Josie thought it was her natural demeanor, not something that indicated a problem with Samantha's injuries. The doctor asked what had happened and where the blood came from.

Josie explained what happened. She realized that the doctor would probably think that Josie and Samantha were lowlifes. Why else would they be in a situation where they would get shot? But there didn't seem much point in bringing up the authorization from the governor. The doctor probably wouldn't believe it. Sometimes it was best not to explain.

The doctor listened to Samantha's heart and her breathing and looked at the chart on which the nurse had already written Samantha's blood pressure.

"You said your left shoulder hurts."

"Really bad."

"I'm going to touch it very gently." The doctor ran her fingertips over Samantha's shoulder and upper arm, feeling around and under the pad and brace that were put into place by the paramedics.

"I believe your left shoulder is dislocated. It's very common. It hurts a lot, especially in people who are very strong. You have significant muscles."

"I should be strong. It's my name," Samantha said. She made a weak smile.

"I'd like you to sit up." The doctor helped lift Samantha to a sitting position.

Josie wanted to get in there and help as well, but she forced herself to refrain from getting in the way. She focused on keeping quiet and holding Unknown.

"Now let's shift you over to this chair," the doctor said.

They got Samantha onto a straight-backed chair.

The doctor sat in another chair directly in front of Samantha. She rubbed Samantha's trapezius muscle and said, "I'm going to take off this brace." She undid some velcro straps. "Are you an athlete?"

"Kind of. I'm on the volleyball team."

Josie wanted to proclaim that Samantha was an accomplished athlete, a fantastic volleyball player. But she managed to stay silent. Let Samantha answer for herself.

The doctor got the brace off. "Now we're going to gently raise your left hand up, bring it across in front of me, and set it on my left shoulder. We'll move slowly." The doctor slowly raised Samantha's hand up to rest on the doctor's shoulder.

"It still hurts, right?" the doctor said.

"Yes. A lot." Samantha's voice quivered. "But better since I got the pain reliever."

"Major pain in a dislocated shoulder is a good sign because it shows you have an anterior dislocation. Those kinds are easily fixed. This will all be over in a bit." The doctor set her left hand on the inside of Samantha's left elbow. It seemed to Josie like the doctor was gently pulling down on Samantha's arm. The doctor reached out with her right hand and massaged Samantha's trapezius muscle, then moved down to her deltoid, then down to her bicep. "I want you to relax. Keep sitting up straight. But relax your arm. Have you ever walked on the ocean beach?"

"Yes. Almost every day. We live in Santa Monica."

"Think how relaxing that is, listening to the sound of the waves, watching the sea foam on the sand, feeling the water wash over your feet." The doctor kept rubbing Samantha's muscles as she spoke. "That's what I want you to think about. Gentle waves on the beach."

Josie realized that the nervous-acting doctor was a master at creating a relaxing mood. The doctor moved her right hand up and down, rubbing Samantha's arm, then her shoulder, and up to the side of her neck.

"When I walk the ocean beach, I take deep breaths," the doctor said. "Let's both take deep breaths. Slow inhalation." The doctor inhaled at the same time as Samantha. "Hold it. Now breathe out slowly."

Both doctor and patient breathed out.

"I listen to the birds," the doctor said. "Sometimes I think the birds are silent, but when I breathe deeply enough, I hear them. Little twittering. Long calls. Talking sounds. I love to close my eyes and listen to the birds talk to each other. I like to imagine what they are saying."

Josie saw Samantha close her eyes. The doctor made an almost imperceptible shift in the way she held Samantha's arm. Josie couldn't tell if Samantha's arm rotated a little toward the outside. Maybe. Maybe not. The doctor kept talking as she massaged Samantha's muscles.

There was very soft sound accompanied by an equally slight movement. Samantha opened her eyes and sighed. Then grinned.

"Feel better?" the doctor said. She was still holding Samantha's left arm.

"Yes. How did you do that?" Samantha asked. "That was amazing."

"In that position, the shoulder wants to go back into its correct location position. All it takes is relaxing the muscles so they let it move where it wants to be."

"Is that like hypnosis?" Samantha asked.

"A little, I suppose. Getting a person to relax is the key to many things."

"I'm going to move your arm across your chest. You hold it there with your other arm. I'll lift this sling over your head. It will help hold your arm in position. Wear it for four or five days, night and day, in the shower too. When you have no more pain, then you can take it off and use your arm for most things. But nothing real strenuous. No volleyball for six weeks."

Samantha nodded.

"Now let's see about this bruise on your chest."

The doctor got a scissors and cut into the neckline of Samantha's shirt. She cut down enough to pull the fabric away from the bruise on Samantha's chest.

"You've got substantial trauma. But I don't see a break in the skin. It's possible you aren't bleeding."

"I don't think I am," Samantha said. "I think the blood is from the woman who was shot."

"Before I go further, have you talked to the police? We're required to report certain injuries."

"Yeah. The police sent me here. You can call them. My mom has their card with the number."

"Did this woman who was shot fall on you? There is a lot of blood."

"She was facing me. I believe she was shot from behind."

The doctor paused. "I'm sorry to sound macabre, but perhaps the bullet went all the way through her and splashed blood on you."

"Probably, yeah."

The doctor palpated Samantha's bruise. "Something hit you

hard to cause this bruise. The bruise has edges. It looks like you hit a fence post. Something rectangular. Can you remember anything like that striking you?"

Samantha shook her head. "No."

"You're going to be quite sore for the next week. But based on the swelling, I think your chest muscles protected your ribs. I don't think anything is broken."

"Do I need to do anything?"

"No. Heed the pain. Pain is the message to be careful and go easy. You can take a little ibuprofen as needed."

"Will do," Samantha said.

Twenty minutes later, they'd signed the insurance paperwork and left. Josie used her phone to request an Uber ride. While they waited, they went into the hospital gift store, and Samantha bought a T-shirt that said 'Contains Mostly Working Parts.' Josie borrowed a scissors from the store clerk, and she made several cuts in the bloody shirt. She helped Samantha pull the new shirt over the old, and then they pulled the cut pieces of blood-stained shirt out from under the new shirt.

An older man in a Honda Pilot arrived to pick them up. Josie, Samantha, and Unknown got in the back seat. Josie gave the man the hotel address where they had reservations. The man drove to the local freeway, got on it for a few miles, then got off and pulled up to the hotel.

Josie thanked him, tipped him actual cash instead of entering it on the app, and they got out.

"Mama, I just realized our bags with clothes are in our car."

"Yes, that occurred to me. But we couldn't have taken them in the ambulance, anyway. We'll have to manage. Hopefully, the car will get fixed, and we'll get it and our clothes back soon."

"Can we drive home?"

"I'd like to. But we have to give a statement to the police in the morning."

Samantha moaned. "I lost my phone, I lost my clothes, I'm stuck in an arm brace. What will I do?"

"Take a one-armed shower and eat with me in the restaurant, sweetheart."

EIGHTEEN

They checked into the hotel and then headed to the hotel restaurant.

The restaurant was not crowded, and they immediately seated Josie and Sam in a booth. Josie sat first, and Samantha slid in next to her on the same side, being careful to favor the arm in the sling. Unknown sat obediently on the outside of the bench seat, near Samantha's feet.

"I can't believe that woman was shot," Samantha said. She leaned her head down against Josie's shoulder. She looked sick. "Do you think the killer was trying to shoot Mary Jo? Or was he trying to hit us and accidentally hit her instead?"

"I don't know, Sam." Josie rubbed Samantha's leg.

"It's too painful. I don't think I can eat. I don't have any appetite."

"We have to eat. It's hard when you're stressed. But you can't heal, mind or body, without food."

"I can't heal my mind without my phone."

"We'll get you a new one."

Samantha picked up the menu and scanned it. "Maybe I could eat pizza."

"Pizza it will be."

They ordered a large vegetarian, as Samantha liked. Josie had thought about asking for pepperoni on half, but resisted the impulse. She thought resisting would send a good message of accommodation and open-mindedness. Samantha thought it was wrong to eat animals. Josie thought she was probably right even though she loved meat, especially the bad stuff, like bacon and sausage, salty and processed.

While they waited, Josie looked in her personal phone and found the number for the governor's aide and dialed.

Even though it was late, the phone was answered in the middle of the first ring. "Sonja Gonsalves."

Clearly, Josie thought, this woman had no life beyond work.

"Hello. This is Josie Strong calling."

"Oh, my God, the governor's office just got a call from the sheriff in El Dorado County. They told me what happened, and they wanted to verify that you are working with us. Are you okay?"

"My daughter was hurt, her shoulder dislocated, her chest badly bruised. But she'll be okay. The situation is upsetting, to say the least."

"I'm so sorry this happened."

Although the woman's words expressed dismay, Josie didn't think the woman's tone was sufficiently stressed to match her words. But she was all about efficiency, which, while not the opposite of emotion, certainly didn't incline one toward emotional responses.

"I'm calling to see if you and the governor want me to continue looking into this situation. Of course, we'd like to come back to L.A. to rest and recharge. But I'm thinking that once we adjust to the assault, we could perhaps keep investigating. Maybe I'll feel differently in the morning. But I thought I would ask."

"Let me call him, and I'll call you back."

"He answers at this time of evening?" Josie said.

"When I call, yes."

"Okay. I'll wait for your call." They clicked off.

Josie touched Samantha's sling. "How does your shoulder feel?"

"As long as I don't try to move it, I don't have any pain. It's amazing what that doctor did. I thought my shoulder was totally ruined. Instead, it's going to be okay!"

Josie's phone rang.

"Hello?"

"Professor Strong, this is the governor."

"Thanks for calling."

"I'm so sorry about what you went through. I can't believe

that Mary Jo was killed. This must be so hard for you. And then to have your daughter's shoulder injured. You have my deepest sympathy. Although it seems obvious, I suppose I should ask, do you think this assault tonight is connected to the murder of Mary Jo's husband?"

"Yes. I could be wrong. But it seems far too much of a coincidence otherwise."

"I agree. Nevertheless, if you want to abandon this case, I completely understand. In fact, I recommend it. I shouldn't have put you in such danger."

"Actually, while before I was feeling coerced and frustrated, now I'm committed," Josie said. "When someone shoots at me and my daughter, I'm very determined to find him."

As Josie said it, she sensed Samantha at her side, shaking her head in dismay.

There was a pause before the governor responded. "I think you should sleep on that thought. If you still think that when you wake up, the terms will remain the same. We'll support you, cover your medical expenses, and pay the fee we agreed upon regardless of whether you find this guy or not."

"Thank you. I'll let you know my decision tomorrow."

"Thank you."

Josie clicked off and looked at Samantha. The girl was leaning down, petting Unknown with her right hand. Josie touched Samantha's thigh. "Are you still okay? You look like you're in pain."

Samantha looked unsure. "My chest hurts. My brain hurts. I'm distressed at the idea that we might continue this horrible thing. Searching for a killer who is trying to kill us."

Josie didn't know how to respond. She thought it was horrible as well. But it was now personal.

Samantha added, "Maybe ask me again after I've had some pizza."

Josie nodded, gave Samantha's leg a squeeze.

NINETEEN

Samantha looked around the restaurant. "When is our pizza going to come?" She sounded weary and exasperated.

"I thought you said you didn't have an appetite." Josie made a slight smile.

"That was before. This is now, after I've been thinking about pizza."

"It takes time to make a good pizza." Josie was tired. She rubbed her eyes. "Do you think I'm terrible? That I want to try to find the killer?"

"Mama, someone just tried to kill us. Common sense says we should be running for cover and hiding."

"Is that what you want?"

As Josie said it, she saw Samantha's jaw muscles bulge.

Samantha spoke in a low voice that sounded more like a hiss. "But the other part of me thinks, someone just tried to kill us! We should find him and kick his ass!"

"But this isn't life lessons from the movies where we can act as if we're superheroes."

Samantha turned and looked Josie in the eyes. "Maybe we are."

"Okay. I mentioned the woman who might be able to help us. She was a student in my class that was just canceled."

"The Army woman?"

"Yes. When my class was canceled, she realized that I was dealing with strange circumstances, and she volunteered to help."

"What would you do? Call her up and ask her to help?"

"Yes."

"Should you call Mr. Ellison? Didn't he offer to help if you even needed it?"

"He did. But my sense is that Cor Kontos might be better for this."

Samantha nodded but didn't speak.

Josie looked in her phone and found the number for Cor Kontos. She dialed. Josie didn't want to put the phone on speaker in the restaurant. But she held it so Samantha could overhear.

"Cor Kontos," the woman answered in a commanding voice.

"Hello, my name is Josie Strong. I met you at UCLA…"

"Professor Strong, Medieval history," the woman interrupted.

"Sorry I'm calling late."

"Late by Army time. But in some L.A. circles, you're just getting going. What can I help you with, Professor?"

"Josie, please."

"What can I help you with, Josie?" The woman's voice was rushed and clipped, not the way Josie had remembered her.

"When you spoke to me after I had to cancel my class, you said that if I ever needed help, I could call you."

"Yes, I remember. Of course, you should call. I'm at your service. What happened? The governor got you into a tight spot?"

"I, um, yes." Josie was trying to gather her thoughts. She didn't think that the woman would remember the incident with the governor asking Josie to get into his limousine. And Josie hadn't remembered the woman as being so quick with her words. It made Josie lose her focus. Maybe Cor Kontos had been drinking or doing some other drug. It was late, after all. "Yes," Josie said, "the governor did get my daughter and me into a tight spot. I've found myself in need of someone who has your skills. It's totally beyond social decorum for me to ask you to…"

Samantha interrupted with a loud whisper, "Stop with the professor speak, Mama!"

Cor was speaking on the other end of the phone.

"What?" Josie said, feeling awkward. Both Cor and Samantha were talking at the same time. "I'm sorry, my daughter said something, and I didn't hear you."

"Don't worry about decorum," Cor said. "Just tell me what you'd like. If I can help, I will. If it doesn't work, I'll tell you."

"Okay. Thank you," Josie said. It didn't feel like she was talking to the student she'd remembered. It was more as if she was talking to someone… in charge. Like someone in the Army. "Thank you so much," Josie said again. "Let me think how to explain this. My daughter Samantha and I are near Placerville, which is east of Sacramento, on the road up to Lake Tahoe. At the request of the governor, we're investigating the murder of a Forest Service ranger, which is a type of law enforcement officer. But you probably know that. Anyway, Sam and I went to talk to the ranger's widow. As we spoke outside the house this evening, the woman was shot and killed, and my daughter was injured."

"Did you see the shooter?"

"No. He was apparently hiding in the forest."

"The house is surrounded by forest? Or cliffs? Or other buildings?" Cor asked, her words fast, her tone impatient.

"The entire area is generally forest," Josie said. "So the shooter was probably some distance away. But I don't know where."

"The woman was shot by a sniper," Cor said as if to clarify.

"I suppose so. I don't know about these things. I think there's a low ridge or a gentle slope a good distance from the house. Maybe he was on that ridge. There is no cell reception there, but I got through to the local police on the house landline. The police came, along with the paramedics. We've been to the hospital, where Sam was treated for a dislocated shoulder, and we're now at a hotel restaurant. We need to make a statement to the police tomorrow, so we'll be here for some time tomorrow. And we don't have the use of our car, because it was shot, too. The windshield was shattered. Maybe more, but I couldn't see in the dark."

"Did the sniper shot happen after dark?"

"Yes. Anyway, I plan to rent a car if ours can't be fixed soon. But my main concern is that I want to go back out to the house as soon as possible tomorrow and see if we can find where the shooter was hidden in the forest. I'm thinking that might provide some clues as to who he is or why he came after us. I know this is a big request of you, but I have no skills in this area. I'm thinking you do. So I thought I'd ask. If it doesn't work for you, I..."

The woman interrupted, "If I leave in the morning at four a.m., I'll beat the rush hour. My computer says it's four hundred twenty-five miles to Placerville. Tell me your hotel name and address. I'll be there about noon."

"Oh, that is fast. And so nice of you."

"I'm an Army Joe, Josie. My job for much of the last twenty years was reconnaissance, threat assessment, camouflage, disinformation, terrain analysis. The thing you're asking? Finding a sniper nest and seeing what it reveals? This is territory in which I have some expertise."

"That's very nice of you." Josie felt intimidated speaking to the woman. Maybe it was the way the woman radiated competence even over the phone. "What do you need from me?" Josie said.

"I still need you to tell me where I'm going," Cor said.

"Oh, right. Sorry." Josie picked up the cocktail napkin from the restaurant table and read off the name and address of the hotel.

"And the address of the house where the shooting occurred?"

"I forget. It's in my purse. Hold on." Josie found the slip she'd written on. "I actually don't have the address because the governor didn't know it. But I have the directions." Josie read them off over the phone.

"I'm getting search results as you describe this. Okay, I'm bringing the house location up on my computer. I can see the house on Google's satellite image. Where were you when the shots were fired?" Cor asked. "Describe it as thoroughly as you can."

"We were outside in the parking area. Maybe fifty or sixty feet out from the front door and garage. There's a short wall on... let me think, the sunset colors were to the left as we walked out the door. So the wall was to the northeast as you go out past the garage. We were standing by it. My daughter and I had our backs to the short wall and were facing the parking area. The woman we'd been visiting was facing us. Her back was toward the forest that's in the distance behind the parking area. She was shot from behind, and the impact of the bullet pushed her toward us, sending Samantha and her over the wall and down the slope."

"You said the woman was killed."

"Yes, it was horrible. Blood from the woman splattered all over my daughter."

"Meaning the round went all the way through the woman."

"Yes," Josie said.

"Did you hear the gunshot?" Cor asked.

"I'm not sure. I might have heard a distant crack. But I'm not sure. If I did, it certainly wasn't very loud." Josie turned to Samantha. "Sam? Did you hear a gunshot?"

"I can't remember. If so, it wasn't loud enough to notice."

Josie said, "Did you hear that, Cor?"

"Yeah. If you were to guess, would you say the distant crack you might have heard came to you at the same time the woman was hit, or after she was hit?"

"It would just be a guess. But I think maybe a little after she was hit."

Josie spoke into her phone. "You're asking because you can use the travel time for sound to estimate the distance, right?"

"Right," Cor said. "Now tell me another thing to help establish position. Imagine you're standing where the woman was shot, and your back faces the entry door behind you. You're the center of the clock face, so the door behind you is six o'clock. Does that make sense?"

"Yes. I can visualize that position."

"Good. Now visualize where on the clock dial was the shooter."

"I'd say he was somewhere off in the forest toward ten o'clock."

"Perfect. That fits with the terrain map on my screen. I'll see you at your hotel around noon tomorrow."

"Thanks so much." Josie had barely gotten out the words, when the phone went dead. The abrupt disconnect reminded her of the way Cumberland Durand would hang up without saying goodbye.

TWENTY

After Josie put her phone away, Samantha said, "Cor sounds—I don't know—different from any other woman I know. Her name is different, too."

"She told me it's short for Corinthia, a city in Greece. Her father is Greek. Her mother is Puerto Rican."

"But she grew up in America?"

"Right. I'd guess Brooklyn, New York, from the sound of her accent."

The waitress brought their pizza. They ate it as if they were starving, even though Sam was slowed by having her left arm in the sling.

"Unknown's food is in the car," Samantha said.

"Then we better give her some pizza," Josie said. "We can give her water in the room."

Josie cut two slices into smaller pieces, which Samantha gave to Unknown. Unlike most dogs that immediately gulp their food, Unknown ate hers slowly. Almost delicately.

Josie was worried she'd never be able to relax and sleep, so she had a glass of Liebfraumilch and then another. She signed the bill.

The hotel provided spare toothbrushes and such, and they went to bed soon after they got to their room.

They shared a king-size bed.

"Mama, where will Unknown sleep?"

"On the floor?" Josie said, realizing that the words somehow sounded harsh.

"There's no cushion, no dog bed. It's cold and drafty. She should sleep on the bed with us."

This was something Josie hadn't thought about before. A dog in her bed.

"I guess she could sleep on our bed. But only on the bottom. Your side."

"Mama, you're so strict. You've got rules for everything."

"That's a mother's job."

"Okay, Unknown, up on the bed!" Samantha said. She patted the blankets at the foot of the bed.

Josie turned on her side and watched through half-shut eyes.

Unknown put her front paws on the bed and stood up on her rear legs. She looked at Sam and Josie for a long time. Josie couldn't tell why the dog was so hesitant. Did she have pain? Or was it painful memories connected to a bed? Josie remembered the warmth that Bill, Unknown's former owner, showed the dog. Josie couldn't believe that Bill would have done anything to make Unknown so tentative. But Bill was Unknown's second owner. Maybe Unknown came to Bill with bad experiences. Dogs were like people in that trauma as puppies could scar them for life.

Unknown gave a push with her rear legs and came up on the bed. The dog had no exuberance, no enthusiasm. Just quiet acceptance tempered with major caution.

"Here, baby," Samantha said. The girl patted the blankets at the bottom of the bed. "You lie here. We gotta keep Mama from getting bent out of shape about having a dog on her bed."

Unknown lay down and looked toward Josie. The dog didn't look afraid, but Josie felt like she'd done something terrible to remind the dog of a painful past.

When they turned off the light, Samantha snuggled up to Josie.

"I can't sleep," Samantha said. "That woman died right in front of us! It was terrible."

"Yes, it was." Josie held Samantha, stroked her forehead.

"Mama?"

"Yes, sweetheart?"

"I know you saw death up close on our last two cases. But had you ever seen someone die when you were my age?"

"No. It must be very upsetting for you." Josie thought of

the two attackers she'd shot with her crossbow in the previous months. In neither case had Samantha been close enough to witness it. But she had been traumatized nevertheless.

Josie said, "Mary Jo's death was a horrible trauma to witness. Any pain you feel is justified. Give yourself some slack. You have every reason to feel traumatized."

Samantha nodded. "When Mary Jo was shot and her body pushed into me, it was like she was instantly dead. I can't get the image out of my head."

"I'm so sorry," Josie said. "Death is hard to face. A person is here, and then they're not. When you first meet them, their body seems to be the essence of them and then, when they die, their body is suddenly just a body, and their essence is gone."

"Do you think some part of them is still around? Something more than their body?"

"You mean, in a spiritual sense? Like their soul?" Josie asked.

"Yeah. Maybe not like they're floating up to heaven or walking on clouds. But could some essence of them remain in some other way?"

"I think that as long as they remain in our memories, then something of them lives on."

"I have a friend in school who's really religious. She thinks her grandmother is looking down at her from heaven. Like her grandmother is always there in the sky."

"If the grandmother is in your friend's thoughts and memories every day, then that's almost the same, don't you think?"

"I suppose." Samantha was quiet for a while.

"Mama, we never go to church. Are you at all religious?"

"You mean, like thinking God is a white guy with a long beard? No. But even if the image was a Black woman with a big afro, it still wouldn't work for me. It would be the same for Buddha or Allah or Yahweh or Shiva. But I have a very strong regard for principles of goodness. Philosophers have often noticed that all religions have the same common principles. Thou shalt not kill, and so forth. One philosopher calls them the common decencies. Yet many religions have developed on opposite sides of the Earth from each other yet still have the same common decencies. So it's clear that people are hardwired to know the difference between right and wrong, what's good and what's bad, and they incorporate that into their religions."

"So you don't think you need God to know the difference between right and wrong?"

"No. I think morality is intrinsic to who we are. But I recognize that most religions offer guidance that some people need."

"If you believe in those common decencies that religions share, why don't you follow organized religion? Why don't we go to church?"

Josie paused to think. "I think it's because, to me, a lot of organized religion has a kind of attitude of exclusion. In most religions, you're expected to believe in their god, and you're expected to believe it on faith, and you're supposed to take no other gods before the god they are talking about. I find that..." Josie stopped talking.

"What, Mama? I'm your daughter. You can say anything to me."

Josie thought about it. "I often think of the Native Americans from centuries ago. And our ancestors in Africa. They all had a rich set of beliefs about the sacredness of the natural world. Weren't their gods okay? What must it have been like to have missionaries come through and tell them their spiritual beliefs were wrong? How did they feel when strangers appeared and said they were supposed to believe in the different god and that they couldn't believe in any other kind of god? I like to think that most missionaries sincerely believed that they were saving these people. But I also think that Native Americans and Africans must have found that hard to hear."

"Like native people weren't smart enough to figure out the world in their way?" Samantha said.

"Yes. I think people should be given access to knowledge and ideas and then be allowed to choose what they think. Encouraging them to believe in your god is fine. Telling them about your own beliefs and your faith is fine. But telling them that they can't believe in any other gods is not showing sensitivity to what people think. It could be Christianity or Judaism or Islam or Hinduism or Buddhism. If they act like they know better than you do about what you should believe, that's kind of an affront."

Samantha was quiet a long moment. "Is Mary Jo in your thoughts?"

"Yes," Josie said.

"I'm glad, Mama. She's in my thoughts, too."

And then Josie heard Samantha's breathing change as she fell asleep. Josie turned her head just enough to kiss Samantha on her forehead.

Unknown lay at the bottom of the bed. Josie could see a little glint of light reflecting off the dog's eyes. She realized that Unknown was watching her.

Without making any sudden movements that might wake Samantha, Josie slowly pushed herself up to a sitting position, reached down, and rubbed Unknown.

"Thank you, Unknown," she said, "for being Samantha's friend and companion."

The dog lowered her jaw and rested it on Josie's foot, which was under the blankets. Her eyes remained open and alert. Josie felt a new level of affection for the dog.

Josie lay back down. As she tried to get drowsy, she was endlessly grateful for the gift of her daughter. And she was grateful that Samantha had found a constant companion in this silent, reticent dog.

TWENTY-ONE

The next morning, Josie and Samantha and Unknown had an early breakfast in the hotel breakfast bar.

"You're being very careful of your arm," Josie said.

Samantha looked down at her arm in the sling. "It hurts more than when I went to bed. But my whole body is still sore from doing the pancake dive in volleyball, too. So it's probably sore for multiple reasons."

The sergeant who they'd spoken to the night before showed up with their suitcases from the Prius. He carried both with one arm and opened the hotel door with the other.

"Sorry I didn't think of this last night," he said.

"Thank you. I didn't think of it, either," Josie said.

"Your car is at the Toyota dealer out on Highway Fifty. I'll give you a ride to the station so you can give your statements."

"Now that you've brought our clothes and my walking shoes, would it be okay if we shower and change? Maybe you could run an errand or something."

"Sure. I'll stop back in an hour."

"Before you go, we never got properly introduced. I'm Josie Strong, and this is my daughter Samantha."

"And this is Unknown," Samantha interrupted.

"There's a name that makes you think," the man said.

"Yeah," Samantha nodded. "We don't know much about her, so..."

"She's Unknown. Makes sense. I'm Sergeant Ham Garner. El Dorado County Sheriff's Office. The sheriff got a call about you from the governor. Now you're the talk of the day. Sheriff says we're to do whatever you want. Pleased to meet you."

Josie shook his hand.

The sergeant looked at Samantha's sling and didn't reach

out. "Looks like the hospital patched you up pretty good. But shaking hands might be too much movement, huh?"

Samantha nodded. "But I'm determined to be playing volleyball again soon."

"And I'll be cheering for your team." He made a little wave. "See you back here in a bit."

Josie and Sam went back to their room, got cleaned up, and went back out to the hotel lobby.

While they waited for the sergeant to return, Josie called their home landline to talk to Amelia, their new boarder.

Amelia answered with such a cheerful demeanor, Josie thought she should try to learn from it.

"Am I calling at an okay time?" Josie asked.

"Yes. I am just about to leave for work. I've got the afternoon shift."

Josie said, "Sorry we didn't call last night. We've had to deal with some unexpected things."

"You are okay?"

"Yes." Josie saw no reason to tell Amelia about their trauma. "And our condo? You made the sticky front door key work?"

"Yes. It is so very nice of you to let me stay. You can know all is well. I even sat out on the deck last night and listened to the surf. I'm very lucky you are letting me stay. And tell Samantha her room is perfect."

Josie saw the sergeant return.

"I will tell her. Someone we're waiting for just arrived, so I should go. I'm so glad you're settled in. Talk to you soon."

"Thank you again," Amelia said before they clicked off.

The sergeant walked up.

"We were out to the crime scene early this morning," he said. "We found this." He handed them a phone.

"My iPhone!" Samantha said. "Oh, no, it's totally destroyed!" The phone was shattered and bent. It looked like it had been hit in the center of the back with a hammer. And it had dried blood on it.

"It was shot," Sergeant Garner said. "Our best reconstruction is that you were holding it when the other woman was shot. The round exited the woman's body and hit your phone. Do you remember holding the phone?"

"Maybe... Yeah, I think I was. But I often hold the phone. So it might be that I'm thinking of what's normal more than I'm remembering, you know, the details before the woman was shot."

"Either way," the officer said. "That phone probably saved your life. Unfortunately, the slug was damaged beyond recognition when it hit your phone, so it doesn't tell us much about the shooter, other than that he used a large caliber weapon. But we won't be able to trace the bullet to a specific weapon."

"What about the bullets that hit my car?" Josie asked.

"The one that went through the two windows flew out over the slope down toward the river. We'll never find that. The other bullet went through the driver's window then into the passenger door where it punched through a support rib, which stopped it. There was no exit hole, so we took off the door panel and there it was. It was also smashed flat. So it doesn't tell us much beyond the weight of the bullet."

Josie stared at the phone and looked at Samantha. "Remember what the doctor said? That the bruise on your chest has edges like from something rectangular?"

Samantha raised the phone in front of her. "If the bullet hit it in this position, it must have slammed the phone out of my hand and against my chest." Samantha held the phone against her chest. "That bullet must have hit really hard to go through Mary Jo and then hit my phone hard enough to cause the bruise." Samantha had a renewed look of distress.

Josie rubbed her good shoulder.

Sergeant Garner drove them to the sheriff's office, where they each gave their rendition of the shooting to another sergeant named Jane Gayle. Samantha held tight to Unknown while Gayle asked questions and worked the recorder.

When they were through, Gayle turned to Josie. "We understand you're working for the governor."

"Yes. The governor knew the woman who was killed. She had asked the governor if he could help her, and she wanted him to call me and ask me to help in finding the man who killed her husband a few days ago."

"That's curious. Why would the shooting victim want the governor to call a history professor?"

"The woman had read a news story about us. My daughter and I witnessed something in a murder case in L.A. Then the murderer targeted us. We investigated and caught him." Josie didn't think it would help to say that it had actually happened twice.

"You are a crime investigator?" Sergeant Gayle seemed suspicious.

"No. Not by training. Not by choice, either. We were just unlucky in what we witnessed. Later, we were lucky in being able to track him down. But the governor thinks we have the magic touch. So he asked us to try. I couldn't exactly say no to the governor."

Gayle regarded them for a long moment. "So the woman who was just killed was married to the ranger who was shot and killed a few days ago in Tahoe, and you were looking into that."

"Right."

"Have you learned anything about that murder?"

"No."

"Anything about the widow?" Gayle's tone made Josie think that the woman was skeptical of everything Josie said.

"No, nothing about the widow."

"Do you have any idea of why someone might want to harm Ranger Francis Telman or his wife Mary Jo?"

Josie shook her head. "No. No idea at all. But we've barely done any investigating."

"Will you let us know if you learn anything of interest?"

"Of course."

"Where can we contact you?" the sergeant asked.

Josie gave the woman her phone and email. "We'll be at the hotel near Placerville until our car is fixed or until we can get a rental."

"Thank you. We'll be in touch if we have more questions."

Sergeant Ham Garner drove Josie and Samantha and Unknown back to their hotel. He said he knew someone at the car dealership and hoped he could motivate that person to get their car repaired sooner.

"Oh, the governor wanted you to have Mary Jo Telman's keys. He said you might want access to their house and cabin for your investigation or whatever it is that you do." He handed Josie a ring of keys. "I believe one of those keys is for the house where Ms. Telman was staying when she was killed, the house that belongs to friends of Ms. Telman's."

"What about the owner of the house? Have you contacted them?"

"Not yet. Somebody was going to look up the name in the county records, but I haven't heard, yet. We called the landline and left a message on the answering machine in hopes that the owner would get the message remotely. If they contact you and show up at the house, please let us know." He gave her a sheepish look. "It seems unusual to be giving you a key to someone else's house. But whatever the governor wants…" He left the statement unfinished.

Josie thanked him, and he left.

TWENTY-TWO

Cor Kontos showed up at noon. Josie and Samantha and Unknown were watching from the hotel lobby. They saw an Army-green Jeep pull into the curved drivc in front of the lobby doors. It came to a fast stop.

The Jeep was large and tall and shiny as if the woman cleaned it daily. There was no top and no windows beyond the windshield. It had short doors and a big black roll bar.

Cor Kontos reached up and grabbed the roll bar. She did a pull-up and leg lift until her feet cleared the side door. Then she swung out and jumped to the ground. She was wearing the kind of clothes Josie remembered from when they met before. Large black boots, khaki jeans with cargo pockets, and a camo-colored sleeveless top showing her muscular arms, which seemed to have even more tattoos than Josie remembered from when they'd first met. Josie thought the woman would be freezing, driving an open Jeep while wearing nothing but a sleeveless shirt.

"That's the woman who took your class?" Samantha said in a voice so low it was nearly a whisper.

"Yes," Josie said.

"She looks totally kick butt. Like if you messed with her, she'd take you down."

"Take you down," Josie repeated. "That means to kill?"

"Yeah. Life lessons from the movies," Samantha said.

"Cor spent twenty years in the Army, and now she teaches self-defense. So yes, she's pretty much of a kick-butt woman."

Cor came in through the lobby door, saw Josie, smiled and walked over.

"Hi, Cor. Thanks for coming." Josie reached to shake hands. Cor ignored the outstretched hand and bent down to give Josie a bear hug.

After they separated, Josie said, "I'd like you to meet my daughter Samantha."

Cor looked at Samantha's arm sling, held out her fist, and said, "Put it here, girl. Any daughter of my favorite prof is someone I respect."

Samantha used her good hand to bump fists with Cor.

Josie noticed that while Samantha, at 5' 11", was a couple of inches taller than Cor, she was only half as wide. Samantha was a strong 120 pounds. But Cor was like a rock by comparison, probably 170 pounds of solid muscle.

Cor squatted down and made a wavering humming sound as she gently touched Unknown on the top of her head. "And who's this girl?"

"That's Unknown," Samantha said.

Unknown sniffed Cor's boots and did a small tail movement.

"Mama, look! Unknown is wagging at Cor."

"I have that effect on dogs," Cor said. "They sense I'm closer to a dog than a person."

"How did you know she was a girl?" Samantha asked. "Because she's got kind of longish fur that, you know, makes it hard to tell."

"It ain't what the fur might cover up, it's the demeanor. She acts like a girl. A reserved, careful, thoughtful girl. But like a lot of girls, I can tell that she can be tough if she has to." Cor held her hand in front of Unknown's nose for sniffing, then ran her hand down Unknown's neck.

"When I enlisted, there weren't a lot of female soldiers. But there was a lot of focus on male/female differences. The Army was struggling with the issue. Still is. The result is you get good at identifying gender. 'Course, we've got Joes whose gender isn't what you'd expect from how they look."

Josie watched as Samantha frowned and nodded. It wasn't a frown of disagreement, it was a frown of thoughtfulness.

Cor looked at Samantha's arm brace and the bandage poking above the neckline of the 'Contains-Mostly-Working-Parts' T-Shirt, which Samantha had put back on over another T-shirt despite taking a shower and changing her clothes. "You okay?" Cor said. "Looks like you busted up your shoulder."

"Pretty much."

Cor looked from one of Samantha's shoulders to the other. "The shoulder brace is on your left side, but the bandage poking out of your t-shirt is on your right."

Samantha said, "When the woman got shot, she was pushed into me, and I fell over a wall and hurt my shoulder. But the bullet that went through her hit my iPhone, which punched me here where this bandage is."

"Your phone stopped the bullet."

"Yeah."

"And saved you," Cor said. "Like a Bible or something."

Samantha pulled her crushed, bent phone from her pocket and held it up. "It's kind of my Bible, so yeah."

Cor took the phone and stared at it. "And I thought I'd seen everything in the Army. But you just blew that idea up like an IED. If you were a Joe, they'd give you a Purple Heart."

Josie noticed that Cor's words, while frank, were spoken more softly than the way she spoke on the phone the night before. Maybe it was because she was rested. Or sober. Or talking to a kid.

"Did they find the bullet that hit the phone?" Cor asked.

Samantha nodded. "Yeah. They said it was totally mashed."

"The sergeant said that all they could tell was that it was a large caliber weapon," Josie said.

Cor nodded understanding.

"They're working on my Prius," Josie said. "So we won't have transportation for a few days."

"Why I'm here," Cor said. "You can ride in my Jeep. Have you two eaten?"

"Breakfast, not lunch," Josie said. "Maybe we should stop at the supermarket and get a deli sandwich."

"I saw an In N Out Burger from the highway."

In her peripheral vision, Josie saw Samantha grin and do a fist pump.

"But you're a vegetarian," Josie said quietly to Samantha.

"You don't eat burger."

"I eat their grilled cheese."

"Since when do you know there's grilled cheese on the In N Out menu?"

"Since Christy's boyfriend took us to one in Marina Del Rey."

Josie was shocked even though she knew she shouldn't be. "Did you go on the bus?"

"No. He drove."

Josie's voice came out at loud volume. "Christy has a boyfriend who's old enough to drive?"

"Jeremiah's only sixteen, but don't worry. His dad won't let him take the Porsche. He has to use the old diesel convertible. It's slower than my bicycle. I think it might be a Mercedes. But I couldn't tell 'cuz the logo thing got broken off when Jeremiah got too close to a truck. I guess the car's hood went right under the back of the truck."

"Is Jeremiah…" Josie stopped herself.

"Don't worry, Mama. He's okay. It's not like he's all tatted up or anything."

"Tatted up?"

Cor bent her arm and lifted up her elbow as if to show Josie her tattoos.

Josie felt dread seeping in. "So this boy is partially tatted up."

"He's only got one tattoo that I've seen."

"What is it?" Josie was envisioning skulls and women being devoured by snakes.

"It's just a Twisted Sister band logo."

"Whoa," Cor said. "A bad boy wannabe."

Samantha paused, then said, "But I was sitting in the middle, so I couldn't really get a good look at him. That car is so old, it has the long seats that go all the way across the car."

"Cool," Cor said. "An old Benz oil burner with bench seats."

Josie knew she should drop the subject. She'd never heard of a band called Twisted Sister. Or a Benz oil burner. "Where is this tattoo?"

Samantha glanced at Cor. "On the back of his thigh. But don't worry, it wasn't up on his butt, or anything."

Josie couldn't breathe. She knew that Samantha probably liked shocking her a little. But Josie's wind was knocked out just as surely as if she'd done a pancake dive on a volleyball court.

Josie suddenly thought she'd failed as a mother. Failed as surely as if she'd personally taught Samantha the art of shooting up heroin.

Maybe she could change the subject. She waved her hand toward the corner in the lobby where they served breakfast. "Cor, if you need something to eat sooner, they have muffins and coffee in the, uh…"

"Mess hall," Cor said as she glanced toward the hotel coffee counter. "Had enough of that food in the Army. Eating bran muffins isn't living. In N Out Burgers is living."

Cor turned and walked toward her Jeep. Samantha and Unknown followed. Josie lagged behind, still trying to breathe. Her daughter was the perfect age when she was about 8. Now that Samantha was 14, it stressed Josie's health. When Samantha made it to 16, Josie felt that she was bound to asphyxiate in a panic attack.

When they got to the Jeep, Cor said, "It's cooler here than down on the valley floor, and my ride doesn't have its wrap on, so you might get chilly." She reached into the open back, unzipped a bag, and pulled out an Army jacket with a camouflage pattern. She handed it to Samantha. "Skinny girls need insulation."

Josie was surprised to see Samantha put her right arm into the jacket sleeve and drape the jacket over the sling on her left arm. The jacket arms were inches too short, and the jacket was big enough to wrap around Samantha one and a half times. But it would keep her warm.

Cor said, "You can sit in back, Samantha. The seat is tiny, but it serves its purpose. You might have to turn sideways to fit legs that long. And hold your dog tight. Josie, you ride shotgun." Cor opened the passenger door, which was a half door with no visible glass. As Josie got in, she saw Samantha looking at the

Jeep as if wondering how to get in the back.

"I know the sling gets in the way," Cor said to Samantha. "But you're tall enough to just climb over the back."

Cor grabbed the roll bar and did another gymnastics swing that deposited her into the driver's seat.

Samantha carefully climbed into the back, using her good arm, then tried to coax Unknown to jump in. Unknown looked at the imposing height of the Jeep's tail gate, then trotted around to Josie's door, which was still open. She jumped in and worked her way back to Samantha.

Cor started the Jeep and sped off. She drove fast and hard, and the wind whipped through the open Jeep. Josie realized that Cor had memorized the map. She knew exactly where to turn. They pulled into the fast food drive-thru ten minutes later. Cor ordered two burgers and a large order of fries, Samantha got her grilled cheese and fries. They turned to look at Josie. All Josie could think about was Samantha jammed thigh-to-thigh with a Twisted Sister fanboy who didn't know how to brake his Mercedes in time. Josie had no appetite. But she ordered a burger.

They picked up their food at the window and ate while they drove.

Cor seemed to drive even faster as she ate. Josie's burger cooled to outdoor December mountain temperature before she finished it. But Samantha and Cor were already done, and Samantha seemed happy, which—Josie tried to tell herself—was all that mattered. At least she was alive. A diesel Mercedes convertible probably didn't even have a seat belt for the middle of the front seat.

Twenty minutes later, they pulled into the drive to the house where Mary Jo had been shot. There was yellow crime scene tape stretched across the front of the house and garage and over to encompass part of the parking area.

Cor parked back from the tape and jumped out.

"This is creepy being back here, Mama. I feel shaky."

"I agree, Sam. Very upsetting."

TWENTY-THREE

"Maybe we shouldn't be here." Samantha's anxiety was pronounced. "What if the killer is waiting for us to come back?"

Josie reached her arm to the back seat and squeezed Samantha's knee. "I suppose anything's possible. But I doubt it. The shooter knows that a lot of people, the sheriff's deputies, and us, are looking for him. I think we're safe."

Samantha crawled out of the back. Unknown jumped down. Unknown looked over toward the area where Mary Jo had been shot, but didn't move. It was as if Unknown didn't want to be there, revisiting the scene of death.

Cor walked around the parking area, looking over at the ridge, then at the short stone wall. She stepped over the crime scene tape and walked to the wall.

"Do you think the police are done here? Even though the crime scene tape is still up?" Cor asked.

"I don't know."

"According to the gov, you're his official crime-scene investigator, right?"

"Yes," Josie said. "I guess so."

Cor stood next to the wall. "Was this where y'all were standing when the sniper took his shot?"

"That's where Sam and Mary Jo were standing," Josie said. "The gunshot knocked both of them over that wall." Josie pointed to a spot about twenty feet away. "I was trying to pick up my lipstick where it fell out of my purse and rolled away."

"I don't recall ever seeing you wear lipstick," Cor said.

"Mama ain't brave enough to be a lipstick lady," Samantha said. "She's got one lipstick that's lasted for thirty years."

"Are you two done discussing my deficiencies?" Josie said.

Cor looked over the wall and down at the slope. "Can you both come here and stand in the same positions where you were last night?"

They did as asked.

Cor walked in front of them, facing them. "Is this where the other woman stood?"

"A little to my right," Samantha said. "Your left."

Cor took a step to the side. "Here?"

"Yes."

"Did you see where on her body the bullet struck?"

Josie said, "When I saw her lying down on the slope, after she was dead, the hole in her chest was about here. Probably near the top of her sternum."

"How tall was this woman?"

"Taller than me. I'm five-four. More like your height. Do you agree, Samantha?"

"I'd say shorter than Cor by an inch or two."

"I'm five-nine. So you think the woman was about this tall?" Cor held her hand up.

"Yeah," Samantha said.

Cor put her finger on her sternum. "Adjusting for the height of the other woman, the bullet's exit wound would be about this height." Cor looked around. "The parking area is sloped, making the area where I'm standing higher than where you two are standing. The bullet would have exited me here and struck Samantha's phone, which she was holding near her chest, where the bandage is. Is that right?"

"I think so," Josie said. "Sam?"

"Yeah, I agree."

"Okay, Josie, you come stand here. Turn so you're close to me. See where my finger is on my sternum? This point on your shoulder is the same height. So you hold your finger on that point of your shoulder."

Josie did as told.

Cor walked over to Samantha. "I'd like you to step to the side about six or eight inches. Then hold your fingertip on your shoulder at the same height as your bruise."

Samantha did as instructed.

"Does it seem to you both that the imaginary line from Josie's fingertip to Samantha's fingertip is roughly the path the bullet traced?"

They both nodded.

"Now I'll stand next to Samantha so that I can sight from her fingertip to Josie's fingertip."

Cor got into position, moving her head a little back and forth. "As I do this, it looks like the shooter was over on that ridge as you said earlier. I'm guessing he was just a little down from the tall pine with that bent top."

Samantha looked at the ridge.

"Josie, would you like to look?"

"There isn't much point. I don't have good vision. At this distance, I'd just see green trees with no sense of detail."

Cor asked, "Samantha, what is your opinion?"

"I'd guess the shooter was a little to the right of that tree with the bent top."

"Okay, good. We'll hike over to that point and see what we find."

"I saw this in a movie," Samantha said. "They shine a laser through the bullet holes and look to see where it goes. That tells where the shooter was."

"Yeah, but that's a mock up. And our measuring system isn't accurate when it's based on memory. If a single bullet had made two holes in a wall, then you can shine a laser through the holes, and that would be much more accurate. But you can't see a laser dot at a distance in the sunlight, anyway. So unless we can borrow a laser range finder, our approach is as good as it gets. We're not even taking into account the distance and how much the bullet arcs under the pull of gravity."

"But bullets go straight," Samantha said.

"No. They fall just like anything else."

"No way." Samantha shook her head in disbelief.

"You ever play baseball?"

"Softball."

"Okay. Let's say the batter hits a line drive. The ball goes straight out. Where does it end up?"

"If the pitcher can't catch it, the ball hits the ground someplace out by second base."

Cor nodded. "What if the batter wants her ball to go over the back fence?"

"Then she's gotta hit a major-league fly ball."

"And what path does that ball take?"

Samantha held out her hand and moved it in a large curve, arcing up and then down.

"That's what a bullet does."

"Really? You can't be serious," Samantha said. She did a little jumping bounce like the animated kid she was. "Come on. Everyone knows that bullets fly. They don't just drop to the ground." She looked at Cor. "Am I wrong? Don't they fly?"

Cor smiled. Josie was glad to see that it was a warm smile. Samantha's innate charm was working her magic with the Army woman just like it did with everyone else.

"So that's a physics thing?" Samantha said.

Cor picked up a stone and dropped it. "Yep, it's a physics thing called gravity."

"You're making fun of me," Samantha said, grinning.

"No, I'm making fun with you."

"What do we do next?" Josie asked.

"Are you up to hiking?"

Josie nodded.

Cor unfolded some papers on which she'd printed maps. She spread them on the hood of the Jeep and pointed. "Here is where we are at the house. The ridge where we think the shooter was runs here, northwest to southeast. I think the easiest way to get there is to hike back up the drive, cut across through this low area, then hike over to the next ridge. Once we reach the high ground, we'll hike down the ridge and look for openings in the trees, the bent pine tree, view windows that would show this house and parking area. Sound good?"

"Sounds good," Josie repeated. "Will we leave your Jeep here?"

"Yeah." Cor walked over and reached under the corner of

the left rear bumper. It looked to Josie like she was grabbing an item, but her hand came back empty.

"Anti-theft switch," Cor said in answer to the unspoken question.

"But there's no windows and roof and stuff," Samantha said.

"Don't need them. Anyone comes within ten feet of the Jeep, their picture is uploaded to the internet. Any closer, the guard dog does his thing."

"I don't get it." Samantha pet Unknown. "My baby isn't much of a guard dog."

"The Jeep has its own guard dog. When he growls, he seems close enough to rip out your throat. I've never seen a man who wasn't unnerved by him. The Jeep's got some other Army tricks as well. But I don't want to demonstrate them, as they would upset you. Your hound, too."

Samantha looked at Josie. Josie shrugged.

"Ready?" Cor turned and walked back down the sloped driveway.

Josie and Samantha followed. It was a struggle for Josie to keep up, because Cor walked quickly. The driveway went up from the house, leveled off, then dropped down. Cor followed it for 50 yards, then turned off and headed out through the forest.

"C'mon, Mama, you gotta speed up," Samantha said, as Cor got increasingly far in front of them.

Josie tried to move quickly, but the footing was uneven, and she didn't see well in the forest shadows.

Cor went up a slight rise. The ground rose to a low ridge. At the top, Cor slowed, then stopped. She held her hand out to her side. Josie didn't understand what Cor was doing. Then Josie realized it was a hand signal that meant Stop. Probably an Army thing.

"I think she wants us to stop and wait," Josie said in a low voice.

"Why are you whispering, Mama?"

"I don't know. I guess I'm feeling a little on edge."

"Do you think someone else might be out here in the forest?" Samantha looked around at the dense trees.

"I… Let's just be a little quiet and see what Cor does."

Samantha whispered, "Do you think Cor has a gun? In one of those concealed holsters?"

"I don't know, Sam," Josie whispered back. "I've heard that off-duty police officers carry guns. Maybe off-duty Army people do, too."

Cor was above them, mostly obscured by trees. She looked at the ground, then slowly moved along the ridge as it went slightly uphill. Cor reached out to move bushes aside, stepping tentatively as if the forest floor contained nasty surprises. Cor turned around and came back. She stopped again at her original position, then continued on. She reached out her arm behind her and waved, beckoning Josie and Samantha to follow her.

The three of them followed the top of the ridge as it dropped slightly. Josie and Samantha stayed behind Cor. At one point, Cor stopped, and Josie and Samantha caught up with her.

"It seems like you're looking for something in particular," Josie said.

"Just following the shooter's trail. I don't want to step on evidence."

"He came this way?" Josie felt uncomfortable.

"Yeah. He's sloppy. He just stepped in some places that took a boot print. And he broke some branches. Now we're on his trail. If there's anything I want you to avoid, I'll reach behind me and point so you can move to the side as well."

"Got it."

Cor began moving again. Her head was bent down. She looked at the ground more than anywhere else.

They wound through boulders and around trees. Occasionally, Cor ducked under branches. At one point, she stopped and studied a tree trunk. She reached out and plucked what looked like a bit of lint off the rough bark. She pulled a plastic baggie out of her pocket and put the lint into the bag.

A few minutes later, Cor stopped. Josie and Samantha stayed back. Samantha held Unknown's leash.

"This is it," Cor said. She pointed at the ground. "This ground has been swept with a branch to obscure his prints. But these two vague dips are at the same distance as a typical bipod support for a large rifle. The bipod wiggled enough that it dug into the ground. He should have been more thorough with his branch sweeping. You can even see a vague larger area here." She pointed. "This is where he lay on the ground."

"You're saying this was where he was when he shot at us?" Josie said.

"Yeah." Cor pointed through the trees. "Take a look."

They turned. There was a clear view window. Very far away, the house was crisply defined in the afternoon sunlight. The windshield of Cor's Jeep glinted. Despite Josie's poor vision, she could see that the sun illuminated a straight line. She realized it was the short stone wall close to where they'd stood when Mary Jo was shot and killed. To look at it from the shooter's perspective was very unsettling.

Cor used her binoculars to look toward the house. She scanned left and right, then lowered the binoculars and looked at the ground around the impressions in the dirt. Josie and Samantha stayed back.

"I don't like it," Cor said.

"What?"

"I don't like realizing he's had experience as a professional sniper."

TWENTY-FOUR

"What does that mean when you say professional sniper?" Josie asked.

"It means military." Cor turned, still looking at the ground. "He left no shell casings and no litter. The guy was a little careless with his movement through the forest. Like he didn't worry that we could trace his tracks. But he was careful not to leave any evidence that could be traced."

Cor turned to look at Unknown, who was sniffing a low area where the dirt was darker with moisture. Cor walked over and stared. "What you got, girl? Hello. Here's a partial boot print." Cor bent over, hands on her knees, and stared at the ground.

"Is it okay if we walk over there?" Josie said.

"Yeah. I don't think there's anything we need to avoid stepping on."

Josie approached and looked where Cor pointed.

It was a curved line, possibly the edge of a heel.

Samantha leaned in to look. "That boot print comes from a Vibram sole. I have heavy shoes with Vibram soles."

Cor said, "Probably a majority of hikers have boots with Vibram soles. Nothing distinctive that could connect to an individual."

Samantha pointed. "Is that a bug?"

Josie pulled out her phone and took a picture of the print. She looked at it on her phone, zoomed in on the image, then looked again at the print.

"The top of this rectangle of dirt came from the part of the sole that recedes the most," she said, talking to herself more than anything.

"Right," Cor said.

Josie took another photo, then expanded the image on the

screen. "You're right, Samantha. There's definitely a little bug stuck in that mud."

Cor looked closely. "Do you know the bug or something?"

"No."

"It could have been on the dirt when the guy stepped here."

Josie nodded.

"Or it could have been stuck inside the farthest recess of his boot sole, and it was only when the guy stepped onto moist dirt, that the dirt squished up into his boot sole and grabbed the bug."

Josie zoomed in with her phone camera and took a closeup of the bug.

"You think the bug could reveal something?" Cor asked.

"Probably not, but you never know."

Samantha said, "Like, what if that bug is a rare insect that's—I don't know—Russian or something, and it's only found on a certain kind of plant that is used in Russian restaurants? And you go to those restaurants and find a chef who used to be a military sniper!" Her grin was huge.

Cor turned to Josie. "Where'd you get this girl? She's something."

"She is something. I agree with that." Josie's thoughts flashed back to a vision of Samantha in a Mercedes convertible talking tattoos with her friends. Josie looked around at the area. "The sheriff's team probably hasn't been here. So I shouldn't take that bug."

"Technically, maybe not," Cor said. "But practically speaking? I know some cops. I can't see them thinking a bug could tell them who murdered the woman. There's bugs everywhere, right? What's another bug?"

"Maybe I can carefully take the bug without marring the boot print?" Josie asked.

"Cops have lots of cases and criminals to catch. You only have one. My sense is that the governor would much rather have you take that bug and try to do something useful with it than leave it here." Cor pulled out the baggie with the tiny piece of lint she'd pulled off the tree trunk. She handed it to Josie. "You can put it in here, if you like. It won't hurt the lint I took."

Josie took the baggie. Inside was a speck of blue, the lint Cor had pulled off the tree trunk. Josie found a nail file in her purse and used it to slice off a tiny bit of boot-print dirt that contained the bug. She slid it into the baggie. "Why did you take the lint?" Josie asked.

"It's like the bug. I don't know. But blue lint in the forest is unusual."

Samantha said, "When you find the Russian chef with sniper training, and he's wearing a blue fleece jacket, you'll know it's him!"

Cor smiled. "While you bag the bug," Cor said, "I'll text the coordinates to the cops. I've got a GPS app on my phone, so I can get the exact position." She started tapping on the phone keypad. After a minute, she looked at her phone. "One bar of reception. It might work. Tell me if this text works for you. 'To the El Dorado County Sheriff's Office. My name's Cor Kontos, helping Professor Josie Strong, who was targeted by gunfire at a private home near Placerville, California. Professor Strong has already explained to your office that she's on special assignment from the governor's office. She has asked me to provide support for that assignment. We have discovered the location from which the shooter fired his shot, and I'm writing to provide you with the GPS coordinates so you can investigate. We looked the site over without touching anything. In my opinion, the only thing to learn from the site is that it is approximately three quarters of a mile from the house, a distance that suggests the shooter has military sniper training. Feel free to contact me with questions. Signed Cor Kontos, Sergeant First Class U.S. Army RET."

Cor looked at Josie. "Did I miss anything?"

"No. Perfect," Josie said.

"What would you like to do next?" Cor asked.

"I'd like you to advise me. Tell me what you can discern about this shooting. This shooter."

"There's not much to tell. As I said in my text, the shooter was almost certainly ex-military. He likely used..."

"Wait, please," Josie said. "Back up. Why do you say he was military?"

Cor gestured at the house in the distance. "As I said, the house is about three quarters of a mile away, or thirteen hundred yards. While expert snipers can shoot from longer distances, thirteen hundred yards is still a serious distance and usually far beyond the expertise of any big game hunter. Hunters shoot well at a hundred yards and often can hit a target at three hundred yards. A really good hunter might make his target at four hundred. But thirteen hundred? That is highly specialized territory that requires a great deal of training and practice."

"Why?" Samantha said.

Josie loved that Samantha felt free to ask what Cor probably thought was a flip, much-too-casual question.

"Are you into sports?" Cor asked.

Samantha grinned. "Yeah! I'm on the volleyball team at our school."

"Can you think of a truly great volleyball player?"

"Of course. Kerri Walsh Jennings. And Misty May-Treanor. Probably the best players ever."

"Do you have a really good player on your team?"

"Sure. Martina Harmon. She's three years older than me. She's my role model."

"Could Martina Harmon go up against Jennings and May-Treanor?"

Samantha guffawed. "Of course not. Not even close. They're like, not even in the same universe."

Cor nodded. "That's the difference between a really good hunter and a trained sniper. Not even in the same universe."

"You've got me curious," Josie said. She gestured toward the house in the distance. "What makes a long shot like this so difficult?"

"A host of factors. First, a bullet traveling that far will probably drop sixty feet."

"Sixty feet!" Samantha said. "Oh, that's the fly ball thing." She grinned.

"Yup," Cor said. "So you have to set your scope to aim way

above your target. But, of course, you need to use a range finder to learn the exact distance to your target so you can calculate the exact drop. As a bullet goes through the air, resistance slows it down, meaning it will drop more than a static calculation will suggest. It also depends on what round you're shooting. Some bullets maintain muzzle velocity better than others."

Cor looked around as if taking in the entire sky.

"Then there is the wind," Cor said. "Even a tiny breeze blows a bullet off course. You can look at the weather forecast and see that it predicts wind of 8 miles per hour out of the northeast. Which is what I found last night when I checked the weather history for this area and the approximate time of the shot. But who ever saw a completely steady wind? And if you're shooting to the east, a northeast wind will not only blow your bullet off course, but the headwind component will slow it even more than still air will slow it. You're using trigonometry to calculate how a northeast wind affects an east-traveling bullet."

Cor looked away from the house and back to Samantha. "Here's another consideration. When you feel your pulse, what are you actually feeling?"

Samantha looked puzzled. "I don't know. A little bump under your skin, I guess."

"What makes it seem like a bump?"

"Because the blood pumping through the artery down below makes the skin move?"

"Right. How much do you think it moves?"

Samantha shrugged. She held her thumb and forefinger up, showing a tiny gap.

"That looks like less than a tenth of an inch. Does that seem reasonable?"

Another shrug. "Yeah, sure."

Cor lifted her arms up in the position of holding a rifle. "The rifle touches the sniper's body at both of his hands and at his shoulder and maybe the side of his neck or jaw. The shooter has a pulse in all those places. Imagine if the bump of the shooter's pulse were only a hundredth as much movement as you're describing. That would be only a thousandth of an inch.

But if you move the barrel of a sniper's rifle a thousandth of an inch, a shot will miss the target."

Josie saw Samantha's face register amazement.

"Then there's temperature changes," Cor said. "As you move through air, you sometimes go into pockets of cooler air and warmer air, right?"

Samantha nodded.

"Each transition from one temp to another will throw your bullet off."

"I guess I didn't realize all that stuff. You're right. Being a sniper is tricky business."

"Wait, there's lots more." Cor was smiling. "We haven't gotten to the Coriolis Effect."

"What's that?"

"The Earth turns, right? After you fire your shot, your target is moving because the Earth is always turning. By the time your shot gets to the target, the target is in a slightly different place."

"You gotta be kidding," Samantha said. "The bullet gets there almost immediately. Yet you're saying the turning Earth makes a difference?"

"Absolutely."

"Wow. You're right. This is complicated stuff."

"While there may be exceptions, pretty much the only place where a sniper gets the appropriate training is the military."

Josie said, "So the shooter is military. Or ex-military. Is there a way to search for soldiers with sniper training?"

"I wouldn't know about that."

As Cor said it, Josie thought of her former student, the computer wizard Cumberland Durand. Maybe he would have an idea.

"You started to mention the kind of gun the sniper had," Josie said. "We were told that the two bullets that were recovered were hopelessly deformed. So there isn't any chance of tracing them to the gun?"

"It's true that you need a bullet in good shape to tell you much about the gun. It's very likely that the shooter used a common bolt-action rifle and stock optics. But I could be wrong. My guess is he'd choose something that shoots a three-oh-eight or a similar caliber, which is a large bullet with good flight characteristics and good penetrating power."

Josie felt herself flinch at the words.

Cor continued, "Despite having a great deal of training, he would have had to perform many tests and put in hours of practice to suss out the quirks and characteristics of the chosen rifle. But once he became very familiar with his weapon, it would do the job. Then he would dispose of it."

"I don't understand."

"If spent bullets are in good shape, guns can be traced by ballistics. But guns can also be traced to some degree by purchase. Even a smashed bullet might contain enough material to suggest its caliber, which suggests guns that might have shot it. So if you find a potential shooter with the right training, and he's got a gun that might have fired that caliber, you get a possible ID. Guns have serial numbers that gun dealers record. If the gun is stolen, there is information available to anyone who wants to backtrack it. And if you have an exotic gun, people pay attention. Gun dealers will know about it. They talk."

Samantha said, "Like you wouldn't want to rob a bank while driving a yellow Maserati. Better to steal an old Camaro, wear gloves and a wig and a face mask, and use that. Then leave the old car in a parking lot where there are no security cameras, change your disguise, walk to a different lot, steal another old car, drive that to a bus station, and pay cash for a ticket to Las Vegas, rent one of those trailer homes, and then live large using your stash of unmarked twenty-dollar bills."

Cor looked at Josie.

Maybe Josie's look revealed her alarm.

Cor grinned.

"Life lessons from the movies." Samantha said.

Cor said, "If I'm ever in deep doo doo, I'm calling Samantha to help me disappear."

Josie realized she was shaking her head, and she made herself stop. "You said a shooter would actually throw a gun away?"

"If he's smart, yeah. If the shooter has a common gun, and

he disposes it after a killing, it's very difficult to figure out who the killer is, regardless of whether your bullet evidence is good or not."

"What exactly do you mean when you say dispose of the gun?" Josie asked.

"The best way is to drop it out in the ocean or into a deep lake. Or bury it in a grave. Under the coffin. But of course, most shooters are loathe to throw away their weapon. It seems like such a waste. But nevertheless, that is the smart thing to do. Then again, this shooter took more than one shot. A smart sniper only takes one, then makes his escape whether his shot was successful or not."

Josie felt a little overwhelmed. A shooter had tried to kill her and Samantha, and what Cor said made it seem like there was little hope of ever catching him. "Is there anything else we should know?" Josie asked.

"Not that I can think of. But I'll let you know if I do. What else can I do to help?"

"Drive us back to our hotel? If our car is fixed, you could take us to the dealer. Once I get to cell reception and pick up our car, I can try to find an entomologist to look at this bug." Josie patted her pocket where she'd put the baggie.

"What's an entomologist?" Samantha asked.

"Someone who studies insects."

"What do you imagine an entomologist might say about the bug?" Cor asked. She glanced at Samantha. "Aside from any association with Russian sniper chefs who wear blue fleece clothing."

Josie smiled. "No idea."

"When is your car supposed to be ready?"

"I don't know."

They walked back to Cor's Jeep, got in like before, and Cor drove to Placerville. They stopped at Starbucks to grab food and warm drinks because Samantha was cold from riding in back.

Josie called the car dealer and was told the Prius needed several parts that had been damaged and that it would be another two days minimum.

"Now our next move is to rent a car," Josie said.

"I have no commitments for the next few days," Cor said. "How 'bout I serve as your driver?"

Josie thought about it. Cor was being very helpful. Too helpful? She showed up near the governor's car at UCLA. Was it possible she was working for him? Following Josie at his request? But Josie called Cor in L.A. No way could Cor have known that would happen. Then again, maybe Cor was in the Placerville area, watching Josie and Samantha, when she answered her cell phone. Maybe she only pretended to be in L.A.

It was an upsetting thought. But even if Cor was a plant—which didn't feel realistic to Josie—her presence was reassuring. Was that a stupid thought? Josie wondered. She felt like she was losing her center.

"The governor gave me an expense allowance," Josie said. "I'll pay you for your time and expenses."

"Whatever works for you," Cor said.

"Okay. Thanks very much. Let me spend a little time on this bug question."

Cor turned to Samantha. "Let's you and me give her some space. We can talk volleyball."

They stood. "Did you ever play?" Samantha asked as they walked toward the door and the Starbucks parking lot beyond.

"Yeah. I tried to be a setter. They get all the action, right? But I sucked at it..." They moved out of hearing.

Josie set her phone on the table. She set the baggie with the bug next to it. She thought it would be good to see if she could figure out what kind of bug it was before she called an expert, especially if experts weren't available to talk on the phone.

She searched on insects and went to multiple websites looking for photos and drawings of bugs. There was an astonishing range of bugs out there. It didn't take long to find a hundred bugs that looked like the little black bug in the baggie. How could one possibly tell the difference? She'd need an expert.

Josie searched the UCLA faculty, made some calls, left voicemails. A little more searching revealed that UC Riverside had a bigger entomology department. That would be an easy drive once they were back in L.A. It also appeared that Josie's alma mater, UC Davis, had entomologists. That was closer to where they were now.

Another listing mentioned Lake Tahoe. That was closer still. It wasn't a school. Just a name under the heading of entomologists. The name was Street Casey Ph.D. What kind of name was Street? Under the name was the curriculum vitae, which said he had gotten his Ph.D. at UC Berkeley, which suggested he knew his stuff.

Josie dialed the number. It rang twice and was answered.

"Street Casey," a woman said.

It took Josie a second to adjust to her incorrect assumption about the entomologist's gender.

"Hello. My name is Josie Strong. I teach medieval history at UCLA. I'm trying to find help in identifying a bug that was found at a crime scene near Placerville. I wonder if you can help or direct me to someone who can?"

"Certainly. I can probably help you with that. Can I ask you what is the condition of the bug?"

"It's dead as far as I can tell. It was in a muddy boot print. So it's caked with dirt. I put it in a baggie. I can email you a photo. Would that help?"

"Yes, let's try that. Let me give you my email address."

"Great." Josie tapped it out as the woman recited it.

Josie hit 'send,' and she heard a little ring sound over the phone.

"Got it," the Casey woman said. "It's hard to see identifying details in the photo. But it's definitely an insect."

"Oh," Josie said, feeling confused. "I…" she stopped.

"Sorry, I'm not being clear. You said you had a bug. There are many small animals that people call bugs but which are actually arachnids or other non-insect arthropods. However, I can see that this guy has six legs, which indicates an insect. The insect is damaged enough that it's hard to tell much from the photo. It looks a little like the Order Mecoptera."

"What is a Mecoptera?"

"They're called Scorpionflies. No relation to scorpions. How big is this guy overall?" the woman asked.

Josie lifted up the baggie and imagined a ruler next to it. "I'm not good at this. But I'd guess about a quarter inch long."

"That fits. There are several hundred species. It would be hard to tell more than that without looking at it in person."

"If I brought it to you, do you think you could identify it?"

"Yes, I imagine so."

"Would that fit in your schedule in the next day or so?"

"Late tomorrow morning would work," the Casey woman said. "Say, eleven a.m.?"

"Great. Where do I go?"

"I'm on the South Shore of Tahoe, on the Nevada side of the state line. If you're coming from South Lake Tahoe, you take a right up Kingsbury Grade. My lab is in a commercial area on the left." The woman gave Josie an address.

Josie wrote down the address and the directions. "Thanks so much, I'll see you there at eleven."

Josie clicked off and went outside to where Samantha and Cor were talking. Samantha was standing up, her uninjured arm out, demonstrating some kind of volleyball move, and Cor was nodding.

They seemed to turn toward Josie only reluctantly.

"You get a result?" Cor asked.

"Yes, I did." Josie held up the baggie with the bug in it. "I need to bring the bug to Tahoe. I talked to an entomologist named Street Casey. She's willing to take a look at it."

"There's a name. She couldn't tell you about the bug over the phone?"

"I emailed her a photo, and all she said was that this bug is a scorpionfly from some kind of group called mecoptera."

"Does it sting like a scorpion?"

"All she said was that scorpionflies are not related to scorpions. So that might suggest that it doesn't sting."

"When do we go?" Cor asked.

"Tomorrow morning. If that works for you, we'll see if the hotel has another room."

"Sounds like a plan."

TWENTY-FIVE

As Cor drove back toward their hotel, Josie said, "A sniper seems almost mythically powerful. He's able to take life from a great distance. From beyond where we can even perceive a threat."

Cor nodded. "The myth may be real. In Afghanistan, there was a supposed Army sniper who had a mythical reputation. They called him Typhon."

"The Greek monster god," Josie said.

"Wow, you've heard of him. Yeah. Some mythology geek said Typhon is half god and half monster. A scary dude who struck fear into all. This Army sniper definitely had the fear thing down."

"Did he exist? Or was he just legend?"

"From everything I heard, he exists. But no one knows who he is. Or was, if he's no longer alive. No one even knows who gave him orders. Standard Army doctrine is that military action is teamwork, and everyone has a backup. Snipers would seem like the lone-wolf exception, but even they usually go out as a team of two, a sniper cell consisting of a shooter and a spotter. The spotter helps identify the target and also provides enemy surveillance. But the talk is that Typhon must work alone, because otherwise there'd be Joes who'd actually know him. As it is, they've had to deduce his skills from evidence left behind and from rumors."

"What is there to deduce?" Josie asked. "Don't all snipers do the same job? Kill people from a distance?"

"Yeah. But from what I know, snipers also carry a short-range weapon for close-quarter combat. The chances of using their sidearm may be low, but they assume the possibility. Typhon apparently works in crowded cities. So he's been surprised and taken incoming rounds. They've found mushroomed bullets at his shooting sites. But there was no blood on them. So they know the guy wears a vest and armor. That's not always standard with snipers, because they often work from really tight and cramped positions that limit their movement. And they often are in positions where they wait for many hours or even days before their target presents itself. That makes snipers avoid armor. But this guy was apparently once in heavily populated territory and was surprised at night. Three enemy combatants stumbled onto him and took their shots. A security cam captured his tactical light and his gun fire. It appeared he held his light with his right arm outstretched to his side to draw enemy fire to his side. Just as he wanted, the enemy fired at the light. The shots went wide. While they fired multiple rounds, he used his other arm to put a single shot into each enemy. From the security cam, it looked like he used a Glock. Nine millimeter. Three shots. Three dead enemies. Then he ran away."

Josie tried to stay calm as Cor related the details. She reiterated as if to set the details in her memory. "So he holds the light with his right hand and shoots with his left, making him left-handed."

"Yeah, that's what you'd think. But part of his legend is that he's ambidextrous with his shooting, and wily, too. The Typhon we hear about in the Army is the kind of guy who'd switch his shooting hand just to mess with us."

Josie nodded. "You mentioned vests and armor. That just refers to something made from a kind of super tough cloth, right?" Josie said. "I've always wondered how a vest can stop bullets."

"The Kevlar fabric absorbs their impact similar to the way a tennis net stops a tennis ball. The impact can still knock a person over and cause a major bruise. The vest works because lead bullets are malleable. If the bullets have hardened points, they can go through the vest."

"Oh? I always thought that a bullet-proof vest was impenetrable. I guess that was more of a superhero notion."

"Vests will stop most bullets but not hardened ones. A steel knife can cut most vests, too. If you want more protection, you need a vest with built-in armor."

"Like the armor of a medieval knight?" Josie said.

"Yeah." Cor came to a tight curve and didn't slow down. Josie hung on to the inside door handle and her seatbelt as the Jeep flew around the turn, its wheels squealing.

Josie looked back, relieved to see that Samantha and Unknown were still onboard.

Josie said, "did security cameras ever show Typhon's face?"

"No. According to what I heard, they couldn't even tell if he was white or black or brown. He was just a dark shape at night. Even when he moved, his ghillie suit made him mostly invisible."

Samantha said, "What's a ghillie suit?"

"You've probably seen them in movies. The suits are made of fabric that moves and is covered with colors and textures that mimic whatever environment the soldier expects to be in."

"Oh, yeah," Samantha said. "One movie had soldiers out on a snowy landscape, and they were totally invisible! Then they stood up, and it was such a surprise to see them where it seemed like there was only snow. They looked like snowmen made of confetti."

Cor nodded.

"Is this mythical Typhon still in the Army?" Josie asked.

"Again, all they have are rumors. But it's such a rich bunch of rumors, people wonder if Typhon himself made up the stories as part of building his legend. One of the stories is that he adopted the god-like Typhon pseudonym as a sign of contempt for the world that controlled his life for so long."

Cor looked off at the horizon, her brow deeply furrowed, as if she were seeing a distant war zone.

She continued, "There haven't been any Typhon kills in several years. So maybe he took a lethal hit. Or maybe he retired. It's said he hated the brass, hated the hierarchy. He supposedly hated government types because they're the ones who taught him to be a killing machine and made him do it. It makes sense he would quit when he got the chance. It's hard to imagine

Typhon retired, playing golf in Florida or someplace. But it's possible."

"It seems logical that the sniper who killed Mary Jo Telman would have intended to kill her, right? It wasn't accidental. He wasn't trying to hit me or Samantha."

"Meaning..." Cor said, apparently not clear about what Josie was getting at.

"Meaning that, assuming his purpose was to kill Mary Jo, then why did he shoot at me when I got in my car? It's not as if I was going to find him out on that ridge in the dark."

"I don't know the answer to that. I think military snipers often plan to hit their target with a single shot, and then when others show up soon after, the sniper doesn't fire any more shots. To do so would be to give the enemy more information about his location. One logical possibility is that he didn't want to leave you alive because you would have information, however vague, about the experience."

"So trying to kill Mama was covering his tracks," Samantha called out from the back.

"Yeah. I think so."

TWENTY-SIX

They got a room for Cor in the same hotel and ate dinner in the same restaurant as the night before. As before, Josie ordered a glass of wine. She felt a little self-conscious about it in front of Cor as if it might affect how Cor thought about her. Josie imagined that the Army instilled great discipline among soldiers. Did that discipline extend to temperance? Josie rarely drank, but she thought it would help her relax. Then Cor ordered a beer, which, happily, helped Josie relax more.

The waiter brought the drinks. Cor picked up her beer and drank half of it down at once.

That signaled to Josie that temperance wasn't part of Cor's habits. And when the waiter brought dinner, Cor ordered a second beer.

They talked strategy while they ate. After dinner, no one had room for dessert, so they headed to their rooms.

They were on the road the next morning. Cor had pulled out a fabric roof cover that included clear vinyl windows. She rolled up little half-windows from the short doors. When the Jeep was enclosed, it was still cold and windy. But with the heater on, it was comfortable, if noisy.

The highway to the South Shore of Lake Tahoe went up a long, winding canyon. Not far from the highway was a river with continuous white-water rapids. The road got steeper as it went higher. Even though it was not yet officially winter, they saw snow on the tops of the mountains. A few miles farther, they crested the Echo Summit Pass at 7400 feet, and dropped down into the Tahoe Basin. In the distance below was the huge lake with a deep blue color, surrounded by snow-covered mountains. It was even bigger and bluer than Josie remembered from years before, when she visited during grad school at UC Davis.

The town of South Lake Tahoe was comprised of a long strip of stores and restaurants and motels. In the center of town, the road crawled next to the lake shore. The water was ultramarine blue, the sky dotted with white puffy clouds, and distant mountains white with snow.

"That's one of the biggest lakes I've ever seen," Samantha said.

"I read about it," Josie said. "It's twenty-two miles long. That would be similar to the distance from the beach in Santa Monica, past downtown, and all the way to Ellison's warehouse loft in Montebello."

Samantha went quiet as if superimposing Lake Tahoe over the Los Angeles basin.

They came to a built-up area with hotels and a pedestrian plaza and a gondola that stretched up a nearby mountain. There was a long line of skiers waiting to ride the gondola.

"Look, how funny," Samantha said. "Those skiers are waiting to go up the mountain, but there's no snow on the ground."

"Depends what the snow line was during the season's early storms," Cor said. "Could be there's ten feet of snow up on the mountain." She leaned forward to look up through the windshield. "In fact, I can see white up where that gondola is going."

"Right," Samantha said. Then she exclaimed, "I suddenly recognize this! This is Heavenly Ski Resort. My friend Myra and her family come here to ski at Christmas. They're probably coming up here in a few days. Myra showed me the pictures. She said you can ski from California to Nevada and back. Maybe we could ride up the gondola!"

Josie said, "It looks like it's just for skiers."

"We could ski!"

"You could," Josie said. "Whenever I'm on a slippery surface, my goal is to not slide anywhere. I'd prefer to stay in one piece."

Cor looked in the rearview mirror. "Maybe I'll go skiing with you someday, Sam. We could learn together."

"That would be cool," Samantha said, using Cor's favorite

word.

Cor drove past a sign that said they were entering Nevada. A mile farther, they turned onto Kingsbury Grade and found the commercial area where the entomologist was located. Cor parked.

"Want me to come in?" Cor said.

"No thanks. I'll be fine."

As Josie opened the door, Unknown made her eager whine from the back. Josie looked out and saw an open door in the building. A very tall man stood in the doorway. He was facing a small woman who was as thin as Samantha. Next to the woman was a small yellow lab. Next to the man was a giant dog, white with black splotches.

"Check out the Great Dane," Cor said. "That is one huge dog."

"Mama!" Samantha said in a loud whisper. "I have to let Unknown go meet that dog! I've never seen such a big dog! And why does his ear sparkle?"

The man with the Great Dane kissed the woman and turned to leave.

Unknown made another one of her eager whines.

"Your hound wants to play," Cor said. "Or at least visit."

The three of them got out of Cor's Jeep.

Josie walked toward the building as Samantha held Unknown's leash and walked toward the Great Dane.

"Excuse me, sir," Samantha called out. "My dog would like to meet your dog."

The man paused.

"Actually, I would like to meet your dog," she said. "Would that be okay?"

The man's dog was so tall, the man was holding him by the collar. His dog was looking at Samantha and Unknown, and he was wagging vigorously. "It's more than okay," the man said. "It appears he insists on it."

Josie felt a little worried as she watched. The Great Dane was much bigger than Samantha. Or her. Or Cor.

Samantha walked Unknown up to the man and dog. Josie

stopped to watch and listen.

"What's his name?"

"Spot. He also answers to His Largeness."

"He's got an ear stud!" Samantha said. "I've never seen that on a dog. That is so… Cool."

"He accidentally got a hole punched in his ear, so my girlfriend got him an earring."

Josie was amazed to see that Unknown had no fear, no hesitation. The Dane lowered his head and sniffed Unknown. Unknown did her tentative wag and reached her head up high to sniff the giant dog.

"Mama," Samantha called out. "Unknown likes him, and she's not afraid of him!"

"If you take off her leash," the man said, "they can play."

"Really? He won't hurt her?"

"No. He likes all dogs."

"Can I, Mama? Let Unknown play? I mean, we've never seen her play. But can we try?"

Josie nodded. "Sure."

Samantha unhooked Unknown's leash, and the man let go of the Great Dane's collar, and the two dogs did a kind of slow, formal dance, the small one walking around the giant one, first clockwise, then counter-clockwise. The giant one walked his front paws out, lowering the front of his body. His rear legs stayed straight, resulting in his back being impossibly arched. He still wagged.

"Why won't your dog run?" the man asked.

"We don't know," Samantha said. "Her former owner was killed in Canada, so we took her in. She seems pretty normal in some ways, but she won't run, she won't bark, and she won't play. No fetch, no Frisbee, no chasing with other dogs."

The man put his hand back on his dog's collar, then squatted down and held out his hand for Unknown to sniff. Unknown kept her distance.

"How does she react to other men? Versus women?" the man asked.

"She's friendly with women and kind of suspicious of men.

But we have one friend, Mr. Ellison, who is older, and she's okay with him. She even wags for him. It makes me worry the way Unknown is so reserved."

"Don't worry about it. She's probably just an introvert. Happy to go through life with a certain remove. Happy to observe from a distance."

Samantha reached out to stroke the man's dog, whose head came up to the middle of Samantha's abdomen. The dog wagged and stepped sideways next to Samantha and began to lean against her. Unknown stepped back to make room.

"Your dog obviously isn't an introvert!" she said.

"No. He expects to be the center of attention wherever he goes. Run, play, eat, sleep, get hugged and petted. Then repeat."

After a few seconds, the door to the building opened, and the thin woman and the yellow lab came back out.

"Blondie sees you all having a good time, and she wanted to join in," the woman said.

The yellow lab ran over, sniffed Unknown, then spun in a circle. The lab and the Dane ran around and dodged this way and that. Unknown walked after them. She seemed content, but, as always, she didn't exhibit much enthusiasm.

The woman came over. "What's your dog's name?"

"Unknown," Samantha said. "We adopted her up in the Quetico Wilderness in Canada after her owner died. He had adopted her before and didn't know her name. So he called her Unknown."

"She seems happy," the woman said. "But a little tentative about running and playing."

Josie replied. "She's kind of a mystery."

"Your voice sounds familiar," the woman said. "Are you the UCLA professor who called?"

"Yes. Josie Strong. And this is my daughter Samantha and our friend Cor Kontos."

"Street Casey. Good to meet you all."

They shook hands.

The woman gestured toward the man, who stood several

yards away. "This is Spot's enabler, Owen McKenna."

The man held up his hand and made a little wave and nodded. "Good to meet you all," he said. "I have to leave for an appointment. So Spot will need to cut this play date short. I hope that's okay."

"Thank you, Mr. McKenna," Samantha said. "I'm so glad Unknown got to meet His Largeness!"

The man took his dog by the collar, got into another Jeep, this one with normal doors and a roof—and multiple holes that looked like they'd been made by bullets—and they left.

Street Casey called out. "You can all come into my lab, if you want. Feel free to bring your Unknown."

Samantha looked at Cor, then said, "We've been driving a long time, so I think I should take Unknown for a walk. But thank you!"

Cor and Samantha headed off into the forest with Unknown.

Josie followed the woman into her lab.

When the door was shut, Josie's first thought was that the space had an unusual aroma. There was an antiseptic, alcohol smell. It mixed with a smell that Josie couldn't identify. More organic, like soil. Musty. It wasn't unpleasant. But it wasn't a smell you wanted indoors. Was this the smell of bugs? Josie wondered.

The yellow lab was standing in front of Josie, wagging. Josie reached down and stroked the dog's head. Satisfied, the dog walked over to a large wicker bed with a round mattress in it and lay down. The dog lowered her jaw to her front paws, but kept her eyes turned up and focused on Josie.

"I've never been in an entomology lab," Josie said as she scanned the place. There were workshop counters that held what looked like high-tech equipment. There were two microscopes. Each had two eyepieces. One had a cord connecting it to a computer. On another counter was a mini-fridge and a microwave. Josie didn't mind the idea that the entomologist might refrigerate her subjects. But cooking them? Maybe it was just for heating up coffee. Maybe the fridge was just for lunch.

There were many shelves full of glass jars with lids, and inside them a multitude of things, some twigs and some leaves and many dark specs that Josie didn't want to look at up close.

"You brought your bug..." the entomologist said.

"Yes. Thank you for seeing me." Josie pulled the baggie out of her pocket. She handed it to the woman.

The woman looked at it, walked over, and held it under a bright light at the end of a flex-tube lamp.

"A scorpionfly, as I thought," she said. "Let's get a look under the scope."

She opened the baggie and tilted it so the bug slid out onto a white card. She set the card on the base of the scope next to the computer. She turned on a bright light that was attached to the microscope, then moved the computer mouse.

The computer screen came on, and a vague image appeared. The woman adjusted a dial on the scope. The bug became focused, hugely magnified, looking quite intimidating with a large pointy nose and a nasty stinger.

"Definitely a scorpionfly."

"That thing looks like it could sting like a scorpion."

"Looks like it, but no. What looks like a stinger is the enlarged genitals of the male scorpionfly. They have nothing to do with scorpions. And they can't sting you. But the male is, well, impressive in that regard."

"Oh," Josie said and then felt embarrassed.

"What's interesting is that this is a snow scorpionfly. They show up in winter and spring. They eat moss and they scamper across snow, hence their name. This is quite early in the season for them. But of course insects are variable in their patterns. Where did you find him?"

"Down by Placerville."

"Do you know the elevation of the area?"

"No." Josie thought about it. "As I remember, when we drove out of Placerville, the road went up a little and downhill, as well. So it would probably be similar to Placerville. Does that tell you about the insect?"

"Yes to the extent that the insect isn't native to the area

where you found it. Many of the areas near Placerville are below eighteen hundred feet." The woman looked over at the little critter on the microscope. "It sounds like you found him below that elevation. But this insect only lives at high altitude. That means the insect was brought to the area. It's quite unlikely that the snow scorpionfly would have gotten there by itself."

"Where do snow scorpionflies normally live?" Josie asked.

"In places like Tahoe. I think you said you found this boy in a boot print?"

"Yes."

"Then that boot was up in the higher mountains before this poor baby was left for dead in Placerville."

Josie noticed the woman spoke of the insect like it was a sweet pet that no one should ever want to hurt or abuse.

"When you first called me," Casey said, "you mentioned that this insect was found at a crime scene."

"Right."

"How does the insect connect to that?"

"A sniper in the forest shot and killed a woman."

The entomologist frowned, and her eyes looked sad.

Josie continued, "The insect was in a muddy boot print that very likely belonged to the killer."

"So it appears," Casey said, "that before the killer fired the shot, he was probably up here in Tahoe."

"Right," Josie said as she thought about Francis Telman being killed in Tahoe. And just days later, his wife Mary Jo was killed.

"I'm curious," the woman said. "You said you teach history at UCLA. How did you come to investigate a murder?"

"A long story… A few months ago my daughter and I witnessed something that made some men try to kill us. We were able to find them and bring them to justice. The governor heard about it. He asked us to investigate the killing of a Forest Service ranger in Desolation Wilderness."

"I heard about that killing," the entomologist said.

Josie said, "A couple of days ago, we were talking to the ranger's widow when she was shot by the man whose boot print propbably left this bug. It's likely that the same man killed her husband. The ranger's widow was a friend of the governor. She was the connection between the ranger and the governor."

"And now she's dead," Casey said. "What a sordid situation. I probably shouldn't volunteer another person's help without asking him first, but that man you just met? The one with the Harlequin Great Dane?"

Josie nodded.

"His name's Owen McKenna. He's a former Homicide Inspector with the San Francisco PD, now a private investigator here in Tahoe. He knows all the local cops. If you have any law enforcement questions, he might be able to answer them or point you in the right direction."

"That is very kind of you to offer help. His help."

"I'll give you his card." Casey lifted a group of cards out of a coffee mug and handed one to Josie. Then she looked over at the microscope. "Do you want to take your scorpionfly?"

"I don't think so. You already gave me the only useful information I could get from it. Do you mind tossing it?"

"I'll add it to my collection. I don't have this particular version of scorpionfly."

"I came to the perfect expert."

"Maybe." The woman grinned.

"I should let you get back to work. How much do I owe you?"

"Nothing. I'm happy to help."

"But the governor is paying my expenses. It will get paid by the state of California."

"Then bill them for your time and donate it to a library or other good cause. But between you and me? Let's call it professional courtesy. From a bug scientist to a history scientist."

Josie was uncomfortable. She didn't know what an entomologist in Tahoe earned, but it was likely far less than the high salaries UCLA professors were paid. Nevertheless, protesting free service might seem patronizing.

"Speaking of history," Casey said, "do you have a specialty?"

"Medieval history."

"You need a Ph.D. to teach that, right?"

"Generally, yes. I did mine at UC Davis. I wrote my dissertation on medieval weapons. I saw on your CV that you did yours at Berkeley."

"So there you have it. We're UC comrades. I'm not going to charge you for looking in my microscope."

"You're too kind. Thank you so much. I hope to return the favor some day."

They said goodbye, and Josie went out, looked toward the forest, and saw Samantha and Cor coming toward her.

"What did you find out, Mama?"

"It's a snow scorpionfly. It lives at high altitude. Places like Tahoe."

Samantha was quick to say, "So the man who got the bug stuck in his boot murdered Francis in Tahoe and then came down the mountain and shot Mary Jo."

"Maybe yes," Josie said.

Cor raised her eyebrows. "You two are a natural crime-fighting duo. You've just found a likely link between the murder of Ranger Francis and his wife Mary Jo. They were both murdered by the same killer." Cor looked at Josie. "What do you make of that?"

"I think it reveals that both Ranger Francis and Mary Jo knew the killer."

TWENTY-SEVEN

They got back in Cor's Jeep.

Cor asked, "Where to next?"

"I'm hungry," Samantha said. "We should find some lunch and then take Unknown for a walk somewhere. This lake's gotta have a beach."

"Good idea," Josie said. "It's already two p.m." She handed her phone back to Samantha. "You're the captain and navigator. You could find a food venue and a good place to walk."

Samantha had spent only a short time on Josie's phone when she announced, "The Safeway supermarket in the middle of town has a deli. We could get sandwiches and food for Unknown, and there's a beach walk practically across the road."

An hour later, they had left Cor's Jeep at the supermarket, found a picnic table near the water, and eaten turkey sandwiches and chips. Samantha had found a miniature bag of dog food. She opened the top and mixed in some turkey. After Unknown ate a small amount and seemed satisfied, Samantha closed up the dog food bag, and they walked along the beach. Josie soon felt winded. She realized that walking at 6,200 feet of elevation meant much less oxygen than the air has at sea level. But she didn't want to slow to a stroll, because she would feel embarrassed in front of Samantha and Cor.

Eventually, they stopped.

Josie said, "I'd like to stop at the cabin where Mary Jo's husband Francis lived when he was in Tahoe. That's the place where he saw the man who stole the car at the Reno gas station."

"The man who killed him?"

"Yes."

"Did the gas station have video?"

"The governor's aides said it was out of order when the car was stolen."

"Okay, let's check out the cabin." Cor pointed with both of her index fingers, first to the left, then to the right. She raised her eyebrows in question.

"Oh, sorry," Josie said. "I saw on the map that Emerald Bay is on the southwest side of the lake. Please drive back through town. That's where the highway heads to Emerald Bay."

"Got it." The three of them and Unknown got back in the Jeep. Cor pulled out of the lot.

"The road to Emerald Bay," Cor said, "do you know what it's called?"

"I could find it on my phone," Samantha called out from behind them, "but I can't because my phone was destroyed. I'm suffering phone withdrawal."

Josie said, "The artist Salvador Dali said that suffering builds character." Josie once again handed her phone back to Samantha.

"See what I have to put up with, Cor?" Samantha said.

"Your life doesn't look that bad from up here," Cor said as she glanced in her rear view mirror at Samantha.

"Now you're both ganging up on me," Samantha said. "Neither of you knows what it's like. I'm living a life of communication poverty."

Samantha paused to tap and swipe on Josie's phone.

Samantha continued as she tapped on Josie's phone. "And phone withdrawal is in addition to my normal challenges. I have to cope with a doting mother. And all the electronic toys. A popular charter school. A position on the volleyball team, which is coached by a former pro. A condo so close to the Santa Monica beach that we can never escape the horrid sound of the surf. Imagine how nice it must be for kids who are privileged and can just live in silence in a trailer out on the desert somewhere."

Cor started laughing.

Samantha added, "With sweet rattlesnakes and real scorpions and so much heat you can cook by just setting your food outside."

"She's a funny girl, professor. What's that called? When you down-talk yourself?"

"Self deprecation?" Josie said.

"Yeah." Cor turned toward Josie. "When you took me aside and told me you wished you could trade her in, I thought, wow, that kid must be bad. But I think you should reconsider. She might eventually come around."

Josie turned just enough to see Samantha look up toward the rear view mirror, put her fingers in her mouth, stretch out her cheeks, and waggle her tongue.

After Samantha handed Josie's phone back, Josie got Sonja Gonsalves in the governor's office on the phone and explained what she wanted.

Sonja said, "I know I wrote that address down. Hold on."

Josie waited. Cor drove through the gathering dusk.

"Here it is," Sonja said on the phone. "I was told that the road was not well marked. I'll read this to you. 'Drive north out of South Lake Tahoe on Emerald Bay Road. Take it around the head of Emerald Bay. Then head up the north side of the bay. Look for a small dirt road that heads off to the left.'"

Josie repeated the words as Sonja spoke so that Cor and Samantha would hear them. She thanked the woman and clicked off.

"So we turn north on Emerald Bay Road," Cor said. "In fact, it's right here," Cor said, as she swerved over into a right turn lane at a stop light. "These winter days are short. The sun is nearly setting. It might be dark by the time we get there."

"I'd like to check it out anyway," Josie said. She thought about the possibility that the murderer could be in the area, but the chances seemed remote. And having Cor with them was very reassuring.

Emerald Bay Road was a winding highway that went through a neighborhood, then past beaches and a resort with many cabins, and then started climbing. They went around four sharp switchbacks and came to a high ridge. Despite the twilight, they were high enough that the remaining light from the sunset lit the vast stretch of Lake Tahoe with a dark gray-blue shimmer. A smaller lake appeared down to the left side. Emerald Bay appeared far down to the right side. Both the lake and the bay were hundreds of feet below them. The backdrop was a wall of mountains, white with snow. The sun had set behind the mountains, and the snowy landscape turned bluish.

"This road is narrow," Samantha said. "It looks like we could fall off in either direction. We'd roll all the way down to water. Kind of scary." After a moment, she added, "But beautiful."

"Never saw anything in the mountains of Afghanistan like this," Cor said. "They had lots of cliffs and steep mountains. But it was desert. No lakes where I was."

Josie's hands gripped the armrest on the door handle with her right hand and her seat belt with her left hand. She felt a little vertigo. Maybe if she shut her eyes...

They came to a rock wall on the left and a dropoff to the right. Down in Emerald Bay was an island that Josie had seen in pictures. She remembered reading that on the shore of the bay was a replica of a Norwegian castle that was built by a rich woman who funded Charles Lindbergh's first solo flight across the Atlantic Ocean. But Josie couldn't see the castle below her. The dropoff was too steep.

When she did open her eyes, the view was amazing by any measure. No wonder Tahoe was choked with tourists, she thought.

Josie said, "Sonja said that we turn left on a small Forest Service trail that goes back toward the mountain. There are some old cabins back in there. She said the road isn't plowed." Josie looked out at the landscape. "But it doesn't look like the snow is very deep."

"My Jeep can probably handle it," Cor said. "I've got the Goodyear Wrangler DuraTracs on all four corners. Practically bullet proof. So this girl shouldn't have any problem." Cor patted the dash.

Josie tried not to act appalled. Calling the vehicle a girl, talking about it like it had a personality, patting its dashboard like it was a pet. That kind of anthropomorphizing was so different from Josie's world, she could barely comprehend it.

Yet, even as she had the thought, she realized that it was likely that far more people understood Cor Kontos's world view than Josephine Strong's world view. Josie also realized that her view perpetuated the stuffed-shirt reputation attached to professors.

"Maybe I should get Wrangler DuraTracs for my next iPhone," Samantha called out from behind them.

Cor laughed. "Right on. Bullet-proof that puppy." Josie sensed Cor looking from her rear view mirror, then over to her. Cor said, "The volleyball player in the back seat is funny."

Josie made a single, solemn nod.

"I think this is our road," Cor said. She slowed, and turned left onto a narrow path. Twilight was shifting toward darkness, but the headlights illuminated the white snow.

Cor reached down and moved a gear shift. Josie didn't know what it was. Low gear. Or four-wheel-drive. Cor glanced again in the rear view mirror.

The Jeep went slowly, but it never seemed to spin its wheels as it went up a slope covered in snow. The trail went back into the woods a quarter mile or more. As twilight turned to darkness, the forest seemed to close in on them.

Cabins appeared in the dark. "What are we looking for?" Cor asked.

Josie looked down at the notes she'd made when talking to Sonja Gonsalves. Then she looked up as they drove by cabins.

"I think it's this next cabin," Josie suddenly said. "This looks like what Sonja described."

Cor pulled over and stopped in front of a small old cabin with a very steep roof and a stone chimney. Josie was about to unsnap her seat belt and get out when Cor suddenly shifted into reverse, hit the accelerator, and backed up very fast. Cor hit the brakes, spun the wheel, and the Jeep went into a backward, skidding slide on the snowy road. Cor turned the wheel again, the Jeep spun around 180 degrees, she shifted into forward, and sped back down the trail toward the highway.

"What are you doing?!" Josie cried, fear making it hard to breathe.

Cor pointed. "That pickup down close to the highway has

been following us. Now he's turning around and heading back to the highway because he sees us coming." Cor's hands gripped the steering wheel hard. Her steering movements were tense and shaky. "He's been behind us for some time, not close, but always there." Cor turned hard, hit the brakes, skidded around an S-curve, sped up again. "When we pulled onto this little trail and he turned after us, I knew it wasn't a coincidence."

"What are you going to do?" Josie tried to stay calm as they raced toward the highway. Josie braced herself and worried about Samantha in the back seat. Josie thought they were going much too fast.

The truck turned left as it got to the highway.

Just as it seemed they would shoot all the way across the highway, Cor turned the wheel to the left, and the Jeep skidded sideways and slid out onto the highway. Josie thought Cor was reckless, but she noticed that Cor wasn't losing control of the Jeep. Maybe Cor had gotten Army training in evasive driving or high-speed pursuit.

"We're going so fast," Josie said, her teeth clenched, her hands locked onto the armrest and seat belt.

"I'm just driving fast to see how hard he gets on it. See what he's made of." Cor was squinting through the windshield at the night. Unlike the dirt trail, the snow had melted on the black highway, which snaked left and right through a forest white with snow. "If he's a wimp, we catch him, get his license number, maybe interrogate him. If he's a Le Mans wannabe, we lose him. Or maybe he launches off one of these steep curves and tries to fly through the air down to the big lake."

"I'm quite… I'm quite scared," Josie managed to say, her voice barely audible over the roar of the racing Jeep. She noticed that Samantha hadn't made a sound from the back seat.

"You want me to stop? Let him get away?"

"I… Yes. I'd like you to stop."

Cor immediately took her foot off the gas. The Jeep slowed, coasting ever slower. Cor found a wide place on the shoulder and pulled in as the Jeep came to a stop.

"I'm sorry for stopping you," Josie said. She had a sudden

memory of when she was a child and she didn't want to participate when other kids were physically daring.

"This is no problem, Josie," Cor said, her voice reassuring. "It's okay to not pursue him. Driving fast at night on a snowy mountain road was probably a bad idea. It just gets my anger up, somebody following us after you've been shot at. But this is your gig. My job is to help, not direct."

"You're trying to be nice," Josie said. "I appreciate that."

"I'm telling the truth. Let's put this to good use. He knows we're on to him. So he won't be back soon."

"Shouldn't we call the police?"

"Not much point," Cor said. "We have no license plate, no vehicle ID other than the fact it's a black pickup, no personal ID, no knowledge of any value. We have no indication of any crime, no evidence of wrong doing. All we have is our gut sense that this guy could be connected to the sniper down in the foothills. And even if the cops should have a reason to pull him over, he'll have a cover story, legitimate and rehearsed."

Samantha said, "What if he has a gun?"

"That would be worth noting," Cor said. "But he will have the gun taken apart, the components locked in a gun case, tucked out of sight. He's not going to have it lying on the seat of his pickup. And even if cops —who have no cause to get a search warrant—somehow found a gun, the shooter will have a permit for it. It will look legitimate. Maybe it will be legitimate. But it's a moot point unless we could find the guy, catch him committing a crime, and discover the gun without having a search warrant. We don't even know where to look for the guy."

"What do you think he wanted?" Josie asked.

Josie saw Cor glance in the rearview mirror before she spoke.

"I think he was on recon. Watching us. Trying to see what we know."

"Do you think he was going to try to kill us?"

"No."

Josie thought Cor's answer came too fast. As if she thought the opposite.

"Not now, anyway," Cor added. "Now that he knows we've seen him, he'll be much more careful and stay away from us."

Samantha said, "If he has binoculars, he would see that there's three of us and a dog. And he would see Cor's camo clothes and think he probably shouldn't mess with her. Like she could have her own rifle in the Jeep. Or be carrying a piece on her person."

"Carrying a piece?" Josie was continuously surprised at Samantha's lingo. Josie noticed that Cor didn't comment.

"If he's the sniper," Cor said slowly, "and if he wants to harm us, he'll target us from a long distance. It won't be driving on the road. He'll figure out where we are, and he'll set up in a shooter's blind."

"What's that?" Josie asked.

"Someplace where he can see us but we can't see him. Like the ridge where he set up to shoot Mary Jo."

Samantha said, "Some hiding place where he could lounge in his blue fleece jacket and snack on his gourmet Russian lunch while waiting for good conditions."

Cor made a light tap on the dashboard as if it were punctuation for Samantha's comment. "The Sam and Josie show is taking shape. Maybe you should be taking notes, Josie. Write down Sam's jokes."

"That would just encourage her."

"You don't want to encourage her?"

"To be a doctor, maybe. Or an astronaut. Not a comedian."

"What about a professor?"

Josie shook her head. "Professors are…"

"Go ahead and say it, Mama."

"Professors are a little too full of their own world."

"Because they know a lot of stuff, and the school pays them a lot of money for knowing it?" Cor said.

"Yes, I suppose so."

"Let's go look at that cabin. Are you okay with that?" Cor reached over and touched Josie's leg.

The touch felt reassuring to Josie even as it also seemed a bit forward. Josie reminded herself that this was yet another aspect of being normal. These were the behaviors of people who had normal relationships. Because Josie had no friends to speak of, she needed to stay aware of the reasons why. She needed to be open-minded and not be too comfortable with her own introverted ways.

"Yes, let's go back to the cabin," Josie said.

Cor put her hand back on the wheel, waited until a truck passed them, did a U-turn on the highway, and headed back toward Emerald Bay. She turned into the same road, drove back to the cabin, and parked.

Cor pulled a flashlight out of one of her cargo pockets. "I have an extra light," she said. She reached into the glove box and pulled out a small, narrow light. She handed it to Josie.

"Give it to Sam," Josie said. "Sam showed me that my phone has a flashlight."

Cor handed the flashlight to Samantha.

Josie got out, switched on the phone light, and turned a full circle, scanning the nearby ground.

The forest and cabin were coated with a couple of inches of fresh snow. The underlying snow pack seemed deep. But it had crusted over so that Josie only sank in a few inches. She didn't know how that happened. Probably warmer temperatures softened the snow, and then colder temps froze it solid.

There were footprints in the fresh snow around the cabin. Someone had been up to the cabin door and walked around its perimeter.

The air was cold, the temperature dropping fast. The last place they'd been that was cold was Yosemite. But this was much colder. As if reading Josie's mind, when Samantha got out of the Jeep, she said, "Whoa, it's even colder here than it was in Yosemite. Why is that?"

Cor said, "Tahoe's farther north. And we're around three thousand feet higher than Yosemite Village. Higher elevation usually means colder."

Samantha pulled on the jacket Cor had given her the previous day. The jacket only draped her left arm and the sling, but Samantha got it zipped up. Cor was still wearing her sleeveless camo shirt.

Cor walked toward the cabin. "Lots of footprints in the snow. But the snow is too soft and cold to take a clear image." The cabin door was flanked by piles of split firewood. Cor tried turning the doorknob. The knob was locked. But the door swung in at her touch.

"No need to break in. Some dude beat us to it."

Josie inhaled and looked around at the snow-covered night. "Do you think it was the person following us?"

Cor shrugged. "I'll check it out. Wait out here."

TWENTY-EIGHT

Cor stepped to the side of the cabin door. She pushed on the door, and stayed back as it swung open. She shined her light inside, reached in, found a switch, and flipped it.

Lights came on in the right half of the cabin. Josie stayed back with Samantha and Unknown as Cor stepped inside. A few seconds later, more lights turned on, spilling out a window on the left side.

"All clear," Cor's voice called out.

Josie walked to the door and waited, unsure of what to do. Cor appeared in the doorway. She shined her light on the door jamb. It was splintered, and the metal plate was bent. Cor pushed on the wood and metal. It flexed.

"Whoever came here before us pried the door open. The damage isn't significant. I don't think they used anything bigger than a large screwdriver. I'll get my tool box. I can maybe bend the metal plate back enough that the door latch will catch. It won't be strong, but it will hold the door shut and keep snow from blowing in until someone can get a carpenter out here." Cor gestured toward the inside. "Place is empty," she said to Josie. "Check it out."

"Cor, you walked in with almost no hesitation. Didn't you think you could get ambushed? Or shot?"

"Always possible." Cor shifted her weight from one leg to the other.

Josie noticed that Cor moved her foot like she had the previous day, rotating her foot as if stretching her ankle. It reminded Josie of when she'd gotten to know a student who was a dancer. The woman had a sprained ankle, and she kept rotating it as if to judge her range of movement.

"Does your foot hurt?" Josie asked.

"No. But sometimes… It catches and makes a snapping sound. Started happening in the Army. Anyway, I noticed that there were two sets of footprints in the snow," Cor said. "One set went into the cabin. Another set came out. The ones that came out stepped on top of some of the previous prints. So it's pretty clear that there was only one intruder, and he left the way he came."

"You think it's okay for us to go inside?"

"You're the official on special assignment for the governor. If push came to shove and the governor got involved, you'd probably pull rank on anyone else. Even the sheriff. And you're not even breaking in. Someone already did the honors."

Cor seemed to linger outside the door as if wondering if the pursuer in the pickup would return. A breeze came, colder than before. How Cor stayed warm with bare arms, Josie had no idea. It was probably a combination of muscles and metabolism.

Josie walked inside, followed by Samantha and Unknown.

The cabin was small. It had an open design with large log trusses that held up the roof, which appeared to be uninsulated. The logs and the roof boards were unpainted. The wood had once been varnished. And while it had darkened substantially over the many decades since it was built, the wood was still beautiful.

The cabin appeared to have two sections, the larger section to the right, a smaller one to the left. Samantha and Unknown quickly cruised through the cabin, while Josie took her time looking.

The main part of the cabin was a large room with plank pine flooring and a large, circular braided rug in front of a stone fireplace. In front of the fireplace were an old couch and an armchair. Both armchair and couch had reading lights on tall stands.

To one side of the fireplace was a tall bookcase. Josie walked over and looked at the titles. They were an eclectic mix. Novels, contemporary and classic, histories, biographies of historical figures. There was a small section of poetry. It seemed a perfect combination for reading by the fire.

At the front of the cabin was a kitchen that consisted of a counter with a sink, a small gas oven and stove top, and several cupboards attached to the wall above. On the stove top was an enamel orange tea kettle and an old-fashioned, aluminum drip coffee pot. On the counter next to the stove top was a metal stand from which hung five mismatched coffee mugs, only one of which was the orange of the tea kettle.

There was a small window above the kitchen sink. The window had old, orange drapes that had probably never been cleaned in 50 years.

Dividing the kitchen area from the living room was an old plank table that served as dining table and desk and anything else that required a place to sit down at a flat surface. The table was stained from countless years of meals and other activities. Four chairs were tucked under the table. They had wooden backs. Three had orange seat cushions, stained with years of dropped food. Josie noticed that the orange, though bright, wasn't quite the same orange as the kitchen components. It may have been a superfluous observation. But it made Josie think that, while Francis Telman seemed neat and orderly, he didn't care much for cleanliness.

On the table were miscellaneous piles of paper, letters, bills, and a few books, all neatly stacked. Perhaps most notable of all was that there was no TV.

Samantha and Unknown came out of a small central doorway that led to the left side of the cabin. Samantha sat on the couch. Unknown stood in front of her, reaching with her head to sniff the cushions.

Samantha patted the couch fabric with her right hand. "No one's gonna care, baby. Make yourself at home."

Unknown, always tentative, lifted a single front paw and carefully placed it on the couch as if stepping out onto thin ice and testing to see if it would hold. She waited as if to see if someone might disapprove. When no one objected, she put her other paw up and climbed onto the couch in a crawling maneuver. She went from standing on the floor to lying on the couch in one smooth motion. She looked up at Samantha for approval. Samantha rested her hand on the dog's back.

Josie walked toward the rear of the cabin. She found herself in a small, square area that led to a bathroom on one side and a bedroom on the other. The furnishings were spare and old but comfortable. The bed had a spread that was a handmade quilt. Josie looked in the closest and pulled open several dresser drawers. Sweaters, jackets, and jeans, all sized for a man. There were knit hats, baseball caps, gloves, and two rectangular cloths made of heavy nylon and with Velcro straps along one edge. Josie assumed they were some kind of snow gear, maybe for keeping snow from getting in boots. On the floor of the closet was a pair of snowshoes and some large plastic boots, no doubt for skiing.

One wall of the bedroom had a window, and beneath it stood a desk with a built-in two-drawer filing cabinet. Josie pulled open the drawers. There was a sparse collection of hanging folders. Josie flipped through them. There were bills and Forest Service notes and tax filings. Josie opened several of the tax folders. She was never good with taxes. But from what she could see, the returns were for Francis. Mary Jo's were somewhere else.

An IRS form showed that Francis earned $66,000 per year working as a ranger for the Forest Service. His only deductions seemed to be the standard IRS deduction and real estate taxes on the Tahoe cabin, showing that the Tahoe cabin was in his name. Telman reported no substantial dividends or interest income. Josie found an IRA portfolio. Francis made regular contributions to his IRA fund, which seemed to Josie to be quite small for someone who might depend on it in later years. But she realized she likely had a skewed perception from her position at UCLA.

Josie used her phone to take photos of all the pages on the ranger's tax return. She didn't think they would reveal anything. But it was possible.

Francis Telman appeared to be a hard-working guy who had no surprising financial investments. His largest asset was the Tahoe cabin.

Josie remembered that the Telmans had another house Mary

Jo had inherited from her father. It was closer to the town of Foresthill, where Telman's Forest Service job was headquartered. Josie intended to look at it the next day.

But as Josie looked at this Tahoe cabin, something about it seemed unusual. There was some similarity between the modern foothill extravaganza where Mary Jo had been shot and the Tahoe cabin that Josie couldn't identify. She was turning to go outside, when it came to her. Neither place had any electronics. In addition to no TV screens, there were no computers, no iPads or Kindles, no security cameras.

Almost certainly it was a coincidence, a Tahoe cabin owned by the Telmans and a large modern foothill house owned by unnamed friends of the Telmans, and neither of them having what nearly every house in the country had. The likeliest explanation was that both the Telmans and the Bay Area couple viewed their respective places as getaways to escape being constantly connected to the rest of the world. Josie was curious whether the Telmans' other house would have the standard wide-screen TV and other electronics.

Josie remembered that Mary Jo had pulled her husband's phone out of the secret cubby and handed it to them. Samantha had gone through that phone and emailed Francis's contacts to Josie. Josie realized that she should also look for Mary Jo's phone. She had no idea where it would be. At the friends' modern house near Placerville?

Josie told Samantha and Cor that she was ready to go. They got in the Jeep, with Unknown once again in back with Samantha, and Cor headed back out to Emerald Bay Road and then up and over Echo Summit and down to the foothills, where it was substantially warmer. Josie thought the foothills seemed like fall instead of winter, as it was up in Tahoe.

Josie was unable to reach Sonja at the governor's office, which only made sense considering the late hour. She left a message asking directions to the Telman's Foresthill house.

Cor said, "Shall we grab grub in your hotel digs? Or you want something else?"

Josie hesitated, unsure of what to say.

"The thing is," Samantha said, rescuing Josie, "Mama has a thing for bacon, but otherwise she and I are pretty much vegetarians. It's part of the professor package."

To Josie's great relief, Cor laughed. "No hay problema," Cor said. "Veggie works. I've been chowing down Impossible Burgers at this beanery in Hollywood. Amazing how good veggie burgers taste."

"Mama, if you give me your phone, I'll find us a joint."

Josie handed her phone over the seat. She was thinking about the word joint, how it used to mean prison. Where did Samantha pick up these words? Josie tried to put it out of her mind.

"Got one," Samantha said a few minutes later. "Oh, Mama, you're gonna love this. You know that guy who writes stuff?"

"Like that guy who was in that movie?" Josie said, repeating one of their favorite jokes.

"Right!" Samantha said. "This is the guy you talk about sometimes. A medieval guy."

Josie sensed Cor glancing up to the rear view mirror.

"Isn't his name Dante?" Samantha said.

"Yes. Dante Alighieri. He was an Italian poet from the thirteenth and fourteenth centuries. Probably the most important medieval writer."

"Okay, get ready, Matey," Samantha said. "This place is called Dante's Divine Comedic Gourmet Vegan Pasta and Pizza."

"I'm sold already, Cap'n," Josie said. "Dante's most important poem was called the Divine Comedy. So the restaurant owner has some literature chops."

"The thing is, it looks kinda upscale," Samantha said. "White tablecloths and red leather chairs and wine glasses on all the tables."

"I've got a sport jacket," Cor said. "When I put it on over my camo, people think I'm a rock star. I get special treatment."

Josie thought that any special treatment was more likely due to Cor's big black Army boots and the way she telegraphed a tough attitude. "It's probably your charisma more than your jacket," Josie said.

The dashboard lights were bright enough that Josie could see Cor grin. Cor lifted her fingers to the side of her head and made like she was a movie starlet checking non-existent curls. She spoke with a high, squeaky voice, heavy with Long Island accent. "Aw, professaw, ya think I got charisma?"

"Yes, I do."

Cor went back to her regular voice. "Okay. Dante's it is."

When they got to the restaurant, Cor pulled up to the valet park and removed a black sport jacket from her bag as the others got out. Cor pulled on the jacket, which Josie thought looked sharp with the black boots. Cor slapped the car keys in the palm of the skinny teenage kid at the valet park podium. "I check my odometer. I'll make you drop and give me fifty for every mile you drive this."

"I can't do fifty pushups," the kid said.

"Then you best put this ride in the closest space and guard it with your life."

"Okay." The kid looked at Samantha and Unknown. "The thing is, dogs aren't allowed inside. It has to be a certified service dog, bib and all. Luigi is real strict."

Cor leaned close to the valet. "I'm Cor Kontos, Sergeant First Class U.S. Army, and this is my service dog. We are assigned to this woman who is a professor working as a special consultant for the governor. If Luigi wants to make a fuss, we'll call the governor's office. His aide will pull up the list of health department restaurant examiners, and they'll come and do their thing. You know about the inspection levels, right?"

The kid shook his head.

Cor said, "The silver level brings two inspectors who look at everything and interrupt the diners' dinners. They're really quite annoying. They send the message that restaurants need to be mindful of their hygiene standards. The gold level shuts the restaurant down for three days while they write up reports. Reports go in the local papers and on TV. Some of the restaurants survive. The platinum inspection is what the state does when they want to put a restaurant out of business. Regardless of the approach, Luigi will be told that the inspections were triggered by the car park valet's obstructive response to a customer."

The kid made a solemn nod. He looked at Unknown, then turned toward the restaurant door. He walked over to the doorman and spoke quietly.

The doorman nodded.

The kid came back and said, "Ralph will seat you in our private Dante dining room with dedicated personal waiter." He looked directly at Cor. "And I'll put your Jeep in one of the reserved spaces and personally guard it."

"Thanks."

Cor hooked one of her arms through Josie's elbow and put her other arm around Samantha's waist. She walked them to the door. Unknown stayed next to Samantha.

"How did you know how to do that?" Josie asked as they walked.

"It's a standard threat/intimidation dynamic to get people to do what you want. We used it all the time in Afghanistan. Different situations, but similar technique. We called it, 'Scare 'em and Snare 'em.'"

"That was pretty kick-butt, huh, Mama?"

"Yes. Definitely kick-butt."

The doorman nodded at them as he opened the big entrance door that had a carved profile of a man with a large nose. Dante, Josie thought.

They were led into a large private room, served excellent food and drink, including large steel bowls for Unknown's veggie meatballs and pasta bolognese, and water. Josie drank another glass of Riesling, completing three nights in a row with alcohol, which was unusual. Cor had two beers.

Later, Cor drove back to their hotel. Her last words before she went to her room were, 'Keep your head down,' which didn't make Josie feel comfortable. Josie thought it was likely just a figure of speech. But it was also a good warning to be careful.

TWENTY-NINE

Before they went to sleep, Samantha used Josie's phone to call home and see how Amelia was doing. Josie was pleased to hear their pleasant tones. They seemed to get along just as they had before Amelia moved into Samantha's room.

The next morning, the automotive shop called to say that Josie's Prius repairs would be finished the following morning. Josie arranged to pick it up at 9 a.m.

Her phone beeped with a voicemail. It was Sonja from the governor's office. The voicemail must have come when Josie was out of cell coverage. Sonja left the address of Mary Jo and Francis Telman's Foresthill house, the one Mary Jo had inherited from her father. Sonja also mentioned that the governor had asked the sheriff's office to give Josie the keys that Mary Jo had. Sonja thought—but didn't know for certain—that the key to the Foresthill house was probably among those keys.

After the incident the night before with the vehicle following them to Telman's Tahoe cabin, Josie asked Cor to accompany them to the Foresthill house. Cor said she was free until her next self-defense class two days later and she'd be happy to drive.

They walked to a nearby restaurant for breakfast, then headed back to the hotel. Cor had gone to fetch her Jeep from the parking lot. She pulled up in front of the hotel.

They drove north out of Placerville, through the foothills to Coloma, where gold was discovered in 1848 and started the massive Gold Rush.

The early winter weather was crisply cool. But the sun was hot in a deep blue sky, very different from the L.A. weather of moderate temps, soft blue skies, and sunshine that was muted by the misty air that blew in from the Pacific.

A half hour later, they pulled up to the address in Foresthill that the governor's aide had given Josie.

The house that Mary Jo's father had owned was a modest-sized rambler, probably built decades before but in very good shape. There was a detached garage to one side, and on the other side of the garage, a shed. All of the structures were painted soft light green with dark green trim, like colors the Forest Service would choose. Because Josie's vision wasn't very good, and because the front door was shaded, she gave Samantha the keys. Although all of Samantha's movements were one-handed, it seemed having one of her arms in the sling was not constraining at all. She had the door unlocked seconds later.

Cor stood to the side, a self-appointed guardian. She told Samantha to stay put while she searched the house. She went in and came out a minute later. "All clear," she said, just as she'd done the evening before at the cabin above Emerald Bay in Tahoe.

Josie and Samantha and Unknown all walked inside.

Unlike Telman's Tahoe cabin with its log structure and strong rustic flavor, this house had little personality, no doubt the choice of Mary Jo's father who'd owned the house before his death. There were three bedrooms. The largest of them had a bathroom, making two bathrooms for the house.

The master bedroom had a queen-size bed, carefully made up, the bed covers taut. The bedspread was gray with tiny red squares. The sheets and pillowcases darker gray.

In one corner of the room was a desk and chair.

On the desk was an old landline phone, a banker's-type desk lamp, and two yellow pads. Next to the pads was a single Bic pen. But there were no notes.

Josie sat in the desk chair and pushed back to make the chair recline. But it was stiff and wouldn't recline easily. She looked underneath the seat. There were levers to adjust the chair settings. Josie recalled that her own desk chair at UCLA had been too stiff for her to recline until she found the adjustment spindle underneath the chair and loosened the setting so a lighter person could recline it. This chair had not been adjusted for a lightweight woman. Mary Jo was taller than Josie, but thinner.

She probably weighed less than Josie. Either she never wanted to recline the chair or she never sat in it. Josie concluded that it was another indication that Mary Jo didn't spend any time at this house.

In the desk drawers were a few standard office items. Stapler, paperclips, scissors, a partial roll of stamps, some #10 envelopes. Nothing personal.

Josie stood and walked around the room. She opened the closet door. It was empty.

Josie walked to the next bedroom. It also contained a queen bed. It was unmade. Clothes hung off the upper corner of an open closet door. The closet was a disorganized collection of men's clothes. Same for the dresser.

Samantha walked in, with Unknown trailing behind her as if wary of what might be in the house.

"Find anything?" Samantha asked.

"Some clothes. Men's clothes. It looks like this room was Francis's bedroom, while the master bedroom is empty. Bed made, but nothing else. Nothing in the closet, either."

"That's weird," Samantha said. "I went into the third bedroom and it's empty, except for old office stuff. Where is Mary Jo's stuff? It was her father who owned this house, right?"

"Yes. So shortly after Mary Jo's father died, Francis moved into the house she inherited. But Mary Jo didn't move in."

"Do you think she lived at the Tahoe cabin? No, you don't need to answer that. I was there. There was nothing there that connects to a woman like Mary Jo."

"Tell me," Josie said. "What do you mean when you say, 'a woman like Mary Jo?'"

Samantha frowned, thinking. "Refined, feminine but not girly, upscale with her clothes and hair, the kind of person who owns lots of nice stuff. Mary Jo would have matching dishes and silverware but without patterns. Drapes or blinds with no patterns. But she wouldn't go for the lumberjack look. Mary Jo definitely doesn't fit in the Tahoe cabin. That was obviously a man's place."

"That's what I think, too."

"Mary Jo fits with her friends' modern house."

Samantha and Unknown walked out and turned toward the master bedroom.

Josie went into the third bedroom, which was used as an office, apparently for Francis. On an old wooden desk were two small fishing trophies engraved with Francis Telman's name. His desk had an old computer with the old, curved glass monitor. Josie turned it on. It crackled with static electricity as the screen came to life. The screen slowly went from dark to light. It said Windows 95. The computer was decades old.

Josie clicked on the documents folder and found nothing except some early Windows files, logs and such that made no sense to Josie. There was no internet connection, no browser, nothing even remotely modern. Josie looked at the printer. It was disconnected from the computer and unplugged from the wall.

It seemed clear that no one used the office. Francis must have done all of his desk work at one of the Forest Service offices.

Like the Tahoe cabin, the bedroom with Francis's clothes was obviously used.

Where was any sign of Mary Jo's existence? Where were her clothes? Where was her car? Where did she work? What was her work? Her phone?

If Josie hadn't met the woman and seen her shot to death, she'd think the woman didn't exist.

Josie walked into the kitchen. It was poorly stocked, both in terms of cookware and groceries. There was nothing revealing. The refrigerator had food that Josie associated more with men—hotdogs, Ribeye steak, Budweiser, a 12-pack of powdered donuts—than with women like Mary Jo, who Josie imagined drank herbal tea and ate raw broccoli and carrots and nibbled gourmet chocolates that came in decorative boxes.

Josie walked back into the living room where Samantha sat with Unknown at her side.

Samantha pointed toward the kitchen. "All the dishes match. But a lot of them look unused."

Cor stepped in from outside.

"Find anything?" Cor asked.

"Only that I think no woman lives here. Francis Telman moved some of his clothes here. But Mary Jo didn't live here in the normal sense. And there is no sense of a married couple, either. No notes to each other. No photos showing them together vacationing. No family pictures. No books. This place is like a motel. Antiseptic. It doesn't make sense that nothing of Mary Jo is here."

"Maybe they were planning to sell the house." Cor looked around at the living room. "But the furniture is still here."

"I wondered about that. Sometimes people will sell a house furnished. But that wouldn't explain why Francis Telman's clothes are in one of the bedrooms. And it doesn't explain where Mary Jo lived."

"I looked around the Tahoe cabin," Samantha said. "I'm pretty sure she didn't live there, either."

Cor said, "Maybe Francis moved his things in right after they married, and she hadn't gotten around to it. Maybe her stuff is still in her apartment, wherever that is."

Cor said, "But she'd still have some clothes with her. Her car, too."

Samantha frowned. "Mary Jo looked like the kind of person who would have a fancy house with expensive furniture."

Josie thought about it. "Maybe Sonja has an idea of where that might be."

Josie found the number for the governor's aide and dialed. She once again expected that she'd be routed to voicemail.

But Sonja answered just as she'd claimed she would.

"Hi Professor Strong, this is Sonja Gonsalves."

"Oh, thanks for taking my call."

"Certainly. How can I help you?"

"First, a progress report. We've visited Francis Telman's cabin in Tahoe."

"Oh, your car is repaired. That's great."

Josie was about to mention Cor Kontos when she thought to err toward privacy. There would be nothing to gain by explaining about Cor. "Actually, it won't be done for another day or so. We used a loaner car from the repair shop. The sheriff gave us Mary Jo's keys. So we went to both the Telman cabin in Tahoe and the house near Foresthill, the one Mary Jo had inherited from her father."

"Oh, I forgot about that. Mary Jo's father died right before their wedding, and he left the house to Mary Jo. Didn't she and Francis move into that house after their wedding?"

"It looks like Francis moved some of his things in there," Josie said, "but not Mary Jo. The Tahoe cabin is similar in that it's got men's things but no women's stuff. So I'm wondering if you or the governor have any idea of where Mary Jo lived. Maybe a house or apartment she lived in before she and Francis got married. If we could look at Mary Jo's previous residence, we might get a sense about why Mary Jo was killed. And that might also settle any questions about whether Francis's shooting was random."

"Yes, of course. Looking at Mary Jo's place would be an obvious step, wouldn't it? I recall the governor mentioning Mary Jo's apartment, but I don't know where it is. Let me get him on the other line and ask him."

"No rush," Josie said. "I don't want him to feel pressured."

"No pressure at all. Just hang on a bit. I'll be right back."

The line went silent. Josie waited. She mouthed the words 'I'm on hold,' to Samantha and Cor.

A minute later Sonja was back.

"I'm sorry to say he didn't have any information."

"Mary Jo must have an address listed somewhere," Josie said.

"You'd think so. The governor seemed embarrassed not to know. He's going to look in his computer and see if he can find anything. He'll call me back. But he's busy, so I don't expect he'll call back until this evening."

"Do you have any ideas?" Josie asked. "Maybe the State of California has records of its citizens and their addresses?"

"Maybe. Tax records, certainly. But I assume they are confidential. I have no idea how to pursue that. I'll ask the governor when he calls back. In the meantime, let me think. I suppose you could go back to her friends' house where she was staying. There has to be something that Mary Jo would have left there. Something that would give an indication of where she lived."

"It's pretty intimidating," Josie said, "to go back to where she was shot. For my daughter especially."

"Of course. I totally understand. When the sheriff's office called our office, they said your daughter was wounded. Physically. No doubt psychologically, too. Tell you what. I'll call some other people I know in the governor's office. Maybe I can find out something without waiting for the governor to call back."

"Okay, thanks."

Josie said goodbye and hung up.

"Did she have anything helpful, Mama?"

"No. Her only thought was that Mary Jo would have had some personal things at her friends' house. Something that would indicate where she lives."

"In her wallet," Cor said. "And from your description of her, Mary Jo would carry a purse." Cor looked at Josie. "The only time you were inside was before Mary Jo was shot. We should definitely check it out."

"Sam, are you okay with that?"

"Yeah. We already went to the driveway to figure out where the shooter fired from. The inside of the house will be less traumatic than that."

"The sergeant gave me the key." Josie said. "Shall we go back there now?"

Cor nodded.

THIRTY

Cor drove them back through the foothills to the modern house owned by Mary Jo Telman's Bay Area friends.

The house was the same as before, but the yellow crime scene tape had been taken down.

From Cor's Jeep, they could see a red light on the security camera above the front door.

"Is the security system armed?" Cor asked.

Josie thought about it. "I don't remember that light before, but I might have easily missed it. No one said anything about an alarm password. So unless the sheriff's officers were able to contact the house owners and they came within the last day, the alarm would still be off."

"I'll go in first," Cor said.

Josie was happy to have Cor serve that role. Just thinking about going in the house again made Josie feel a little shaky. She pulled out the key that Sergeant Garner had given her.

Cor took the key, jumped out of the Jeep, and jogged to the entry. She unlocked the door and slowly pushed it open.

No alarm. Just silence.

Cor disappeared inside.

"After that hike to where the shooter was," Samantha said, "I should feel more comfortable. But..." she stopped.

"I know, hon. Just remember that Cor is with us. She makes us safer."

After a couple of minutes, Cor reappeared in the doorway and waved. "All clear," she called out.

"It's like in the movies," Samantha said. "We keep sending Cor to be our advance scout."

Josie and Samantha and Unknown got out of the Jeep. Samantha used her good arm to grab Josie's hand. They hurried to the front door and went inside.

"Nice place," Cor said as she circled around the fountain in the entryway. She looked up at the plant hanging beneath the skylight, walked past the kitchen area and over to the wall of glass that overlooked the river in the canyon below.

Josie realized that when she and Samantha had first come to the house, she was so focused on her interaction with Mary Jo that she hadn't paid much attention to the house beyond noticing the entry fountain and the marble floors.

Later, when she was shot at and was scrambling around the house on her knees in the dark, Josie saw nothing that lodged in her memory. All of her memories were upstaged by the horror of seeing Samantha get pushed over the stone wall, covered in Mary Jo's blood.

But now, as Josie saw Cor turn and look around, Josie looked at the various walls, which were broad expanses of yellow color mixed with sections of natural maple boards about twelve feet high. The living room was trapezoidal in shape and had three main walls that joined at unusual angles. Each wall had a very large abstract painting with orange and magenta and lavender pigments. The other two walls of the living room were glass, huge panels that rose from the marble floors to a ceiling made of maple boards. There was a glass door in one of the glass walls. The door led to a broad deck that had a grand view of the river canyon below.

Cor frowned. "This place is a mash up of angles. I don't see a square corner in the place. I have an architect lady in one of my self-defense classes. One of the other women was asking her about building a custom house, and the architect talked about how building rectangles is relatively cheap and building unusual angles is expensive. It would take a serious bank account to buy a place like this. Any idea who the owner is?"

"No," Josie said, shaking her head. "Obviously someone who is financially successful."

"Being back inside after Mary Jo was killed makes me nervous," Samantha said.

Cor nodded. "Can I help look for something?" she asked.

Josie answered, "I think we should be looking for anything personal as opposed to generic. Something that belonged to Mary Jo or that gives us information about her."

"Like a magazine address label or clothes or some engraved jewelry?"

Josie nodded. "Yes. Exactly."

While Samantha seemed to wander with Unknown following her, and Cor began a focused search, Josie began at one end of the house, the garage. Inside was a late-model Volvo. Deep blue, polished to a high gloss. It was unlocked and had few items in it. A pair of sunglasses that didn't indicate gender. A small box of Kleenex tissue. Did men like Ranger Francis Telman carry tissue in their cars? Josie had no idea. If not, that suggested the obvious, that the Volvo was Mary Jo's car.

The registration card was made out to Carmichael Two LLC. Josie wondered what that meant. An automotive leasing company? There were just a few other items inside the garage, a broom, a garden trowel, some leather work gloves, small-sized. The gloves almost certainly belonged to a woman.

Back inside the house, Josie opened kitchen cupboards and drawers and looked at the contents.

"Mama," Samantha said, "remember the secret cupboard that Mary Jo opened up? We should check that."

Josie reached under the writing desk as Mary Jo had done. She found a latch and flipped it to the side. The hidden cupboard door once again opened.

Cor had come nearby. "Whoa, that's cool."

"Yes. Mary Jo opened this to show us her husband's phone."

The shelves contained the same items. There was nothing revealing to look at except for the phone. Josie pressed the button to turn it on. It showed a very low charge.

"Sam? Remember you emailed me Francis Telman's contact list? I'd like you to spend some more time on this phone and see if you can find anything else interesting. Be fast, because it needs a charge."

Samantha nodded, took the phone, and sat down on the

couch. Unknown sat on the rug next to her.

Josie moved from the kitchen to the dining area where there was a modern buffet. Josie looked in the drawers. From there, she moved to the bedrooms. There were two on the main floor, one of which was nice but basic, with furniture that could be found in an upscale hotel.

The other bedroom was like a hotel suite with a king-size bed, a sitting area near another wall of glass, a huge bathroom with a Jacuzzi tub that had water jets and a large shower made of 12" Tuscan tiles, with two shower heads that sprayed from opposite walls. It was in the closet that she found confirmation of what she'd suspected after looking in the kitchen.

The closet was huge with a three-sided section covered in floor-to-ceiling mirrors. There was an upholstered bench in front of the mirrors. On two walls were multiple hanging rods with uncountable clothes. Another wall had built-in shelves that held clothes like sweaters that don't work well on hangers. A custom section had angled shelves to store and display shoes, of which there were several dozen. There was a tree of dowels for holding bags and purses and other accessories.

But the main thing Josie noticed was that all the clothes and shoes appeared to be the same size, the size of a woman like Mary Jo. Even though the clothes weren't especially feminine, there wasn't a single item that would typically be used by a man.

Josie left and walked downstairs on a wide, open stairway that was shaped like a big U, two flights that were connected by a wide landing. Hanging above the center of the staircase was a large, modern chandelier that looked like it was made of blown glass. It reminded Josie of the stairway in the Beverly Hills house that Cumberland Durand, his siblings, and their mother lived in before the loan sharks seized the house in payment of the father's debts.

Josie looked through two guest bedrooms, each of which had its own bathroom.

There were no personal items in the guest rooms. They were set up for either show or for guests. One of the bedrooms seemed to be used for storage, with empty cardboard moving boxes stacked in the closet.

In the center of the lower floor was a large sitting area with a fireplace.

Like the main floor, the two large downstairs walls each had a large painting, about six by eight feet, abstracts with explosions of color, mostly yellow and blue. On either side of the fireplace were large windows that looked over the drop-off down to the river. There was another glass door that led to a deck that mirrored the deck one floor up. Josie turned the deadbolt and went outside. The air blowing up from the river canyon was cold. She gazed over the railing at the river, which seemed almost straight below. Josie turned and looked up to the side at the area below the wall where Samantha and Mary Jo had fallen after the gunshot that killed Mary Jo. In the daylight, the steep slope looked even more dangerous. Had they tumbled just a bit to the side, they might have rolled hundreds of feet down and died. The thought was more bracing than the cold wind.

Josie walked to the other end of the lower deck. There was a gate built into the railing and beyond it three steps that went down at an angle to the deck. Josie opened the gate and walked down. The steps brought Josie to the lowest corner of the house. There was a short flagstone walkway. Josie followed it around the corner of the house. She came to a small patio. Unlike the rest of the outer walls, this part of the house had a solid stucco wall, a foundation wall, painted terra cotta. In the wall was a steel door, also painted terra cotta.

The door had a heavy-duty deadbolt lock above the doorknob. Josie tried the doorknob. It was locked. Josie imagined that the steel door led to a mechanical room or a storage area, a place to put yard tools and such. She tried the front door key in the deadbolt lock, but it wouldn't work.

A narrow stone walkway and stone steps went from the patio up the slope next to the house. There was a railing to keep people from slipping off toward the steep dropoff below. The walkway climbed up toward the driveway on the other side of the house.

Josie went back inside and tried to see where the steel door would lead. It was not clear. The angles of the house were too confusing to easily understand the layout. Nevertheless, Josie could find no access to the storage area from inside the house.

Josie went back up the stairs to the main floor.

Samantha said, "Find anything, Mama?"

"Not much. There's a little patio off the lower deck and some kind of storage room with a steel door. Probably one of those places to store lawn tools. I'm almost certain a single woman lives here. No one else."

"No guy stuff?"

"Correct. Everything is bright colors. Lots of light yellow and sky blue. Of course, nothing says that a guy couldn't like those, but in practice I think it would be quite rare." Josie turned toward the main bedroom. "All the clothes and shoes are a woman's, as well, and all the same size. Even the dishes in the kitchen and the linens in the closets are things that a woman would be more likely to choose."

As Josie and Samantha talked, Josie sensed Cor watching them from over by the window wall. Her look went from Josie to Samantha and back as if watching to see how a mother and daughter communicated. For all Josie knew, Cor could have a daughter herself, but it didn't seem like it.

Samantha said, "Didn't the governor refer to the house owners as Mary Jo's friends? Meaning two people?"

"Yes."

"So maybe both were women."

"I wondered that. But something about the various items makes me think only one person lives here. In the master bath, there is just one face towel, one washcloth, one bath towel, one toothbrush. And the downstairs bedrooms haven't been used at all."

"Maybe this house is owned by one woman, and the governor just assumed otherwise," Samantha said. She rotated in a full circle, taking in the breadth of the house again. "It's pretty neato that a single woman would have an impressive house like this. Not that there aren't a ton of rich women who could afford it. But most women are—how do I say it—too reserved and practical to have such a fancy place just for one person."

As Josie listened, she got stuck on Samantha's use of the word neato. She stopped herself from commenting on how Samantha continuously picked up words from her classmates. There was nothing wrong with that, of course. But it sometimes made Josie feel like she wasn't the prime influence in Samantha's life. She wanted to be number one in Samantha's world. Maybe she still was. But it bothered her that she could see that slipping away.

"Anyway," Josie said, "I don't think Mary Jo was visiting her friend here. I think she was staying here by herself. And I don't think the house owner stays here on any regular basis."

"That's a curious situation," Cor said.

"Right. Not only are all the clothes the same size, they have a similar style. If the house owner ever stayed here, there would be two kinds of personal effects."

"Wow," Samantha said. "Imagine someone having a house this fancy and you don't even use it! Its only use is to let your friend Mary Jo stay there."

"Curiouser," Cor said.

"I think it's more strange than that," Josie said. "I'm guessing this is actually Mary Jo's house, and she just told the governor that the house belongs to friends. This house shows signs of her. The other house and the Tahoe cabin only show signs of her husband Francis. But much is missing." Josie was aware that both Samantha and Cor were waiting to hear what it was.

Josie said, "I still see no indication of what Mary Jo did for a living. Or how she spent her time. What was her work, her hobbies? She's like a cipher, a phantom. If we hadn't seen her die, we wouldn't even know she existed. It would be like someone filled this place with furniture and furnishings and clothes just to make it look like a real person lived here."

"No personal stuff," Cor added. "The things that connect to how Mary Jo spent her time."

"Right. If I could find her..."

Josie stopped, found a pad of paper, wrote, 'I'm going to put my phone in Cor's Jeep. Private World concerns.' She showed the paper to Samantha and Cor, then walked outside, opened the passenger door, and slid her phone under the front passenger seat.

When Josie got back inside, Samantha spoke.

"Are you worried about someone listening in, Mama?"

"Not especially. But I'm still sensitized after our last experience. It can't hurt to reduce our exposure, right?"

Samantha nodded.

Cor looked from Samantha to Josie, then back, watching and listening, making no comment.

Josie wasn't worried about Cor's phone. No one in Josie's world knew about Cor.

Josie said, "If I could find Mary Jo's phone, then maybe I'd have a clue." Josie walked around the living room. She held her hands out, palms up. "This place doesn't even have a desk, never mind an office. We can't find so much as a checkbook and a stack of bills."

Outside the living room was another deck, which mirrored the one at the lower level. Josie pushed out through another glass door and walked to one end of the deck, turned, and walked back. Josie stood near the railing and looked back at the house, looking at the juxtaposition of the various shapes. She rotated and looked down at the river canyon. The pleasant sound of whitewater rapids a thousand feet below was a constant soft accompaniment to the spectacular view. It would be a great place to live. Private. Beautiful. But sterile, with nothing personal in it.

"I can tell you have an idea, Mama," Samantha said when Josie came back inside.

Cor was leaning against one of the big windows. Samantha and Unknown were in the kitchen.

"Maybe Mary Jo has a hidden cubby here someplace."

"Yeah! Like the secret kitchen desk cupboard. Okay, do that professor thing," Samantha said. "Where you turn things around to analyze them. Pretend this is your place and you wanted a hidden cubby. How big would it be, and where would you put it?"

Cor looked from Samantha to Josie, watching as if she found mother-daughter dynamics interesting.

Josie looked at the dining table, then turned toward the kitchen cabinets. "I'd want someplace to put a file cabinet. Maybe it could be a rolling file cabinet." She pointed. "Like that trash compactor only twice as wide. It could be hidden in plain sight. I'd use it to store personal papers and other things, and they would be safe from a burglar."

"Maybe she's gone paperless," Cor said. "Gets all her forms and bills via email."

"But she'd still have some kind of paperwork. I know professors who've done that. Everything is online in the cloud. Their bills are mostly set up for autopay. But they still have a regular checkbook for the accounts you can't do online. They still keep paper receipts from stores that don't do everything by email."

Cor made a slow walk around the main floor. She went out on the deck and looked down at the storeroom door that Josie described. Cor came back inside, went down the stairs, and was gone for a few minutes. She came back up and went into the master bedroom. Next, she looked in the other main-floor bedroom. She came back out, took a turn around the kitchen and then went into the garage.

Samantha gave Josie a questioning look. Josie made an I-don't-know shrug.

Cor returned from the garage. "Like you say, this place is hard to figure out. I thought maybe I could find something in the back of a closet." She pointed to the island area near the kitchen. "Like these closets and pantry," she said. "Walk around and the angles make it seem like there's wasted space behind them. Same for the refrigerator. Why would they build like that? Just to confuse a future home buyer?"

"In the movies, they always find a grate that looks like the covering for an air vent," Samantha said. "But the grate comes off to reveal a hiding place." Samantha walked over to the area near the laundry room and looked up. "That grate in the ceiling is big. If that was in the wall next to the floor, it would be perfect."

Josie had an idea.

"Sam? I'm thinking about how smart Unknown is."

"Of course. Why?"

"I'm thinking of teaching her a new challenge."

"Okay. But you know she's not real eager like some trained dogs. My friend Anna has a dog that'll do flips and turn circles on her hind legs for a treat. Unknown isn't like that. But we've seen her do the finding thing. She can sniff a million things that we can't."

"What does she find?" Cor said.

"There's one thing she's incredible at finding…" Samantha paused, then spelled letters. "P-O-P-C-O-R-N."

"You mean popcorn?"

"Oh, don't say that!" Samantha shot a glance toward Unknown. "I hope she didn't hear you!"

"Now I get it," Cor said. "Sorry." Unknown was looking up at Cor. "I hope I haven't ruined anything. I'll turn away and ignore her. She'll think she misheard me." Cor turned so her back was toward Unknown. "How does the finding thing work?" she asked as she faced the window wall.

"We play a game. Mama distracts her. Talks to her and stuff. Then I sneak around and hide pieces of the… stuff you can't say out loud. After I hide them, I have her sniff a piece. Then I give it to her and tell her to find the rest. She trots around and finds all the hidden goodies. She's amazing at it."

"I'm thinking," Josie said slowly, "that we could get Unknown to search for Mary Jo's clothes."

"But Mary Jo is dead and gone."

"Yes. But her scent would still be here. If Unknown could find Mary Jo's scent, maybe she'd find someplace we've overlooked. I'm guessing Mary Jo hides her papers and such. But this is such a big house they could be anywhere. But no matter how well they are hidden, they wouldn't be hidden to a dog, right?"

THIRTY-ONE

Samantha's eyes were wide as she looked over at Unknown.

"This is fun," Cor said, as she hitched her hip on the seat of one of the bar stools at the kitchen counter. "Professor Nancy Drew. In the Army, I got to watch how search and rescue dogs work, how they get a dog to search for a missing person."

Josie waited to see where Cor was taking the line of thought.

Cor said, "I figured out that the basic principle was to take a piece of clothing that belonged to the missing person and put it over the dog's nose. Just like Sam said about the P-O-P stuff. They make sure the dog gets a good sniff, then they tell the dog to find the person. And the dog runs off to search. I saw some amazing things. The dogs were incredible." Cor looked at Unknown.

Samantha said, "You think we should just grab something from the closet?"

"No. Those are probably all washed. We'd need to find something that hasn't been washed. Let me look."

Cor walked over to the laundry room and went inside. She came back out holding a shirt. "This was in the basket, and it smells worn." She handed it to Samantha.

"Mama, should I do it like the food find?"

"Yes. I would say it exactly the same."

"Hey, Unknown," Samantha said. "C'mere, girl. We're gonna play your favorite game."

The dog walked to Samantha. Samantha rubbed her with her good hand, then bunched up the shirt. She put it in front of Unknown's nose. "This is Mary Jo's shirt." Unknown gave it a delicate sniff.

"C'mon, girl. Take a good whiff." Samantha wrapped the shirt over Unknown's nose and part way up her head. "Okay. Do you have Mary Jo's scent?" Samantha put her hand on Unknown's back and gave her a shake. "Find Mary Jo, girl! Find Mary Jo!"

Samantha straightened up. Unknown looked up at her.

"Go for it, Unknown! Find Mary Jo!"

Samantha gestured, swinging her good hand and the arm in the sling from side to side, motioning the dog to look.

Unknown glanced over at Josie and then Cor, as if feeling self-conscious around them.

"Go, girl. Find Mary Jo." Samantha patted her thigh and started walking through the house.

Unknown walked alongside. She looked confused as if she didn't understand a game in which she wasn't finding a food treat. Samantha went through the kitchen. Unknown looked back again. Toward Josie.

Josie wondered if she and Cor should go outside to be less distracting. Then again, that might be even more distracting for the dog.

Unknown turned and looked at the laundry room where Cor had found the shirt.

"Unknown, find Mary Jo," Samantha said from the dining area. "Go on."

Unknown sniffed along the bottom edge of the kitchen cabinets. Probably looking for food, Josie thought.

"See if she responds to the master bedroom," Josie said.

Samantha walked that direction. She went past the open door.

Unknown turned into the door.

"Mama, she went into the bedroom. Maybe she does know what we mean!"

Josie and Cor stayed back.

"Find Mary Jo," Samantha said. "Do you need a refresher? Take another sniff of the shirt. Good girl. Find the scent. Really? You want to take a nap?"

There was a pause.

"Mama! Unknown just jumped up on the bed! She's sniffing Mary Jo's pillow! Good girl! Okay, back down on the floor. Good girl. Find more scent. Atta girl." Another pause.

"She's in the closet! Sniffing around. Mama, we've got a star search-and-rescue dog!"

Pause.

"Okay, find more scent," came Samantha's voice. "Atta girl."

Unknown came out of the bedroom and walked back into the kitchen. She sniffed around the fridge and the cabinet that held the oven.

Josie and Cor watched without speaking. Josie knew that Mary Jo's scent would be all over the kitchen. But it seemed obvious that there would be innumerable food smells that would also attract Unknown's attention.

Unknown came back to the living area. She showed no enthusiasm, but she seemed to have focus.

"Maybe you should take her downstairs," Josie said.

Unknown looked toward the door to the garage. Or was it the laundry room?

"Cor, were there other dirty clothes in the laundry room?"

"Yeah, she's probably smelling those."

Samantha bent down and once again held the shirt on Unknown's nose. "Go girl! Find the scent."

Unknown walked over to the open laundry room door. Then past it. Unknown sniffed along the floor and along the wall. She gave the wall a lot of attention.

The wall next to the laundry room was made of vertical maple boards, coated with gloss varnish. The wall was just like the wooden walls elsewhere on the house.

The boards were about 3 inches wide and had half-inch gaps between them. The gaps were recessed and black, whether from a black paint or just the shadow.

Josie had a good view of the area near the laundry. She didn't move.

"Whoa," Cor said. "This is different."

Unknown moved slowly, came to the door to the garage,

turned around, and went back. She once again walked past the laundry room door and sniffed the wall.

Cor walked closer and watched.

Unknown repeated her movements, focusing on the base of the wall.

Cor said, "Either Unknown has taken a very strong interest in walls, or Mary Jo did something to leave her scent on that wall."

Samantha came over, bent down, and pet Unknown. "What are you smelling, girl?"

Cor walked into the laundry room and then came back. Josie looked in the laundry room, then walked into the garage. She came back inside, walked past the laundry room, past the wall where Unknown was sniffing.

Opposite that wall was a utility closet. Next to it, a coat closet. Next to that was the kitchen pantry. Josie opened a cupboard door and stared at the cans and boxes on the shelves. She was thinking about the house layout. The refrigerator was on the other side of the pantry. The closets and fridge and microwave cabinet comprised an island. Josie went back into the kitchen and walked around the island. Other than imagining that it would be grand to have so much space compared to their little condo in Santa Monica, nothing about it was remarkable.

Josie looked again at the laundry room. It had no windows. It was above one of the downstairs bedrooms and on the same end of the house as the downstairs storeroom with its outdoor access.

Unknown was still sniffing the wall near the laundry room. What was on the other side of that wall?

Josie walked farther, past the island, out to the entryway with the sculpture fountain, and the hanging plant, and the skylight above. She turned and looked back through the angled passageway, toward the living room.

Something didn't make sense.

Josie tried to visualize the line of the outside wall of the house. She walked out the front door, looked at the garage placement, then came back inside.

The area where Unknown had sniffed didn't line up.

"Your mother has a certain look," Cor said to Samantha.

"It's one of the standard professor looks. Solving a problem," Samantha said. "Spill the beans, Mama," Samantha said.

Josie pointed to the wall where Unknown had been sniffing. "I think there is a space behind that wall."

Samantha's eyes widened. "You think Unknown found a hidden cubby?"

"Maybe."

"What do we do?"

"Figure out how to get into it."

Cor walked over to the wall and looked at it up close. "It's too dark here to see anything in detail. I've got a tac light in my Jeep. I'll be right back." She walked out the front door.

Josie and Sam both looked at the wall up close. Sam ran her fingertips over the vertical maple boards, left and right, up and down.

Cor came back. She turned on her light. It produced a brilliant blue-white light that was like a search light. She shined it back and forth then focused on the edges of the wall. One side of the wall was the door molding for the laundry room door. On the other end of the wall was a vertical trim board. Between the laundry room door and the trim board was an uninterrupted expanse of vertical maple boards, all spaced a half inch apart.

Josie said, "Imagine if you wanted to have a cupboard door that was like the hidden cubby in the kitchen. A wall like this would be a perfect disguise. The door could swing out and the edges of it would be in those half-inch gaps. They are recessed and painted black. We could never see the edge of any door."

"But we'd see the top and bottom edge," Samantha said.

Josie looked up. "Not if the top of the door were at the ceiling and the bottom were at the floor. Then we wouldn't see it."

"True. But wouldn't that be overkill for a hidden cupboard?"

"I suppose."

"If there's a door here, there would be some wear or scuff

marks that would give us a hint," Cor said. She knelt down on the floor and shined her light at the intersection of wall and floor. "There's a quarter-round molding along the base of the wall. A door could swing back away from the molding. And as you stepped through, you'd lift your foot over that molding."

Cor trained her light along the edge, feeling the molding with her fingertip. She spoke as she inspected. "If you accidentally stepped on the quarter-round molding, your shoe might dent it. Then again, here's a more interesting thought. If there weren't any door here, the dust and dirt that accumulates at the intersection of floor and wall would be undisturbed. Like this area here." Cor moved her fingertip, then stopped. "But if a door swung away, that same dirt and dust wouldn't get impacted. And you'd have a clearly-visible crack, like here." Cor ran her finger about three feet along the wall, stopped, then came back. She shined her light. "Do you see this dark crack?"

Samantha leaned in. "Yeah, it looks totally like that area doesn't accumulate dust." Samantha looked at Josie. "It looks like this part of the wall moves away." Samantha looked up at the vertical boards and the gaps between them. "If there's a door here, it would be totally disguised."

Cor pressed on the wall in multiple places. "It feels solid. If there's a door, it's well built. I wonder how we could find it? We could go back downstairs and see if something about the wall layout would give us a clue."

"I think a better way," Josie said, "would be to think in the manner that Samantha suggested. Pretend we're the person who built the house. If they wanted to put in a door for a secret closet, they would plan it so it could be opened by a catch that is well hidden. There would be no point in a secret door with a release that is easy to find. So we should look for a good hiding place for the catch. But even though it would be hidden, it would be in a place that's easy to reach. No one is going to want to get down on the floor to unlock the door."

As Josie said it, Cor stood up from where she'd been kneeling. She started running her fingers along the gaps between the vertical boards. Sam did the same. As Josie watched them, she had an idea. She walked into the laundry room and looked around. It seemed like a logical place to hide some kind of door release. But the laundry room walls were smooth plaster board. There was no obvious handle or knob. Josie felt around the laundry tub. Nothing.

The only interruption in the wall surface was the light switch, the exhaust fan switch, and the electrical panel. Was it possible there was an electrical door switch?

The electrical panel door was a heavy sheet of metal, painted gray. Was the panel door smudged? Skin oil? Or lotion? She looked closely. It seemed there was dust near the handle. Dust wouldn't normally accumulate on the smooth painted surface. But a surface that had been touched with moisturized fingers would catch and hold dust.

Josie tugged the panel open. There were two rows of circuit breakers. The same kind she'd seen many times before. She looked at the little labels describing the circuits. Bedrooms. Bathrooms. Kitchen. Living room. Dryer. Washing machine. Well pump. Furnace. A/C. Outdoor lights. Garage.

In the left row of circuit breakers, the third breaker up from the bottom, had a label that had just one letter. A capital D. Could it be for Door?

Josie gently touched the breaker. It didn't snap to one side like a typical breaker. It was some kind of flexible switch that, once pushed, returned to its former position.

Josie flipped it, preparing to be plunged into sudden darkness or to hear a sudden silence as appliance motors turned off.

"Hey, Mama!" Samantha shouted from outside of the laundry room. "You better come here. This ain't no hidden desk cupboard or filing cabinet cubby."

THIRTY-TWO

Josie stepped out to see Samantha staring at the wall where Unknown had been sniffing.

A large, floor-to-ceiling hidden door was swinging inward, revealing a stairway that led down between angled walls.

"Mama!" Samantha shouted over her shoulder.

"Right here," Josie said.

Samantha was pointing with her good hand.

Cor leaned into the opening. Found a light switch. Flipped it.

The stairway was illuminated and a light came on down below. The stairway was wide enough to be easily accessible, but Josie felt a little afraid.

"I'll check it out," Cor said. She headed down the stairway.

Josie leaned in and watched Cor disappear downstairs.

Not long after, Cor called out. "C'mon down. All clear."

Sam, despite not having use of the arm in the sling, rushed down the stairs, followed by Unknown. Josie was last.

The stairway went down in one flight of steps. At the bottom, Josie saw that they were in a large comfortable room, about 18 X 24 feet. It had no windows, but one wall was covered in a large photo of Lake Tahoe. The photo made it seem as if the room were outdoors.

Josie looked around. It was the office that was missing from Mary Jo's life. A large desk, laptop computer and printer, and two four-drawer filing cabinets filled one corner. To one side was a single upholstered easy chair with a floor-lamp light, a hassock, a small table, and a bookcase with books and magazines and newspapers. On the opposite wall was a door that stood open. Visible through the door was a twin-sized bed, a night table, and a dresser and an armoire. Next to the armoire was a door. Josie looked inside. It was a closet with a few clothes and other items.

On another side of the main room was a kitchen counter with a sink and microwave. There were kitchen cupboards and a medium-sized refrigerator. Beyond the fridge was a steel door. The one that Josie had seen from the outside. Next to the door was a folding chair.

Josie opened the door. They all looked outside.

"This is an entire hidden apartment," Josie said. "Mary Jo's office, kitchen, bedroom, storage. It comes complete with an outdoor patio where she could sit and get some fresh air and look down at the river in the canyon below."

"It's called a safe room," Samantha said.

Josie looked at her.

"I've seen these in the movies," Samantha said. "Safe rooms are sometimes obvious with big bank-vault doors. But most of the time they are secret rooms. No one except the owner knows they exist."

Cor asked, "What kind of a person would have a secret room and a house like this?"

Josie thought about it. "Someone whose life had secrets. Someone who might have wanted to live in a house like this but didn't want it to look like her house. So she had a secret apartment where she could put anything that connected to her, and where she could hide if she were under threat. The rest of the house could look more generic. But if one of her enemies came into the house, she could go through the secret door and hide in the safe room."

Samantha said, "If we hadn't come, and if Mary Jo had sensed a threat from the shooter, she could have come down here and hid. She'd still be alive." Samantha's voice was thick.

Josie walked over and hugged her. "We were trying to help her. She asked the governor for our help. We were just following her request. Maybe we did it wrong. But our intentions were good. And now we've found her nest of secrets."

Cor moved the mouse on the computer. It came to life and showed a passcode screen. "Looks like this part of the nest will remain hidden," she said.

Cor moved to one of the filing cabinets. On it was a small framed photo. "Is this Mary Jo?" she asked.

Samantha walked over and picked it up. "Yeah, that's Mary Jo. Check out the man. He looks like a movie star. I wonder if that's her husband who was murdered." She handed the photo to Josie.

The photo was a black-and-white portrait of a couple. Mary Jo stood next to a man. Her husband Francis? She had her arm around his waist. They were both smiling. Mary Jo was wearing a long dress with an abstract pattern of bright colors not unlike the big abstract paintings in the house. She wore loop earrings, and her hair was up, which then curled like ribbons dangling down the left side of her head. The man was wearing a dark sport coat over a light shirt. Around his neck was a bolo tie with an oval gemstone clasp that looked medium gray in the photo. Josie thought it might be turquoise. The man wore a fedora. He was rakishly handsome, a white version of Idris Elba.

Josie turned the picture over. On the back, hand-written in pen, was 'The catch of your lives—definitely keepers—on your special day.'

Josie put the photo back and opened the top file drawer.

"What are you looking for, Mama?"

"I don't know. A look into the personal world of Mary Jo and Francis Telman. Whoever killed them had a reason. I'm looking for that reason."

"Can you give an example?" Cor asked.

Josie shrugged. "I don't know. Let's say Mary Jo was involved in some kind of legal skirmish. A lawsuit or something."

"Oh, I get it," Samantha said. "Like if Mary Jo sued somebody and that person was so mad they killed her."

"Or hired her killer," Cor said. "Remember, almost no one has the level of sniper skill to make that shot."

"Right." Josie looked around the office. "I'm also wondering where Mary Jo gets her mail. I see that the bin under the paper shredder is nearly full. But maybe there is an address somewhere."

Samantha opened the top drawer of the adjacent cabinet. She flipped through files as Josie did the same. In a few moments, Sam moved to the next drawer down. A moment later, Samantha tried the drawer below that.

"That was a fast search," Josie said. "Find anything?"

"Not really. There's some stuff about the Pony Express Casino in Reno, Nevada. But nothing much else. What did you find, Mama?"

"There's something here about LLCs. It's like a state-by-state comparison."

"What's an LLC?" Samantha leaned over to look at the paper Josie held.

"A Limited Liability Company. All I know about them is they are a kind of corporation. I think business owners use LLCs to give them some protection against lawsuits. They also use them to obscure ownership."

Josie opened the rest of the file drawers. She pulled out any documents that might connect personally to Mary Jo or Francis Telman.

"Bingo," Cor said. She'd been sifting through the paper shredder bin. She handed Josie an envelope. "This fell down behind the bin with all the shredded spaghetti," Cor said. "It must have slipped out of the shredder."

Josie looked at it. The writing was somewhat faint, as if the envelope printer was running low on toner. Josie's vision had always been weak. Maybe it was getting worse? She held the envelope close to the desk lamp.

Carmichael Two LLC

P.O. Box 3499101

Placerville, CA 95667

The return address was the California Tax and Fee Administration.

Josie realized that Mary Jo received her mail at the nearby town post office.

The envelope had been neatly sliced open and was empty.

"Now I remember this name," Josie said. "Carmichael Two LLC was on the car registration in the Volvo in the garage. Even without the contents of the envelope, this is the first thing we've seen that might give us a peek into Mary Jo's life."

They continued to go through Mary Jo's office. What seemed of particular note was that they found no debit card, credit cards, bills, phone, etc.

"There's gotta be another hidden cupboard," Samantha said.

Cor nodded. "I agree. But I can't find it."

They all continued to look. Josie hoped that going through the paperwork carefully would reveal secrets about Mary Jo's life. But there wasn't time now. They put a bunch of the paper records in a box, and Cor carried it up the secret staircase. They turned off the light, and Josie flipped the switch on the laundry room electrical panel. The door swung closed and shut with the clicking sound of latches closing.

They looked through the rest of the house once again. Finding nothing, they went back to their hotel.

Josie gave her phone to Samantha, then stepped outside and used her burner phone to call Cumberland.

She explained what had happened since they last talked.

"You looked up information on a Forest Service Ranger who was murdered," she said.

"I remember," Cumberland said. "He married the woman named Mary Jo, who doesn't seem to exist in the databases. Not under that name, anyway."

"Right. Unfortunately, Mary Jo Telman was also murdered." Josie decided there was no point in telling Cumberland that Samantha was nearly killed as well.

Josie continued, "I've found something I'd like to know about, and I'm hoping you can apply your magic techniques to learning about it. Mary Jo Telman, the woman who was killed, had an envelope addressed to Carmichael Two LLC, which I believe is a Limited Liability Company." Josie held the envelope close to see the printing. She read off the address. "I'm interested in anything you can learn about it. I'm also wondering if Mary Jo might be the owner of the LLC."

They exchanged a few more words, then disconnected.

THIRTY-THREE

The three women and Unknown were in the hotel restaurant having dinner when Josie got a return call on her burner from Cumberland.

Josie felt awkward, knowing her regular phone was in her purse. But, on her last case, Cumberland had shown her that phones could be monitored by anyone who was proficient with technology. The result was that Josie and Samantha had developed the habit of not using their regular phones if they thought they were dealing with highly-sensitive information that someone might want to overhear.

Cumberland was calling the burner phone she'd used to call him.

"I looked up the Carmichael Two LLC," he said when Josie answered.

"That was fast. Thanks so much. Did you find anything?"

"Sort of. The Carmichael Two LLC is a California corporation that is owned by another LLC in Nevada."

"What?" Josie was prepared to be surprised but not that kind of surprise. "A Nevada company owns a California company?" Josie said.

"Right. That might be kind of common. But I don't know about that stuff."

"Who owns the Nevada LLC?" she asked.

"That's tricky. I don't get all the terms. But it's run by what's called an undisclosed manager. I assume—but don't know—that the undisclosed manager is the owner."

"Why such a shell game?" Josie asked, not expecting Cumberland to have an answer.

"I don't know. But I think it's about making it hard for someone to sue the owner of a California property."

"Because they can't figure out who really owns the property?" Josie said.

"Something like that."

"Am I out of luck?"

"Maybe not." Cumberland made some typing sounds that were surprisingly loud over the phone. "You said the name of the LLC is Carmichael Two LLC. I found out that Carmichael is a suburb of Sacramento. So I looked around and found some other LLCs that might be connected. They all have names that are suburbs of Sacramento. There's a Rocklin One LLC, a Folsom Three LLC, a Fair Oaks Four LLC, a Rancho Cordova Five LLC. All of them are also owned by Nevada LLCs."

"Did you find anything that could link any of them to Mary Jo Telman?" Josie asked.

"No. But you asked me about Carmichael Two LLC. So there was some connection."

"Yes. We found the address in Mary Jo's office. This gives me a lot to work on. Thanks so much."

They hung up, and Josie explained to Samantha and Cor what she'd learned. She sensed that both of them shared her frustration.

After they ate dinner, they retired to their rooms.

As Josie was getting ready for bed, she got an email from Cumberland. There was no hello.

'The Carmichael Two LLC runs an extended care facility in Carmichael. Each one of those other LLCs I mentioned runs another extended care facility.'

Josie thought that the businesses he was referring to were what are often called nursing homes.

His email continued.

'Here's the list:

Choose Serenity Home

Choose Tranquility Home

Choose Composure Home

Choose Repose Home

Choose Quiet Home. All are in the Sacramento suburbs whose names are the LLC names. Hope that helps.'

There was no sign-off from Cumberland.

Josie closed her email. She lay back on the bed and thought about it. It appeared that Mary Jo Telman owned nursing homes. What was the motivation for that? Were nursing homes simply good businesses? Josie had heard about the enormous expense for someone to live in such a facility. Josie knew she was naive about nursing homes. She'd always assumed they were basically glorified apartment buildings with a nursing facility and a commercial kitchen attached. The residents mostly ate in a communal dining room, and they socialized in a communal recreation room or out on a communal lawn. And when someone needed medical care, the staff had nurses to provide it. Or, perhaps they contracted with a medical group to provide regular doctor visits. The expenses of running such a business were, no doubt, very high. But with a large group of financially-sound residents, the net profit could possibly be impressive. Was that Mary Jo's goal? To have a large monthly profit? Or, was there something else? Maybe Mary Jo had an emotional reason. Perhaps she'd had a frail friend or a deceased mother or other relative who had lived in one of the nursing homes and it was that experience that drew Mary Jo to provide a good living situation for others.

Without the benefit of information about the business of nursing homes, Josie imagined it would require a great deal of investment to own a nursing home. Multiply by five homes, and it seemed that Mary Jo would have had to be wealthy to get into the business. Either that or she would have had to take on an enormous amount of debt.

Regardless of the reason Mary Jo owned nursing homes, Josie didn't know how to proceed. She couldn't just call them up and start asking questions, hoping to find out if any of Mary Jo's employees had a reason to kill her. Maybe Cumberland could help with that, too.

It was getting late. Samantha was asleep, and Unknown seemed drowsy at her feet.

Josie got out of bed and moved over to sit in a corner where their room had a small desk and chair.

Josie used her burner phone to dial Cumberland's number. He'd once told her that he didn't have regular hours and he sometimes worked in the middle of the night. She hoped that if he didn't want to be bothered, he would let her call go to voicemail.

He answered, "Hi, Professor."

Josie said hi in a low voice, hoping not to wake Samantha. She tried to chat with Cumberland a moment. But it was a one-sided chat. She made some small talk. Cumberland didn't say anything.

"Thanks for emailing me about these nursing homes that are owned by the LLCs," Josie said.

Cumberland didn't respond. Maybe he was distracted by something else. A video game or something. Or maybe he simply had no response to a statement that didn't ask for one.

"I was trying to think of some way to turn the nursing home list into useful information. The idea made me wonder if a disgruntled employee might have killed Mary Jo." Josie paused. Cumberland still didn't say anything. Josie continued, "If we could we get a list of employees, do you think it would be possible to somehow cross reference their names against military records?"

"Why the military? Was Mary Jo Telman in the military?"

"I don't know. But she was killed from a long distance by a trained sniper, and my Army friend says that there are only a limited number of people in the world who can make that kind of shot, and they all learned the skill in the military."

"So you're wondering if any of Mary Jo's employees were snipers in the Army?" The way Cumberland said it, it sounded like he thought it was a ridiculous idea.

"I was kind of thinking that, yes," Josie said.

"I don't know how secure military data is. Even if I can get into their satellite feeds, their human resource records might be hard to crack. What would it be called in the Army? Soldier records? Employee records? I don't even know what Army people are called."

"I don't know, either," Josie said. "What about nursing home employees? Is that something that would be in an accessible database?"

"It would probably be harder to get employee records from nursing homes than from the military. Small businesses like that have small computer systems. The computer they use for records might not be online. They might even keep employee files in a file cabinet. Paper records. Isolated systems don't allow an easy way in."

"You're saying that to break in, I'd have to physically go there and look in their files."

"Maybe. Paper systems are very crude and not useful for data analysis. But they're really secure compared to computers. Computers can be hacked from the other side of the world, and you usually can't find the hacker. People always forget that. Paper records in a file cabinet seem so outdated. But to hack them, yeah, you'd have to break into the building and the file cabinet. One thing I can look for is external human resource service companies that might handle the payroll for nursing homes."

"Okay, thanks, Cumberland."

"Sure. There is one more thing I found out since I sent you that email."

"What?" Josie said.

"When I looked into databases for Mary Jo Telman, I saw references to four laundromats and a casino, all in Reno, Nevada. I haven't found LLCs for them, but I'd guess they exist. I'll keep looking and let you know if I find anything."

"Thanks, Cumberland. Good info. I owe you."

After a pause, Cumberland said, "Bye," and hung up.

Josie never would have thought of such businesses for the wife of a Forest Service ranger. Laundromats were like wallpaper in her perception. She'd seen them all her life and used them on occasion. But they were mostly invisible to her. Part of the backdrop of any town. Never noticeable unless you were looking for one. To think that Mary Jo invested in laundromats put a kind of spotlight on them. And a casino in Reno really stood out. Why would someone who owns nursing homes and laundromats be in the casino business? Josie didn't know what to make of it. Then she remembered that Samantha had seen something about the Pony Express Casino in a file drawer in Mary Jo's secret office. Who keeps information about a casino in their office file drawer? The owner or employees.

Josie opened her laptop and spent some time Googling the names Cumberland had given her.

Choose Serenity Home, and the others with the similar nomenclature. Tranquility, Composure, Repose, and Quiet.

They all shared the same website, filled with photos of smiling middle-aged and older people apparently enjoying life. It looked like nothing could be better than spending time with friendly people. Assuming you had the financial resources, you could move to one of these facilities, and you wouldn't have to worry about anything again. The website made it seem like you'd have no pain and no stress about anything.

But Josie knew it was the golden age myth. Life didn't come with clean, neat endings. Everyone had to cope with unexpected struggles. It was impossible to live the happy life depicted on the websites without a great deal of luck and good health.

Worse, Josie thought, was that consigning oneself to such a cocoon would probably make you lose your purpose, your work, your reason for existence. But then maybe most people in these facilities had already lost their purpose before they went into the place. Or maybe they never had any purpose.

Josie couldn't imagine that. But she also realized that such homes solved a problem that many families faced. How to avoid putting one's age-related struggles onto their children. Or, viewing it from the younger perspective, how to best take care of parents when they could no longer take care of themselves.

Josie read through the website, looking for any information that stood out. She didn't know what it would be. But someone killed Mary Jo and her husband and then tried to kill Josie and, possibly, Samantha, too. Was it possible that the killer was among the smiling employees shown in the website photos?

Looking at the happy website photos while considering if one of the employees could be a killer was like looking at smiling family photos and wondering if one of the family members was an impossibly-overbearing mother, or an intolerant father who popped pills to get through the day, or a drunk cousin, or an uncle who'd spent twenty years in prison.

Or someone so disgruntled they used their military training to kill others.

Josie switched her computer search to the map view. She started with the Choose Serenity Home. The facility was several miles outside of downtown Sacramento. She wasn't looking for anything in particular. And nothing of interest popped up. She next searched on the Choose Tranquility Home. Again, nothing notable.

Josie thought there might be something to learn about Mary Jo Telman's ownership of laundromats.

Maybe laundromats and nursing homes naturally went together and Josie had simply never noticed. A nursing home would certainly need substantial laundry facilities. If you have to make the investment in a laundry for your nursing home, why not open it to the public and make extra money?

But the problem was that Cumberland said the nursing homes were in Sacramento and the laundromats and casino were in Reno. Based on Josie's glance at the map, those two cities looked to be 100 miles apart. None of the laundromats would be of use for the laundry needs of the nursing homes.

Josie looked up other nursing homes with no connection to Mary Jo. She studied maps and read about the business practices of nursing homes. Nothing seemed noticeable.

Josie guessed that nursing homes required high capital outlays but, if they were well run, could produce large profits.

But they also appeared to be a difficult business, constrained by dozens of regulations and watched by state and federal inspectors from health departments, building departments, and social welfare services. Even their finances were subject to scrutiny. And nursing homes probably collected much of their revenue from insurance companies and state and federal agencies that ran programs like Medicaid and Medicare. That alone seemed like a nightmare. Perhaps they also billed residents or their families or guardians directly. Josie had no grasp of the complexities involved in acquiring their revenue and routing that income into their bank account.

Josie didn't know anything about casinos either, but she doubted that they received much income from insurance companies. However, they were probably complex businesses as well.

By comparison, laundromats were much simpler. Install machines, maintain them, collect the cash, and make the bank deposits.

Josie closed her computer and thought about it. Nursing homes and laundromats shared the feature of being service businesses. They were both essential in any city, and neither was glamorous. Josie could see no other similarities.

What Josie did understand is that laundromats, in contrast to nursing homes, were more like casinos in one major way. They were cash-focused businesses. The money arrived in the form of coins and dollar bills, and debit and credit cards. A laundromat would require a different accounting system from a nursing home.

Why would Mary Jo Telman own both kinds of businesses? And was there anything about those businesses that would possibly get her killed? Or was her murder something personal that had nothing to do with her businesses?

Another question was Mary Jo's secret life. Why did she have a house where she apparently lived alone and not with her husband? Why did the house have a hidden apartment that was accessed by a secret staircase? Who owned the house?

To Josie's sensibility, a secret apartment indicated a monumental difference between the life of Mary Jo Telman and other people. Was the woman really paranoid? Or did she merely have a pronounced focus on privacy, as indicated by having businesses with ownership protected by LLCs.

Josie got back into bed and lay back, propped up on two pillows. She laced her fingers together behind her head and searched for a different perspective.

Laundromats. Nursing homes. Casinos. Dramatically

different businesses. Situated in two cities a hundred miles or more apart, in different states.

Yet all were connected by their ownership structure of LLCs. And one person seemed to be behind them all.

Why?

Josie turned off the bedside light. The room was plunged into darkness. Gradually, Josie's night vision—poor as it was—revealed the room dimly lit by lights here and there. The red clock lights, the blue LED at the bottom of the TV, orange numbers on what looked like a DVD player, some kind of blinking white light over by the desk, the Wifi modem perhaps.

As the dark room became alive with a wide variety of lights, Josie sensed her own perception changing.

She began to realize that no one would casually create a world where they owned nursing homes in one state and laundromats in another and put all of them into LLCs.

It was obviously a careful plan, a well-thought-out design. Which meant that each aspect was part of a plan.

Do what Samantha said, Josie thought. Do the professor thing. Analyze. Mary Jo must own laundromats and nursing homes for a specific reason. The cities of Reno and Sacramento were chosen for specific reasons. Mary Jo's house near Placerville existed for a specific purpose. It must be that, because all of the businesses and real estate were part of a larger plan, all of the pieces would fit together like a jigsaw puzzle.

Josie dozed off thinking about it.

She woke up at 3:00 a.m. with an idea of just what the big picture might be.

THIRTY-FOUR

Josie got out of bed, trying not to wake Samantha with her movement. She walked over to the small desk and turned on the desk lamp. She glanced toward the bed, hoping that she hadn't awakened Samantha.

Josie saw that Unknown was still watching her, just as she had been a few hours before.

Josie made notes on her pad of paper.

-Laundromats are primarily a cash business.

-Nursing homes work with doctors and pharmacies and dispense drugs to their residents.

Josie leaned back in the little desk chair. She glanced over at Samantha who was still breathing heavily. Unknown was still watching Josie.

Josie wrote questions:

-Could drugs be skimmed?

-Could a nursing home, or a nursing home employee, take the drugs for any given patient and dilute them, giving the patient a reduced dose and keep the rest?

-Could an employee give the patient a sugar-pill placebo and keep the entire prescription?

-In addition, could a nursing home help increase drug prescriptions? Work with a corrupt doctor to obtain excess drugs?

-Once a doctor prescribed drugs for a patient, perhaps the prescription could be copied, and a counterfeit prescription used to obtain more drugs?

With the complexities of dealing with hundreds of nursing home residents, many or most of whom need drugs, it would be very hard to track. And the few people, like pharmacists, who might get a sense of what was going on could possibly be paid to look the other way.

If any of the nursing home residents were not lucid, they would be especially easy to manipulate to obtain drugs in their names. Nursing home staff could say that the patient complains of pain. The patients might not have the mental focus to report that their supposed pain is non-existent or that they hadn't been given the drugs that were prescribed in their names.

The illicit drugs could be sold undercover in a manner such that the drug dealer/buyer didn't know where the drugs came from. Very few people would be aware of what was actually happening.

Josie continued her list:

-Could a nursing home sell those drugs on the street?

Although this might be a far-fetched scenario, it could explain a relationship between nursing homes and laundromats and a casino. The nursing homes would be the source for illegal drug sales, and the laundromats and casino would exist to launder the cash receipts.

Josie pondered how drug sales might work. She didn't even know which drugs would be sold on the street. But she imagined that many drugs—opiate-type painkillers, for example—would be popular.

It was something she had no knowledge of. But she had an imagination. She made more notes.

-A nursing home could have a trusted confidant who takes the excess drugs and spreads them through a street-dealer network in Sacramento and in Central Valley cities like Stockton, Fresno, and Bakersfield. Sacramento nursing homes would be well-placed to provide for such a network.

As with the illegal drug business, Josie didn't know anything about money laundering. But she understood the concept. A business with ill-gotten cash can't do much with the money unless they can make it look legitimate. So if you illegally acquire lots of cash, you could possibly report it as income at your laundromat or casino, pay the appropriate taxes, and the cash will then appear legitimate.

She continued with her notes.

-How much money do illegal drug sales earn? No idea.

-But four laundromats and a casino could probably deposit many thousands of dollars in cash each day and no one would question it.

Josie did a mental game of calculating what kind of income a laundromat produced. She thought about when she'd been in laundromats on vacation. She made a guestimate of how many loads of laundry a laundromat might do in a twelve-hour day, multiplied by several dollars to wash and dry a load, and came up with a rough guess of $400 per day. Multiplying by 365 days a year, she guessed a laundromat could gross $150,000 a year.

Next, she turned on her computer and Googled "average coin-operated laundromat revenue." There was a wide range of estimates. But several were in the range of $300,000 per year, twice her estimate. The difference between Josie's estimate and the online estimates was almost certainly due to Josie's lack of knowledge about laundromats.

But it could also be that average laundromat revenues were skewed upward by some laundromats getting cash deposits from other sources. Like illegal activity.

She wrote:

-Nursing homes could fuel drug sales, and the money could be added to laundromat and casino bank deposits.

Next, she searched on nursing homes. There appeared to be no significant news in that world. She scrolled down through the various links, went forward a page, then another page, then stopped.

There was a heading that said, 'Care Facility Cook Still Missing.'

Josie clicked on it. An article from a Sacramento weekly came up.

There was a photo that showed a couple in their mid-fifties. The caption said, 'Zoe and Juan Soto are offering $500 for any information about their missing daughter Elena who disappeared from work after her shift at the Choose Serenity nursing home ten days ago.'

Another picture was a closeup of a smiling woman in her

twenties. Josie thought she looked bright and happy and sweet. Her thick black hair appeared held up in a net like a chef might wear.

The caption said, 'Elena Soto on her 24th birthday.'

What caught Josie's attention was the $500 amount. In an era when wealthy people will pay $500,000 for the return of a stolen pet dog, $500 stood out as a paltry amount.

But for parents who were very poor yet felt desperate, $500 might be a huge sacrifice. It seemed worth checking out.

THIRTY-FIVE

Josie went back to bed and slept fitfully.

Come morning, she was watching the clock and lying still so as not to wake Samantha.

She got out of bed at 7:00 a.m., moving slowly. Samantha remained asleep. Josie made coffee in the hotel coffee maker, carried it to the little desk, and once again turned on her laptop computer.

Samantha eventually got up, moving very slowly.

"You okay, hon?" Josie asked.

Samantha rotated her shoulder in the sling a small amount. "My shoulder hurts."

"I can rub it."

"Thanks. First, I'll try some stretches. It'll probably loosen up after that."

Samantha, who had recently been drinking a little coffee now and then, poured some from the pot Josie had made. She sipped, winced, frowned, and started coughing. "What is this stuff?" she said, sounding horrified.

"Standard hotel brand," Josie said. "No like?"

"It tastes like old bugs."

Josie nodded and kept her face blank as she said, "Sorry, Cap'n, I agree that new bugs taste much better." Josie reached for her phone. "Okay if I make a call?"

"Aye, Matey." Samantha added a creamer packet to her coffee and put it in the microwave to heat it up.

Josie dialed the number listed for the reward for information about the missing employee at the Choose Serenity Home. It was a 775 number, which Josie didn't know. The call was picked up after five rings.

"Hello?" A woman's voice, soft and tentative.

"Hi, my name is Josie Strong. Is this Zoe? I'd like to talk to you about Elena."

"You saw my advertisement."

Josie was afraid that if she didn't say the right thing, the woman would hang up. "Yes."

"I no longer am looking for Elena," the woman said.

"She came home?"

"No. But she sent a letter to say why she is gone. Do you know Elena?" the woman asked.

"Not personally. But I know a person who worked for the same company."

"Lucas?" the woman said.

Josie tried to think of the most effective response. "Someone who knows Lucas. Would it be possible for me to meet you and talk to you?"

The woman didn't immediately respond. Josie thought she'd probably gotten crank calls from people who saw her ad and were just trying to get an easy $500.

"I'm a professor from UCLA, and I'm working on a project for the Governor of California. That project may connect to Elena's place of employment." As she said it, she realized that Samantha would call her phrasing professor speak. She rephrased, "My work has to do with where Elena works."

"The Serenity Grill?"

"Yes. I'd like to stop by and talk to you."

"Okay." The woman gave her an address in Reno.

"I'm near Sacramento. A place called Placerville. I don't know how long it will take me to get there."

"That is a very long way to come to ask questions."

"It would be worth it to me."

"It is two hours and twenty-five minutes from Sacramento to Reno," the woman interrupted. "I know because I had a cleaning job in Sacramento for twenty years. I had to drive there and back once a week. I don't know about Placerville. That's east of Sacramento. Probably the same time to drive. But if you go at rush hour, the number eighty freeway can be very long to drive."

"My car is in the repair shop, and I'm picking it up at nine this morning. I can head to Reno after that, so I might be there around noon."

Josie and Samantha met Cor for breakfast. It was a cool day, but the sun was hot, so they got their food to go. They ate outside where there was a grouping of picnic tables. Unknown stood nearby and ate with them. Josie explained her plans.

"I'll drop you at the auto repair shop," Cor said. "I've got an Army friend I'd like to visit in Red Bluff, which is a city north up the Central Valley. After that I have to head back to L.A. Does that work for you?"

"Yes. Thanks so much."

They finished their breakfast. Cor drove them to pick up their car.

"I'll see you back in L.A.?" Cor said.

"Yes. Thank you more than I can say."

They went their separate ways.

Instead of working their way north to Interstate 80, they drove back up the winding Highway 50 to South Lake Tahoe, continued over the mountains to Carson City, Nevada, and connected to another freeway that went north to Reno.

While they drove, Josie told Samantha her suspicions about the nursing homes being a mechanism to obtain drugs, which could then be sold on the street. The cash could be laundered through laundromats and a casino.

"And that," Samantha said, "would be enough incentive for someone to kill Mary Jo and nearly kill me in the process." Samantha sounded disgusted.

"I think so, yes," Josie said.

Samantha said no more. Josie thought it was a dramatic loss of innocence for a child Samantha's age to be confronted with such evil violence.

Less than three hours later, Josie and Samantha pulled up to an apartment building just east of downtown Reno. It was a square, solid building made of blond-colored bricks, probably built in the time of World War II or earlier. The place was four stories high.

"Do you think we should leave Unknown in the car?" Samantha asked. "The weather is cold enough we don't have to worry about her overheating."

"Agreed," Josie said.

Samantha rubbed the dog, told her to be good, and locked her in the car.

The front door of the building had an old security system with a keypad for entering a code. But the door lock was broken and the door did not close enough to latch. Josie pulled it open and walked inside. Then she stopped and thought. She got out her phone and dialed the number for Zoe.

When the woman answered, Josie explained that she had arrived at the building and would be at Zoe's door shortly.

They found the apartment in the basement at the back of the building. The hallway had dim bulbs behind metal grates to keep them from being broken. Every other bulb was dark, either burnt out or broken, Josie couldn't tell which.

"Mama," Samantha whispered. "I can't imagine living here. It's so dark! I feel bad for these people."

"There are much worse places to live," Josie said.

She knocked on an old wooden door that had a thick coat of glossy varnish over a dark walnut stain. Initials and crude symbols had been gouged into the wood.

The peep hole darkened, and then the door opened. The woman standing there wore a stained yellow apron over dark blue pants and shirt. Her bare feet were in old white Adidas with the backs broken down so they were worn like slippers. The woman held a dish towel in her hands. She was probably in her late forties, a little older than Josie. Like Josie, she was compact and short and somewhat overweight. Unlike Josie, she had graying hair and wrinkled skin the color of aged cherry wood, a beautiful tone that might have come from a mix of Native American and Latino ancestry. She reminded Josie somewhat of Shulu Ojai, the Chumash Indian artist whose studio was not far from Josie and Samantha's Santa Monica condo.

As the woman wiped her hands on the towel, Josie saw the roughness that comes from decades of hard labor. Also, unlike Josie, the woman was obviously an accomplished cook as the glorious aromas of chili peppers and other seasonings washed over them.

"Hi Zoe. I'm Josie Strong. And this is my daughter Samantha." Josie made a little wave. "Thank you for seeing me. May we come in and talk?"

The woman nodded and stepped aside. As Josie walked past her, she sensed the woman looking her up and down. Josie was glad she wasn't wearing professional clothes. Her jeans and shirt were nice and not the least bit worn, but hopefully they weren't off-putting to a person of less economic means. Yet even as Josie had the thought, she realized that her demeanor, as Samantha had often pointed out, was apparently a total giveaway. Josie had tried many times to act like a regular person and not talk like a professor. She had even asked Samantha to judge how she sounded and walked, which had given Samantha a near-incurable giggle fit. Now, when Josie really wanted this woman to open up to her like a friend, the woman was probably judging her and thinking she'd keep a wary distance. But Josie knew that Samantha was her secret weapon. Samantha could make a granite sculpture of a warrior relax and drop its guard.

Zoe's apartment was small and cramped but neat. As with many basement apartments, there were two small windows set up high on the wall. The glass was etched, and there were reinforcement wires crisscrossing the glass. One of the windows was cracked. There were shadowed areas on the glass as if junk had been kicked into the window wells outside and blocked the light. On the walls hung many photos of a girl and a young woman, likely all the same person. The young woman had long, curly black hair and dramatic dark brown eyes that crinkled at the corners when she smiled. She looked vaguely like Amelia Gomez, Josie and Samantha's new house guest.

Samantha leaned close to the photos. "Is this your daughter? She's so pretty. And the dog is charming, too."

Zoe smiled. "Yes. Elena and her dog. Snazzy was a Miniature

Schnauzer. Snazzy is gone now seven years and…" Zoe looked off, thinking. "And two months."

Josie made a knowing nod. "We get so attached to our pets."

"We left our dog in the car," Samantha said. "She's a rescue dog, and her name is Unknown."

"Pets give the love that is always on, and they don't give you the talking back," Zoe said.

Josie gave Samantha a hint of a grin.

"Why look at me?" Samantha said. "Oh, because I talk back? Or because you think I don't give unconditional love?"

Josie smiled. "I think you're perfect."

"Yeah, right."

Zoe realized they were being humorous, and she began to grin.

Josie was glad that they'd brought some levity to the woman's day, even if just a trickle.

On the wall with the photos were multiple hanging needlepoint cloths that had thin wooden rods top and bottom as if they were scrolls. Stitched into the cloths were sayings. The stitched words were in elaborate script and written in Spanish. Josie couldn't make them out. Stitched into the fabric around the sayings were colorful symbols. Mayan? Josie couldn't tell.

Zoe Soto gestured at a small couch. "Would you like to sit? I have some tea."

"Yes, please."

They sat. A few minutes later, Zoe brought over a dark brass tray with geometric designs engraved around the perimeter. Josie thought the tray designs also looked Mayan. On the tray was a ceramic teapot and three small ceramic cups. Zoe sat down on a rickety wooden chair and poured tea.

For a moment, Josie remembered that the last time she and Samantha had tea, it was at Mary Jo's house, just minutes before she was shot dead. Josie tried to push the thought out of her head.

After they'd sipped, Zoe said, "What is this work you have with Elena?"

"The governor has asked me to help investigate a crime involving some nursing homes."

"You are a police woman?"

"No. I teach medieval history at UCLA. But the governor thinks my area of study could be useful in this crime."

"What is the crime?"

Josie didn't know how to answer. If she said murder, that would make Zoe potentially fearful for her daughter's life. "We are investigating organized crime. We suspect that nursing homes may be a cover for illegal activity."

Zoe frowned as if considering nursing homes in a new way. "And you are to take the cover off?"

Josie loved the way the woman used words. "Yes, I suppose that is exactly what I'm trying to do."

"And they had these crimes in… the medieval time?"

The woman was too smart to let anything Josie said go unexamined. The woman looked at Josie, then at Samantha. Her eyes seemed to travel along Samantha's arm and sling.

Samantha said, "The governor sometimes turns to professors for help because professors don't think like regular police." She paused. Josie wondered if she was making up her lines on the fly, or if she was re-purposing something she'd heard in school. Samantha continued, "Different thinking leads to new kinds of approaches." Samantha looked at Josie. "Right, Mama?"

Josie realized it was a true statement that nevertheless revealed nothing that would be upsetting to the woman. Brilliant. "Definitely," Josie said.

Zoe Soto looked at Samantha, then turned back to Josie. "You think my daughter knows something of these crimes?"

"No. But she could probably give me helpful information about the nursing homes."

Zoe frowned. "How could she do that?"

"Just because she works near men who might be doing bad things."

"But now she is gone. So you can't ask her."

"She left without telling you first," Josie said. "That's why you placed the ad."

"Sí. But now I think she is okay. Or I hope she is okay."

"You mentioned a letter. She didn't call you?"

"Sí. At first, I was very worried. When I hadn't heard from her for two days, I called her roommate Lucinda, and she didn't know where Elena was. Then I called her work, and the receptionist didn't know, either. So I called the police where she lives and made the missing person report and the reward notice. It turned out that Elena's letter to me was put in the wrong box in our building. It came to me two days after that."

"Was the letter about where Elena went?"

"Sí. It explains that she is going to live in a retreat for the spirit."

Josie said, "Is this like a religious retreat?"

"I think so."

"You haven't talked to Elena?" Josie said.

"No."

"Is that unusual?"

"Sí. I don't like it. But you know how it is with children..." Zoe glanced at Samantha.

"I'm so sorry about Elena's absence. Would you be willing to show me the letter?" Josie asked. "Or is it too private?"

"It's not too private. You will understand when you read it." Zoe walked over to a drawer in the kitchen, pulled out an envelope, and handed it to Josie.

The envelope was worn as if it had been opened many times. Josie pulled out a piece of folded paper that was limp from handling. Like old paper money. Josie unfolded it.

The letter was written by hand with black ink on blue-lined paper.

Dearest Mamita,

This is a difficult letter to write. As you know, I've been struggling a little at work. I still love my job, but Lucas Herman has been making me more uncomfortable with his pressure. Constantly touching, constantly making the kind of statements that have a secondary meaning. Too much attention! I was getting to the point where I thought about quitting. But one day a different opportunity came up.

Bruno Masser, who is Lucas's boss and maybe the highest-up boss of all, came to the Serenity Home. He had some of the employees come in to an office, one at a time. I was one of those employees.

Mr. Masser asked me questions about what I wanted in my career. Things like how much responsibility I wanted and was I single or did I have a boyfriend, and did I have kids or was I planning to have kids. Things like that. Basically, I think he wanted to know how much commitment I was willing to make for my career. I said my job was very important to me.

That was when he offered me a different job. It is to cook for a spiritual retreat that the company is developing. I would go and live and work at this retreat where there is no communication. No phone because there is no cell signal there. No snail mail, either. Apparently, the isolation is supposed to be part of the appeal of the retreat.

The initial commitment would be six months. He said he would give me a big raise if I chose to go. But he also said all information about this retreat has to be kept private. I would also have to sign something called a non-disclosure agreement, which basically means I can't tell anyone about the experience. I think they are worried that other companies would try to steal their idea, whatever it is.

If, after six months, I am comfortable in the new job, I can continue working at the retreat, and he will give me another raise. He said his hope is that I will spend a long time there. He said there will be regular sabbaticals for the people who work there. Times when I could take time off and come and visit you. He also said the money would keep going up.

Mamita, I've been thinking about this very hard. It would be a real sacrifice for me, walking away from my friends and social life. But Mr. Masser said that is the nature of certain spiritual journeys. And certain career journeys as well. Sacrifice followed by reward.

But the biggest sacrifice would be not being able to talk to you for six months! And part of my agreement with him is that I can't talk to you about it in advance.

After lots of thinking, I've decided to give it a try. I will make lots more money. I will get away from daily contact with Lucas Herman. And whenever I move on to another job, in six months or whenever, I'll have a huge amount of new job experience that will benefit me wherever I go.

And, who knows, maybe I'll even learn something about spiritual things. You know I've struggled with my faith. Maybe this will give me meaning in a different way.

I've signed Mr. Masser's non-disclosure agreement, so I can't talk to you on the phone. The company is sending me to the retreat in two days. I know of one other employee who is also going, a young man who does custodial work for the Serenity Home.

All I can do is send this letter and hope you understand that this is one of those unusual career opportunities. Please know that I will talk to you in six months when my first assignment is over.

I love you very very much!

Elena

Josie said, "It must be very hard to get this letter."

Zoe nodded. "Sí. Very hard."

"This means she's already at the retreat."

Zoe nodded again, looking very serious.

Josie gestured with the letter. "Does Elena use email?"

"Yes, for her work. And she does the texting. I have the texting, too, but you know texting is not so good for letters. That is why she sent me the letter."

"Do you know her email address?"

"No. I don't do the email. My husband Juan knows. He has her email in his phone. Elena gets her email with her phone. But no cell signal at this retreat means she can't get email, either." Zoe glanced at a wall clock. "Juan gets home from work in three hours."

"Could I please ask what you know about Lucas Herman and Bruno Masser?" Josie asked.

Zoe Soto shrugged. "Not very much. Lucas is Elena's

everyday boss. Or maybe I should say was. I think that is the big reason she decided to go to the retreat. She says Lucas is nice, but he is touching too much. When he walks by. When she is working in the kitchen. Whenever her hands are busy, he is behind her, touching. She is unhappy about that."

"What about Bruno Masser?"

Zoe shook her head. "I have not heard about Mr. Masser until the letter. You know what I know."

"Does Elena have a boyfriend?"

Zoe looked uncomfortable. "I am embarrassed to tell you this. I wondered about boyfriends. So one day, I looked at her phone when she was in the bathroom. There was one number she got more calls from than any others except me and Lucinda."

"Do you know whose phone number it is?"

"No. I wanted to ask her. But I was afraid she would think I was snooping. Which I was. I'm so embarrassed."

Zoe sipped her tea. Josie and Samantha followed suit.

"I don't like to snoop, either," Josie said. "Unfortunately, the California governor's request to me involves snooping."

Zoe made a slow nod.

Josie said, "I could probably find out whose phone number is in Elena's phone, if you would be willing to give me that number."

Zoe nodded. Her face looked very serious. "I know the number by memory." She got a scrap of paper and wrote the number down and also wrote Elena's and Lucinda's numbers. "I am hoping you are not going to tell Elena I have done this bad thing. I don't want to keep secrets. But I feel her knowing this would be more bad than good."

"I won't tell her."

Zoe stood up. She walked over to the wall with the pictures and looked at them. Zoe spoke toward the wall.

"When your daughter grows up, you will find these things to happen. Mothers look at life from the east and daughters look from the west. They each think they are seeing the same things, but it is not the same. The daughter sees opportunities. Places to go. Her life expands. The mother sees the daughter going away. Her life does not expand. What is the word. Her life is shrinking."

Zoe turned and looked at both Josie and Samantha. Her eyes were red and puffy.

"Could I ask where Elena lived before she went to the retreat?"

"A town called Folsom. Near Sacramento. Where the Choose Serenity Home is. She shared an apartment with two roommates. One is a hairdresser. The other is a fingernail artist. Before we got the letter, Juan and I called her roommates and her boss and her friends. No one had heard from her. She was disappeared."

"I'm hoping you are more comfortable now that you know she went to a retreat."

"Not happy. But more comfortable, sí."

Josie was wondering if Zoe knew anything that might add information about Mary Jo Telman's life and work.

"When you told the police that Elena was missing," Josie said, "you probably told them where Elena worked."

"At the Serenity Home, sí."

"Did they say anything about the home?"

"No. I need to tell them I got a letter and they can stop looking."

"Did the police show any interest in the Serenity Home?"

Another head shake. "It was like they never heard of the home."

Josie said, "Did Elena mention anything about the home that might suggest any crime at the home? Any talk of theft or bad people? Anything that made her feel bad or worried?"

"No. She loves her work. What she doesn't like is Lucas Herman always wanting her to go to date with him."

"I wonder if he may have also gone to the retreat?"

Zoe's face darkened. "Oh, I hope not! She didn't say in her letter. That would be terrible. He could be touching when there is no one else around to make him stop."

"Oh, I'm sorry. I didn't mean to suggest that." Josie reached over and touched Zoe's knee.

"Do you know what Lucas's official job is?"

"Only that he is important in the company. Maybe just below Mr. Bruno Masser, the highest-up boss. Elena said Lucas was at the Serenity Home a few days every week. But he also goes to other homes the company has."

"Are those the homes called Choose? Like Choose Serenity?"

"Sí. They are all Choose."

"Did Elena ever say what Lucas Herman does at the other homes?"

"No. I am to think he checks on them to make sure everything is okay."

Josie was wondering about Mary Jo Telman's business organization. "Do you think there is a bigger company that owns the nursing homes?"

"I don't know."

"In the letter, Elena mentioned Bruno Masser. Did Elena ever mention any other names of the company's employees?"

"No. But she did say something was strange. She said Lucas talks of the morning email."

"What does that refer to?"

Zoe paused. "I don't know. That's why I remember the strangeness. But I am to think that the highest man at the company doesn't come to visit very often."

"Is this Bruno Masser?" Josie asked.

"Maybe. Or maybe someone higher than Bruno Masser. Someone who stays in his office somewhere. Maybe he just sends out the email each day. Maybe he doesn't, you know, go to the homes." She frowned. "Could you do that in business? Not leave your office?"

"Not in the world of teaching. But maybe in other lines of work."

"I've never been working any business besides cleaning, so I don't know how the bigger business is to work."

Samantha spoke up. "It seems to me you could run a business with email, especially if your job was making decisions." She turned to Josie. "I'm thinking about Amelia's plan to start a coffee shop. A coffee barista has to be there to make the coffee. But if the shop owner had employees she trusted, she could get info from them, make her decisions, and give them instructions through email."

Josie thought about Mary Jo. She seemed shy. Running a business by email might be attractive to someone who didn't like to mix with people. If Josie could figure out Mary Jo's email password, she could possibly learn a great deal. But that didn't seem likely.

"Did Lucas ever say anything that worried Elena? Or was it just the touching?"

"I think, the touching."

"Was Lucas Herman the person who hired her to cook in the cafeteria?"

Zoe suddenly looked very worried. "Elena explained what she is doing in her letter. But you are asking all these questions. Does this mean you think she's in trouble?"

"Not at all," Josie said, maybe too quickly. She didn't want to upset Zoe. "I'm just thinking about the crime I'm supposed to investigate. The more I learn about the nursing home, the better. I was only wondering about the extent of Elena's duties."

"It is just to cook. She told me she is hands full just running the cafeteria. And Lucas told her she is perfect at the job. He said he'd worked with cooks in the military, so he knew what was involved."

That comment stood out.

Josie asked, "Did Elena ever say what he did in the military?"

Zoe Soto shook her head. "I think he just said it to brag. He is to act like the big man with many experiences so he can impress the girl. And she is just a cook who should be glad someone wants to touch her."

Zoe frowned and shook her head as if the very thought made her ill. "Elena didn't like that. She said it was… I forget many English words. To make a person very not happy. Now I remember. She said it was creepy. It made her think of arguments in the home."

"Who argues?"

"Lucas and the other workers. I think he is the argue kind of person."

"Was Elena friends with the other people who worked at the home?"

Zoe nodded her head vigorously. "Sí. Everyone loves Elena. Maybe too much, if you are thinking of Lucas."

Zoe looked up at the wall of photos. She seemed to focus on one of a little girl who was holding an umbrella and twirling. Zoe took a deep breath as if to face something difficult.

Josie sensed Zoe's discomfort, but didn't know what it was. "Is there anything else you think I might want to know about the Choose Serenity Home?"

Zoe started to talk, paused, started again. "You might want to know a scary thing Elena told me. She said Lucas Herman wanted to go with her to lunch. He said they would talk business. So she got in his car. But he didn't drive to a restaurant. He drove to country road and pulled over. Then he got too close, too touching. He talked to her about his guns. He told her he was a hunter in the Army. Hunts from a long distance."

"What did he hunt?"

Zoe looked at Josie as if it were obvious. "I think he hunted what the Army always hunts. People."

THIRTY-SIX

Josie reached over and took Zoe's hand in hers and held it.

"I'm so sorry," Josie said. "That must be very hard. I will try to learn what I can about the retreat where Elena works. And I will let you know what I find out."

"Gracias," Zoe said.

Josie was enough unnerved by what Zoe told her that she couldn't think clearly. The look on Samantha's face made it obvious that she was unsettled, as well. Knowing that Zoe's daughter Elena worked with a man who was into guns and claimed to be a long-distance hunter in the Army was very disturbing. Knowing that the man likely worked for Mary Jo Telman made him a suspect in Mary Jo's murder.

Josie needed time to think about it. She made a few vague comments, then told Zoe again that she'd be in touch. She thanked Zoe for her time, and they left.

As they walked to their car, Samantha spoke in a loud whispered voice. "Hunting people, Mama!"

"I know. I can barely breathe. But we have no evidence."

"What would we do to get evidence?"

"Connect the two people. Lucas Herman and Mary Jo Telman."

"I have an idea," Samantha said. "We learn more about Lucas Herman and try to find some reference to Mary Jo. Or we learn more about Mary Jo and try to find a reference to Lucas Herman."

"Yes, I think that's exactly right." Josie was thinking that the most useful bit of new information was the phone number Zoe had gotten from Elena's phone, the number from which Elena got the most calls.

When they got to the car, Samantha let Unknown out, clipped on her leash, and the three of them walked through neighborhood streets as Josie called Cumberland Durand.

"Hi, Professor. Where are you?"

"Reno."

"Are you okay?"

"Yes" Josie said. "Whenever I call, you wonder if I'm okay. I must pester you such that you wonder."

He was silent a moment. "Sometimes you're not okay."

"True. You're right."

"If you're okay, then you must have a question."

"I do. I have a phone number, and I don't know who it belongs to. Is it possible to find out who owns the phone? And, also, is it possible to track that phone?"

As was his norm, Cumberland didn't immediately respond.

"First question first. I can probably find out the owner of a phone, but maybe not. I'll let you know. As for your second question, all phones can be tracked. Landlines are attached to a physical address. The accuracy of tracking cellphones depends on lots of factors, such as if the phone is in a city or in the country. Cities have lots of cell towers and lots of wifi sources. Rural areas do not. It also matters if the phone has GPS. Old ones don't."

"I thought maybe a phone had to place a call or something to get tracked."

"No." There was crinkling noise in the background. "All you need is the phone number."

"But the phone has to be turned on, right?"

"No. Phones are like any computer. They're never completely powered down. You can turn them off, but that just stops several of the apps. The internal clock, some GPS processes, the calendar, and other stuff still works."

"What if airplane mode is turned on?"

"Doesn't matter. When you turn it off, some of the background stuff goes into low-power mode and works slower, but stuff stays on. Leaks from National Security Agency employees say they can track phones that are supposedly untrackable and are turned off and have the batteries removed. In my world, it's commonly assumed that the phone service providers and the manufacturers all put trojan apps in phones, and those trojan apps still stay on when you power down the phone. Even if you take out the battery and SIM card, there is another small backup battery that's built into the system. The trojan apps are still able to phone home every ten minutes or so. That way they can get data on you regardless of what you do. Selling that info to advertising companies is a good source of revenue. They also use the data in designing future products."

Josie had a recollection. "One of my colleagues mentioned putting your phone in a foil pouch to block the signals."

"Doesn't work," Cumberland said. "Try it. Then have Samantha dial it. Most times, most places, the call will still go through. But it will run down your phone's battery faster."

There was more crinkling noise, then a snapping sound. Maybe he opened a new stack of Saltines and popped open a Diet Coke.

"If I give you a phone number to trace, what happens?"

"Okay."

"Okay, what?" Josie said.

"Give me the phone number. I'm loading a tracking app."

Josie read off the number that Zoe had gotten out of Elena's phone, the number that Elena got the most calls from.

Josie heard Cumberland munching crackers.

"That phone doesn't show on my app."

"May I give you a different number?"

"Yeah."

Josie read off Elena's number.

"I don't show that phone, either. What company is the carrier?"

"I don't know. I could probably find out for the second number but not the first."

"It's no big deal. I'm just curious."

"What does it mean when you can't trace a phone?" Josie asked. "Is the tracking app not good? Or has the carrier canceled the service?"

"The app is good. It doesn't matter if the carrier has canceled the service. Or if the phone has been reset or wiped. It only means that radio signals can't get to or from the phone."

"How would that be?"

"The likeliest explanation is the phone is in a complete cell signal shadow, away from the sky and its satellites and any wifi or blue tooth signal."

"A phone can be tracked through wifi or satellites?"

"Yeah. A phone sort of reaches out by periodically beaming a short little radio signal every few minutes. If that signal gets noticed by any network in any way, bingo. The phone's location is discoverable."

"Because the radio signal includes the phone's identification?"

"Right."

Josie was trying to understand the details. "Even if the phone is near a wifi signal, it would have to be public wifi, like Starbucks. A private wifi would require the password."

"No. Passwords only grant you access to go to websites and such. Even without the password, phone pings are still noticed through private wifi. But if the phone's owner is taking a tour of a cave, then that phone is more or less hiding."

"Are you saying cave in a metaphorical way? Or literal?"

"Both. You put a phone in a cave, power it down, take out the battery and the SIM card, and leave it for a long time, it will be very hard to trace unless there's wifi in the cave. The other possibility is if the phone is inoperable."

"How would that happen?"

"Maybe it suffered severe damage. The phone might have gotten struck by lightning. Or maybe it got cooked in a fire. Or enough water for a long enough time will do it. My friend dropped one of his phones into a toilet and accidentally flushed it. He had one of the old small phones, so it went down the pipe. He said he got a signal off of it for fourteen minutes, then the signal went away. Probably because the sewer carried it away."

"If you can't track a phone, can you still tell who owns it?"

"Yeah. Hold on."

After a long wait, Cumberland said, "One phone is registered to Elena Soto. The other is registered to Carmichael Two LLC. That's the same LLC we talked about before, right?"

"Yes." Josie realized that meant that the phone number Elena got the most calls from went to a phone owned by an LLC. Thus the phone was probably owned by Mary Jo Telman.

But Mary Jo's phone would only have power if it was plugged into a charger all this time.

"You said a cell phone has a backup battery."

"Yeah."

"If a phone wasn't charged for a long time, would that backup battery still have power?"

"I don't know," Cumberland said. "Eventually it would discharge completely."

"Would that make it untrackable? Like being in a cave?"

"Probably," he said.

"If either of these phones were to show up in tracking, could I follow the owner as he or she moves around?"

"Yes. But be aware that some tracking apps are much more accurate than others. If you're around a crowd of people, it won't be very helpful to know that the person is within one hundred fifty feet of you. But if you can narrow it down to ten or twenty feet, that's much more useful."

"Yes, that makes sense."

"You might also want to know that if the person you're tracking has the right app, they can tell you're tracking them. They can find out who you are and where you are. Tracking goes both ways."

"Oh, I wouldn't want that," Josie said.

"I have a phone you can borrow. It has a beta version of the best new tracking app. I've also got it set up so it blocks being tracked, so the trackee can't find out who the tracker is. Are you coming home? I could give it to you. And I should show you some things."

"I'll take you up on that. I'm hoping to be back tomorrow."

"Okay. Call when you get here."

Josie thanked him, but he'd already hung up.

THIRTY-SEVEN

The next morning, Josie and Samantha checked out of the Placerville hotel and headed home. Unknown curled in Samantha's lap in the front passenger seat. They drove down the Central Valley at a leisurely rate, yet by evening they were on the Santa Monica beach walk with Unknown.

The waves off the Pacific were big, and they crashed with such fury that it made Josie think that Poseidon and Neptune, the gods of the sea, were agitated. She thought of the artist Shulu Ojai who said that the Chumash Indians could read the waves. Samantha held Unknown's leash and was unnaturally quiet. Josie felt very unsettled. She kept thinking about being shot at in the Sierra. It was so frightening and disturbing that it was impossible to shake. In some ways, it was not much different from what happened in Yosemite. But it felt different. Maybe because Samantha was safe in Yosemite but nearly killed near Tahoe. Every time Josie looked at Samantha's sling for her shoulder dislocation, that was an additional reminder.

Josie kept thinking about the letter Elena Soto had sent her mother Zoe. On its face, the letter explained why Elena had dropped off the radar. Yet Josie worried about Elena Soto as well.

Although it seemed a wild idea—and Josie had no actual evidence—it still appeared that the shooting victim, Mary Jo Telman, could be running a drug and money-laundering ring. Whether or not her husband Francis had been involved in the business wasn't clear. But both of their deaths by shooting suggested as much.

Elena Soto could have decided to leave the nursing home and take on the new job at a spiritual retreat to simply leave the daily hustle of life like so many people do. But she might have been kidnapped and held prisoner by Lucas Herman. Or Bruno Masser. Elena's mother Zoe had told Josie and Samantha that Lucas, one of Mary Jo Telman's chief employees, was focused on guns and claimed to be a long-distance hunter. Did that suggest that Lucas was a sniper? It certainly seemed like it.

Was Lucas now in control of Mary Jo's business? Did he kill the Telmans and continue to run the business as usual so that he could steal the profits? Did the other employees even know who Mary Jo was? Josie could think of several advantages to running a business anonymously, hiding its ownership behind Limited Liability Companies and communicating business decisions by email. But a potentially large disadvantage was that someone could kill the leader, step into her position, continue sending the emails, and no one would be the wiser.

Unfortunately, it was all guesses.

The next day, they were again on their beach walk as Josie mulled over the murders of Francis and Mary Jo.

Years ago, Josie had studied the Greek and Roman mythology that predated and shaped the Middle Ages. So much of past human activity was wrapped up in many different gods. Did that help people understand the world? Could it still? Josie stared at the roiling Pacific waters. Maybe the gods of the sea, Poseidon and Neptune, were angry. Maybe they were trying to tell Josie something.

Josie's phone rang. The screen said it was Cor.

"Hi Cor."

"You made it back okay?"

"Yes. Thank you. And you taught your classes."

"Two today. One each the next two days. Then we break for the Christmas holiday and don't start up again until January sixth."

"I keep forgetting about Christmas."

"That just shows you've got more important stuff on your mind. You got a plan?"

"I'm working on it," Josie said. "I'll meet with the tech guy I told you about, Cumberland Durand. He's going to show me how to track cell phones. Depending on what I learn, I might head back to Sacramento."

"Let me know?"

"Sure."

Josie hung up. Samantha and she had gotten to the end of the beach walk. They turned and headed back.

Samantha said, "My school has just two more days before the Christmas break. I could go back for those two days, right? We'll be here in L.A.?"

"I think so, yes. I'm hoping to meet with Cumberland tomorrow so he can show me how to use tracking software. That will take much of the day to drive across town to Ellison's place in Montebello. If you go back to school before the Christmas break, that might make the headmaster more comfortable. He cares about you."

"You think so? I always think he doesn't even view us as students, if that makes any sense."

"How does he view you?"

Samantha thought about it. "We're like a kind of property. What's that called? Business assets. He looks at each of us in terms of what we can bring to the school's reputation."

"What do you bring in his mind?"

"I'm not sure. The school is pretty white bread. So I'm one of the two poster Black girls. I play volleyball and get good grades, too. Plus, he's always focused on what the kids' parents do. It's like he's memorized which kids' parents are doctors and which run giant corporations. The last thing I heard him say was a comment about Christy Barron's mom."

"Not about her looks, I hope," Josie said.

"No, he's not that crass. But it's like he's totally aware that her last movie made a zillion dollars. And he can never be around me without mentioning that my mom is a UCLA professor."

"He says that?"

"Yeah. He'll introduce me by saying, 'This is Samantha Strong. She's the one whose mother is the history prof at UCLA.'"

Samantha paused. "It's like he knows that the best way to

sell the school is to sell the occupations of the parents. That makes other parents want to sign up their kid. It's kind of a competition for parents."

"You're kidding." Josie was uneasy just thinking about it.

"No, I'm not kidding. Sure, he wants good kids for his students. But it's more important to have big-time parents."

"I can't believe he thinks of me as big time."

"Not you, personally, Mama. You're more a kind of concept."

"A poster-parent concept?"

"Yeah. The school's single mom who's got a big-time job."

"Wow, that's rather bleak, reducing kids to the occupations of their parents."

"I suppose. But it's the truth. Like it or not, this is the way the world works, right?"

"How'd I get such a smart kid?"

"Lucky, I guess." Samantha's grin was huge.

"You look like the Cheshire Cat."

"But will my grin still be here even if my body disappears like the cat in Alice and Wonderland?"

"Knowing you, probably."

"What's next? Do we go get me a new phone?" Samantha didn't wait for Josie's response. "Of course we can, dear," Samantha said, imitating Josie. "Your phone is your Bible. Hate to have you suffer more… what did you call it, dear? Deprivation?" Samantha looked at Josie and began nodding her head in an exaggerated way.

When Josie still didn't respond, Samantha nodded even more dramatically.

"Okay, stop, you're making me seasick."

Samantha started bouncing on her toes. "Hear that, Unknown? We're getting a new phone!"

THIRTY-EIGHT

"Is the Apple store open in the evening?" Josie asked. "They should be open when I come shopping!"

They left the beach and headed to the Apple store at the Third Street Promenade. Samantha carried the old phone that was bent and shattered by the bullet. An hour later, the Apple employees were buzzing with excitement about their phones offering bullet protection. Samantha never looked up as she and Josie walked toward their condo, so transfixed was she by the new device.

"Sam, you're going to get run over if you don't watch where you're going."

"Sorry, Mama, this phone is so cool!"

"Isn't it just the same as your old one?"

"No. Not at all. I'm going to have to arrange to get shot every year."

"Don't make me think about it. I'm having nightmares about it, just like you." Josie didn't want to think about Samantha's whimpering and panicked cries in the middle of the night. And now that they were back home and sleeping in their own rooms, Josie wouldn't hear Samantha's nightmare stresses. But Amelia would...

Back home, Samantha and Amelia were buzzing about Samantha's phone. They sat on the couch and explored it together.

Josie went out on the deck and called Cumberland Durand.

"Oh, Professor," he said when he answered the phone. "Are you, um, okay? And Samantha, too?"

"Yes, Cumberland. We're fine. Thank you for your concern. We just got home. How are you and Aiden and Cara doing? Is it still okay living at Ellison's?"

"He's nice. It's good. But I think he kind of lost his lifestyle. I think he liked being alone."

"He probably knows it won't go on for an extended time." As Josie said it, she thought maybe she was wrong. "Would it be okay for me to meet you and learn about tracking phones?"

"Sure."

Josie was once again thinking about how Cumberland refused to take payment for all he'd done for her. She said, "The governor has given me an expense account. He's expecting me to use this money. It shows him that I'm working on his problem. So I'll be distributing some of this to you."

"You found us a place to live after the loan sharks took our house to pay off dad's debts. Mr. Ellison is nice. But he wasn't looking for a family to live in his warehouse. He's doing it because of you. So I owe you because I owe him. It's a logical progression."

"If you don't want it, you can put it in an account for your siblings. Where can we meet?"

"Mr. Ellison's place has lots of room."

"I'd like to not distract him."

"We could meet at the library," Cumberland said.

"Yes, but I want to talk. Libraries like silence. How about a coffee shop?"

"Oh, sure. They don't have Diet Coke, but I can drink tea." Cumberland told her where to go.

They picked a time the next morning.

"Bye," Cumberland said and hung up.

Josie, Samantha, and Amelia had dinner of grilled veggies over pasta with olive oil. They mixed a portion into Unknown's dog food bowl, and she ate it in a perfunctory manner. Josie and Samantha knew people who claimed that their dogs ate so fast it was as if they nearly inhaled their food. Not Unknown. She was polite. Tentative. Agreeable. But she had no enthusiasm, whether for playing or eating.

After dinner, they all sat out on their little balcony. Happy voices from the Santa Monica pier drifted over on the breeze. Josie hoped the sounds would resurface in Samantha's dreams to provide some push-back from the horror of what happened during the shooting.

The surf was still breaking in loud, large curls, indicative of a rough ocean hundreds of miles out to sea. The breeze was weak enough that the air felt dry, all sea mist having dropped back to the sea. And while the air was cool, it was very warm compared to the Sierra and Lake Tahoe, where the air was constantly cooled by the snow blanket covering the mountains.

Josie watched some gulls doing their aerial ballet as Samantha and Amelia explored Samantha's new phone.

Josie had Francis Telman's phone, which Josie had taken out of the kitchen cubby in Mary Jo's modern house. She opened up Telman's email. As Mary Jo had said, Francis didn't like using passwords.

There was what seemed to Josie like a standard assortment of junk in the inbox. Some of the emails looked legitimate. Josie clicked on some of them. A few were work related, newsletters from environmental organizations, notices from the forest service. A quick count suggested he was getting only three or four emails per day.

There were no emails that appeared to be truly personal.

Josie clicked on the sent file. There were many fewer emails that Francis had sent. Just one or two per day. Francis was not much of a correspondent. Josie opened a few of them. Nothing was notable.

Josie also searched on Francis Telman's name and then Mary Jo Telman's. It appeared that Mary Jo and Francis didn't email each other or even copy each other on emails they'd sent elsewhere. And Josie could see no indication of social media use. They were both very reserved with their internet activity. Josie remembered that she'd seen no TV in their houses or the Tahoe cabin. Nor did she see any sources of music. She wondered what either did for entertainment. Read books? Go to the movie theater? Listen to music online? Even if they'd done those things, they still kept a low profile in all ways. Were they both complete introverts? Were they a perfect match for each other? Or did they both lead secret lives?

Josie pressed the button on Telman's phone to turn it off. She realized that any useful information was likely to come from the traditional approach to investigation. Talking to people, watching people, following people.

She held that thought as she went to bed, while Samantha and Amelia stayed up and talked.

THIRTY-NINE

The next morning Samantha went to school, and Amelia went to her job at the coffee shop. Josie took Unknown in the car and drove across town to Montebello.

Cumberland was at the coffeeshop, ensconced in his laptop computer as if he were locked in a room. There was a half-empty cup of tea near the computer. Cumberland didn't look up until Unknown sniffed his leg.

"Oh. Hi, dog." He gave Unknown a single pat on the top of her head. Then he made a single wave at Josie.

Josie knew not to wait for an invitation to sit down at his table. Josie pointed to the floor at Cumberland's feet. "Unknown, you sit here."

The dog looked up at her, then down at the floor, then sat such that she was touching Cumberland's leg.

"I'll get some coffee and come back. Do you want more tea or anything?"

Cumberland shook his head. He was back to being focused on his computer and a phone that was on the table next to it.

Josie left. A few minutes later, she returned with coffee and two blueberry scones.

"I got us a treat," she said.

Cumberland picked up a scone and ate it in three or four quick bites. Josie realized he had more energy for eating than Unknown had.

"When we last talked, you said you had a certain phone that I could use to track other phones."

Cumberland made a single nod. "I'm setting it up. It will take another minute." He sipped some tea, then picked up the second scone and took a big bite out of it. Josie had been about to eat it. Better in all ways for Cumberland to have it.

He made a few more taps on his computer keyboard, then put the phone into his backpack and rummaged around. He pulled out another phone and handed it to Josie.

Josie took the phone. It looked normal.

Cumberland wrote on a piece of paper. 545659. "This is the passcode. The phone has been scrubbed, so I know it doesn't have any apps that can be used as spyware. It also has a SIM card that traces to Hedy Lamarr who lives in San Francisco's Presidio."

"You mean Hedy Larmarr like the name of the famous actress?"

"That was the origin, yeah."

"Was this stolen from a real person?" Josie was horrified.

"No. It's all fake. The fake Hedy Lamarr's address is actually a secret computer war room buried beneath Crissy Field at the Presidio in San Francisco. It's maintained by the Army."

"Is that real? The secret underground room?"

"As far as I know."

"And you use this address because…"

Cumberland shrugged. "Some guys I know from UCLA. We thought it would be an effective privacy screen. We could use the address and give the person an identity that would become a honeypot."

"Thus the choice of Hedy Lamarr's name. Because she was beautiful, right?"

Cumberland was shaking his head. "No. We used her name because she was an inventor. Back during World War Two, she invented spread spectrum and frequency hopping, technology that eventually led to wifi and blue tooth."

"The actress?" Josie said, surprised and delighted. "Or is that a joke? I only know Hedy Lamarr as a movie star."

"I wouldn't know. I haven't seen any of her movies. But she was a tech genius."

"Was it her beauty that made you call her a honeypot identity?"

"No. I didn't know she was beautiful. But if you say so... We called it a honeypot identity because it's a kind of baited computer trap. Someone might find the identity intriguing, so they look into it."

"Like an animal smelling a honeypot."

"Right. But this kind of bait comes with tracking. Anytime someone tries to hack into the phone of Hedy Lamarr, who supposedly lives in the Army's secret room under Crissy Field, it triggers a cascade of events that allow us to track the hackers. We learn all about them, and all they learn is fake stuff we created."

Josie held up the phone. "So if someone tracks this phone, you will actually be tracking them."

Cumberland nodded. "But I installed some code on this phone that makes it very hard to track."

"Did Hedy Lamarr really invent those things? What did you call it? Frequency hopping."

"Yeah. She was amazing."

"A good actress, too," Josie said.

"A lot of important stuff traces back to what she invented." He ate the last of the second scone, then looked very serious. "When I was looking at crime stuff in El Dorado County, I saw a sheriff's report about a sniper killing. And your name was mentioned."

Josie nodded. "The woman I talked to you about, Mary Jo Telman, was shot and killed."

Cumberland made a severe frown.

"We got shot at as well. Samantha was nearly killed. Her phone was hit by a bullet."

Cumberland looked shocked and worried. "Samantha's still alive, right?" His alarm was obvious.

"Yes. She dislocated her shoulder, but she's okay."

Cumberland nodded. "Good. I like Samantha."

"Me too," Josie said with a little grin.

"I can't imagine being shot," he said. "Like, someone walks up to you, pulls out a gun, and shoots you. It happened to you in the Santa Monica mountains and then up by Bear Lake. If it happened to me, I would lose my thinking. Just to have someone put a gun in my face..."

"Not that it matters, but this shot was from a long distance. By a military-trained sniper, best as we can tell."

"Why do you say it was a sniper?"

"A woman I've come to know, Cor Kontos, was in the Army. She said the person who made the shot must have been an expert marksman and would have had military training."

"A sniper killing is a different category from a cop killing?"

Josie nodded. "That's why I asked if there's a way to search for people who got sniper training in the military."

"I haven't looked, yet. I'll see what I can find out. Didn't you say that the woman's husband was a cop and he was killed?"

"Yes. A Forest Service ranger."

"Was that also a sniper killing?"

"Not according to what the investigating police said. The husband was shot up close. With something called a nine millimeter. So the M.O., as police say, was completely different."

"A long distance sniper could also shoot someone up close," Cumberland said. "The two killings could be by the same person."

"True."

"Cops are killed kind of often," Cumberland said.

"Yes."

"And it's often assumed that they're killed because they are cops."

Josie sipped her tea. "I assume that, too."

"But if the ranger was killed because he was a cop, then why was she killed?"

"That's one of the questions I want to answer."

Cumberland's watch started beeping. He looked at it, a big techy-looking device with multiple dials set against a backdrop of a huge wind turbine that spun slowly. He pressed a button to turn off the alarm. As Josie looked more closely, she realized the dials and wind turbine were all just representations on a digital face.

"I need to go pick up Aiden and Cara from school," he said as he closed his laptop and slid it into his backpack.

"May I come with you?"

Cumberland gave Josie a look that seemed to her like confusion, as if he couldn't imagine why she would come.

"It only takes one adult to walk them to Mr. Ellison's."

She said, "It would be fun to see them and walk with you all."

Now Cumberland looked even more confused. Josie realized that Cumberland didn't find any particular joy in being with other people. So he wouldn't understand that Josie did.

In case he wanted her not to come, she gave him an out by saying, "But if you think they'd rather I weren't there, no problem."

"Oh. I don't think they'd mind. We just walk. So you won't, you know, cause a problem."

Josie stood, and Unknown stood. Josie left a few ones on the table.

Cumberland looked at it and frowned. "I already paid for my tea."

"It's just a courtesy tip for the person who cleans the tables."

More confusion. No point in explaining to a grown young man about the custom of tipping. Maybe he'd seen people tip and never understood why they did it. More likely, he was oblivious and hadn't noticed.

They left the coffee shop, walked to the corner diagonally opposite from the coffee shop, then headed down through a warehouse district that was gentrifying. There were multiple, small, painted signs that hung out perpendicular to the buildings, advertising businesses. A used bookstore, a free medical clinic, a shared office space with computers and conference rooms and a copy center, a restaurant called Indian Curry Star, another coffee shop, a daycare co-op. One business with large windows was called Urban Design Studio. Visible inside were hip-looking women in torn jeans, pump heels, and beautiful silk shirts leaning over huge angled drafting tables with techy lighting hanging from arched supports.

Two blocks down they came to a dirty gray stucco building

that looked like another warehouse. But the building had a large cheerful hand-painted sign that said Montebello Middle School in deep blue letters against a sky blue background. Under the title, painted in golden yellow, it said Home of the Best Kids in the County. The painter had made an artful change. The word County had been crossed out and changed to Country.

"Fun," Josie said, pointing at the sign.

Cumberland looked at it. "Yeah," he said.

Josie thought he'd likely never noticed it before.

When they came to the school's door, Cumberland looked at his watch. Then he leaned against the gray wall.

Josie stifled her impulse to fill silence with needless comments. Five minutes later, the door opened, and students rushed out, some heading toward buses, some toward waiting cars. Cara came out with another girl. She said something, made a little wave, and the girl walked toward a waiting car. Cara turned toward Cumberland. He gestured toward Josie. Cara saw Josie and made a slight, shy smile, which pleased Josie more than she could say.

"Hi Cara. I don't know if you remember me. I'm Josie Strong." Josie remembered that Cara was nine or ten. But she seemed older than when they'd first met on the beach a few weeks before.

Cara nodded. "You're the professor. My brother talks about you." Cara bent down and rubbed Unknown. "Hi, Unknown. I don't really know about dogs. I hope I pet you okay."

Aiden came out, waved at Josie, then joined Cumberland. They started walking. Josie and Cara followed.

"I had a meeting with Cumberland," Josie said to Cara, "and he said I could come and walk home with you."

"Yeah, sure. Some bad guys took our house from my dad, so now we're living at Mr. Ellison's warehouse. It's not too far from here. I don't have my own room like at home. I just have a corner in the loft, but it's okay. Mr. Ellison put up a divider that makes it so I have my own space. But I no longer have my own bathroom. I don't mind too much. Aiden says it's good for us to have new experiences."

"Cumberland is probably glad to have new experiences, too."

Cara glanced at Cumberland, who walked with Aiden, ten paces ahead of Cara and Josie. In a soft voice, Cara said, "I don't think Cumberland thinks about stuff like that. He's kind of in his own world. Computers and stuff. He doesn't care about anything normal. He doesn't talk normal, either. My friends say he should be a rock star. I told them he doesn't know how to play guitar. They say he could just hold a mic and jump around and shake his hair. I told them he doesn't like being around people, and he doesn't like to jump and shake, and that he would never say a word, and they say that's cool. He could just be eye candy."

"They're probably right," Josie said. "He wouldn't have to sing at all. It would be a new music form. A rock band with a nonverbal front man."

"Nonverbal," Cara said. "In school we learned about a poet like that. I think her name was Emily Dickinson. The teacher said she was a shut-in. I'm going to read her poetry. A shut-in for a rock band would be a new thing."

"Yes, it would," Josie said. "Definitely a new thing."

As they walked, Cara said, "Cumberland says he took a class from you about how to make really cool medieval weapons."

"Well, I don't know how cool they are. I study medieval history. But people in the Middle Ages did fight wars. And they did make weapons. The whole reason I teach the class about weapons is that it's an easy way to get students interested in history."

"Because college students are into guns just like adults, right?"

Josie was surprised at the girl's perspicacity. "Yes, I suppose you could say that. Tell me, are you and Aiden comfortable staying with Mr. Ellison? Or do you wish you had a more normal house?"

"Mr. Ellison is very nice. And I like the warehouse. It's pretty cool. But someday maybe we'll have a normal house again. Maybe not so big with a swimming pool and all. But I don't know how you get a normal house."

"You can rent them or buy them," Josie said.

"Who would do that now that dad is in jail and mom is living with her friend?"

"Maybe Cumberland would."

"I think he makes a lot of money," Cara said, "but I don't think he would know how to get a house. You have to know about normal stuff to do that."

"Cumberland knows about many things."

"Not normal things."

They came to Ellison's building and made the long trek up the stairs to his warehouse loft.

Cumberland slid open the big door, which was unlocked.

Josie called out. "Hi Ellison, it's me, Josie. I don't want you to have an unwelcome surprise." Josie unclipped Unknown's leash. She tapped Unknown on her side, gestured toward Ellison's loft, and said, "It's okay. You can explore."

Unknown looked up at Josie, wariness in her eyes.

"Go. Look around."

Unknown walked very slowly forward, a step, a pause to look around, another step.

"Hi Josie," Ellison's voice came from behind the rolling wall that was currently in front of the kitchen, which was itself delineated by a large rolling counter/sink device like what one might find in a restaurant.

Ellison came out from behind the rolling wall. He was wiping his hands on a towel. He looked freshly showered and was dressed in clean black jeans and a black T-shirt that contrasted with his thin helmet of very white hair.

Josie walked over and gave him a hug.

"You could never be an unwelcome surprise," he said. "Is my new family showing off the local school and such?" he asked.

"And such," Josie said. "And Cumberland is teaching me the intricacies of phone tracking software."

"You gotta watch that guy. I think he lives in the world of what he can do with computers and not so much what he should do."

Josie noticed that Cumberland was heading up the long stairs to the loft, apparently unaware that people were talking about him.

Josie said, "He studies computers, so that's his focus. If he'd been studying world history, his main takeaway would be about human behavior. And people who study behavior aren't much more perceptive about the difference between can and should."

"Ah, history and behavior. That which dogs us all." Ellison gestured toward two large leather chairs that faced windows that looked toward downtown L.A. "Sit for a bit?"

Josie nodded and stepped over to the chairs.

"Rough trip north?" Ellison said.

"Yes." Josie told him the basics.

"So sorry to hear it. But you and Samantha are okay?"

"On the surface, yes. I imagine our emotional undercurrents will be in turmoil for some time."

FORTY

Cumberland came back down the stairs.

It was a moment before he spoke. Josie thought he was probably trying to think how best to explain complicated technology to a Luddite. "I could show you how to use the Hedy Lamarr phone."

Josie pulled over one of the conference chairs that Ellison kept in a stack and sat next to Cumberland. She took out the phone he'd given her and handed it to him.

Cumberland entered the passcode on the phone he'd given her. "I put tracking software on this phone. It's pretty easy to use. You click on this icon, and you get a map and a little box. Type a phone number into the box and be patient. The system has a slow handshake. A blinking dot on the map will indicate the location of the phone we're tracking."

"Can we test it here?"

"Sure. What phone number do you want to track?"

"Let's try Samantha's." Josie typed in the number and hit enter. Nothing changed. "You said to be patient," Josie said.

"Yeah. Tracking will have variable latency and location accuracy," Cumberland said.

"Meaning what, exactly?" Josie asked.

"Just that when I get a location for a person's phone, it will only mean that the phone was at that place earlier. One, two, three minutes before. Maybe ten minutes or more."

"So I could go there, and my target might have left."

"Right."

"Okay. How accurate will the location be?"

"When you see the blinking dot, it usually wouldn't be accurate to less than thirty feet. And sometimes one hundred feet or more is likely."

"Is this a GPS technology?"

"It uses GPS and cell towers and multilateration."

"Multilateration?" Josie thought it sounded like a word designed to be inscrutable.

"That's just hyperbolic positioning based on TOAs… Oh, never mind the tech stuff."

"On TV," Josie said, "they make it look like cell phone tracking is instantaneous and super accurate." As soon as Josie said it, she realized it was a rude comment. It might come across to Cumberland like she was disappointed.

All Cumberland said was, "On TV, sure."

"Meaning stuff on TV is fictional."

Cumberland didn't respond.

"I really appreciate your help, Cumberland," Josie said. But she knew the statement didn't make up for being insensitive about that help.

Several seconds later, he said, "I don't want my help to put you and Samantha in danger."

"We'll be careful. We're hoping it might keep us out of danger."

The phone screen went blank. Then a map appeared. A blinking red dot appeared on the map. Josie couldn't tell anything about the map.

"You can do the finger zoom on the map."

Josie did as he said, zooming out. Out farther. There was Los Angeles. The blinking dot was west of downtown. Josie zoomed in. Farther. Now she recognized Santa Monica. Zoomed in more. There was the street of Samantha's charter school. The blinking dot was on the school building!

"Oh, God, this is creepy. Anyone with this software could find out where Samantha is. A person could watch where Samantha goes."

"It's a good thing to remember about phones," Cumberland said. "They are useful. But they tell the world where you are."

"Unless we do like you've said in the past. Leave them at home."

"But no one ever does. Most people don't mind having their

lives revealed to everybody. They post stuff on social media because they want their lives to be revealed. It's like saying, 'Look at me, look at everything I do.' They don't want privacy."

"But when it's your own daughter..." Josie stopped talking.

"Yeah," he said.

Josie was staring at the blinking dot. It was mesmerizing and very uncomfortable to think that anyone on the planet with this software could find where Samantha was.

"What about when the phone you're tracking moves?"

"You can pull up a history." Cumberland picked up the phone and showed her how.

Josie stared at the Hedy Larmarr phone. A dotted line appeared. It went outside the charter school building, west and south to their condo.

Even more creepy, Josie thought. "If you see a line that shows where a phone traveled and it's a long way from the current blinking dot, is there a way to know which way the phone went?"

"Yeah. Zoom in. If you zoom enough, you'll see that each segment of a dotted line has a little half-arrow on it, showing the direction the phone traveled."

Josie went back to the blinking dot. "What does this circle around the dot mean?"

"The circles show elapsed time. A small circle means the phone has been stationary for ten minutes. A medium circle shows a pause of thirty minutes. The largest circle means it paused for an hour or more."

"And the little numbers?"

"Time stamps."

"Cumberland, this is perfect. How long does this last?"

"Your map will refresh every time the target phone moves more than one hundred feet."

"Is there anything else I need to do?"

"No. Just keep the phone charged. The tracking feed definitely uses juice. As a rough rule, eighty percent charge should give you three hours."

"Thanks so much. You said that if someone tries to track this

Hedy Lamarr phone, you will be able to find out."

He nodded. "Yeah, I can see who is trying to track it."

"But I'm wondering if they can still get this phone's location."

"Based on my testing of this new software, no. But I can't promise that. This number you want to track," he said, "that's a bad guy?"

"I don't know. This is the number you looked up. You found out it belongs to Carmichael Two LLC. It could be a bad guy or someone innocent."

"If he turns out to be bad, you won't confront him, right? You'll call the police and tell them his location."

"I will once I'm confident he's the bad guy. But the police need evidence to get a search warrant, I'd have to get evidence before the police would do anything."

He nodded acknowledgment. "You can't just dial nine, one, one and say you think someone is a bad guy and you think they are in a particular place."

"Right. The police are also looking for this guy—whoever he is—but they haven't caught him yet. They don't know who he is. Also, I'm doing all of this at the request of the governor because the governor says the police have had no luck in finding the shooter. The result is that I have to pursue the bad guy myself. Once I establish that he's the guy I want, then it will be time to notify the authorities. And while the governor wants me to ask the police for help when I need it, he also wants me to call him or his aide as soon as I know who the shooter is."

"This scares me," Cumberland's voice was soft. Josie thought she could hear it waver.

Josie was surprised at Cumberland expressing concern. The young man with the Autism Spectrum-remove and what he described as his dysfunctional brain was showing emotional warmth. Josie wished she could give him a hug. Which, of course, would just make him more uncomfortable.

"Don't worry. I won't do anything foolish. If I sense any danger, I'll call the police," she said.

Once again, they didn't speak for a moment, a silence that

felt awkward to Josie but probably felt normal to Cumberland.

That evening, after Josie got back to her condo, they went down to the beach walk, Samantha and Amelia on each side of Josie. In a desire for Private World mode, they'd all left their phones at the condo. Samantha held Unknown's leash. Josie pulled out the Hedy Lamarr phone.

"I thought you said no phones," Samantha said.

"This one is different." Josie explained it was Cumberland's Hedy Lamarr phone, linked to an Army address of an underground room in the Presidio in San Francisco.

"What does that mean, an underground room?"

"I don't know. It could be real. It could be fictitious. I'm not sure Cumberland knows, either. The main thing is, anyone trying to track this phone will have major problems. It's something to do with some computer code that Cumberland put in it. Cumberland showed me how to use this phone to track other phones. But if anyone tries to reverse the tracking and see where the tracking request comes from, they will be blocked."

Amelia said, "I've heard that name, Hedy Lamarr. Why is the phone named after her?"

"It's not an official name. It's what Cumberland calls it. Hedy Lamarr was a movie star back in the nineteen forties. Cumberland says she was a tech genius. Back in World War Two, she invented some important tech stuff. I think Cumberland said that Wifi and Blue Tooth came from her inventions."

"A woman movie star invented tech stuff?" Samantha said. "That is so cool!"

Josie wasn't sure if Samantha was more impressed that a woman would invent computer tech stuff or that a movie star would. Either way, it was not all good by Josie's estimation.

Amelia pointed at the phone. "What's it for?"

"Before I tell you, think of this like classified information. Cumberland went out on a limb to do this for me. No one but us three can ever know about this."

"Got it," Samantha said. She looked at Amelia.

Amelia nodded. "I promise not to tell anyone."

"This phone has tracking software. The blinking dot is Samantha's phone."

Samantha's eyes widened. She reached for the Hedy Lamarr phone, zoomed in on the map. "This is scary stuff."

"Can you track any phone?" Amelia asked.

"I think so."

"Let's try my friend's number in upstate New York."

Josie handed her the phone, and Amelia typed it in.

After ten seconds, the map shifted. There was a blinking dot. Amelia zoomed out a few times. "This is her city, her phone. What if you don't want to be tracked? Can you unsubscribe?"

"No. Cumberland says they can track any phone, even if it's off and the battery has been removed. He says phones have little backup batteries so the phone can keep reporting its location. He calls it phoning home. The only way to foil the system is to leave your phone at home or at work. They can track your phone but not you personally if you don't have your phone on your person."

Samantha said, "This is about tracking Zoe Soto's daughter Elena, right?"

"Yes. But even more, I want to track the other number Zoe gave us. Remember, she said when she looked in Elena's phone, there was one person who called Elena more than anyone else. Cumberland already tried tracking both, but he said neither phone showed up."

"Maybe the tracking software isn't that good," Samantha said. "Or the phones are turned off and they're not as easy to track as Cumberland says."

"No way to know," Josie said. "I'll try the numbers again." She typed Elena's number into the Hedy Lamarr phone, then held the phone in front of her as they walked.

A minute later, there was still no blinking red dot.

"How could her phone not show up?" Samantha said.

"Remember the letter Zoe showed us? Elena wrote that the spiritual retreat where she was going had no cell reception. Cumberland said that even satellites pick up phone signals. He said that if you don't want your phone to show up, you have to bring your phone to a place with no cell signal, no view of the sky, and nowhere near any wifi source." After a moment, Josie said, "I'll try the other number that Zoe gave us."

"The number that called Elena the most," Samantha said.

Josie nodded as she typed in the number.

Ten seconds later, there was a blinking dot.

Josie zoomed out, then back in.

"Now the phone shows up!" Samantha said. "It's moving."

They all stared at the screen and the blinking red dot.

"Where is that?" Samantha asked.

"That's San Francisco. We need to find out if that phone belongs to Lucas Herman," Josie said.

"The man who touches Elena," Samantha said.

"Right. We could drive toward that blinking red dot and maybe find the owner of the phone that way. Or we could search online just in case Lucas Herman ever posted information about himself and included this phone number."

Samantha spoke slowly. "In addition to knowing where Elena is, Lucas Herman will know a great deal about the nursing homes. And because he bragged to Elena that he was a hunter in the Army, he might be the sniper, or he might know who the sniper is." Samantha looked at Josie. "This is scary, Mama."

"Yes, it is."

"And if this is Lucas's phone, how would we get any of that information out of him?"

"I haven't yet figured that out. All we really know about the phone is that it is registered to Carmichael Two LLC."

"If we can connect this phone number to Lucas, what would that mean?"

Josie didn't like her next thought. "It would mean we have more traveling to do."

FORTY-ONE

When they got back to their condo, Samantha and Amelia each pulled out their own phones and did the thumb dance.

Josie reached over and took Unknown's leash from Samantha's grip. Samantha didn't appear to notice. Josie bent down and rubbed Unknown.

A few minutes later, Amelia said, "I found it."

"What?" Josie said.

"A LinkedIn page with Lucas Herman's smiling photo, a list of his bona fides, something about the Choose Serenity Home, and the phone number you were wondering about." Amelia turned her phone so Josie could see it.

Josie looked at the photo. It was small and not very focused. But something about him seemed familiar.

"I've got another connection," Samantha added. "He put the same number on Facebook. We nailed him, Mama."

"Thanks to you both. Here's what that means." She handed the Hedy Lamarr phone to Samantha. "The blinking dot is our destination."

Samantha took the phone. She zoomed in and out. "The dot is blinking on the north side of San Francisco. But it's not moving. And there's a circle around the dot. Let me zoom out again. The phone is near a place called Pier Thirty-nine. Not too far away is a street called Lombard. And another called Embarcadero."

"I know where that is," Josie said. "Pier Thirty-nine is part of Fisherman's Wharf."

"I've heard of Fisherman's Wharf," Samantha said.

"But I've never taken you to San Francisco."

"I still know about San Francisco."

"How is that?"

Samantha sounded smug. "Mrs. Doubtfire. Dirty Harry. The Rock. Bullitt. And that one with Mark Harmon and Sean Connery. The Presidio. Those hills are so steep, you can make your car go airborne."

"I don't think we'll be doing that," Josie said.

Even though Josie and Samantha often watched Netflix movies together, Josie felt so disconnected from main-stream entertainment. "You've watched all of those movies? The only one I remember seeing was Mrs. Doubtfire. With Robin Williams, right?"

"Mama, you're so—I don't know—sweet and innocent. Of all those movies I mentioned, Mrs. Doubtfire is the only one that isn't about chasing a killer."

"I hate to think that your impression of San Francisco is that it's full of killers."

"Isn't that why we're going there? To chase a killer?"

Josie felt a sudden embarrassment. "Well, yes, I suppose that's what we're doing. But that's not a general characteristic of San Francisco. I think it's pretty safe compared to most big cities."

"Anyway," Samantha said. "Those movies taught me a lot about San Francisco."

This time, Josie didn't grin. "Basic Life Info from the movies," she said.

Samantha made an exaggerated single nod as if Josie had just said the most obvious thing possible. "And we've been doing all this stuff in the wilderness. The Santa Monica Mountains, San Bernardino Mountains, the Yosemite Wilderness. And now—what was it called—the Desolation Wilderness in Tahoe. So it will be good to go to a city for once."

"In years past, the definition of the word wilderness was an inhospitable place," Josie said. "But depending on what we might find in San Francisco, that might be a kind of wilderness of its own."

FORTY-TWO

The next morning, they said goodbye to Amelia, who said she would watch over the condo.

Unknown got in the back seat of the car as if she had learned that their routine involved regular trips to Northern California.

Josie turned north on the 405, repeating their previous drive.

Samantha was on her new phone. "I can't believe we're still hunting a cop killer, Mama. Would you still do this if the governor didn't threaten you about your job?"

"No."

"Doesn't that make you question how a person should—I don't know—pick their priorities?"

"Yes, it does. I think about it a lot. I'm trying to keep my job. I could never find any other work that pays half as well. That means our home, our food, your school, your volleyball, they're all dependent on my job. If the governor put my job in jeopardy, everything else would be in jeopardy. So yes, I'm always wondering if my priorities are right. I'm dragging my kid off to strange places to track down bad guys, putting our lives in danger to keep everything balanced just so. Is that crazy? You've already gotten seriously hurt, and that made me think I may have made a terrible decision. But if we both survive and maintain our world, and if I live until I get my pension, then I'll probably think it was the right thing to do. But will I still have doubts? Yes, of course. That's what I do. I doubt myself. I've never felt very secure. And should I be telling you these things? Probably not."

Samantha was still looking at her phone. Josie couldn't tell if she heard what Josie said or not.

"Okay, Mama, San Francisco, here we come. I'm looking at Fisherman's Wharf. You can get there different ways. But you gotta go over big bridges. It turns out San Francisco is mostly surrounded by water."

"That wasn't in the Basic Life Info package?"

Samantha smiled. "I do remember that lots of movie images show water. Alcatraz and stuff. Anyway, we have to choose what bridge to go over to get into Frisco. The one that is most familiar from the movies is the Golden Gate Bridge."

"The Golden Gate is too far north when we're coming from the south. Check out how to get to the Bay Bridge."

"Okay. Found it."

"And by the way, you should know that a lot of locals don't like the name Frisco. They call it San Francisco or The City. They think Frisco is disrespectful, as if it refers to the early days before San Francisco was sophisticated. And I kind of agree, even though I grew up across the Bay in Richmond, and the people in my neighborhood were well aware that San Francisco had a bit of a superior attitude. Then again, they probably deserve to decide what to call their town. It is a big, sophisticated city."

Samantha frowned. "Like they're so special that 'The City' refers to them instead of a thousand other cities?"

"Something like that. Names are important to people."

"I guess I don't like it if someone calls me anything but Samantha or Sam. One kid at school called me stick girl because I'm tall and skinny. I almost called him fat boy back."

"But you didn't? Why?"

Samantha seemed to think about it. "Well, it wasn't because I'm so grown up and mature or anything. I think I was afraid he'd escalate it and, you know, call me other things."

"Smart. Often, the best response to bullies or bigots is to ignore them and walk away. It's difficult not to fight back, but sometimes that's the best way to get ahead in an unfair world."

Josie sensed Samantha turning sideways in the seat and looking at her. "But some things you can't walk away from," Samantha said.

Josie nodded. "That's true. Like when someone shoots at

you with a sniper rifle. So we're off to The City to find him."

Samantha leaned toward the backseat. "Hear that, Unknown? Calling cities by the correct name is required. The wrong name ist verboten!"

Josie was excited to hear her daughter speak new phrases. "You're learning German?"

"Nein. Just more movie influence, ja? Have you been to Fisherman's Wharf?"

"Yes, but years ago. It's mostly a big tourist attraction. Restaurants and shops and entertainment out on the pier."

"Like our pier?"

"Oooh, tough comparison. The Santa Monica pier is more about rides, and it has a more relaxed feel."

"The whole SoCal laid-back vibe, huh?" Samantha said.

Josie turned to look at Samantha. She was about to comment, then stopped. "Maybe. It could be that San Francisco tourists are more serious in some way. Another difference between Fisherman's Wharf and our pier is that there are Sea Lions that live at Fisherman's Wharf."

"I remember we watched a thing on Sea Lions in school. I can't remember why they live at Fisherman's Wharf."

Josie said, "I would guess that it's because there aren't any Great White Sharks or Killer Whales there."

"In other words, it's a safe zone for Sea Lions," Samantha said. "They're like us. They don't want predators. But we're going there to find a predator. A sniper's gotta be as bad as a Great White Shark."

"Probably worse," Josie said.

"What's your plan?"

"I don't have one. First, I want to get a look at the man."

North of the town of Santa Nella, Josie merged into the left lane to get on 580, which turned west toward the Bay Area.

Samantha said, "I'm looking at the sun and thinking it will be almost set before our ship arrives in our new land. You got a preference for where we stay when we're in port?"

"Nope," Josie said. "Maybe you could find a good harbor."

Samantha giggled. "That wasn't part of my captain's training."

So Josie explained how one finds lodging, and she talked Samantha through it, from searching hotel websites, to judging hotel attributes, to considering transit options and parking facilities. Josie explained service fees and credit card use and which rewards points were useful and which were closer to scams. Soon, Samantha was reading hotel reviews aloud.

"Lots of four and five-star reviews are good," Josie said. "But they're not very informative because they all say the same thing, that it's a great place. Some of the critical reviews are more informative as they alert you to potential problems that you might not otherwise think of."

"Like…" Samantha said.

Josie was looking in the rear view mirror. There was a dark vehicle behind them. A large vehicle, like a pickup. It had been in the same relative position for several minutes. That was unusual considering that Josie usually drove only the legal speed limit, which caused nearly all vehicles to go around them. Did the following vehicle look like the one that had followed them up at Emerald Bay? Or the one that followed her across L.A. to Ellison's warehouse in Montebello? Josie couldn't tell. She wished Cor were with them now. Cor would know what to do.

Josie kept her focus on driving.

What was it Samantha had said? Oh, the question about what one could learn from critical reviews.

Josie said, "Let's say some reviews mention that a hotel allows dogs and its front rooms look out over the street and have great views. But a critical review might indicate that those rooms are noisy. No problem for the guests who like to party all night and enjoy the vista. But a big problem for those people who want to sleep."

"I get it," Samantha said.

By the time Josie had driven to Oakland and gotten on the Bay Bridge, Samantha had booked them a room in a hotel in the North Beach neighborhood, with valet parking and not far from the Coit Tower and the Wharf.

As they crossed the Bay Bridge, Josie studied the rear view mirror. Once again, there was a dark vehicle several vehicles back. But she couldn't tell if it was the same one as before.

In the middle of the bridge span, they cruised through a low fog bank that lay on the water like a big fluffy blanket. The cloud top just below them was swirled by a giant freighter that looked to be only a short distance below the bridge deck. Then the fog was pierced by the three masts of an antique frigate that looked to Josie's inexpert eye like the USS Constitution from centuries ago. The cloud dissipated as they got to the west end of the bridge. The dark vehicle in the rear view mirror was no longer visible.

FORTY-THREE

They found their hotel, and an hour later they had left their car with the hotel valet and checked into their room. They walked toward Fisherman's Wharf. Unknown seemed energetic at Samantha's side as if all the new scents were interesting.

"What's the big deal about Fisherman's Wharf?" Samantha asked. "It doesn't glitter like the Santa Monica pier."

Josie said, "I think the main attractions are the restaurants, ferry boat rides, and tourist souvenir shops with T-shirts and hats. Things like that."

"You don't sound very intrigued."

"I think it's somewhat like certain celebrities. Fisherman's Wharf, like the Santa Monica Pier, is famous for being famous. But it doesn't have a great deal of merit beyond some restaurants and a history of seafood."

Josie sensed Samantha frown at her side.

"What do you think is more interesting than the wharf?" Samantha asked.

"Here in San Francisco? Lots. The theaters, the symphony, the opera, the ballet, the museums, of which there are several great ones. The SF Modern, The de Young, the Legion of Honor. I've heard the library is fantastic."

"What's in the museums?" Samantha said. "Art paintings?"

"Yes, exactly."

Did Samantha roll her eyes? Josie couldn't tell.

"San Francisco also has a great new baseball stadium," Josie said, trying a new tack. "Awesome views from about a thousand hills, thousands of restaurants. San Francisco is the tech center of the universe. You already mentioned its movie history. It also has some amazing literary history."

"First art stuff, now book stuff?" Samantha said. She sounded like she doubted that either had much value.

Josie nodded. "The Beat poets like Jack Kerouac and Allen Ginsberg, and writers like Robert Frost, Maya Angelou, Mark Twain, Dashell Hammet, Robert Louis Stevenson, John Steinbeck, Joan Didion. All hung out in San Francisco."

"Professor speak, Mama."

"You're funny. Would you like to see the apartment where Dashiell Hammett lived when he wrote The Maltese Falcon? It's in San Francisco."

"How will we find this sniper man?" Samantha asked, ignoring Josie's literary interests.

"We won't. With luck, Cumberland's tracking software will."

Josie pulled out her Hedy Lamarr phone and turned it on. It still showed the tracking program. The blinking dot was now near Powell Street.

Josie and Samantha headed toward Telegraph Hill and the Coit Tower area and then turned down Powell Street. They walked north toward the place where the blinking dot indicated Lucas Herman's possible location. There was a building made of stone blocks, pinkish beige with green awnings. The colors made it look like an apartment building in a tropical city like Miami. It was three stories tall, with a wrought iron fire escape going up the left rear corner. The fire escape carried a thick covering of green vines. Each apartment had a wrought-iron balcony that abutted the fire escape. It seemed like a good design. If you smelled smoke, you didn't have to run down an internal hallway and figure out which way to go. However, the fire escape vines were so thick, it looked like they could trip anyone trying to descend the stairway.

Josie looked again at her phone, then over at the building.

"You think that's where the man's phone is?" Samantha said. "If so, it doesn't tell us how high up. First floor, third floor?"

"Let's keep walking. If he's there looking out, we don't want him to notice us."

They walked down another two blocks, then went around

the block on Lombard Street, and came back on Mason, which ran parallel to Powell. They slowed and tried to peer between buildings to see the apartment building. Nothing was visible. They went back on Powell several blocks down.

Samantha pointed at Josie's phone, which Josie carried at her side like a paperback book and nothing like the way Samantha and others carried their phones, in front of their chests, the screens always pointing up to be seen at a glance. "Does the tracking still show the phone in the same place?"

Josie raised the phone and looked. "Yes. I'd like to find a location where we could watch the apartment without being noticed." They walked farther. The apartment building came into view a block down. "Like here," Josie said.

Samantha glanced at the building, looked around. "Come stand next to this tree."

Josie did as she said.

"You're shorter, so you can't see my view. But if you move back a step… Another. One step to your right. There."

"Got it," Josie said. She moved around. Went part way down the block. Came back. Looked at the phone again. "If that blinking red dot is accurate, I think it indicates the rear corner of the building. Where the fire escape is."

"But there's three floors," Samantha said. "Which one?"

"I don't know. I think this is the only place on this street where we can see the apartment balconies. Unfortunately, we're pretty visible. We need a cover. Some believable reason to spend time in this location. At the minimum, we should face to the side, so it doesn't look like we're watching his apartment building."

Samantha nodded. They both turned sideways and faced the street as if waiting for a ride. "What if he's taking a nap?"

Josie shrugged. She looked at her phone. "The time stamps show his movement. Lots of movement between eleven o'clock and three. Now it's four. So he could be in for a nap like you suggest."

"I don't want to wait while someone sleeps." Samantha looked at her own phone.

Josie nodded. "Okay, we'll keep checking the blinking dot to see if it moves. In the meantime, let's follow his previous movements from when I first put in the phone number."

They walked around the area, following the path the target phone had taken. Out Pier 39, back and forth near the carousel, over to Ben & Jerry's Ice Cream, west on Beach Street to Ghirardelli Square, back on Bay Street to the Powell/Mason cable car turnaround, then back out on the pier. The time stamps showed the phone had spent 40 minutes in one location on Columbus. They walked there and found a restaurant.

"Looks like our guy ate here. Shall we grab a bite as long as we're here?" Josie asked.

"Duh," Samantha said. "You know I'm always hungry."

"Duh?" Josie repeated. "Is that a movie word?"

"Duh," Samantha said again. "It means, you know, duh. Like, of course."

They walked inside and ordered bowls of chili and fresh, hot cornbread. Samantha made a pointing motion down toward Unknown.

"Make that three servings," Josie said to the waiter. "Our dog is hungry. You can put the third serving in a takeout box, and we'll feed her outside."

The waiter looked around. "It's our slow time. I'll put hers in a doggie box, but I think she can eat it right here, if she isn't too messy."

Samantha shook her head. "Unknown's big on manners. Always neat and clean."

Ten minutes later, they had their food.

"Delish," Samantha said when she tasted it. "And yeah, I know not to use words like duh and delish in my college interviews."

Josie didn't comment.

When the chili had cooled somewhat, Samantha set the takeout container on the floor. Unknown ate slowly and delicately.

"If you see the guy who might be Lucas," Samantha said, "you could dial his number. If you see him answer, then you would know you have the right person. We could watch his building. Maybe we'll see him go out on the balcony. Even if he just looks at his phone but doesn't answer, that would still identify him and tell us the apartment probably belongs to him, too."

"I'll have to think about it. It might be the perfect way to tell if that's his number. But I don't want him to think that someone is paying attention to him."

A half hour later, Samantha pointed at Josie's Hedy Lamarr phone, which Josie had set on the table.

"The red blinking dot is moving."

"Oh!" Josie stood up suddenly, bumping the table and setting their water glasses teetering. She grabbed the phone. "It looks like he's going back to Pier Thirty-nine. What is it with that pier?"

Josie put two twenties on the table, and they left.

FORTY-FOUR

"Maybe this guy we're chasing is a spy," Samantha said, as they rushed out into the street, "and he's meeting his confidential informants who come to America by ship and want to meet in a crowded place where they can talk without being overheard."

Josie looked at the phone and picked up her pace. She thought of Mary Jo's secret life and all of her LLC companies. "That might not be as fantastical as it sounds."

They came to the Pier. The blinking dot was out toward the end of the pier. They slowly pushed through crowds of people.

"Try to act like a tourist so we don't stand out," Josie said.

"How would I act like a tourist?"

"I don't know. Figuring out behavior is the kind of thing you excel at and I'm bad at."

"So..." Samantha raised her arm and pointed out toward the water. "I could point at the boats. Like, Mama, maybe we should take a ride on a boat."

"Exactly. And I could look at the tourist shops." Josie walked over to a rack of Christmas ornaments just outside of a store entrance. With one hand, she touched one that depicted the Golden Gate Bridge but kept her eye on the phone in her other hand. The blinking dot hadn't moved. "We have to go farther out on the pier."

They strolled. Samantha acted like a tourist, looking at this and that, seemingly distracted by minutia.

"You do that very well," Josie said.

"We have a kid in school who did his report on attention deficit syndrome. I'm just acting like he said. No ability to focus at all. Isn't that what tourists do?"

"Probably." Josie looked over at a woman who seemed to be

holding a guide book. She was reading aloud to her husband. Her husband was staring at Alcatraz. "Those two don't seem like tourists. They are much more focused."

"If they're not tourists, what are they?"

Josie shrugged. "Travelers?"

Samantha stopped and listened. "What's that sudden sound? It's really loud. Like a hundred barking dogs. Only not quite like dogs." She made a little tug on Unknown's leash. "You hear those dogs, Unknown?"

Unknown seemed unfazed by the sound. She was more focused on the crowds of people. As Josie looked at her, she thought Unknown didn't look excited. Maybe she was wary of the crowds. Or wary of something else.

Josie said, "I just realized the barking is Sea Lions."

Josie stepped sideways to get out of the path of others who were strolling toward the end of the pier. Samantha followed.

"Look, Mama. This pier has a carousel like the one back home!"

They had come within a few dozen yards of the carousel. Josie tried to look at it while keeping her head turned to the side so it wouldn't appear she was staring toward any man who might be Lucas. Josie squinted in an effort to improve her focus. The carousel was quite similar to the one in Santa Monica, elaborate in design.

Josie didn't point, but she moved her head as if to point with her nose. "Do you see that man by the carousel? I think that's Lucas Herman." The man was thick and looked hard and strong.

Samantha's eyes widened as she looked at the man next to the carousel. "He looks kind of scary. Shaved head and a black dress jacket with only a tight black T-shirt underneath. It's almost like a uniform. But what's the mark on this guy's temple?"

"I can't see him well enough to tell." As she said it, Josie thought the man looked like a standard cliched type she'd seen many times before. A tough guy who desperately wanted to be respected. Like a gangster. Maybe he was a gangster. "Let's not stare. We don't want him to notice us."

"I think the mark on his temple is an arrow tattoo," Samantha said. "Lovely. But the Sea Lions are barking so loud, I can't even hear myself think. They weren't making that much noise a little bit ago. But look, Unknown isn't paying much attention. Even though she doesn't bark, she still listens when other dogs bark. She obviously knows the Sea Lions are not dogs."

They ambled closer to the carousel. Josie pointed down over the edge of the pier.

"There they are. All barking." Josie glanced back at the man near the carousel. He was alone. Probably waiting to meet someone.

Samantha looked over the railing. "There's hundreds of Sea Lions!" Samantha said. "Maybe they were napping before and now it's their social hour."

Josie looked down at what appeared to be floating docks covered with massive numbers of Sea Lions.

Samantha had to raise her voice to be heard. "What was it you said in the car? Something like they hang out here to escape Great White Sharks? Seems to me they make so much noise they would scare off the sharks. Plus they're huge. What do you think they're talking about?"

"You got me," Josie said. "Probably the same old thing. The boys are trying to impress the girls. So they make noise."

Samantha giggled. "It's funny you say that. That's exactly like some of the boys at school. Show off and make noise."

Josie took Samantha's elbow and steered her around a building where the barking was less loud. By leaning sideways, she could still see the man who might be Lucas.

"Are the girls impressed when the boys make noise?"

"No. Mostly we just think it's dumb."

"What does impress the girls at your school?"

Samantha responded in a low voice.

"I can't hear you," Josie said, smiling.

Samantha leaned close and spoke louder. "What impresses the girls in my school are boys who are smart but low key. But we also notice the boys who are good athletes."

"You mean, jocks."

"Well… Jocks are often good athletes. But jocks kind of celebrate being not so smart. The girls in my school don't like that. They like smart athletes."

"Glad to hear it." Josie made another sideways glance at the man. He was looking at his phone. "If the girls like intelligence, does that mean they like geeks?"

Samantha made a face of distaste. "No. Geeks are weird. Only a socially awkward girl has any interest in a geek."

"Like Cumberland?"

"Cumberland isn't a geek. He's a nerd."

Josie was surprised. "There's a difference?"

"Yeah. Nerds do stuff. Cumberland does stuff. Nerds are doing stuff in the tech world. What's that called? Making tech innovations. When the nerds get older like Cumberland, they'll be inventing startup companies. Geeks are more like fanboys. They geek out at whatever is the coolest geeky stuff. Nerds obsess over the stuff they're creating."

"Sounds like nerds are more intellectual," Josie said.

"Yeah, that's what I meant."

"It seems a fine distinction. Hard to keep track of."

"Here's something I just thought of," Samantha said. "We have a couple of geeks in our school who are really into collecting comic books. But we have a really nerdy guy, Yani Huxtable, who is *writing* comic books."

"If girls don't go for geeks, do they go for nerds?" Josie felt embarrassed asking the question. But she was curious about all parts of Samantha's world.

"Not in my experience. But the girls probably respect the nerds more."

"What if a nerd was a good athlete?"

"That would be… What's that professor phrase you use… A contradiction?"

Josie said, "A contradiction in terms? Mutually exclusive concepts?"

"Right. A nerd couldn't be doing much intellectual stuff if he was focused on how to play football. But if a nerd was a good athlete... That would be something."

The subject was making Josie uncomfortable. She wished she'd never brought it up. Josie wanted to disappear back into her world of medieval history. How had she gotten into such a conversation? With her daughter!

"Mama! The man by the carousel is gone. You have to look at your phone!" Samantha said.

Josie raised her phone so they could see the screen.

Samantha said, "He's going back off the pier!" She pointed at the phone screen. "He's crossing this street. Embarcadero. Wait, I'm reading it wrong. It's called *The* Embaracadero.

They moved fast down the pier, away from the barking Sea Lions, away from the carousel, back toward the aquarium.

When they got to The Embarcadero, Josie paused to stare at the blinking dot.

"This way," Josie said. She pointed to the west.

They walked along the sidewalk, came to Ben and Jerry's Ice Cream, and stopped and looked at the phone screen.

"The blinking dot went south down Powell," Josie said.

They crossed The Embarcadero and followed the path on the tracking screen. The blinking dot stopped moving.

Josie and Samantha stopped on the street and looked at the various buildings.

Samantha pointed. "I think he's in that apartment building. That's the same building we looked at before, right? But from the opposite side."

"You might be right. Let's keep going and see the back again."

"Where we saw the fire escape with all the vines."

They walked past the building and found the place where they'd stood earlier, looking at the back of the building with the fire escape. They lingered for an hour, staying where they were just out of sight from the building, but where they could lean out and just see the balcony and the fire escape that led down from it. They took turns watching for any movement of the blinking dot on the tracking software. There was none.

"If he's in that apartment," Samantha said, "he's not staying inside because its raining or too windy. The weather's nice. Not warm like home, but still nice."

"Nice is not a common description of San Francisco weather." Josie glanced over at the building. "Let's keep watching."

Samantha looked bored. "It's hard to just stand here."

"You run and leap and do pancake dives in volleyball, yet you think it's hard to stand?"

Samantha widened her eyes and gave Josie an intense look. "Yes. Volleyball is easy. Standing is hard."

FORTY-FIVE

They spent another hour watching the apartment building.

"I can't stand this anymore." Samantha's voice was heavy with frustration.

"Let's just watch for one more hour. We drove a long way to investigate Lucas Herman.

Samantha made a big sigh. "Okay."

"When we go back to the hotel, I might need to take a nap," Josie said.

"Mama, what's wrong with you? You take naps more and more. Are you getting old, or something?"

"Yeah, probably. Actually, definitely. I'm going to be forty-five on my next birthday. Makes me tired just thinking about it."

"Why are you so tired?"

"All my thinking?"

"Mama, that is such an excuse. Ellison is, like, twenty-five or thirty years older than you. I don't think he takes naps. That's like a whole generation."

"Ellison is a miracle man. In shape. Eats broccoli every day. Walks up the long stairway to his warehouse twice or more each day. Probably does a Pagan dance when no one is looking just to work on his coordination and balance."

"What's a Pagan dance?"

Josie hesitated, wondering how she would explain it.

"Don't worry, Mama. You can use professor speak."

"In the Middle Ages, the Romans began to use the term Pagan to describe anyone who wasn't a Christian or a Jew. It became a kind of catch-all pejorative term for anyone outside of those main religions. A thousand years later, some European people who came to America called Native Americans Pagans, as well."

"There's a girl in my school who says she's Wiccan and worships nature. Would she be a Pagan?"

"Some might think so."

"Another kid called her a witch and taunted her, saying 'Double, double, toil and trouble.' He sounded mean."

"'Fire burn and caldron bubble,'" Josie said, adding to the quote. "It's a taunt the witches use on Macbeth in the Shakespeare play. They are messing with Macbeth's mind, egging him on as he prepares to murder Duncan, the king, and take the throne himself. The kid at your school might be trying to mess with your Wiccan friend. But more likely he's just having fun with a popular line that's connected to witches."

Samantha paused and gave Josie a long look. "Wow, you professor types really do know stuff."

After another hour of watching—which mostly meant that Josie watched while Samantha looked at her phone—they gave up and went back to their hotel.

The next day was more of the same. The blinking dot on the Hedy Lamarr phone showed that Lucas Herman walked the neighborhood from the cable car turnaround to Ghiridelli Square near Fisherman's Wharf. But the man never walked out on Pier 39.

Then he went back to his apartment.

Josie and Samantha watched for nearly two hours. There was no more movement on the phone tracking software.

"Mama, this is getting really boring," Samantha said when they went back to their hotel.

"But we still don't know if it's Lucas Herman."

"One more day," Samantha said. "I can only be a hard-working detective for one more day."

"Aye, Cap'n."

FORTY-SIX

The next day, the blinking dot made the now-familiar circuit. But this time it showed that Lucas went back out on Pier 39 and loitered at the carousel.

Josie and Samantha were careful to keep their distance. They didn't want the man to sense them nearby. Once they saw him, they retreated and watched from a long distance. When the blinking dot moved, they moved even farther away and waited in the shadow of a building. The man appeared where they expected him to pass them. This time, he had a companion with him. The other man was shorter than Lucas, not as thickly muscled, with buzz-cut hair, and no obvious tattoos.

The men walked from the pier to the appartment building.

Josie and Samantha took up their observation position where they could only see the building if they leaned out.

A short time later, there was movement on the 3rd-floor balcony of the corner apartment. Two men walked out and stood next to the fire escape. Josie couldn't see well at such a distance.

"Is that Lucas?" Josie whispered.

Samantha had her binoculars up. "Yeah. Lucas and the guy he was walking with."

"I'll dial the phone number." Josie pressed the buttons. It rang once.

Lucas Herman moved, but Josie couldn't see what he was doing.

"Is he reaching for his phone?" Josie said.

"Yeah," Samantha said, her binoculars fixed on the building.

"He's pulling it out of his pocket. He's looking at the screen. Mama, he's going to answer it! He's touching the screen!"

Josie pressed the cancel button. Her heart was thumping in her chest.

"Don't worry, Mama. That's the Hedy Lamarr phone. So even if he has a tracking app, Cumberland said this Hedy Lamarr phone can't be tracked. Right?"

Josie thought about it. "Now I'm concerned. I think what Cumberland actually said was that if someone tries to track the Hedy Lamarr phone, their efforts can be tracked. But I'm not positive I'm remembering correctly."

"If he can still get our location, he could come after us!" Samantha's eyes widened.

"Then we'll be ready to run," Josie said.

Samantha looked back at the distant building. Her expression changed. "They're doing something different." She raised her binoculars and looked.

"Mama, they've got a gun!"

"Is it a rifle? Or a small gun like a pistol?"

"It's long. A rifle."

"Is he pointing it at us?" Josie felt a little panic.

"No. Lucas is handing the rifle to the other guy. It's like he's just showing the guy the gun. Now he went back inside the apartment. He's back. He's got two more rifles!"

Josie felt shaky. She thought of the killer's rifle she'd tossed into the lake when they were in the Quetico Wilderness.

"Does it seem like they're about to shoot someone?"

Samantha said, "No." She held the binoculars out to Josie. "You should look."

"I want to see, but you have good eyes. You should keep the binoculars. Does it look to you like they're trying to find a target to shoot?"

"No. In fact, that balcony is right next to the solid brick wall of that other building. I don't think they could shoot anything from there. It's like the balcony is just a way to get outside air. Wait, Mama. Lucas went back into the apartment. Now he's coming back out with another rifle! He's handing it to the other guy. It's like..."

"What?" Josie said.

"It's like they're… I don't know. Shopping. Like one man is buying guns from the other."

Josie took a deep breath and let it out slowly. "Lucas is meeting gun buyers at the carousel on Pier Thirty-nine. Then he takes them to his apartment to show them the merchandise."

"It's time to call the cops, right?"

"Not quite yet. The governor told me he wanted me to find and identify the killer and report his location. All we've found is a man using a phone that was previously used to call Zoe's daughter Elena. The man may not be Lucas Herman. And even if it is, we don't know that Lucas Herman is the killer of Francis Telman or, for that matter, Mary Jo Telman."

"You're saying we need more info."

"Yes."

"But this is scary, Mama. Lucas, or whoever this man is, has a bunch of guns."

"I agree. But if we called the police, they can't do anything except knock on his door. They can't go inside without a search warrant. And even if they knock and he opens his door, they still can't do anything else unless they see evidence of a crime when they look in his door. Even the police can't answer the basic question the governor asked. Who is the killer of the Telmans?"

Samantha lowered her binoculars. "Lucas might be one of those guys who won't open his door unless he knows who is knocking. And if he thinks the cops are investigating him, he'll disappear and take his guns with him. We would lose any chance of catching him."

Josie nodded. "That's always the difficulty that law enforcement faces. The protection the Fourth Amendment gives us against unreasonable search and seizure is a very important part of our freedom. But because people are protected against illegal searches, it's hard for police to catch bad guys during the commission of a crime."

"Maybe Lucas isn't doing anything criminal." Samantha was once again looking through the binoculars. "Can't a person sell a gun? Like selling a car?"

"I think there are many more rules about selling guns. Especially in California. I think you have to be a licensed gun dealer."

Samantha nodded, the binoculars going up and down with her head. "Showing guns on an apartment balcony doesn't look like something a gun dealer would do."

"I agree." Josie stopped as a vague idea came to her.

"What are you thinking, Mama?"

"I'm not sure. I know that if a police officer looks in a car or in an open door and sees evidence of a crime or evidence of contraband, they can look further."

"Contraband is…"

"An illegal substance or something that was illegally imported."

"You think Lucas's guns are illegal?" Samantha was still looking through the binoculars.

"Yes. When you're showing guns like a gun dealer but you're doing it in an apartment, I'd be willing to bet the guns are illegal. Stolen. Or bought from someone who is stealing them."

"So your idea is…"

"What if there were a way to get Lucas to leave his guns in plain view for the police to see?"

"That would be good. But how would you do that? And if you could do that, how would you get the cops to come at the right time?"

Josie frowned as she pondered the dilemma. "I'm thinking of a medieval approach."

"Why medieval?"

"Because a person like Lucas would never anticipate being subjected to something medieval."

"Are you thinking about the onager we built in the Quetico wilderness in Canada?"

"No. I can't imagine a way to use a torsion-powered device on Lucas. I'm thinking of something simpler."

Samantha lowered the binoculars and looked at Josie.

"Something like a snare," Josie said.

"I thought snare meant catching something."

"The verb does. In the Middle Ages, people often caught their prey with a snare. A kind of a spring-loaded loop. When the prey walked over the loop, it snapped tight on the prey animal and held it until the trapper came to collect the prey for dinner."

"You want to catch Lucas in a snare?"

"Yes."

"Mama, I don't want to rain on your idea, but that sounds pretty ridiculous. No way is he gonna be easy to snare. And even if you could, how would that make it so cops saw his guns?"

"If I could snare him on his balcony, I could call the police. I'd tell them there was a man trapped in some kind of rope up on a balcony. The police would climb the fire escape, and when they got there to free him from the snare, they would look in the sliding glass door and see the guns."

"That's crazy, Mama." Samantha lowered the binoculars and looked at Josie. "That's, like, the craziest idea you've ever had." Samantha made a little tug on Unknown's leash. The dog looked up at her. "It's crazy, right, Unknown?"

"Didn't you think the onager we built in the Quetico was a crazy idea?"

Samantha shrugged. "Yeah, that was pretty crazy, too. But it worked."

Josie stared up at the apartment building. "The beauty of many medieval concepts is that they are never expected. So they have the element of surprise." Josie looked off. "Plus, for the sake of argument, if the police saw me hunting, so to speak, with a snare, there's nothing illegal about a snare. It's not a dangerous weapon. You can carry a snare down the street without anyone noticing."

"What exactly is a snare made of?"

"A loop of rope. Remember seeing lassos in the movies? Where the cowboy throws the lasso around the neck of a steer?"

"Yeah, so?" Samantha looked puzzled.

"A lasso is just a snare."

"Oh. I never realized..." Samantha said slowly, "If Lucas

was on the lookout for potential dangers, he would think about guys with guns, not a snare."

"He especially wouldn't anticpate a snare on his balcony."

"But how would you get a snare on his balcony?" Samantha was shaking her head in disbelief.

"I don't know. But I'm going to work on the idea."

"How will you do that?"

"Thought experiments."

"I remember you mentioning that before. You come up with a concept and then you think about the ways it might work or not. Mental experiments instead of physical experiments?"

"Yes," Josie said.

FORTY-SEVEN

The next day, they found a hardware store a block off Columbus Ave. Samantha wanted to wait with Unknown near Washington Square.

"I'll just walk her around the block," she said.

"No farther, right?" Josie said.

"Right."

Josie went into a building that had tall, narrow aisles crammed with an enormous amount of inventory. She eventually found a section with spools of rope in various sizes.

"Help you, ma'am?"

Josie turned to see an older man, black like her but darker, short like her but much narrower. Like Ralph Ellison, he had a tight helmet of white hair and irises that were nearly black except for a little milky shape near his left pupil. He looked hard, and he was all edges. If he bumped you with his elbow bone, it would hurt. The man looked her up and down, noticing her clothes, which weren't her professor suits, but weren't worn blue jeans and a T-shirt like what he wore, either.

"Yes, please. I need some rope, very strong."

He waved his hand in front of the rope selection where Josie stood. "Normal rope supplier don't provide rating on these. But you could hoist a Peterbilt engine block with all this type. Nylon and poly mix, too, no rot to worry 'bout. Engine block could swing in breeze like mobile art thing. No worry it crash down."

Josie stared at him.

"A modern look in your garden," he continued. "'Course, soon there won't be no more engine block. Peterbilt goin' 'lectric like all other truck maker, but you get my drift."

The man had an accent that Josie didn't recognize. It sounded Caribbean. Josie didn't know exactly what he meant, his "drift" not at all clear.

"I think you're saying that engine blocks are heavy," Josie said, "which implies these ropes are strong."

The man frowned at her, as if it required extra patience to deal with a dumb customer.

"Uh huh," he said, as he looked away toward some other customers down the aisle.

"These ropes are all shades of white," Josie said. "Do you have any darker ropes?"

"Got this paracord. Black." He took two steps to the right, reached out, and touched a wire rack from which hung packages of thin black cord.

"Is that strong?"

"Only five hunder test. Pro'bly wouldn't hold engine block. But it could tie down a big rig flatbed lumber tarp. Did you know flatbed lumber tarp can weigh three hunder pound?"

"No, I didn't know that," Josie said.

"I used to drive a big rig flatbed."

Josie gave him a polite nod. "What about a color other than white and black? Maybe more brownish?"

"A girl always want right color," he said. "Step here." He moved down the aisle. "This military grade cord. Seven hunder fifty test. They call it camo mix or some fool name. Blend right in with brown stuff. Dirt. Sand. Tree bark on the lumber truck. Couch my ex pract'ly live on, watchin' TV."

The man was certainly different, Josie thought.

The man continued, "She keep gettin' softer, all that sittin'. But she still got nice skin. Not that I ever want marriage again, good skin or not."

"This camo mix is perfect," Josie said.

The man moved his hand sideways and touched another type of rope. "Now if you want something real strong, you can get this wire-core type. Only come in brown, though. No camo."

"What's the advantage of wire core?"

"Main thing is it hard to cut. Need a wire cutter. Pretty much can't do it with a knife."

"That might be just right. Do I have to buy the entire

spool?"

"No, ma'am. I cut to length. How much you want?"

"I'm not sure how much I'll need, so I should have extra. Let's cut eighty feet of the brown wire core."

The man nodded. He put the wire-core cord into a measuring wheel, rotated the handle, and wound the rope around a spool until the meter went to 80 feet. He picked up a wire cutter and cut it off.

"Anything else?"

"I need some regular rope. Something easier to cut."

"Like the camo mix."

"Right. I'll take twelve feet of that."

He nodded and cut it.

"Do you have exercise weights? Or rocks? Something really heavy?"

He frowned. "No weight or rock. What 'bout paver?"

"What's a paver?"

"Some people call it patio stone."

Josie nodded.

The man walked her back to the rear of the store where it opened up onto a kind of garden center that backed up to an alley. The space was filled with plants and bags of potting soil and fertilizer and wooden Adirondack chairs. He pointed to three wooden pallets. Stacked on them were patio stones in three colors. Gray, terra cotta, and brown.

"Brown fit your color plan," he said.

"I'd like five hundred pounds of brown," Josie said.

"No disrespect, ma'am, paver don't sell by weight."

"Maybe you have a scale. We could weigh one and figure it out."

The man's frown deepened. He called out. "Tony! How much this paver weigh?"

There was no answer. Maybe Tony was out of the store. Or maybe, Josie thought, he wasn't willing to answer such a ridiculous question.

Josie looked at the man.

For a moment it seemed like he might stare her down. He

turned and walked back into the store. A minute later, he came back with a new bathroom scale that still had its cardboard and shrink-wrap packaging. He set it down, then carefully placed a paver on top of it.

Josie noticed that despite his age, which was probably closer to Ralph Ellison's age than Josie's, and despite his lack of heavy muscle, he had no trouble lifting the paving stone.

"Sixty-nine pound," the man said.

"Great," Josie said. "That means I would need eight pavers to get up to five hundred pounds. Eight pavers would be about five-fifty."

The man gave her a skeptical look. But he didn't protest.

"I also need something to put the pavers in. Some kind of heavy-duty gunny sack?"

"No sack hold five hunder pound 'out tearing apart."

"A fishing net?"

The man shook his head.

"A tarp that could be sewn into a container of some kind?"

Another head shake. "Five-gallon paint bucket?" he said.

"What does that look like?"

The man took her over to stacks of large white plastic buckets. "Pro'bly two paver fit in each one. Might break bucket. If not, be four bucket to hold eight paver."

"White is too bright," Josie said. "Do they make them in brown? Something to blend in?"

"'Course, girl can't have bright white. I got idea." He made a come-with-me gesture and walked over to the paint-mixing part of the store.

"These bucket got paint spill on them. Less bright."

Josie scanned the group. "I can't have blue and yellow. Can I pay you to paint them brown? So they don't stand out?"

"Be expensive. But Tony like business."

"Let me pay you for my current purchases. I'll leave them here for collateral. Then you could ask Tony about making me four brown buckets. They don't have to be uniform brown. Just make them so they don't stand out like white."

"No white," the man said. "Like your rope."

"Right."

When Josie was done paying for her purchases, she had an idea. It was unusual, but it was something to consider. She leaned close to the man and spoke quietly.

"May I ask your name, sir?"

"Michael Griffith."

Josie wanted to get him talking. "Michael, you said your ex is getting softer. But you don't. How is it you stay so thin?"

He responded in a low voice. "Trick I learn when I drove flatbed truck. Met another driver from Barbados like me. But recent, not like me a generation ago. He tol' me 'bout Mount Gay rum made from black gold molasses. Special cask, too. Give it all the vitamins. He drink a short shot each morn' 'fore he get outta bed. Kill the appetite for donuts. So I try it and like it. Thing is, you can't skip your medicine for even a day, or the donut craving come back. And you don't drink it at night. That plus givin' up TV and steak and all the lot lizard cure my gout and my diabetes. And it give me energy for exercise. Do it ever morn'. Now I thin and tough like guy who taught me the trick. Take on Sugar Ray Leonard if I want."

Josie recalled that Barbados was an island country whose official language was English, but whose residents spoke a kind of creole mix of African languages and English. No doubt, that contributed to the man's unusual syntax.

Josie made a slow nod. "What is a lot lizard?"

"Whore at truckstop."

"How did you end up in San Francisco?"

"Brother need help. He rich. Sorta. And in a chair after a shootin'. So I quit drivin' and move in with him up near the Coit. Filbert is real steep, even steeper than the famous crooked street. His block got step for sidewalk. No way to ride chair. So I help him get around. He give me the room, and money for our food, and I work hardware and other odd job for spending dollar. I still take my medicine each morning and do my exercise. Don't miss the lot lizard at all."

"Do you like living and working in San Francisco compared to driving a truck?"

He shrugged. “Sometime hard. But I all set with place to live in my brother house. And if my brother croak, maybe he leave me his house. Then I still set.”

“Your odd jobs,” Josie said, “are they easy to find?”

The man shook his head back and forth slowly. “People don’t much hire old folk, tough as Sugar Ray or not.” He looked both directions as if to make sure no one was eavesdropping, then spoke in a low voice. “When I out o’ money, I sometime take job on the dark side.” He gave Josie a hard look. “Didn’t do that when I drove truck.”

“What does that mean, a job on the dark side?”

“Somethin’ need doin’ but not ’xactly legit.”

“I’m wondering if you might do a side job for me. It would be nearby, just a single job, but I’d make it worth your while.”

“Depend on the work. Won’t do nothing ’gainst my self respect, dark side or not, and I only do side job for cash.” He paused and looked again at Josie’s clothes. “And I’m expensive.”

“Expensive is okay within reason. And I could pay with cash,” Josie said. “The work would be arranging some of this rope on a third floor balcony. The only access is up the fire escape.”

“What the purpose?”

“I’m trying to catch a criminal who comes to the balcony at night. This guy is bad, so I’m hoping to set up a snare trap and catch him. I know how to make it work. But I’m afraid of heights. I need help to set it up.”

“How bad this criminal?”

“He sells guns to people who shouldn’t have them.”

“You want me to mess with a gun guy.” The man paused. “A gun guy who pro’bly shoot me if he caught me. Like guy who put my brother in a chair.”

“I have tracking on his phone. So I know when he’s gone from his apartment.”

“This guy your ex?”

“No. And I don’t want to hurt him. I just want to snare him and hold him until the police come.”

“Sure sound like you fixin’ to trap your ex.” The man sounded suspicious. “What else matter with him? Bad skin and all? Or just sellin' gun?"

"Just guns."

"This guy white or black or what?"

"White."

Michael Griffith nodded. "White guy pract'ly always have funny skin. Kinda pink."

Josie didn't know how to respond to that.

"I never seen a snare trap," the man said. "How you know how snare trap work?"

"I teach medieval history. Back in the Middle Ages, people used longbows to hunt big meat and snares to catch small meat. I've studied snares at some length. I have an idea of how to set one up to catch a gun seller."

"Gun seller ain't small meat."

"True. But I can't exactly go hunting in San Francisco with a longbow."

The man seemed to look off, as if considering the possibilities of longbows in a city. "Where do you teach snare stuff?"

"UCLA."

He nodded approval. "I like watchin' Bruin football. What happen once you get gun seller in snare?"

"I call the police. They come, see that he has too many guns, and they hopefully put him in jail."

The man made a solemn nod and looked left and right as if it were risky just to think about it.

"I should tell you that there's a risk in helping me," Josie said.

"That obvious. I might get caught on gun seller balcony and he shoot hole in me like my brother. I end up in chair."

Or dead, Josie thought. What was she thinking, asking an innocent man to help?! "Yes," she said. "But there is a kind of reward in it. Not the money, but doing good."

"Help cop catch gun seller."

"Yes. It would be a small step in avenging the shooting of your brother." Josie felt guilty saying it. She was trying to entice a man into helping her trap a criminal who would likely shoot them both if he had the chance.

"Sure would like that," he said. "Too many gun in this city."

"Every city," Josie said.

"Tell me about this snare."

"If you have a piece of paper, I can draw you a diagram."

The man walked over to a counter, picked up a pad of paper with a paint brand printed at the top, and handed it and a pen to Josie.

She sketched. "I want to put the snare on the balcony like this... The line would be disguised in these vines that grow on the wall and the fire escape. The line from the snare will go up and over the balcony on the next floor up, kind of like going over a pulley. Then it will drop down through the vines on the fire escape. When it gets close to the street level, it will be tied to the buckets that hold the pavers. There is another line holding the buckets about six feet above the ground. At the right time, I cut that line that holds the buckets, they drop, pulling the main line down. The line way up above pulls the snare up into the air."

"With the gun criminal in the snare," the man said.

"That's my hope, yes."

"Sound like you really gonna get back at your ex. What happen when you marry white guy with bad skin."

Josie shook her head with emphasis.

"If it don't work?" the man said.

"Then I figure out a different way."

"Where would I be when you cut the line and the snare goes up?"

"At home in bed, sleeping, dreaming about your morning shot of Barbados rum."

"How would I put up the snare without the man shootin' hole in me like my brother?"

"In addition to tracking his phone, I've watched him. Each afternoon he goes to the Wharf. He meets people at the Carousel. I think they are his gun customers. He's gone for about two hours. I think he uses those meetings at the carousel to entice the men to come to his apartment and see his guns. I believe that would be enough time to put up the snare and hide the rope in the vines so he doesn't see it. You would be long gone when I trigger the snare."

"You seen the gun?"

"Yes. Guns, plural. He brings them and his customers out of his apartment onto the balcony so his customers can point them at things like Alcatraz in the distance. I don't know why. Maybe that's a way to judge if the gun is good or not. Pointing them at distant objects."

"What you figure to pay me to do this snare work?"

Josie spoke slowly. "I think it would require an hour of prep and an hour or more to haul rope up the fire escape and put the snare in place and string the line through the vines. Let's say, two and a half hours total at two hundred dollars an hour would be five hundred dollars. I would add in a bonus for the unexpected. Let's call it six hundred. One third down in advance, one third when you start the job, and the last third when the snare's in place and you come down from the fire escape." Josie reached into her purse, opened her wallet, and pulled out two hundred dollar bills. She held them out toward the man.

Michael Griffith pressed his lips together as he thought.

"What if cop come by when I do this work? What if they already know this cat store lot of gun, and they looking for people coming by, and they think I buy gun."

"We'll get some orange cones to put on the sidewalk. I'll have a clipboard with printing and boxes to make checkmarks. You and I will both wear an orange road-work vest. You and I will be a fire escape inspection team."

Michael Griffith looked doubtful.

"If it comes to it, I'm doing this job for the governor," Josie said. "I have paperwork to prove it. I could show it to the police if necessary."

"Governor of California?" He said it with a smirk. "Guy who tol' me about Mount Gay rum said he worked on direct order from the president. And his skin almost good as you. So who do I believe?"

His comment made Josie realize she shouldn't have mentioned

the governor. The idea was too outrageous for credibility. But she was already committed. She reached back into her purse and pulled out the envelope with the governor's authorization papers.

Michael Griffith waved as if to push her hand away.

"You pro'bly legit. Else, you crazy as a witch. Otherwise, why front two hunder and not even know if I show up?"

"Does that mean you'll help me?"

The man looked up toward the ceiling of the store. "I'm off tomorrow. Tell me when and where." He reached out, took the hundred dollar bills, folded them neatly into a small rectangle, and put them in the coin pocket of his jeans.

FORTY-EIGHT

The next morning, Josie and Samantha met Michael Griffith at a coffee shop two blocks down from Lucas's apartment. Griffith wheeled a large open-ended lumber cart with four brown paint buckets, eight pavers, two orange traffic cones, a sandwich sign that said 'Fire Escape Inspection Zone,' a three-foot step stool, two day-glow orange vests, a boat hook, and a coil of line. He set the lever brakes on the cart's wheels and placed an orange cone at each end of the cart.

Josie introduced Griffith to Samantha and Unknown.

Griffith nodded at Samantha. He frowned at Unknown.

As always, Unknown was a study in reticence. She stayed back, no eagerness to meet new people.

Josie glanced at her Hedy Lamarr phone. "Our gun seller hasn't left his apartment yet, so we might as well grab a bite while we wait."

"You care what I eat?" Griffith asked.

"No. It's on me, so fill up."

Griffith ordered a huge meal. Eggs and bacon and hashbrowns, a double order of pancakes, a blueberry muffin, and coffee.

Samantha, still adjusting her diet to what she thought was best for volleyball athletes, ordered a vegetarian omelet and nothing else. Josie wanted eggs and pancakes with syrup, and sausages, and she had no appetite for veggies in her breakfast. But she wanted Samantha to respect her. So she had a vegetarian omelet, as well. She watched Griffith while he ate. Now and then she glanced at Samantha as if to see if she was equally entertained by the man's enormous appetite.

When Griffith was done, he grabbed a handful of the little jelly containers and stuffed them in his pocket along with the blueberry muffin.

"We've got movement," Josie said, looking at the phone. "He's left his building and is heading west. Act discreet because he's coming right past this coffeeshop!"

As she said it, a man went past the windows. He held his phone out in front of him and was talking loudly, but Josie couldn't make out the words. After he went past, Griffith said, "Man looks mean. Don't want to face him on the fire escape."

Josie held out her phone and pointed at it. "This blinking dot is the man. We'll always be able to tell where he is. If the dot stays away from his building, we'll know the man is away."

As they watched, the dot moved across the map and stopped at the cable car turnaround.

"We can go now," Josie said. "I'll wait until after he goes toward the Wharf carousel before you head up the fire escape."

"And set a snare to catch some gun meat," Griffith said.

"You remember your part of the plan, Sam?" Josie said.

Samantha nodded. "Unknown and I hang out at the corner we chose on the next block over, where I can see the man's apartment. If I notice any movement or lights in the apartment, I call."

Josie pulled out her burner phone and handed it to Michael. He took it and looked at it with suspicion.

"I'll dial this number if I want you to abandon your mission," Josie said.

"My friend has a cell phone. But I don't know how it work. How do I answer?"

"If it rings, there will be a green circle on the screen. You tap that to answer. But I don't expect you to answer. I would just let it ring once or twice. My call would be the sign to come down the fire escape."

"Feel like climbing fire escape is goin' in jungle by myself. Good place for somebody come make gun hole in me."

"You won't be alone. I'll be down on the sidewalk all the time."

FORTY-NINE

They walked toward the apartment on two different streets, Samantha and Unknown one block over to take up their observation position. Josie carried her clipboard with a pad of paper on which she'd made some notes that looked vaguely like what a fire escape inspector would notice.

When they got to the apartment building, Josie set out the orange cones and tied some yellow caution tape to them as well as to the Fire Escape Inspection sandwich board and the top of the cart. It cordoned off a little work area that passersby would avoid by walking out in the street.

"Let's arrange the paint buckets and paver weights first. Once they're hanging in place, then we'll be able to attach the main line to them without any slack."

As Josie described it, she was aware that Griffith would be doing all the work.

Griffith used the step stool to get the buckets in place, attached to each other, and tied securely to a single support line that hung from the fire escape supports. The buckets were about eight feet above the ground. Griffith then picked up the heavy pavers one at a time, stepped up on the stool, and lowered them down into the buckets. The heavy buckets pulled the support line as taut as a piano wire. Josie remembered that Griffith had said the line was tested to hold 750 pounds. She hoped that was true.

After the snare was in place, its line would connect to the buckets as well. When the time came, Josie would cut the support line, and the buckets would fall to the ground and jerk the snare line down with it. If all went according to plan, the snare on the balcony would draw tight around the legs of anyone standing within its circle and hoist that person into the air. It wouldn't raise them very high above the balcony, but enough to hold them in the air and make it difficult and time-consuming to escape. Josie hoped it would be long enough for police to come. In their attempt to rescue the snare victim, they would hopefully see Lucas's guns.

Josie picked up the coil of wire-core line with its slip-knot loop that she had helped Griffith tie at the hardware store. She spread the snare and adjusted the size a little.

"I think three or four feet in diameter is about right. It doesn't have to be spread out in a perfect circle. The most important aspect of the snare is that it's not obvious. You can move the line to conform to the shape of the balcony. The cord can lie at the intersection where the wall meets the floor. It can bend around objects like that chair in the corner of the balcony that we saw as we approached the building."

Josie handed Griffith a small baggie with a few leaves. "The other day I noticed a rooftop garden on the neighboring building. There are a few ornamental trees up there. So I gathered some leaves like the ones that grow on those trees. You can scatter a few leaves to hide the snare. Not enough to be very noticeable. Just three or four like what might blow in on a breeze."

Griffith took the baggie and put it in his pocket.

Josie remembered her earlier arrangement about money. She handed him two more hundred dollar bills. "Here's your second payment."

As before, he folded the money and put it in the coin pocket of his jeans.

"Do you have any questions?" Josie asked.

"No." Griffith put his arm through the coil of line so that it hung from his shoulder. He reached up with the boat hook, grabbed the fire escape's descending ladder, and pulled it down to the ground. It made a tremendous squeaking screech as it lowered. Griffith grabbed the ladder, stepped up a few rungs, and then turned and looked down at Josie.

"Tell the cops I want to be buried in the Coit Tower cemetery."

Then he climbed up to the first balcony level, let the ladder rise back up on its counterweight, and began climbing the stairs.

Josie heard a vehicle. She turned just enough to see a pickup with a 'San Francisco Public Works' logo on its door pull to a stop next to her. The driver rolled down his window.

In his left hand, he held a clipboard like Josie's.

Josie kept her face turned down to her own clipboard.

"I don't show any maintenance for this street on my calendar," the man said.

Josie was about to respond that it was a last minute addition to inspection requirements when she realized he could check it with a phone call.

If she pulled out the governor's authorization papers, that would create a fuss and probably generate a multitude of phone calls to bored bureaucrats who would all want to get involved and likely pretend such projects needed their stamp of approval. Much better if she could just get the man to go away.

"It's not on your calendar because this isn't a city project," Josie said without looking up. She thought it best to appear so busy that she could barely respond. She kept her pen on her pad and wrote gibberish.

"What kind of project is it?"

She made more notes. "State-mandated fire escape inspection." She still hadn't looked up.

In her peripheral vision, she saw the man turn his head toward the four hanging paint buckets. "You painting as part of your inspection?"

Josie laughed. "That's funny. Do I look like a painter? How 'bout my man up there? He look like a painter?" She kept making notes, kept her head down. "Fire escapes have to meet the code in section twenty-three B and C of California's Uniform Metallurgical Strength requirements. The state requires us to make unannounced random inspections."

"So unannounced that Public Works doesn't get informed?"

"Right. The locations and dates are determined by certified random number generator software like Fortitude Epic or

Fortitude Epic Two. Not even we know where they're going to be. Can't have any graft on this job."

"What is the strength thing?"

"You don't know metallurgical strength requirements?" Josie continued to write on her clipboard.

"No."

"Not knowing that could be a violation in itself. Paragraphs nine and ten specify a deflection test using five hundred and fifty-two pounds. If you look in the buckets, you'll see eight weights that have been certified at sixty-nine pounds each. Do the math before you check with the state office."

"And that allows you to judge deflection of the metal fire escape?"

"What did I just say? We attach the weights to five critical points on each flight of steps and measure the deflection. That tells us if the fire escape can support sufficient numbers of the building's residents."

Josie could hear the pickup driver taking a deep breath.

"Whatever," the man said. "This city's gonna die under the weight of all the rules." He drove away.

Josie looked up and moved back and forth, trying to see Griffith on the upper balcony. She got a little dizzy looking up, whether from craning her head toward the sky or from nerves, she didn't know. She turned back to her clipboard pad.

Michael Griffith seemed to take forever. A few cars came down the street. While Josie didn't look the drivers in the eye, she could feel them staring at her and looking up at Griffith on the fire escape. The cars would slow as they passed by. Josie imagined them all calling the police to report a crime being committed.

Josie pulled out the phone and checked the tracking screen. The blinking dot showed Lucas was moving from the cable car turnaround toward the Wharf. It was just like the previous two days. He probably met someone getting off the cable car and was walking with them toward the Wharf to have lunch or coffee. Maybe they were discussing the terms of a gun sale.

The blinking dot continued out onto Pier 39. Lucas was

moving away from them and was now almost two blocks away. Yet Josie was worried. So many things could go wrong. Maybe the customer wouldn't want to come to Lucas's apartment. Maybe Lucas wouldn't step out on his balcony for the next several days. Maybe Michael Griffith wouldn't be able to set the snare. Maybe when he strung the line up to the balcony above, it would hang out from the building's wall and be very visible. Maybe it would swing in the breeze, and Lucas would see it and figure out it was a setup, and he'd find Samantha watching from a distance, and he'd kidnap her, and...

There was a screech of metal. Josie looked up to see Griffith putting his weight on the descending ladder. It lowered to the ground. Griffith came down, stepped off onto the sidewalk.

"Did it go well?" Josie said.

Griffith nodded. "Snare next to little table and a plant in pot. Hope it dark when time come."

He got up on the step stool, took the snare line, reached up and tied it to the bucket arrangement. The snare line was next to the temporary bucket support line.

As Josie stepped out to look up at the fire escape and see how visible the snare line was, the Public Works pickup reappeared. The driver's window rolled down again.

"Finish your metallurgical inspection?" the man said.

Josie help up her finger to signify that she was in the middle of something.

"Any signs of rust?" she said in a loud voice.

Michael Griffith paused. Glanced at Josie and then at the pickup driver. "Just normal. Some here, some there."

Josie made a note on her clipboard. Then she said, "Structural integrity?"

Griffith paused. "Normal. No serious problem."

"Hey," the pickup driver said. "Aren't you the guy who works at the hardware store?"

Josie made a big sigh and turned to look the pickup driver in the eye for the first time. "If you had to do this job on the budget they give me, you'd be begging kids at the playground to help. And if you're wondering if we're paying our part-time help enough to satisfy the city and if I'm getting the correct info for the ten ninety-two form, just ask him." She looked at Griffith. "Is the state paying you enough, Mr. Griffith?"

Griffith looked confused and a little worried. He shrugged. "Sure thing."

"Well then tell this Public Works fellow so he can get back to work and we can finish this job."

Griffith turned toward the Public Works man. "The state pay real good, sir."

Josie was gathering their gear and putting it on the lumber cart. She left the orange cones and caution tape in place.

The Public Works man hesitated. "You gonna leave the weight buckets up all night?"

Josie sighed with feigned frustration. "Weight deflection tests are measured over a twenty-four-hour time period. Metallurgical yield over one hour doesn't tell you anything."

"Oh. Sure enough."

He drove off.

"That a close call," Griffith said.

"No." Josie shook her head. "Just a guy trying to justify his job. So he drives around and asks questions." Josie pulled out the last two hundred dollar bills.

"Thank you for your help, Michael," she said as she handed the bills to Griffith. "You were great."

"And you a generous lady." He turned, then looked back. "Nice skin, too. Or is that a wrong thing to say?"

"No, Michael. After what we've been through together, that's a fine thing to say."

He nodded and took the money. "I should take the cart back now, huh?"

"Yes, please. But we'll leave the caution tape up. And I'll return the cones and buckets. The man with the apartment won't even see them if he comes and goes through the front door of the building. I'll probably return the buckets next week."

"No rush. You paid for them."

"Thanks."

He started to push the cart away.

"Wait, I need that box cutter to cut the cord," Josie said.

Griffith looked at her.

"And I need something with which I can reach up and cut the cord."

Griffith lifted the boat hook off of the cart. "Tape the box cutter to this," he said. He unrolled some duct tape, held the cutter against the boat hook handle, wrapped it several times. "Wicked," he said, handing it to her.

"I can still slide it closed so the razor doesn't project." Josie hefted the handle with hook and blade. "Kind of like a medieval halberd," she said.

"If you say so."

FIFTY

The rest of that day, Josie checked the blinking dot many times. It got so tedious that she handed the Hedy Lamarr phone to Samantha and asked her to keep checking it.

"What am I looking for?"

"We just want to know when he goes back to his apartment. Or when he moves if he's going someplace else."

Samantha pointed at the phone. "You can tell by the time stamps, he hasn't moved for some time. I think he's at another restaurant. Maybe we should eat, too."

"Sounds good."

They found a casual restaurant near Lucas's apartment. They carried their makeshift halberd inside. Before they picked a table, Samantha bent down and looked at the floor.

"This table," she said.

"Why?"

"There's a power outlet. Cumberland's phone needs charging."

"I'm glad you're paying attention."

"My phone is my Bible. You don't want to neglect your Bible."

"No, of course not."

When they were done eating, they lingered, talking, rehearsing, killing time.

"You remember our plan," Josie said.

"Yes, Mama. We went over it about ten times. When someone appears in the apartment, I call you. When someone goes out on the balcony and steps next to the little table and potted plant, I tell you." Samantha paused. "But what if someone goes out on the balcony, gets caught in the snare, and it isn't Lucas?"

"It will probably still work. The police will come and see

guns in the apartment. It would be unlikely that Lucas could get rid of them in time."

Samantha nodded. "And after you cut the cord, we meet by Ben and Jerry's Ice Cream next to the Wharf."

Josie felt a growing sense of dread. "I worry about getting separated."

"Mama, don't let your anxiety into this. We discussed the entire plan. It's a good plan. Our fallback position is to meet back at the hotel. But we should be okay. You have your trusty weapon thing and I have Unknown." Samantha bent down, her face next to Unknown's. "Right, baby?"

Unknown looked interested, but she did not wag. It was, Josie thought, as if she understood that something very serious was afoot.

Josie held the boat hook out in front of her. "In the Middle Ages, the closest weapon to this was called a halberd. A two-handed pole weapon with a spear and an ax at the end."

Samantha touched her fingertip to the box cutter at the end of the plastic boat hook. "Very intimidating, Mama."

"You want me to have no weapon at all?"

"No, I didn't mean that. I was just, you know, making light of the situation."

It was late afternoon when Samantha said, "Phone's almost charged."

Samantha reached down and unplugged the phone. As she handed it to Josie, she glanced at it. "He's moving! He turned a corner. He's heading toward his apartment!"

Josie left money on the table, and they rushed out of the restaurant.

They went down two blocks to the place where Samantha would wait with Unknown. They both turned and looked toward the apartment, just visible above another building that was closer and lower. Samantha raised her binoculars.

"Good news, Mama, is I can't see the snare line. It's hiding in the vines. Unless they already found it and took it down."

"Don't say that."

"Just being a realist." She gestured toward the phone. "Where is he now?"

Josie stared at the phone. "It looks like he stopped two blocks over. Wait, he's moving again."

Josie looked off toward the target building. "It will take me a couple of minutes to get to the building and hide under the fire escape. But I have my own phone, so you can call me any time."

Samantha said, "The way he's heading will take him to the front door of his building, not the back where the fire escape is."

"Good." Josie gave Samantha a hug. "Ready, Cap'n?"

"Aye, matey."

Josie turned and left.

She walked down the sidewalk, turned at the first corner, turned again at the next corner in a zig-zag pattern. She didn't think anyone would be watching. But it seemed smart to obscure her general direction.

The approach to the rear of the building was from the side. The street didn't allow a good view of the top of the fire escape. Once she was underneath, she would be completely dependent on what Samantha told her.

As Josie approached, she was glad to see that the orange cones and caution tape and 'Fire Escape Test' sandwich sign were still in place.

The four paint buckets still hung from their support, the line so thin and tight it seemed to Josie as if it could never hold that much weight. Josie reached up with her boat-hook halberd and practiced the movement it would take to cut the cord. It felt awkward. A cutting motion would work best if it came across the line at right angles instead of nearly parallel to the line. But standing almost directly below the buckets made it difficult.

Josie looked again at the phone. The blinking dot was once again stationary, hovering a block away from the building where she stood.

She moved to the side and reached up with her homemade halberd from a different angle. It was harder to reach the line, but the angle was better. She brought the smooth plastic of the boat hook handle into contact with the line and made a gentle sawing motion. When it seemed that she'd found the best position, she lowered the halberd and slid back the box cutter housing so that the razor blade was exposed.

Josie was dismayed to see that the razor blade was old and rusted. As she angled it to see better, it appeared that the cutting edge was not very sharp. But it was too late to do anything about it now. Her hope was that the line was so tight that it wouldn't take much sawing to make the line give way.

The blinking dot was moving again, approaching the front door of the building.

Josie looked up at the fire escape steps above her, trying to see through the metal grating that formed the steps. The structure was probably great for letting rain water run through. But it was not designed for seeing. There was just enough light coming through that she would be able to see if someone stepped out on the first balcony directly above her head. But there was no way she could see anything on the balconies higher up.

After peering up, her neck got quite sore and stiff. She leaned her head left and right, forward and backward in a gentle stretching motion. The movement helped, but it also made disconcerting squeaks and pops in her neck. It was probably a result of not stretching or getting enough exercise.

She ignored the internal neck noise and concentrated on her mission. The thought made Josie's pulse speed up. It was the same anxiety that so regularly darkened her psyche. She took a deep breath, held it, let it out slowly. Repeated.

Josie knew that her target could walk out onto his balcony at any moment. That knowledge made her look up despite knowing she wouldn't see movement. It reminded her of when Unknown knew someone was coming up their condo stairs. The dog would stare at the doorknob even though she knew it might never move.

Josie's phone rang. It was so loud, it could have been a fog horn!

Josie almost dropped it in her sudden fright. Why hadn't she turned down the volume?

"Hello?"

"Mama! I see movement inside the apartment! It's hard to see because of the reflection on the glass."

"Okay, I'm ready with my box cutter. Tell me when to cut."

"The balcony door is still closed. I can't see what's happening. There. More movement. But I still can't tell what's happening. Keep waiting. It's hard to hold the binoculars with one hand. I'll put the phone on speaker, then I can use both hands on the binoculars." There was a short pause.

"Okay," Samantha said, "the phone is hooked on my neck lanyard. Can you hear me? Is your phone on your hands-free lanyard?"

"Yes. What's happening?"

"Nothing. There's some blurry movement behind the glass. Lots of reflection. Now nothing. It's like they went into a different room. Wait. The door is opening! Mama, get ready!"

"I am ready. Don't be too quick to judge. Wait until you're pretty sure the man is standing in the right place. If someone comes out and…"

"Mama! Cut the cord! Hurry! Cut the cord!"

Josie reached up with the homemade halberd. She angled it so the box cutter blade would contact the line holding up the weight buckets. She sawed back and forth. Nothing happened! It was hard to see. The line and cutter were in the shade of the fire escape. Josie always knew her vision wasn't very good, but this was infuriating.

She stepped sideways, tried to get a better view of the darkness above her head.

"Hurry, Mama!"

Josie squinted, trying to see. She held the halberd cutter at a new angle. Maybe now she could see.

"Mama! He's moving! You have to cut now!"

Josie was making another sawing motion when the weight buckets fell.

It was like a wrecking ball. They crashed down, smashed a large ceramic planter near the door to the apartment building. One of the buckets fell more toward Josie than the others. It hit her thigh, slammed her sideways, knocking her to the ground.

Josie fell, sprawling on the building's entry step.

"It worked, Mama! The snare caught the man. Wait. It caught just one of his legs. He's hanging sideways, one leg in the air above him, the other swinging in the air. Ouch, it looks uncomfortable."

"I have to click off and call it in," Josie said.

She was still lying on the ground as she gripped the Hedy Lamarr phone that still hung from her neck. She dialed 911.

"Nine, one, one emergency," a female dispatcher answered. "Please state your name and address."

Josie did not say her name, but she recited the apartment building's address on Powell Street. "It appears that someone fell off the third-floor fire escape balcony on the back of the building. It looks like the man is caught in a rope or something. There's another man, and it looks like they've got guns up on the balcony."

Josie hung up. She pushed herself to her knees and then to her feet. She walked away. She was stiff, but nothing seemed broken.

When she was a good distance down the sidewalk, she turned around and looked back and up.

There were two men, one standing, the other still hanging sideways. They were yelling as if angry at each other. One was trying to get the other disentangled from the snare line. Josie couldn't see the details. It looked like one of the men possibly had a knife at the other man's leg, as if trying to cut the line and not realizing it was a wire-core rope.

Despite Josie's bad vision, it was easy to see the man who was standing. He turned away from the snare victim and looked out over the balcony. His eyes clearly locked with Josie's. He stopped. Then he rushed back inside the apartment as if abandoning the man who was hanging from the snare.

Josie turned away, hurried to the corner, and went around a building. When she was out of sight from the gun seller's balcony, she started running.

FIFTY-ONE

If there was one physical ability that stood out among the many things Josie was no good at, it was running. As she charged down the street, she recalled how a fellow professor had once explained to her that running well wasn't just developed through practice and fitness. Running required a set of bio-mechanical relationships that enabled all of the body's moving parts to coordinate. While effort could improve one's running ability, to run well required that one was born with superior mechanics. And Josie's colleague had politely explained that Josie was not gifted with those bio-mechanical basics. He had further added, unnecessarily, in Josie's opinion, that she was sufficiently overweight that it would make running a significant chore.

Josie struggled down the next block, her lopsided gate making her entire body jerk. At first, she'd tried to hang onto the phone at her neck. But then she lost her grip on it, and it bounced up and down, hitting her chin and nearly cracking her teeth. Her tenuous grip on the homemade halberd made her grunt with effort to prevent it from flying out of her grasp. With one arm saddled with the flimsy weapon, her other arm wind-milled more dramatically.

Yet Josie's instincts told her that the man who'd rushed back into the apartment was coming to attack her. Perhaps he would silence her forever, or maybe maim her in punishment for her assault on his friend and the apartment. While she didn't know if the man chasing her was the person she sought, he might still be a killer. And if he was the sniper, then he'd already demonstrated his disregard for human life multiple times.

Josie gasped for air as her run quickly degraded to a jog and then to a slow trot, and finally to a labored walk. She'd lost track of direction. She couldn't figure out which way Samantha might be, nor which way was the killer's apartment.

She came to another corner, rounded it, and collapsed for a moment, leaning against a fence. If the killer came this way, he could grab her as easily as grabbing a lost child. But she was unable to move until she got some more air, so the idea of fleeing was a moot point.

After many deep breaths, she continued down the block, sensing traffic and commotion at the other end.

Sure enough, as she approached the corner, she saw that she'd come to The Embarcadero street directly across from the entrance to Pier 39 at Fisherman's Wharf.

Josie didn't know the territory near Fisherman's Wharf, but the man chasing her probably did. Yet the crowds offered Josie the best hope of cover.

She paused to let a bus go by, then trotted across the intersection.

Josie headed for the most crowded area and then plunged into the thickest group of people. She forced her way through the people, turned left then right, then left again in a serpentine fashion. Because she was quite short, she couldn't easily be seen by someone scanning across the crowd.

There was a line of people in front of the whale tours company and a big group crowding around the entrance to the Aquarium. Josie pushed through the people. There was a restaurant with a sign out advertising a special on crab. Josie ran past, looking for a place to hide. She came to a magic shop and a big crowd moving slowly toward the carousel near the end of the pier.

The Sea Lions made a deafening cacophony off the left side of the pier. In addition to fearing for her life, Josie couldn't think because the Sea Lions were so loud.

Nearby was a construction zone with yellow caution tape marking off an area near the edge of the pier. Josie pushed on by. She came to the edge of the pier. Down below were huge numbers of Sea Lions. Maybe Josie could hide there? It might be a good place—if she could stand the noise—because no people were down there. Were the Sea Lions dangerous? Josie didn't know. They were certainly huge, the size of cows but with flippers instead of legs. If they were dangerous, that would make it a more valuable hiding place. Who'd want to risk their life near a pack of huge dangerous animals?

She looked again at the construction zone. It appeared they were building a makeshift stairway that went down to the water. The workers had left for the day. Could she duck under the tape and escape down to the water? Once down there, could she sneak back under the pier the way you could at the Santa Monica pier? She didn't think so because she was over water, not sand. But she needed to evade a killer.

Josie looked down at the stairway under construction. It didn't have handrails, and the steps seemed uneven as if they were removing boards and replacing them with boards of a different size. There were missing steps. It looked too risky.

Josie headed a different direction. She grabbed her phone and looked at it. The blinking dot was coming out on the pier. Toward the carousel. The man was almost on her.

Maybe she could hide inside a business. Like the aquarium. But the idea of being indoors with a potential killer spooked her. It would be best to hide in plain sight outside. If she could find a little corner or a cubby, a space behind a dumpster, a utility room. Or maybe she could find a way up onto a roof. There had to be outdoor stairs at the rear of one of the storefronts. She scanned for a potential place.

And saw the man.

Josie inhaled. She froze like a rabbit. If she didn't move…

The man was a couple of hundred feet away, over by a pizza restaurant and a set of boat docks, moving fast, clearly searching, looking at people.

Josie glanced behind her, saw a crowd, and started backing up, making no sudden movement. She held her halberd up vertically, like a hiking staff, moving it behind her, taking a step back with both feet in turn, moving the halberd again. Two young boys raced through the area, one chasing the other, both yelling. One of them slammed into Josie, knocking her back as he sprawled on the wooden pier decking.

The man noticed the commotion and looked her way. His eyes connected with Josie's a second time. He started trotting toward her. He was close enough that Josie could see it was Lucas Herman. There wasn't any chance of him missing her again.

Josie tried not to panic. She ran away from him, past the magic shop, back toward the aquarium. But when she looked behind, he was not there.

She tried to run faster. Carrying her homemade halberd was too awkward. She was in effect a one-armed runner, and her lack of balance slowed her down.

Josie thought that if she could get to The Embarcadero street, she could possibly jump on a bus, or simply run out into traffic. The man wouldn't assault her in the middle of the avenue with a hundred people watching.

Or would he?

As Josie scanned ahead, the man ran out in front of her!

Josie about-faced and headed back out the pier. Should she simply stop moving and scream? Would that put him off? Or would he grab her and put his hand over her mouth? Or worse, would he stick a knife into her as he ran by? Would she fall and die without anyone knowing what caused her death?

As she tried to think of what to do, her focus was interrupted by seeing Lucas Herman up close for the first time. In a sudden moment, she realized why he had seemed familiar before. It was because she had seen him before! Seen him up close. Not with the shaved head and the temple tattoo, but with an unruly mop of hair. Probably a wig. Nice clothes, a white shirt, a black jacket, polished shoes. It took another moment to put it together.

Lucas Herman was the governor's valet! He was the one who was sitting in the UCLA hall during her lectures and who eventually ushered Josie into the governor's limousine at UCLA. The governor had introduced him as Taylor Cooke. Somehow, Taylor Cooke had arranged his schedule so he could work multiple jobs, being a valet for the governor, selling illegal guns in San Francisco, and helping to run a chain of nursing homes in Sacramento while using the name Lucas Herman.

Josie's instincts told her to keep running, even though she

had no idea where to go.

She turned away from Lucas/Taylor. She glanced behind as she ran. He was coming up on her right. She veered to the left. Toward the construction area where they were building the stairs. She was trapped with no way out. There wasn't even the slimmest chance she could escape him, a fit, strong man with a murderous drive.

When Josie turned her head to the side again, she sensed him in her peripheral vision. She was almost to the edge of the pier, and he was about to grab her.

Josie angled a bit to the left to delay by a second or two the moment when he would be able to grab her. She ran straight toward the yellow caution tape. She remembered seeing the uneven boards of the pier deck. She had an idea. An impossible idea. But it was her only chance.

Once again she glanced to the side. He was reaching out to grab her right arm, the arm that held the halberd. She was carrying the halberd, bottom end in front of her, the razor end behind her.

The man grabbed her upper arm and jerked hard. Her motion, combined with his pull, threw her down. As she lost her footing and fell head first toward the deck of the pier, she had a memory of using an electrical conduit as a pike not long ago. Josie jammed the end of her halberd pole down and into one of the notches between the uneven boards that made up the pier decking. The box cutter end of the halberd stuck up and back toward her pursuer.

As Josie's face was about to smash onto the pier, the halberd slammed to a sudden stop, like a medieval pike jammed into the ground and pointed up at the charging enemy.

Josie's weak, homemade halberd was nonetheless strong enough to catch the pursuing man square in his abdomen. Maybe the boat hook bruised his abdominal muscles. Maybe the rusty razor blade of the box cutter sliced into the man. The crude halberd lifted the man up like a very short pole vault.

As Josie slammed down to the ground, the side of her head bouncing on the pier deck, the man arced over her. His momentum didn't carry him far through the air. But it was enough to take him through the construction caution tape, over the drop off at the edge of the pier where there was normally a protective railing, and he fell to the Sea Lion docks below.

Josie was dazed. Her head throbbed with crushing pressure, pressure that seemed to originate inside her skull. The world looked blurry, wavy. A sense of black night pushed in from the side.

She wanted to get her elbow underneath her and push herself up. But her arm seemed to flop. She realized she was on the edge of the deck, partially dangling off, about to fall.

She tried to focus her eyes, tried to make the blurry vision go away. She squinted. That helped. She saw the man in the black jacket lying motionless on the boards below as multiple Sea Lions scrambled away and barked out their protest at the man's sudden intrusion into their lounging spot.

People were gathering around.

"Did you see that man chasing that woman?"

"He tripped and went over the edge."

"Look, he's moving a little. He's still alive."

"There's a lot of blood on his stomach. It looks like a serious injury."

"This woman's hurt badly. Her head is bleeding."

"Call nine one one."

A loud voice sounded next to her ear.

"Ma'am, are you okay?"

"What?" The Sea Lions were so loud, Josie could barely hear anything else.

"Are you okay? You're bleeding."

"Yes," Josie said slowly, trying to enunciate. But the single word was unintelligible. Her vision was blurry. Maybe her hearing was blurry, too. She couldn't think. "I'm okay." Her words came in slow motion. Even as Josie said it, she realized she was obviously not okay.

"Let me help you roll over. You have blood on your face. You're all skinned up on your cheekbone. It looks bad. Are you sure you're okay? You could have broken bones. Your cheekbone is badly scraped."

Another voice, "She shouldn't sit up. She could have brain trauma. We need to keep her motionless until the paramedics get here. Ma'am, can you hear me? Are you okay?"

Josie spoke very slowly. "He grabbed me and threw me down."

"Do you know him?"

"No." Concentrate. Think about the words. "I think he was trying to steal my purse." As she said it, she couldn't remember even having a purse. She didn't remember where she was, either.

Josie was on her stomach, her head cranked sideways. She wanted to roll over and sit up, but she couldn't move. If she did move, she might fall off the edge of the pier. She got her arm out and up a bit and reached her phone from the lanyard that held it at her neck. She first dialed Samantha.

"You shouldn't move, ma'am. Help is coming. Stay still."

"Mama! Are you okay?" Samantha answered.

Josie focused on her words. Get them out, no matter how slowly. "Hi hon. I'm okay."

"Mama, what's wrong?! You can barely talk! Where are you?"

"I don't know where... I'm... On the pier. Near the Sea Lions." Was she slurring her words? Her lips were numb, like when you get novacaine at the dentist and you can't talk without drooling. "I won't be making it to Ben and Jerry's."

"Mama, I'm coming. Don't move. Stay right there."

"I have to go." Josie clicked off as Samantha was talking.

More people were talking next to Josie. Some of them were shouting.

It took all of Josie's concentration to look in her phone list. She found the phone number for the governor's office and pressed the call button.

"California State Governor's office, Sonja Gonsalves speaking."

"Hi, Sonja." It took a second between each word. Focus. Speak as clearly as possible. Speak loudly. "This-is-Josie-

Strong."

"Ms. Strong. Are you okay? You don't sound okay. Where are you? I'll send help."

Focus again. Slow but clear. "I believe I've caught the sniper, Lucas Herman." As Josie said it, sirens were sounding in the distance.

"I'm on Pier Thirty-nine on Fisherman's Wharf in San Francisco," Josie said. "I'm out near the end by the Sea Lions."

"I can hear them," Sonja said.

"The sniper appears to be wounded from a fall. Me, too." It seemed to Josie like the pain in her head was squeezing her vision. It made no sense to her. But her vision was going black, nonetheless. Blood was running into one of her eyes. Maybe both eyes.

Not far away came two cops on bicycles.

"The police are approaching," Josie said. "I have to tell you..." Her words came very slowly. The pounding in her head was getting worse. Despite Josie's brain fog, she had the clear thought that maybe she was more injured than she'd initially realized.

"Lucas Herman is using an apartment in a building on Powell between the wharf and Washington Square."

"I'm sorry, Ms. Strong. I can't quite understand you."

Josie repeated what she had said, even more slowly than before. She focused on working her lips and tongue. She gave all her energy to trying to make her enunciation more clear. "Lucas sells guns out of the apartment. There's still a man there... caught in a snare..." Her consciousness was fading. "Third-floor balcony... next to the fire escape. I called nine one one from that location. The police may have found him. But if they figure out that I was involved... I could use..." Josie's vision was blurry and wavering.

"Understood," Sonja Gonsalves said. "You need some intervention. This is one of the things I'm good at. Sit tight, and take your time answering the police questions. I'll have two agents from the California Bureau of Investigation there in a few minutes. They will have the authority to take charge of you.

You and I will talk more later."

"Thanks, Sonja," Josie said, so glad for Sonja's calm and confident demeanor. "Oh, one more thing. Lucas Herman's real name is Taylor Cooke, the governor's valet."

"What?! Are you sure? I can't believe..."

Josie clicked off. In a minute, the bicycle cops were kneeling down, checking Josie. Josie saw movement beyond the cops. Samantha and Unknown came running. Both daughter and dog practically dove down next to Josie. Samantha caressed Josie's head, staying away from her smashed face. She was saying something, but Josie couldn't tell what.

Josie tried to speak, but all went black and silent.

FIFTY-TWO

The first thing Josie saw when she opened her eyes was Samantha sitting on the edge of her bed. Samantha was holding a book and was reading aloud.

"'The geology of California is dominated by the result of plate tectonics. Those slow collisions between vast pieces of the Earth's crust thrust rock thousands of feet into the air and created the Sierra Nevada, the highest mountains in the lower forty-eight states. The immensity of…' Mama! You're awake!"

Josie watched Samantha drop the book and scoot over next to her. She moved very quickly.

Or, possibly, it was only fast compared to Josie's brain.

Samantha squeezed onto the edge of the bed and hugged Josie.

"How do you feel, Mama? Are you okay? Can you see me? Can you hear me? Mama! Say something. Do something." Samantha sounded desperate. She kissed Josie's neck, then her forehead. She was careful to avoid the side of Josie's face, which was covered in bandages.

Josie wanted to turn her head, but she didn't think she had the energy.

She could turn her eyes. She was in a hospital room. There were tubes and wires running from her to monitors with digital readouts. One of the machines had a floating graph. Another made a soft little chirp with each of Josie's heartbeats.

"Where are we?"

"A hospital."

"Where?"

"San Francisco. Mercy Trauma Center."

"How long have I been here?"

"Two days. Mama, I was so scared. I was worried you would

never wake up."

"A good time to learn about plate tectonics." Josie spoke slowly.

"They told me I should read to you, that it would help you. But I think they mostly thought it would help keep me from freaking out. I found the book down in the hospital lounge. They have a shelf of books. It was either California natural history or romance novels with hunky guys on the covers."

"Good choice. I'd learn more from California natural history than from hunky guys." Josie tried to think back. "I remember Lucas chasing me and falling off the pier. Then what happened?"

"There were a bunch of people crowding around and cops talking to you. And there were paramedics. It was horrible, Mama, I thought you were going to die! I've never been so scared in my life. Then two agents from the Bureau of Investigation came. They acted like you belonged to them. They were bossy. But they let me and Unknown ride in the ambulance with you. Later, they came to check on you here. So I guess that means they were okay."

"Why am I still in the hospital?"

"You hit your head, Mama. Real bad. There was pressure inside your head. I don't know the details, but they had to cut into the side of your skull to let the pressure off. Then it was wait and see, and… Oh, I just remembered. I'm supposed to let the nurse know when you regain consciousness." Samantha reached for a switch on a cord and pressed a button.

"My face hurts," Josie said.

"That's because you smashed your cheekbone so hard it broke. So after they cut into your skull, they did surgery on your face to put things back where they belong. After you heal from the surgery, they say a plastic surgeon can make you look as good as new."

It seemed overwhelming to Josie. "When do I get out?"

"I asked the nurse when you might get better. She said you had to wake up, first. But after that, maybe a week. Maybe less."

"Why so long?"

"I think they're worried about your brain, Mama. So they have to keep you under observation."

Josie tried to nod her head, but everything hurt too much.

Two nurses, a man and a woman, came into the room, not running but moving quite fast.

"Good morning, Ms. Strong. So glad you are awake. How do you feel?"

Josie tried to respond, but the nurses started asking more questions before she could answer the first question. They checked the machines, looked at the fluid level in a plastic bag, and they kept talking through it all.

"A doctor will be by, shortly," one of them said when they'd apparently decided Josie would live.

When Josie was alone again with Samantha, she asked, "Do you know if they got Lucas?"

"Yeah, Mama. They got him. One of the Bureau agents came by to ask you some questions, but you were still out. So I pestered him for information. Eventually, he told me that Lucas was in custody, and his San Francisco apartment was full of illegal guns, just like we thought. They also found guns in a Sacramento apartment he rented. The agent said that Lucas stayed there for his nursing home job and when he worked out of the governor's Sacramento office. The agent was looking into where Lucas stayed when he was in L.A. Maybe there are guns there, too. Anyway, the agent said you wouldn't have to worry about Lucas ever coming after you again."

"Good," Josie said softly. "That's very good."

"Oh, he also said the guy we caught in the snare was real bad, wanted for armed robberies."

"More good," Josie said. At that, she went to sleep.

FIFTY-THREE

Two days later, Josie was feeling much better. She'd eaten a few small meals. She could think well. But she kept falling asleep.

Her face still hurt where they'd done surgery. Her head still throbbed.

Doctors examined her a few times. The surgeons said her head would continue to hurt but that it would lessen with time. They changed the dressing on her face and said that it would be a couple of months before they might decide on whether she would need more facial reconstruction.

Twice, they wheeled her to another part of the hospital to do some imaging of her brain. They were efficient and all about business. Only one nurse took the time to joke and try to make Josie smile.

He was just finishing changing the dressing on her face when he said, "You've probably heard the one about a nurse, a doctor, and a priest who went into a bar," he said.

But the day was already long. "I don't remember that joke," Josie said and fell asleep again.

The next morning, Josie woke agitated. She'd had a bad dream. She lifted her head and was relieved to see that Samantha was still in her hospital room, sleeping on a cot they'd brought in. Unknown was also on the cot, curled at Samantha's feet.

"How is it that you talked them into letting you stay here?" Josie asked, after Samantha was awake and they were sipping coffee together.

"Easy. I refused to go. The very first day, when they started asking me questions about which family member I would go stay with, I called the number on your phone for the governor's office. Ms. Gonsalves answered, and I told her I was just a kid and couldn't exactly go back to our hotel and stay there alone. About a half hour later, the hospital people brought in this other bed, and they put up an extra drape to make a kind of dressing room, and they brought a little dog bed for Unknown. And they even let me order Chinese takeout. And a cop delivered it to this room! Imagine having a cop deliver you takeout food in a hospital."

"I guess that's the power of the governor," Josie said.

Samantha shook her head. "I don't think so. I think that's the power of Sonja, his aide. Men posture, while women get things done."

Josie smiled. "Is that a line you heard someone say?"

"No. It's just obvious."

A minute later, Josie's phone rang.

Samantha reached into Josie's purse and pulled it out. She looked at it and handed it to Josie.

The screen said, 'Sonja Gonsalves.'

Josie tapped the button. "Hello, Sonja."

"I hear you are awake and getting better."

"Yes. Thank you for helping after I called you. It made things much easier."

"You're welcome. I'm sure you and I will talk more after you're healed. But I'm calling you with news that will help you sleep. First, the governor and I have determined that you were right. Lucas Herman was actually Taylor Cooke, the governor's valet. The governor was appalled and astonished. He and I are both so grateful that you figured this out."

"Good," was all Josie could mutter.

"The bigger news is that one of the guns that was in Taylor Cooke's apartment has been linked to Mary Jo Telman's shooting death. I've spoken to the ballistics analyst. He said that often times they can't get a one hundred percent positive ID on a particular gun. Especially when the bullet is significantly deformed. But it's his opinion that the bullet is a likely match, the gun itself is a likely match, and there are some other details about Cooke that apparently reinforce his judgment. Cooke's choice of ammunition and weapon, things like that."

"What happens next?"

"Cooke is in jail in San Francisco. It's not yet clear exactly where he will stand trial. There is a lot of evidence against him, physical, circumstantial, and also threats he made to Mary Jo Telman. It's my understanding that defendants in cases like these often plead guilty, in which case there'll be no trial. I'll stay in touch as the case develops. Regardless of the outcome, Taylor Cooke will spend the rest of his life in prison."

Sonja Gonsalves paused.

"Another thing you will want to know about," she said. "The Bureau picked up one of Taylor Cooke's associates. A man named Orlando Avione, someone who Taylor knew from his Army days. Apparently, from the moment the governor wanted to engage you, Cooke worried about your tenacity and the possibility that you would disrupt the business empire he intended to steal from Mary Jo Telman. So Cooke hired Avione to follow you and report all the information he obtained. Among other things, Avione did physical surveillance. You may have noticed a black pickup following you wherever you drove."

"I did," Josie said.

"That was Avione. He pled guilty to some type of unauthorized surveillance charges. He has no previous criminal record, but with the penalty he faces and the fact that Cooke is no longer employing him, we believe he won't bother you anymore. In the meantime, you have the governor's heartfelt thanks and appreciation. You have served the state of California well. The fee the governor discussed with you has been deposited in your account along with a substantial bonus."

"Thank you," Josie said.

"Yesterday," Sonja said, "while you were recovering, I also had a long conversation with your daughter. What a charming, smart young woman."

"Yes, she is," Josie said, looking over toward Samantha.

"She filled me in on your movements leading up to finding Taylor Cooke. She mentioned the woman named Elena Soto, who was working for him."

"Yes, Elena's mother is very worried about her."

"That's what your daughter told me. Samantha said the mother's name is Zoe Soto, and she lives in Reno. I want you and Samantha to know that the governor's office will establish Elena's whereabouts and make certain she is okay."

"I'm glad to hear it," Josie said.

"If you have any questions, call anytime," Sonja said. "Thanks again for your service."

They said goodbye and hung up.

Samantha's phone rang.

She tapped the screen, and said, "Hello? Perfect. I'll be there in a minute." She hung up, then stood up.

"Where are you going?" Josie asked.

"I ordered decorations delivered. They just arrived. I'm going to the nurse's station to pick them up."

"Why decorations?"

"Oh, Mama, you really did hit your head hard. Today is Christmas. We have to decorate."

That was a surprise to Josie. Almost a shock. She'd completely lost track of time.

Samantha hooked up Unknown's leash, and they went out the hospital room door.

"You won't be gone long, will you?" Josie said. Why she felt so insecure, she didn't know.

"We'll only be a minute, Mama."

Samantha and Unknown left. A minute later, there was a short tap on the door. It opened, and Samantha and Unknown returned. Samantha carried a decorated bag with ribbons and other items poking out the top. "Oh, we also have some presents coming."

"You had those delivered too? How extravagant."

"More than you think, Mama. The presents are being delivered by Santa and his helpers." Samantha looked out the open doorway and made a little wave.

In walked Ellison wearing a pointed, red Santa hat with sparkling white trim and a white ball at the end. Behind him was Cor. She wore her standard, sleeveless camo shirt but had a long line of plastic tubing wrapped over her shoulders. Inside the tube were blinking red lights. She carried a food container with a snap-on lid. Behind Cor was Amelia, who held a big insulated coffee container. And behind Amelia was Cumberland, Aiden, and Cara. Each person in the line also carried a small present wrapped in plain Kraft paper decorated with cartoon ink drawings.

"Oh, you all are so perfect," Josie said. "Aiden and Cara, you came all the way up here from L.A. I'm so glad to see you both. And Cumberland! You are the person who made it so Sam and I could find Lucas. You helped us so much. Thank you for coming." She wanted to ask him to come hug her, but she knew he would be too embarrassed.

"Hi, Professer," Cumberland said. "I'm glad you're okay."

Josie's eyes flooded with tears. She couldn't find any words. Eventually she said, "Thank you, again. How did you all get here?"

Amelia answered. "Cor drove us all. Cumberland and Aiden and I squeezed into the back seat of Cor's Jeep. Cara rode in the front with Ellison and Cor. I don't know how she did it."

Cara spoke up, "Cor put a little pillow on that center plastic thing, and I sat there."

Amelia said, "And Cumberland's legs are so long, he can rest his feet on the dash. He squeezed them into the front seat between Cor and Cara. But we got here in no time at all because Cor drives fast!" Amelia's eyes were wide.

"Yeah, we broke some laws coming up here," Cor said. "Too many people for my seat belts, and I have trouble getting stuck behind slowpokes."

They each set their presents on the little sideboard table under the room's window.

Ellison said, "Samantha said our presents had to be small because you have a small condo. And we were prohibited from using metallic-colored wrapping paper or plastic-based ribbon. She further required us to use re-purposed paper shopping bags or some other second-hand paper."

"I didn't require those things," Samantha said. "It was just a suggestion."

Ellison glanced at Samantha then turned back to Josie. "A suggestion that came with the admonition that we would incur the wrath of Hutash, the Chumash goddess should we commit shiny-paper, package-wrapping heresy."

Josie wiped her eyes. "I love you all."

Cor sat at the foot of Josie's bed. "I heard what you did. You are one tough woman, Professor Strong," she said. "You're not ready for Flanders Fields just yet."

Samantha frowned and looked at Cor.

"A World War One battlefield," Ellison said in answer to Samantha's unspoken question. "Immortalized by a famous poem. I'd recite it, but it makes me cry."

"Probably," Cor said, "Samantha's curious about how I came to the reference. After all, I'm not a bookish person." Cor turned to Samantha. "In an effort to raise up the intellect of her students, your mother read part of the poem in one of her classes."

Samantha made a slow nod. "You can't separate the woman from the professor." She turned to Ellison. "I expect this of Mama. But how is it that you know this stuff?"

Ellison shrugged. "I like to read."

Unknown had walked over to Cor and was sniffing her container.

"What's in the container?" Josie asked, wanting to change the subject.

"Amelia made cookies," Cor said. "Alfajores. You want?"

Josie said, "I've been wanting Amelia's cookies since before she was born. Her coffee, too."

"Some of us have been wanting Josie's friendship since before she was born," Ellison said.

Josie once again struggled with tears. She reached up, and Ellison bent over and hugged her very softly and carefully.

He said, "Samantha told me that you always thought Christmas was a special time for just you and her. I asked why. She explained that you said that Christmas represented a time just for family, even if family was just the two of you."

Josie nodded. She lifted the hand that wasn't tethered to

medical equipment and wiped her eyes.

"So I asked Samantha if I might qualify as family. And do you know what she said?"

"No, what?" Josie said.

Samantha answered. "I told him, 'Ellison, I'm Cap'n around here, and if I say you and Cor and Amelia and Cumberland and Aiden and Cara are family, then First Mate here will just have to deal with it.'"

Josie gradually got a grip on her emotions. "And what are we going to do for Christmas beyond opening these lovely presents? Order more takeout?"

Ellison sat on the bed and held Josie's hand, careful not to disturb the IV drip needle that went into her vein. "The weather's pretty sweet in Santa Monica this time of year," he said. "When they give you the go-ahead, how 'bout I drive your Prius, and Cor drives her Jeep and we divvy up the crew between the two vehicles. Then we all go home and have a picnic on that glorious warm beach?"

About the Author

Todd Borg and his wife live in Tahoe, where they write and paint. To contact Todd or learn more about the Josie Strong thrillers or the Owen McKenna mysteries, please visit toddborg.com.

A message from the author:

Dear Reader,

If you enjoyed this novel, please consider posting a short review on any book website you like to use, such as Goodreads and Amazon. Reviews help authors a great deal, and that in turn allows us to write more stories for you.

Thank you very much for your interest and support!

Todd

Made in the USA
Columbia, SC
28 August 2024

40575773R00212